I0582140

BEFORE NOW

C. G. BLAINE

OF MEN AND WOLVES #1

Copyright © 2025 by C.G. Blaine

Published by Gray Page Books LLC

All rights reserved.

Cover Designer: Kate Decided to Design

Photographer: Cadwallader Photography, LLC

Editing: Rebecca at Fairest Reviews Editing Services, Ellie at My Brother's Editor

Sensitivity Reading: Jayla J, Whitney Lynn

No part of this book may be reproduced or transmitted in any form or by any means, electronic or mechanical, including photocopying, recording, or by any information storage and retrieval system without the written permission of the author, except for the use of brief quotations in a book review.

This book is a work of fiction. Names, characters, places, and incidents either are products of the author's imagination or are used fictitiously. Any resemblance to actual persons, living or dead, events, or locales is entirely coincidental. Except for the original material written by the author, all mention of films, television shows and songs, song titles, and lyrics mentioned in the novel are the property of the songwriters and copyright holders.

Ebook ISBN: 978-1-950847-32-7

Paperback ISBN: 978-1-950847-33-4

For those who bend when they want you to break.

1

REMI

THE SHRILL SCREAMS from outside the venue cut off when the heavy metal door slams behind me. I force a deep breath, regaining my cool after shoving through the group of women camped outside the back exit to the arena.

I glance over my shoulder at the guard who followed me inside, leaving the other to deal with the fans. He's in an all-black T-shirt with *Security* sprawled on the back in white with the Czech translation above it. His eyes sweep over me before he juts his chin in the opposite direction.

As I turn, he dodges around me and starts down the long, narrow hallway. I shadow behind him, rechecking my phone. The video has been pulled up and ready to go the other twelve times I've looked since leaving the hotel, but I need something to focus on. A distraction from the nerves that accompany the soft thump of bass, growing louder with every passing second.

Once we turn a corner, a few people are rushing around the corridor, some carrying flashlights and others with cables and gear.

This is my first time backstage during a concert. I always imagined it would be busier, though I guess people are already where they need to be by now—keeping the show going with lights and sound.

I'm watching a tech fast-change batteries in a radio when we stop in front of another guy with an earpiece. The guard at my side lifts the shoulder closest to me. "She's for the band."

I glare up at him for making it sound like I'm *for* the band, but he just smirks and shrugs.

"My English," he says in his thick accent, "it's not always perfect."

He stalks back in the direction we came, and the man he left me with chuckles.

"He's a dick," my new keeper says, a bit of a southern drawl sneaking through. His attention follows the other guy a little longer before it drops to me. "You're the documentary director meeting Christian?"

I nod, and his lips turn up at the corners.

"This should be interesting." Then he hooks his head for me to follow him.

He keeps a much more leisurely pace than the previous guy, seeming perfectly at home roaming the venue. If he's private security, which I'm guessing he is with the Texan accent and plain black Henley, he's likely strutted plenty of unfamiliar hallways.

When we hit a door at the end, he pulls it open for me and unleashes the full volume of the concert. The music pulses in my chest, a rush of cooler air hitting me as I step into the dimly lit area. With most of the light spilling off the side of the stage, my eyes fight to adjust. The rafters towering above us are barely visible, and the only other clear marker is a red *Exit* sign shining on the far side.

"Here," the guard says, clicking on a flashlight.

He takes the lead again and crosses toward the sign. The stream of light hits us on our way past a metal set of stairs that lead onto the stage. I squint against the brightness until I make out the band. And all those nerves kick it up a notch at the sight of them, real and in front of me.

Of Men and Wolves weren't complete unknowns when they left for the European leg of their tour, but over the past few months, they've gone from up-and-coming to arrived. They have four songs on the charts; their music is all over social media and a constant on the radio, and they've added six more stops on the last leg of the tour once they return to the States.

Now the documentary.

I stop by the bottom step, curious for a preview of them live. A friend had tickets to a show in NYC last year, but I was working a wedding that weekend in Jersey. I still heard their song "Echo" that night at the reception. Like a majority of the weddings I filmed that summer, the couple picked it for their first dance. It was an interesting trend, considering the song's about a guy watching a girl he's never met, imagining falling in love with her.

Semi-romantic if you only listen to half the words, I suppose.

The band's playing the second verse of it now, and the lyrics that were burned into my brain pour through the arena, wrapping around the crowd of ten thousand.

I never asked to fall for a smile and those innocent eyes.
Had to find out the hard way the ghost of love never fades.
You left me chasing your echo while he holds you through the night.
You let him take away the pain, even though I wrote you a lullaby.

A whistle drags my attention away from the stage and to the guard. His shoulder is propping open the door under the sign, his head tipped to the side while he waits for me.

I'm about to catch up with him when I glance onstage one more time. The bassist has backed closer to the speakers, giving me a straight shot of the singer. He has his red and black guitar slung across his chest, a hand on the microphone stand. Only instead of starting the final chorus of the song, he's looking offstage in my direction. Like *right* at me.

He lets go of the mic and pushes the dark, shaggy hair off his forehead. His brow draws in just as a tech bumps into me.

Another pushes by me on the other side, flying up the steps. Realizing how in the way I am, I rush after the guard and offer an apologetic smile.

"Easily distracted," I tell him.

He snorts, letting me pass him into the hallway. "Right."

"I thought they would be finished by now."

"There was a sound issue after the opening band. They only have one song left."

We stop at an open dressing room with sparse furniture and photos hung all over the walls.

"Christian's finishing up a call." He glances at the yellow velvet couch set alongside the far wall. "You want to hang here for a bit or chance being swarmed by the band when they come offstage?"

"Here," I answer fast. "I mean, this is fine."

The guard ushers me inside and leans in to grab the knob. "Stay here so I don't have to track you down. Cool?"

My eyes close at the same time as the door, and I let out a long breath. I collapse onto the center cushion and pull one of the throw pillows into my lap. Then I stare at a water spot on the ceiling, questioning whether Heath is completely out of his mind for sending me alone or only partially.

Originally, the director-turned-film-studies professor was supposed to be leading the charge on the documentary. Heath Erickson used to work on everything from music videos to indie horror flicks, and even though he "gave it up" for a house in the suburbs, he still can't say no when a label calls.

My job as his TA quickly shifted from grading freshmen's silent films to tagging along for music video shoots. He fired me at the end of the semester, only to rehire me as an intern for the next one, and then again for a summer program. The man found ways to keep me as his assistant without costing him a dime until I finished my degree last year.

Now he cuts me checks himself. The pay is shit, and he knows it. He also knows he could quit paying me altogether and I'd still show up every time. It's about the connections and experience, not the almost nonexistent cash flow.

For money, I waitress and freelance as a videographer for an event planner on weekends. It affords the rent on my tiny apartment in Tribeca. Nothing glamorous, but if I need to drop everything for a last second flight or reshoots, at least I'm not giving up much. Unlike Heath, leaving behind a wife and two kids—with a third on the way.

That woman has put up with a lot of his shit over the years. Red eyes across the country, missed birthdays and anniversaries, models throwing themselves at him, hoping for their big break. She finally hit her limit this time. Not that I blame her. She's nearly six months pregnant, and her husband announced he was signing on to tour the country with a rock band for the next four. He's lucky she only *threatened* to throw him out.

So, even though the record execs begged my boss to direct a documentary to release alongside Of Men and Wolves' next album, it's me on a yellow velvet couch with clammy palms. Feeling like I haven't spent the past few years meeting managers and herding musicians around a set.

Sitting becomes too much, so I walk around, searching the frames on the walls for a picture or signatures of artists or performers I recognize. I half-smile, seeing a few, and as I'm reaching for one to get a better look, a pair of voices stop outside the room. A few seconds later, the door flies open. The guy stops short when he sees me. His eyes travel down and pause on my legs.

"Well, fuck, I wasn't expecting *those* when I walked in." He starts striding toward me in his black silk dress shirt, unbuttoned one more than necessary at the top. "Please tell me you dress like this every day, because we need those legs on tour."

I let out an unimpressed, "Excuse me?"

The guard's standing outside with his back against the wall, and he turns enough so that the side of his face appears in the doorway. "Fucking professional, Christian. She'll slap you with a harassment lawsuit before even meeting the band."

Christian. The band's manager. I've seen pictures of him, though in person he has a younger face, his dirty blond hair longer. He has half of it pulled back, and his sleeves rolled up to his elbows.

Despite still scanning me over, he stops a respectable distance away. "My humblest apologies," he says, a smug grin appearing as his eyes finally make it to my face and stay there. "I thought I was meeting a dude with a goatee until about five minutes ago."

He has far more tension in his voice toward the end, but the annoyance is warranted if they only told him now that I was taking over the project. They signed off on me directing two weeks ago after Heath offered to consult from the safety of suburbia.

"Remi Sinner." I slide my palm into his waiting one, but he more strokes the back of my hand with his thumb than shakes it. "The band sounded great," I add, pulling my hand away.

"They always do." Christian studies me for a beat before he claps. "So..." He pauses and holds his arms out to the sides. "Impress me, baby. Tell me how this is all going to go down."

The second he brings up filming, a portion of the nerves dissolve. I reach in my bag for my phone to show him what I shot and edited together last week for a visual.

"The label's vision was very on with the current documentaries a lot of musicians have been filming and releasing on streaming services. A camera crew follows the band around, and they give prompted confessionals. Nothing wrong with it, but I propose going in a different direction."

I hit play on the video of the kids at the skate park and hold my phone out for Christian. He slips it out of my fingers, flipping the screen. A few seconds with nothing but the sounds from the speakers pass as he watches, and I can't read his reaction.

"We'll shoot with handheld cams," I explain to him, "including from the band's points of view when we can. It will be candid and raw—them showing a genuine depiction of their journey. Honestly, the overproduced, safe, and scripted side of singers and artists has been done to death. People want something real. They're losing interest in the commercialized bullshit constantly shoved down their throats."

"Amen," the guard says from the hallway.

"Hand cams and unfiltered," Christian mutters. He glances up, squinting, and then checks the video again. "This is how you're gonna make my guys look like they're worth the money the label's pouring into this?"

"Well, I'm sure they'll do that themselves. I'll just be there to capture it."

After a beat, he breaks into another grin, looking all the way up this time. "You keep talking like that, and you won't only have me hard, but I might fall in love with you, Remi Sinner."

The guard meets my skeptical gaze, followed by his eyes dramatically rolling. Borderline inappropriate must be the norm with Christian, then. Not shocking when it comes to music managers.

"You've won me over," he says, already checking his phone when he hands over mine. "The guys have a few questions before they sign off on the whole thing. Mostly they want to know how in their faces you and a film crew plan on being."

"*Before* they sign off?" I ask.

When the label's producer called last week, she made it sound like the deal was done. Mac Records just wanted to fly me to Prague to meet the band and answer any questions they might have about filming.

Christian lowers his phone, noticing my confusion. "We would never agree to someone coming on the road like this without meeting them first. You won't be some roadie on tour they dodge while walking to the stage. You'll be in their shit twenty-four-seven—witnessing God knows what between the bus and hotels. Don't take it personally, doll, but they could very well tell you to fuck off in a few minutes."

My cheeks heat as I realize this isn't the "chill little meet and greet" I was promised. It's a fucking interview.

"Let me guess, they told you this was in the bag?" Christian looks like a man who just regained control of his kingdom, giving me a wink. "No worries, beautiful. I can't imagine anyone telling you no."

Then he adjusts his posture. In a split second, he shifts from frat boy to intimidating and in charge, rolling down his sleeves and fastening the buttons at one of the cuffs as he walks away.

The guard straightens and tips his head to the side, waiting for me to follow Christian out of the room. "Honestly," he says, once I reach the hallway, "that went better than I thought it would."

"Yay for me," I deadpan on my way by him.

The band's dressing room is only a few down from the one they stashed me in. Christian grabs the knob, pausing before he turns it. "Let me brace them for the switch-up, and then let her in."

"Aye aye, Commander Douche," the guard says.

"Real fucking mature, Colton." Christian slips inside.

The door bounces rather than latching behind him, leaving an inch-wide gap. My eyes stay locked on it, muffled voices leaking through but the words unclear. All of my anxiety exists in that tiny space until Colton clears his throat. When I look up, he props his shoulder against the wall.

"You're an anomaly, you know?" He crosses his arms, and before I can ask how, he tells me, "You're walking into the lions' den without planning to lose your clothes."

I narrow my eyes at him, but the comment takes some of the edge off. And with the half-smile he gives, I think he meant for it to.

He nods for me to go in, and I blow out a breath.

"Thanks for the pep talk, Colton."

He smirks, pushing the door open for me. With my first step, Christian spins around, and two more sets of eyes shift to me.

Felix Mills and Dev Ferris look up, the drummer and bassist with their legs spread wide on the couch.

I pause, awkwardly half in and half out, until a hand presses to my back. Colton nudges me forward, and as he pulls the door shut, he whispers, "Give 'em hell, lioness."

The latch clicks behind me.

"Perfect timing, Sinner." Christian saunters over, his grin as wolfish as the first time I saw it.

He hooks me around the waist, drawing me into the center of the room. The bassist and drummer slouch deeper into the cushions, neither making a move to meet me part way for introductions like Christian had. Suits shake hands, and it's a dead giveaway what side of the line you land on, art or business.

Off to the side of them is a table covered in knocked-over beer and liquor bottles and whatever else their rider required. The opposite wall has a few bags on the floor with clothes strewed around them, a guitar case, and a pair of drumsticks tossed into the mix. It smells like booze and sweat, an intoxicating scent I'm familiar with from dressing rooms at video shoots.

Christian rests his hand on my shoulder once we stop. "I was just telling the guys about our little surprise."

Felix already has his lips curled up. "Quite the fucking surprise."

His black hair is pushed back and still damp from sweat. He lifts his hips as he readjusts on the cushion. From the rundown their agent gave me, he's the wild one of the group. Whenever they have downtime, he finds creative ways to blow off steam, legal or not.

Beside him, Dev chuckles, a sheen across his forehead, the lighter blond of his tips stuck to his glistening skin. "Yeah," he says. "It's like the tour gods realized we had way too much dick around lately."

"Who says I don't have a dick?" I ask, tipping my head to the side.

My mouth perks when his eyebrows shoot up, and Felix snorts

out a surprised laugh. Dev leans forward, ready to fire something back until Christian cuts him off with an exasperated sigh.

"Do *not* say whatever you're about to."

Dev holds up his hands in mock surrender, feigning innocence.

"And Colton thought I'd be the problem," the manager mumbles beside me.

Dev slumps back then, whispering something to Felix that makes them both chuckle, and Christian's still shaking his head when he rotates toward me.

"Now, with those incredible first impressions out of the way, we'll let you do what you came here for." He winks, backing away. "Floor's yours, gorgeous."

I can't help but roll my eyes as he drops into a chair, angled near the couch.

Whoever decided I should talk to these guys after a show had no idea what they were doing. They're still keyed up from performing, and I'm between them and whatever they usually do to come down from the high. The musicians on set are similar after a long day, not quite the same as a sold-out concert, but it still leaves their adrenaline pumping.

It's why I avoid musicians' dressing rooms immediately following a shoot. The number of times I've gotten an eyeful of ass is almost impressive.

"Like I already mentioned to Christian," I start, "I want to go a different direction than what the label was talking to Heath about. Most of the filming would be more low-key than you're probably used to. We'd rely on hand cams or spy glasses."

"Spy glasses?" Felix gives me a look. "What are we, fucking assassins now?"

"That's just what they're called," I tell him, "but they'd give a really cool perspective. Like you are the lens—"

The door off to the side of them jerks open, and when I look over, my gaze hits a bare torso, the skin tan and stretched tight over muscle. As my attention drops lower to the word tattooed just above the low-slung jeans, a maroon T-shirt pulls down over it. My eyes jerk the rest of the way up to his face, and the same eyes from the stage are locked on me.

Adams North.

The lead singer and guitarist for Of Men and Wolves is shoving his hands through his wet hair, straight out of a shower, but he stops moving. The same expression touches his face from before, his lips parting slightly. The room warms from the steam pouring out from behind him, and one of the guys gives him a "Hey, man."

His throat bobs in a swallow before he blinks, and then he glances at the rest of the room like he wasn't expecting them to be there. A split second later, he's back to me, something about him making me more nervous than the others.

I flash a smile, and Adams gives me a quick once-over. His gaze crawls up me, and by the time he reaches my face again, he looks bored, almost dismissive, as he nods on his way past me.

Well, then.

"Feel better?" Dev asks, sliding to the end of the couch to make room.

Adams nods once and settles between his bandmates.

"Adams, this is Remi Sinner," Christian says. Adams's jaw clenches at the introduction, his attention already on his phone, so Christian continues, "She was just telling us her plans for the doc since the label pulled a fast one on us."

As Adams continues to show a complete disinterest in my existence, I lick my lips and force another smile. It's not the first time a musician has acted like I'm shit on their shoes, and I doubt it will be the last.

"Right," I whisper before taking a deep breath. "Well, the shooting itself should be pretty straightforward. The crew and I will tag along, filming you guys through the end of your rehearsals and on the last leg of your tour. And the label said you plan on writing your next album, so we'll be sure to get footage of that. Fans will want a glimpse into the magic behind Of Men and Wolves."

"So you're going to be in our faces while we're trying to write?" Dev asks.

He glances at Adams, and for the first time since he sat down, Adams looks from his phone to his bandmate. They seem to share an unspoken moment before they both turn to Felix, sharing the same one with him.

"Not in your faces," I say fast, not liking the way the vibe in the room is shifting. "On them, maybe. I think it would be pretty awesome if we could get footage from your guys' points of view during concerts and writing."

"Is that where the glasses come in?" Felix asks.

Adams looks up then, and this time his gaze bores into me. His jaw muscles work overtime under the skin, and to say this guy doesn't like me would be an understatement. I have to lower my eyes to my black-heeled boots to regroup before I can nod at Felix.

"If one of you doesn't mind wearing them. I know a guy who can make almost any pair of frames work, and since the label's paying, I say we take advantage of it."

I get a laugh from Christian, and he looks up from his phone to shoot me another wink. It eases my nerves, the room settling back into a more relaxed state again.

"We can use the glasses for anything you might feel uncomfortable having outsiders around for. I know writing lyrics can be personal with you baring your souls, so—"

"No," Adams says, his voice deep and raspy after his performance.

My eyes snap up to him, and Christian shifts in the chair, sitting up straighter.

"No, what?" the manager says. "No to the glasses?"

"To all of it."

"What the fuck do you mean, all of it?" Christian pushes out of the chair, his commanding presence returning, but Adams stays trained on me, making me want the walls to absorb me.

Dev and Felix seem unsure for a second, but then Dev crosses his arms.

"It is a lot going on at once," he says. "We've already done 33 shows with another 28 to go, the label expects us to write while on the road and be in the studio the week after we finish the tour. Now we're going to have a film crew shadowing our every move?"

The room falls silent until Felix nods. "We wouldn't even be able to relax and do stupid shit between shows. Not with someone reporting our every move back to the label."

"I would *never*—" I start, but Dev cuts me off, "Not just you on the road, sweetness."

I swallow and reach for the back of my neck, not sure how to regain control here. The three of them have all sunk back into the cushions now, a unified force eyeing me like I'm the enemy.

"You serious about this, Adams?" Christian asks, staring down at him.

Adams tips his head to the side, his voice rough when he says, "All of us on board or none, right?"

Before I can even think how to get us back on track, Christian sighs and turns to me. "Thank you for coming, Miss Sinner." The finality in his voice sends a cold wave through me.

Then he gestures for the door.

Nothing feels real as I scan over the three men on the couch, the one in the center, glaring at me as much as I am at him. One asshole has a problem with me, and I lost the best opportunity of my career.

I slap on a smile, not willing to let them see how utterly devastated I am right now. "It was really cool to meet you guys. Good luck on the rest of your tour."

Christian guides me toward the door with a hand on my back, his other arm coming around to open it for me. When I step into the hall, Colton's head lifts from the wall he's leaning against, but the grin leaves his face when he sees an irritated Christian following me out.

"No fucking way," Colton says to him. His expression softens when he looks at me, and I shrug, taking a breath as I turn around to Christian.

I shove my hand at him. "Pleasure."

He grimaces, sliding his palm into mine, but when I try to pull back, he tugs me closer, his face serious. "Stay in Prague."

I shake my head, not sure why I would even consider it, but he licks his lips and glances over his shoulder quickly before returning his attention to me.

"Give me until tomorrow, and I'll change their minds. Adams just needs a nudge in the right direction."

"It was Adams?" Colton asks.

Christian doesn't even acknowledge him, his focus staying on me.

I search his eyes and try to gauge how much I should believe him. Playing it safe, I'd say maybe twenty percent, but the little girl running around with her daddy's digital camera is fucking giddy.

"Really?"

Christian nods. "Go back to your hotel and keep your phone on you."

When he steps back, he regains his grin, and I can't believe I'm putting my faith in a band manager, but I manage a small smile. He slips into the room, and my shoulders slump.

"Don't sweat it." Colton nudges me down the hallway. "I'll set 'em straight for you."

I give him a doubtful look, wondering how much sway a security guard has over the band, but I decide not to point it out. So instead, I say, "And if neither of you can change their minds?"

He shrugs. "In the slim chance it happens, you got a free trip to Prague. You ever been?"

Following him around the corner, I shake my head. "I've never been out of the states until yesterday."

"Let me guess, you haven't been anywhere other than the airport, your hotel, and here?"

I don't answer him, and he chuckles.

"Well then, I guess you'll have plenty to do."

We pass the two security guards from when I arrived, and Colton pushes open the exit, the fresh night air hitting me. He holds it open, and his mouth turns up as he shouts over the screams.

"Go sleep in the five-star hotel the label paid for, and tomorrow, download a tourist app or just wander around until you're lost. Experience the world, Remi Sinner."

His words still echo in my ears on the car ride back to the hotel. I lean my head against the window, watching the lights of Prague pass by. Wander. It's exactly what I want to do, but I don't think I could get lost here if I tried.

It might be my first time in Prague, but the truth is, I know it by heart. That's exactly where I've kept this city since the last time I wandered it—only then it was through a phone screen. And I saw every second of it through someone else's eyes.

As we pull up to the hotel, I pull out my phone, and after a quick app search, a familiar logo appears on my screen. Then I hit download, and for a second, the air warms.

2

FOSTER

SHE DIDN'T EVEN RECOGNIZE me. Then again, why would I expect her to? It's not like we've met—not *really*, that is.

I remember everything about her, though, and she's exactly the same as she was five years ago. Same high cheekbones and delicate jawline. The rosebud lips I spent hours memorizing. And, of course, those eyes, devastating with the sadness and tearing their way into my soul no matter how hard I tried to keep them out.

The black bleeding in at the ends of her auburn hair is the only difference I noticed. That and she wasn't Remi Sinner back then.

No, it was Remi Saint who haunted my dreams, waking and asleep.

The elevator dings, dipping to a stop on the lobby floor, and my eyes lift from my phone screen, but I stay against the wall.

I know what happens when I walk into the restaurant, and I'm putting off the inevitable. At least I plan to until Colton rips the phone from my hand.

"Your majesty," he says, dropping into a low bow.

I swipe my phone on the way by, stepping into the buzzing lobby, voices bouncing off the marble floors and cascading from the vaulted ceilings, leading to the skylight two stories above us.

"So, we're going with silent and broody today?" Colton falls into step beside me, his eyes sweeping the faces while I continue to ignore him.

The security is most likely overkill with the sunglasses. And those are deemed necessary after a night of trying to forget reawakened ghosts. Even with them on, the glare through the windows is nearly unbearable.

None of this would matter if today had gone the way it was supposed to have, with me buried under the blankets and the heavy curtains drawn. I ignored my phone for a reason this morning. Fucking Colton let himself into my room, tucking his into my hand.

"Christian Vero," he tells the hostess outside the hotel's restaurant.

Her eyebrows shoot up, followed by her gaze. They land on Colton first before sliding to me, where they settle.

"Of course." She bites her lip when she smiles. "Right this way."

I huff out a chuckle and hold out my hand as Colton groans. He digs in his pocket and slaps cash in my palm and mutters, "Unbelievable," leading the way with another guard trailing behind us but at a distance.

Overkill.

Christian glances up from his phone as we approach, the irritation palpable by the time I drop into the seat across from him at the table. I feign innocence, shaking out the napkin and blinking at him with a smile.

"Foster." It's his entire sentence but represents a full paragraph at least.

I toss my sunglasses on the plate in front of me, not planning to eat, and drag a hand through my hair for about the tenth time today, frustrated as Colton lowers into the chair beside me.

"Why don't you tell me how you think this conversation is going to go, Christian. Save us some time."

He nods, checking if anyone's within earshot other than Colt, and then he leans forward to close the space between. "Of Men and Wolves are doing the Mac Records documentary."

My jaw clenches as he goes on.

"You'll tell the other guys you changed your mind. We worked out an agreement, minimal extra people on tour, no one allowed in during writing sessions."

"If I don't?" I ask.

"You will," he counters. "Because this isn't just you saying fuck off to the label. It's taking money out of everyone's pockets—including that chick from last night."

Just the mention of Remi is equivalent to the lobby glare, and I squint as if I'd been blinded.

"She's fucking good, Foster. And she's hungry for this," he adds. "You watch that video I sent you?"

I nod as Christian relaxes back in his chair. His demeanor even calms enough he eye-strips a woman sauntering past. His attention stays on her long enough Colton clears his throat, and our manager finally brings his focus back to me.

"Then you know she has the talent. Her style is the vibe I thought you, of all people, would want for this thing." He rushes the last few words, looking up when the server stops at the side of the table.

The problem is he's not wrong. Remi has the *exact* style I envisioned when I first heard about the possibility of a documentary. She's perfect for it.

While Christian orders his five-star meal, my gaze lowers to my phone, partially obscured by the table. I tap the screen, bringing the video I was watching earlier back to life. Not the one Christian sent me, but one that cuts deeper than some kids at a skate park. This one's personal. This one has a part of me tainting it.

The battle of the bands sign hangs behind the all-girls punk band on the stage, and then it cuts to the singer's POV, the drums hitting behind her while she nails a riff on her guitar. She turns to the grinning bass guitarist, spinning off to the side. Then the video switches to a camera in the crowd, right in the middle of the excitement and pulse of the show. I swallow, knowing whose eyes I'm looking through at this exact moment.

I thought my mental well-being had finally taken the long-awaited swan dive last night when I looked offstage and saw her at the base of the stairs, watching me perform for a fucking arena full of people. The mic stand might as well have electrocuted me, my entire being in shock. Felix shouted at me, and I glanced away long enough for her to disappear.

It was so surreal. By the time I walked out of the shower, I'd convinced myself she was a full-body apparition. Until I saw her standing in the middle of the dressing room.

"Excuse me."

I look up at a girl standing beside the table. She has a skittish smile and glances over her shoulder to another girl, seated a few tables away from us.

"You're Adams North," she tells me.

When I nod, her eyes light up, her smile spreading before she turns to say something in Czech to her friend. Colton adjusts in his seat like he might need to tackle her, so I pat his leg. "Down, boy."

The girl whips around, pen already in hand, as her friend rushes to her side. "Might we get your autograph?"

I pluck the pen from her, and the new chick steps forward enough to place a napkin on the table. After I sign it, I hand it back and grab the other napkin the first girl is wiggling in her hands.

"From signing IOUs to napkins," Colton mutters under his breath. "So proud."

The corner of my mouth tips up at that, and I shake my head, giving the girls a smile.

"You two catch the show last night?" I ask, sliding the napkin to the edge of the table.

"Yes," the first one says, snatching it up. "You were incredible."

"Wasn't he?" Christian hands the menu off to the server, his eyes dancing over the girls, who seem more than happy with his attention. "Now, you just need to tell him how much you want to see an Of Men and Wolves documentary."

My eyes snap to his, and he smirks with a shrug.

"What? If you won't do it for me, maybe you'll do it for them."

"Oh my God," the girl says before talking to her friend. Then they both nod adamantly with her adding, "That would be amazing."

I try to keep my expression from faltering, not wanting them to think they've done anything wrong by playing into Christian's hand.

"Well, we'll see what we can do about that then." I wink, and they giggle.

Christian talks them up a little longer before they grin at me and wander back to their table. I give them a little wave and then turn a scowl on Christian.

"Cheap shot." My fist clenches under the table, and I notice Colt glance at my hand. We both know he'll swing for me, not risk screwing up my hand. But something about the idea of punching Christian in his smug face is incredibly appealing at the moment.

"It's business." He pauses, seeing the server bringing his scotch. He waits for him to drop it off and then sits forward again, dropping his voice low. "Be pissed at me personally all you want, Foster. But you and I both know this is the best move professionally for every single one of us."

My college roommate with his surfer hair and all chill vibes flashes through my mind, and I try to pick out those pieces of him now in the black jacket, his hair pulled back in a tight bun. But all I see is the pompous version—the one who knows his shit and won't let any of mine stand between us and a payday.

This is the Christian we hired, even if the other is more tolerable.

When I nod, he blows out a breath. "Thank fuck." He drains the scotch glass, lifting a finger to the server for another. "Now, I'll just have to apologize to the sexy little redhead for you acting like a douche last night and hope you haven't chased her off. Considering who the label could have sent, I'd say we lucked the fuck out."

As he pulls out his phone, I swipe to unlock mine. I stare at it for a long moment before opening the app I downloaded the second we landed in Prague. It comes to life, the large purple W throbbing like a heartbeat on the screen until it turns into Wanderer's dashboard.

The second it loads, a notification lowers from the top of the screen. The same shock from last night coasts through my bloodstream, and not trusting reality, I have to read it three more times.

SaintR signed on twelve hours ago—location Prague.

"I'll do it," I say, not even thinking. My eyes lift to my manager across the table.

Christian's brow draws in, his eyes trained on his phone. "Do what?"

"Tell the director we changed our minds." I swallow the lump of doubt in my throat, shoving down the part of me that says I need to leave the past in the past. Let Remi Sinner go on tour with Adams North and Of Men and Wolves without knowing who I am.

But we're both in Prague. Both have the app.

Christian studies me, searching for the angle he'll never find. "You won't pull anything?"

I shoot him a cool smile and slide my shades back on, rising from the table without a word. As I'm walking away, he calls through the restaurant after me, "How are you going to apologize without her number?"

"Don't need it," I reply.

I don't even need to know where she's staying.

Remi Sinner is about to come straight to me, and then we'll learn which one of us is more afraid of ghosts.

3

REMI

WHEN MY PHONE DINGS, I sigh, flopping back on the bed.

I've been editing video all morning, avoiding Heath's messages. Shockingly, I'm not eager to explain to my mentor that I somehow screwed up the chance of a lifetime he handed me. Plus, part of me is still holding out for the band's manager to call, telling me it was all a misunderstanding.

Of course I have the job. I'm perfect for it.

I know I am—even if Adams North doesn't agree.

In case it is Christian trying to get ahold of me, I sit up and reach for my phone on the mattress beside me. Only instead of finding a threat or salvation via text, my entire body takes an electric shot to the nervous system. The last notification I ever expected to see again floats in front of me, my thumb hovering over top of the purple *W*.

I hadn't planned on using *Wanderer* when I downloaded the virtual tourism app last night. I don't even know why I bothered, other than a need for something familiar after that travesty of a meeting. Even if the familiar was from another life.

It was like déjà vu when I typed in my old login info and it still worked, a little nudge from the universe. Now it's practically holding my head under water, the past recreated while I stare at my screen, rereading.

WestF has signed on and is available.

It borders on overwhelming, the spike of adrenaline I get at seeing his name again. Then the ache of regret follows right behind. All the what-could-have-beens bombarding me at once.

The *should*-have-beens.

I close my laptop and open *Wanderer*. Muscle memory kicks in after five years, and I tap on his username to see where he is. Where in the world his life has taken him. Only then, everything turns to a light hum around me as my body fully disconnects from the rest of the world.

Foster's in Prague.

Again or maybe still or I don't know that it matters. He's here. In the same city where I left him. And now, so am I.

I swallow, my mouth dry enough I could choke.

We're in the same place.

All the conversations come flooding back—all the promises—and my legs are unfolding from under me, my body making the decision before my brain. I shouldn't be surprised, though. When it came to Foster, it was never my head leading the charge.

I grab my bag on the way out of the hotel room, and once on the elevator, I check where in Prague he is right now. The app only gives me a general location, but it's enough. There are a few places nearby, and I pick the one closest to him. I input my payment information so the app can charge me, and then I return to his profile, clicking the Wander button.

The W flashes on the screen, fading in and out with my pulse thrumming harder as I cross the hotel's lobby. He'll be getting the notification now, seeing my username and deciding whether to accept the tour.

I stop on the large concrete staircase outside, holding my breath until the purple dialogue box pops up.

You're now wandering with WestF.

The screen fills with a busy sidewalk, and I swear my heart falls out of rhythm as I watch the world through Foster's eyes. He's maneuvering around people, heading toward the Charles Bridge—then to the museum where I sent him.

I rush down the steps. He's not far, so I bypass the hotel employees and the waiting taxis at the curb. My eyes constantly flick to my phone, watching Foster cross the historic bridge. He flashes me the view, showing me what he's already shown me.

Every step he takes after the bridge, I know. He's taken me there before, and a few minutes later, I'm walking the same path. I spin around, my blood on fire when I recognize this part of the city, even though my feet have never touched the ground until now. There's no screen between me and the air or the sun shining down through breaks in the clouds.

Then I stop, staring down at the screen. Foster's walking into the museum, and when I look up, I see the burnt orange tiles in the distance. By the time I reach the doors, he's wandering a long hall, works of art on either side. I'm paying for entry when he pauses, pointing the camera at one of the paintings.

A little girl sits on her father's lap, playing with a porcelain doll. The girl's hair is long and red, the doll's dark and curly. The oils swirl, the colors mixing and fading from one to another to create their features and dresses and precious faces.

I hesitate, my body not quite my own while it occupies the space he was just in.

We're sharing the air.

"Excuse me," I say, turning back to the woman at the entrance. "Could you tell me where this painting is located?"

Her gaze lowers to my phone when I hold it out. Then she gives me a soft smile and shows me a map of the museum, pointing to a hall not far from the entrance. I thank her before making my way there. I stop in front of the girl and her doll, the colors less subdued than the screen would lead you to believe.

"You're not really seeing the art," Foster told me once. *"Not until you're standing in front of it have you truly seen anything."*

He's moved on to an open room, streaks of light visible from large windows set high above. I wander farther down the hall until it widens into the same room. The same light wood on the floor and the same white on the walls with black beams vaulting in the ceiling.

The screen shows a statue of a man on a horse, and when I look up, the same bronze catches my eye, only I'm seeing the opposite side. My pulse spikes, my feet once again moving before I've decided what to do. But I've come this far, and all he'd have to do is look at my profile to see I'm in Prague.

I scan the faces as I move through the room, trying to pick him out. But I've only seen him in pieces—never all of him at once. A glimpse of eyes in a reflection. His lips, turning up in a smile when he'd talk about a new song. The stubble of his jaw when he'd tell me all the things he'd do to me if we ever truly met.

After moving to where he was before, with the bronze horse and man in front of me, I look down, and I suck in a breath.

It's me. On the screen.

My head jerks up, and I search the opposite side of the room before referencing the screen again. He's watching my profile now, catching the fountain in the center of the room in his shot. When I lift my gaze, it lands on a guy in a bomber jacket with a phone in his hand. A cap is pulled down, low on his face, and sunglasses cover his eyes, but my gut tells me I'm looking straight at Foster West.

He starts moving, and the shot drifts to another piece of artwork. It's of a dog and a picnic, sunny sky and green, green grass, but the image shifts within seconds, showing me a new angle of myself. This time, he's behind me. I close my eyes, my heart threatening to rip out of my chest.

I wander away from him, to the hallway and the painting of the little girl. After a minute, the frames he passes on screen look familiar. He's following me. My limbs tingle as I climb the grand stairway to the second floor.

The slight crowd from downstairs thins the deeper into the building I go. When I glance down, I see the carved wooden banister stretching to the second level, a flash of his shoe, and then another shot of me by a sculpture of the female form.

I slowly make my way into a large, empty hall with nothing but baroque-style art. Foster's entering the room as I pass the directory signs against the far wall. I check over my shoulder, making sure he's watching and no one else is around before I turn down a narrow corridor. Then, I slip through the door halfway down, letting it swing shut behind me.

My heart threatens to beat out of my rib cage as I watch him follow, down the hallway, pausing by the sign on the door. It creaks open, and my eyes lift to the row of mirrors in front of me where they hang above the sinks. I catch a quick peek of myself, cheeks flushed, eyes wide when the switch clicks, the room around me and the screen in my hand going dark.

A strip of safety lights kicks on along the baseboards, barely enough to see by and casting the space in a cool hue of blue. Barely enough to see him walk around the corner behind me. I swallow, my fist clenching tight around my phone, and when he steps behind me, my eyes close.

"Hi," I say, weakly.

And I didn't realize how desperate I've been for his voice until he answers, "Hey."

It sounds the same and yet so different, deep and gravelly.

I feel the heat of him first, then a brush of his chest against my back. My body screams for him to touch me, like he promised he would if this moment ever happened.

The first sweep of his hand might as well be an electric current, every part of me settling in the line of contact he draws up my arm. I can't think—only fall into this moment, his skin warming mine. He presses closer behind me, his fingers wrapping over my hip, and I feel his breath against the side of my face, then the light scrape of stubble against my bare shoulder.

I open my eyes to watch him through the mirror. He's taken off the hat and sunglasses, but all I can make out are the lines of his nose, the curves of his cheekbones, the edges of his jaw, with the details just out of reach.

"Foster…" I trail off when his other hand skims up my arm to my neck. The tips of his fingers graze up my jawline before his thumb stops on my pounding pulse.

"Remi."

The tension breaks the second my name leaves his lips. He tightens his grip on my neck and pulls me around, already backing me across the room by the time I face him. He dips down, his mouth grazing my collarbone and moving to my neck as my back hits the bluish-green tile beside the paper towel dispenser. My hands creep up his hard chest and then around to the back of his neck. I still have my phone clutched in one when my fingers push into his hair, and he groans, pinning me to the wall with his hips.

None of this can be real. The wandering boy I wasn't supposed to fall for was long gone. No one I would ever hear from again, no one I'd ever touch.

"Foster."

His name falls out, like my mouth has been waiting to say it again.

"Remi." He nips at my neck, wrapping his hand around the back of my thigh. "Fuck," he whispers, grinding his erection into me.

I keep breathing in more than breathing out—as if my body were more concerned with memorizing the scent of him than using the air. Cedar and leather.

"Foster." It's on an exhale, my lips grazing the side of his face.

He hasn't even kissed me yet when his mouth works its way over my skin to my jaw, and I'm about to wrap my legs around him for more contact when his tongue glides over my skin, and he hums out a satisfied sound.

"Remi Sinner."

I still—all of me in a free fall that feels even less real than everything else.

Foster stops moving too, bringing his face to hover in front of mine. "What's wrong?" Even in the mostly dark room, I can see his mouth hitch up on one side. "That's your name, right? Your *real* one?"

My lips part on a shaky breath, my fingers still in his hair. The lines of his face begin to come into focus, the features piecing together.

"*She's a sinner, pretending to be a saint.*" His voice is still his, but now it also sounds like someone else's, repeating Of Men and Wolves' lyrics.

No, it can't be.

I would have known it was him.

The last time I talked to him flashes through my mind. It leaves me even more chilled inside, my heart twisting as I remember sending him my picture. He texted back like he promised he would—only I never opened the message to see his.

With the memory tightening around my throat, I slowly bring my phone around to his face, closing the app as I do. Light flares over his face, and my eyes lock with his.

Adams North is staring back at me. Only now I know without a doubt it's Foster too.

Then it all slips into place—how the voice on the radio made me want to close my eyes and fall, and I could feel it deeper than I should. Because I'd already fallen. It had already been buried as far down as I could get it.

Foster licks his lips, his eyes lowering to my mouth for a second before they return to mine. "Come on," he says smoothly. "If anyone could figure it out, it should have been you. Foster *West*. Adams *North*. Who do you think inspired me?"

If it felt unreal before, now it's so real it hurts.

My eyes burn, and I shake my head, but before I can even come close to forming a coherent sentence, Foster straightens.

He smirks, and the last parts of me that were still warm with him touching them cool as he backs away. "You're hired, by the way." He turns, walking toward the door. "See you on tour."

I stare after him even after he disappears around the corner. The lights blink on as the hinges creak, and then the latch clicks and he's gone. I close my eyes, gasping for air as everything pours in at once.

Everything.

Every second since my phone buzzed with his last message. Every moment I've tried to forget. It all surfaces no matter how much I try to push it down.

Foster West just tore out of the ground—back from the dead. And he unearthed the rest of what I'd buried with him on his way out.

4

REMI

Before...

I PAUSE outside the front door, my hand on the knob but not turning. The house looks like every other home on the block: the red-brown brick, white columns, perfectly manicured yard. It's the exact shot you'd show at the start of a movie—letting the audience soak in the picturesque view. That way, when they see something not quite right happen on the other side of the brass-knobbed door, they easily dismiss it so you can shock them later.

Misdirection. Show them something beautiful to obscure the ugliness of reality.

Rather than go inside, I retreat down the steps. I follow the little stone path to the side of the house, and in under a minute, I've scaled the decorative trellis to my bedroom window. It easily slides open, and I crawl in, successfully avoiding the rest of the step-house.

I toss my bag by the bed and fall backward onto my mattress.

Unlike the outside, my room is full of reality. My teenage angst has bathed the walls in red, black words scribbled over the paint. Mostly they're notes from Sage, telling me she loves me and claiming me as her best friend in case any competition might wander in. The rest are words that felt too significant to forget. Quotes I've read or realizations I've made about life. All the wisdom I hold after eighteen years of existence.

Important shit.

Speaking of the best friend, I reach for the top hem of my school uniform skirt. Navy and green plaid. Another faux reality.

I slide out my buzzing phone and read the three messages, spaced less than thirty seconds apart.

SAGE

Are you home? I know you get out early on Fridays.

Bitch?

If you're off blowing a football player, I'll be so pissed/proud.

A perfect representation of our friendship in a triple text.

I blow out a breath as I stare up at the coffered ceiling, counting down from ten, and like clockwork—or an overly aggressive teenage girl—my phone starts vibrating.

"You're certifiable," I answer, putting her on speaker.

Sage doesn't miss a beat. "And you're a prep school slut." Then she immediately adds, "Unless you're just in your room on the bed. Then you're a substantial disappointment."

"She means she loves you," a deep voice says.

I smile. "Hi, Miles."

"Hey, Rem," her boyfriend says.

The two of them have been inseparable all week while he's been back. She even had him use his Mr. Teller impression to call her out of school.

They've been dating since last summer when he was home on break from CalTech. He'd skipped a year, so he graduated this spring but spent most of summer on the West Coast at a new internship. Or, as Sage refers to it, his new ho market.

"Did you get the app to work?" he asks.

"Yeah." I sit up, hearing the garage door open. "It's working fine."

"Let me know if the video cuts out. I've dealt with a few reports of it today."

Sage sighs into the mic. "You two need a room or what?"

I roll my eyes, and Miles starts sweet-talking the drama queen on the other end.

"You love the nerd talk." Something rustles, his voice suddenly much closer and lower. "You want to hear me talk about backend servers and bug reports."

"No!" she giggles out.

"Admit it—you're so turned on right now."

They fall into their own little world like they usually do, and once a breathy sigh comes through, I don't even bother with a goodbye.

It's nothing new for us. In fact, Sage and I haven't said goodbye once since we met in the second grade. Not when she left for eight weeks of summer camp, not when my mom and I moved to the town over a few years ago.

A door slams downstairs, and I glance at my closed one. I grab the extra pillows from the top of the bed and go over to shove them against the crack at the bottom, silencing all other sounds from the rest of the house.

As I crash back onto my bed, I grab my phone and open the app Miles installed over the weekend.

The startup he's interning at is developing an app for virtual tourism. Eventually a person will be able to log in, and someone in another part of the world will walk them through a museum or an art exhibit. They could experience Carnival in Brazil while working a late nursing shift in Maine or see the Vatican in the middle of a snowstorm in the Midwest.

It's in the beta-testing stage, only available to a few dozen people right now. I'm one of them because my best friend has no boundaries and volunteered me without my knowledge. She claimed it would be good for me to have more randomness in my life. Really, she thought Miles said virtual *dating*, only realizing her mistake when he was explaining to me how it works.

The purple *W* flashes, and the dots appear at the bottom as the app loads. Then the dashboard appears, welcoming SaintR to *Wanderer*.

No matter how much Miles swore the strangers on the other end couldn't see anything too revealing, I couldn't bring myself to use my real last name when I logged in the first time. I kept thinking how perfect of a setup it would be for a thriller movie. A stranger on the other side of the world tracks me down through the app. Might as well make them work for it.

But also, I wanted a few hours a day as far away from my life as possible. Even if it was only through a screen.

I check to see if anyone is online and available for a tour. Since the testing is broken into smaller groups to help track issues, my options are limited to three surrogates and wherever they might be in the world.

None of them are on, though, and I reach for my bag off the floor. A ding makes me stop and look down at the screen.

WestF has signed on and is available.

Rolling onto my back, I grab my phone again. I tap the notification to bring up his profile. Foster West, twenty-one, currently in Paris. His profile picture is of his shadow—or I assume it's his with the cast of his phone.

Out of the three, he's the one I choose most often. The others are constantly asking me in the chat what I want to see. But he just shows me what he thinks I should look at.

While it's barely two in the afternoon in Ohio, it's already evening there. I wouldn't think any places would still be open, but when I check, there's an available art museum nearby that doesn't close for another hour. I select it before hitting the Wander button.

Typically, it takes a few minutes for it to connect after he accepts the tour, but as I slip in my earbuds, a dialogue box pops up, telling me I'm wandering with WestF. Then the screen flickers to life, and I'm in the museum. The white floor below and windows above filled with the dimming Parisian sky.

There's always a pull when I see somewhere new. Like a part of my soul's begging to go—to see what I'm forced to experience through someone else's eyes. It reminds me of pictures and videos my dad would send me from when he traveled. The way I'd quietly promise myself to really be there one day.

I listen to the heartbeat of the museum while Foster pauses beside a large stone statue. Something abstract and harsh with smooth lines. Then he moves on to a wall of artwork, lingering on each long enough for me to absorb them fully.

It's how I know he's truly looking at them too.

When he stops the camera on a painting longer than the others, I study it, trying to figure out what about the colors he wants more time to appreciate. Why he's spending it on these brushstrokes over the others.

Eventually he starts to move again. He's crossing to the opposite wall when a brunette passes him, her eyes not leaving him and her mouth turning up. She's almost out of sight when the camera follows, keeping her in view longer.

That's the one drawback of Foster—among the culture and city sights are smooth legs in short skirts. I usually ignore them, but this one keeps cutting into the shot. The artwork's always off to the side to include at least her ass.

It starts to look like she'll be a permanent part of the tour, and I roll my eyes. I open the chat between us for the first time, not paying attention to the prompt telling me to say hi to my tour guide.

SAINTR: *Not that she isn't pretty, but a little more art, maybe?*

Miles said a few of the surrogates were sent glasses with a camera in them to test. Foster must be one because as soon as I hit send on the message, the video shifts down to his phone in his hand, and I can see the red dot by the chat icon in the corner.

Instead of opening it, the camera moves back and forth, as if he were shaking his head, and then he looks up again.

"Calm down, Remi Saint," a low voice says into my ears. "We'll go look at Impressionism shit."

Something about the way he says my name makes me smile as he walks in the opposite direction of her.

SAINTR: *Thank you, Foster West.*

When he glances down this time, he opens the chat and reads my messages.

5

REMI

Now...

I HAVE LESS than an hour until the car arrives, but I'm standing in the middle of my torn-apart bedroom, scanning for my red skirt like I haven't had the past four weeks to pack for a four-month tour.

My eyes dart to the sound of my phone, buried under a pile of rejected outfits. I shove them off the bed and swipe to answer before even lifting the phone off the mattress.

"I'm drowning," I say. "Send the Coast Guard."

A deep sigh comes over the line. "You're not even out of the kiddie pool, Sinner. Stand the fuck up."

I lower onto the bed beside my suitcase. "Is this where you tell me you've taught me everything you can, and it's time to make my way in the world?"

Heath huffs out a breath, the closest he gets to a laugh. "You know half of what I do, and I'll be surprised if you make it through the first two weeks without calling me, crying, and begging me to bail you out."

My mentor, ever the nurturer.

I grab a top from beside me and play with the label, distracting myself from the sudden tug in my chest. The same one as every other time I've thought about the documentary over the past several weeks. It starts with a second of bliss, realizing how close I am to what I've wanted for so long. Then it stings when I remember Foster's hands gripping my waist, his calloused fingers dragging over my skin. The way he looked at me before walking away as Adams North.

The rest isn't far behind, and I blink a few times, running my fingernail along the stitches of the tag.

"You'll be fine, Sinner," Heath says when my silence drags out. "If you're not, I'll make sure this tour is the last one of their careers."

"You're lying," I tell him with half a smile.

He flicks his lighter on the other end, and I hear the crackle of burning paper as he lights a cigarette. "Of course I am. I've told you from the beginning I don't do the coddling shit. You either grow a pair and rule the fucking world or get on your knees for those of us who already do."

I blow out a breath and fold the top, laying it aside. "Well, thank you for the attempt. I truly appreciate it."

Spotting red fabric, I go to the dresser, moving the jeans from on top of my lost skirt. I tuck it in with the rest of my clothes and then flip the lid shut before jerking the zipper across.

"You don't need me spouting bullshit at you, Sinner. You know how to get your shots, and you have better vision than anyone I know—other than me. Just do what you do and don't let anyone give you shit about it, got it?"

"And if they spend the entire tour hating me?" I ask. But they is Foster. His parting words have started to sound like a threat the more I've replayed them in my mind. I thought enough time had passed that he would have forgiven me.

I guess I was wrong.

"Who the fuck cares if a bunch of musicians hate you or love you?" Heath pauses to take a long drag. Then he gives me a, "You good?"

I inhale and toss my last bag with the other two beside my door. "The best."

"Now we're both liars," he mumbles.

The world's full of liars and the oblivious.

"Send me footage every few days," Heath tells me. "Stay the fuck out of their hotel rooms, and I'll see you in four months."

He ends the call, and I sigh, letting the phone slip from my ear.

It took a lot of time to learn to sift through for the praise buried deep in talks with Heath. The takeaway from this little convo is he thinks I'm the person least likely to fuck this up. And it shockingly helps more than anything else anyone could have said.

FORTY MINUTES LATER, I've got my suitcases by the door, and I'm fidgeting on the couch.

I'm digging through my messenger bag for the stack of index cards I have all of my notes for the documentary on when the bedroom door across the hall from mine opens. I look up at the bare back slipping through. Xander spins and walks down the hall, dragging a hand through his pink hair. He disappears toward the bathroom, but then he backs up and stops at the open archway to the living room. His eyebrows rise in surprise, and I give him a little wave.

"Hey," he says before glancing back at his closed door. He braces in the archway for a second and then steps into the living room, rubbing a red mark on his shoulder. "I thought you'd still be asleep."

He drops onto the cushion beside me, and I pull my feet up between us.

"They called last night and changed my pickup time to this morning."

"That's why you disappeared early last night?" His lips pull tight, and he groans, scrubbing his hands over his face. "You should have told me, Rem. I thought you left with someone." His amber eyes set on me, his long lashes brushing his cheeks. "I would have come with you."

I shrug as he slides his hand onto my knee. "No point in ruining both our nights."

He glances at the door again, but his gaze darts right back to me. He drops his voice to keep it between us. "Definitely wouldn't have ruined it."

His fingers drag across the back of my hand until the door to his room opens, and I pull away. A girl steps into the hall in nothing but the shirt he wore out last night. She gives an awkward smile when she spots us on the couch together. Xander keeps looking at me, though, so after a second of being ignored, she scurries into the bathroom.

I push him in the chest once she disappears. "Dick."

He chuckles and tips his head back on the couch, closing his eyes. "She knew that's all she was signing up for."

One eye peeks open at me, and I try to fight off a smile but fail. "You're terrible," I tell him.

I swipe my bag off the floor and leave him and his hangover on the couch. He lifts his head so his heated gaze can trail me across the room, reminding me why I left early last night without telling him.

When we moved in together last year, our relationship was far less blurred lines. I'd needed a new place; he had a steady girlfriend. Since he'd taken over as Heath's TA after I started interning, we already knew we got along. Then his relationship ended, and we realized we got along in other, naked ways.

It usually happens when we're drunk and neither of us has brought someone home. A backup body when another falls through. But last night his eyes stayed on me, his hand sinking low on my back and pulling my body against his at the bar.

I *was* the girl he wanted to take home, the toy he wanted because soon he wasn't going to be able to have me. Isn't that part of the human condition? Wanting what we can't touch.

"Hey." Xander follows me to the door and tugs me against his hot chest. "I'm going to miss you."

I sigh, allowing myself to relax into him. "Just keep the girls out of my bed."

"Not a promise I would ever make."

He cracks a grin as I push him away, everything seeming to shift back to the way it should be between us as he gathers up my bags. This is the Xander I signed up for—no strings, no emotions.

I hold the door open for him, and he bounces down the stairs with me right behind him. I'm pulling my messenger bag off his shoulder when a black van pulls to the curb.

The door swings open, and a familiar smile appears. Colton gets out in a short-sleeve black tee, his biceps more intimidating than I remembered. His black hair glistens in the morning sun, and he leaves his sunglasses on and strides over to us, bending for my luggage on the sidewalk.

"Lioness," he says. He slips his shades down to wink at me over the top of them before pushing them back up and grabbing the strap out of my hand.

"I want that one," I tell him.

Rather than answer, he hands the messenger bag off to Christian, who's climbing out of the back seat. He loads the others while the band's manager hooks the button of his jacket. His gaze completes what I'm sure is going to be a habitual scan of my legs.

Ignoring the return of borderline inappropriate Christian, I turn to Xander. "Keep Heath alive for me?"

Even after the hell of being Heath's TA, he agreed to fill in when needed while I'm away. If he thought it was bad before, he has no idea what's waiting for him as an assistant.

Xander nods. "You got it." Then he surprises me and wraps his arms around me again. His lips press to the top of my head, a hand in my hair. "Go be great, okay?"

I ease away from him, and when I turn around, Christian has an entertained look to him. He sweeps his arm across his body, gesturing for me to climb in.

"Sinner," he says, his voice low as I pass him.

It sounds more like approval of my outfit than a greeting. I take my bag back from him, and he smirks. He grips my elbow to help me into the van, but I hesitate when my eyes lock with an icy blue stare. Foster's in the seat on the other side. I blink a few times, still in partial disbelief it could really be him.

Everything I wanted and couldn't touch at one time. Then it all became a memory I hated to even be reminded of. Because memories are like a web, tugging at other ones and bringing moments to the front of our minds that threaten to break us.

He looks away first. His gaze falls and then moves out the window. My eyes shift to the two guys in the third row of seats. Dev and Felix are both zoned out, neither offering more than a nod. I slide into the seat in front of Dev, pulling my bag with me onto my lap.

The band's been back in LA to rehearse the past few weeks. The shows on this leg have some changes from the previous two, accommodating for larger venues. They happened to be in New York for an interview today, so the label set it up for me to fly back with them. I just wasn't expecting all of them to show up to my apartment building.

Christian's already on his phone, sliding into the seat in front of me, and Colton slams the door shut on his way by. He hops in the front, and then we're pulling away from the curb. I twist around enough to watch Xander and my tiny little life slowly disappear. It feels freeing to see it all fade away.

"Boyfriend or wannabe?" Christian asks.

I rotate around, my back touching the cool leather. "Roommate."

"So, wannabe," Christian says.

Foster shifts, and I catch his reflection in the window. Since he walked out of the bathroom in Prague, I've scoured the internet for pictures of Adams North. I've seen him on stage, grabbing coffee, signing autographs, serenading a crowd with his eyes closed, hand on the mic like he's untouchable.

The images have merged with my memories, and even though I don't know the tortured eyes and hard-set jaw of the musician a few feet away, it feels like I should. Like I have this sliver of my soul that suddenly feels foreign inside me. The memories of who he was not lining up with who he is.

When I look up, his gaze meets mine in the tinted glass. Then it happens. The buzz of excitement gives way to the tug. A tug that drags me under and into the words and hurt lurking beneath the surface between us. Foster holds me hostage there, and something tells me he plans to keep me under the entire tour.

6

FOSTER

OUR FIRST TOUR, we spent eight weeks camping out of the back of a van. Driving around in the hottest part of summer to open for the opening band. Most nights, Colton—who played one hell of a roadie in the beginning—would be half passed out on the bare ground while I slurred every word and told him every dream of what my first headlining tour would be. Sold-out venues, screaming fans. He'd always crack an eye open and add, *"Hotel parties we'll never remember."*

Then one song played by the right person at the right time, an influencer slapping it onto a video, lip-syncing my words, and all the far-flung dreams lightning struck into reality. Except I remember each moment of the past few years.

Also, neither one of us ever imagined it'd be a world tour, or we'd wrap it up by crossing the continental US entirely on a fucking bus.

Even as I shake my head, a thrill tingles in my fingertips as I stare at the ostentatious wrap on the side of the massive tour bus. Black with red accents and a ridiculously large image of my face, Dev and Felix only slightly smaller on either side.

"Not tacky or over-the-top in the least," I mutter.

When I hear the pop of gum, I glance out of the corner of my eye. The tiny blonde beside me rolls her eyes. For as annoyed as Lee looks at the moment, the gleam in her eyes lets on how fascinated she is seeing one of her acts blown up in vinyl. I let my mouth tip up on one side, which seems to have the usual thawing effect on my agent.

She heads inside the label's building with a less irritated head shake. I stay a little longer. Let my gaze trail from one end of the bus to the other one more time.

Lee has a strappy heel planted to hold the door when I reach the elevator. Leaning on the railing beside her, I hang my head back and close my eyes, enjoying a brief reprieve from the chaos of nonstop rehearsals and interviews over the past few weeks. A break from the tour rarely means slowing down.

"Are you happy at least?" Lee asks.

I'm thinking about the bus again and the past few weeks of rehearsals when the elevator doors part. My eyes open and instantly lock onto the curves on the far side of the room. Remi's showing Dev how to hook up the mic pack we'll all be using while recording the documentary. Since she met with the execs earlier, she has on a cap-sleeved black blazer and pinstriped pants that flare at her ankles. Business at first glance, but the ripped graphic tee peeks through the opening of her blazer, and whenever she steps, crimson toenails and a toe ring flash. All the rebellion simmering just below the surface.

The muscles of my jaw work beneath the skin as I follow Lee off the elevator. "As close as I can be."

Lee crosses to the window overlooking the building's main parking. The other luxury tour bus sits below. No faces or specific branding on this one other than the same black and red. I trace my finger over the glass, following one of the lines on the bus.

"Close is good enough so long as you act like you're in heaven every time that camera lands on you." Lee folds her arms. Very serious. "The label ate up all the shit about throwbacks, and now…"

Now I spend four months on the road, sleeping on a cot rather than in hotels. No personal space, the combined stench of the entire band, and no more than twenty feet from the worst thing I ever let into my life.

I drop my hand and rotate enough it looks like I'm talking to Lee, but my full attention swings toward the other side of the room again. Felix is fucking with one of the handheld cams, not listening to Remi's tutorial.

"Just remember," Lee whispers, her body a wall between me and the others, "happy or not, this is what you wanted. It might not have come about the way you thought it would, but you need to live with the consequences."

It is what I wanted when I chased her down and begged on my fucking knees, swearing to her I knew I was meant for this. I still know it. Even the idea of being on that stage, me and the crowd, is the only thing that settles me. The only place I've always wanted to be—sweat dripping, air pulsing, and adrenaline pounding.

"I've got this," I tell her. I even manage to drag my attention from Remi to look her in the eye. "Although if you're concerned with someone acting out, this is a conversation you need to be having with Felix, not me."

Lee hesitates a little, checking over her shoulder toward my bandmates. "Maybe. But Felix isn't the golden boy."

I shake my head. I don't even try to hide the grimace. The fact Lee and the label see Of Men and Wolves as two distinct parts has always pissed me off. The three of us come as a package. No trades, substitutions, or buyouts.

Before we end up drawing blood, Lee sighs. "Just remember, all you have to do is make sure this documentary and tour go the way the label wants, and you're fucking set, Adams."

"Right. Just the documentary and tour. And the next album. And the music vids for the singles. And whatever they want after that."

She snorts, her attention traveling to the others across the room. "You want freedom? Be Foster. The label and fans own

47

Adams North. The sooner you accept that, the smoother your ride to the top."

Lee's barely finished with her lecture when she marches toward Felix, who's seconds from tucking the hand cam down the front of his pants. Colton moves to intervene too, but Remi proves them both unnecessary when she swats his hand away, careful to grab onto the camera so he won't drop it. She narrows a glare at him and rips off some tape from under the neck of his shirt. If I had to guess, it was attached to hair given how fast he goes from smirk to snarl. Remi throws him an innocent smile and finishes attaching the mic.

When her gaze lifts to meet mine, her cheeks take on a red tinge, and then she's looking away.

I make her uncomfortable. Fuck if that doesn't piss me off.

Colton's chuckling when he waltzes over to me. "Looks like our little lioness will have all of you in line before we embark on this party bus." He taps a knuckle on the glass and nods to the bus below. "Not as tacky as I expected. Although, they could have thrown a giant picture of your face up there just so I'd have something to laugh at."

I half-smile. "You haven't seen the other bus in the back lot."

My best friend cracks a grin. "Fuck yes. I'm holding this over you until we're dead."

He shoves me, not gently. I'm flipping him off and rebalancing as Christian reaches us. He has on his business eyebrows, slightly lowered with a line creased between. I already know what he wants. Remi's been interviewing all morning to get our thoughts on the documentary. She's already sat down Dev and Felix, even managed to get Christian to play respectable long enough for his shots. I've conveniently been busy every second until now.

"She needs half an hour," he says.

Remi's finished with Felix, and she snags the spy glasses from Dev. With the wave of a hand, she dismisses them. Lee steers them out the door, no doubt to make sure Felix doesn't destroy anything without Remi's supervision. Colt starts to follow them but pauses, tossing a look back at me.

"Can I trust you to play nice, or do I need to hang around?"

"Whose security are you?" I ask, feigning offense.

"She's a nice girl." He shrugs. "Don't ruin her, yeah?"

By the time he and Christian saunter out the door, the room has cleared out. Remi must not realize I stayed back. She pulls her phone out, and a second later the steady drum and bass beat cuts off. It's replaced with a slow intro. Guitars and then soft vocals. Familiar.

"Mazzy Star."

She startles and spins. Her eyes crush closed when she sees me by the window. "I thought everyone left."

"Would have, but apparently the director requested me for an interview." I move toward her and the table of equipment, and her gaze falls to it too.

"We should get you set up with a mic pack. I can show you how to change out the batteries, and then—"

She cuts off as I drag my fingers over the black-framed glasses. They feel so familiar, and as if sinking into a former life, I slip them on. The silence echoes in that moment. I look over to find Remi staring up at me, her lips parted and eyes glued to my face.

"I always wondered what you'd look like with them on."

We stand there a few more seconds, staring at each other. Even after everything, it feels wrong not to be touching her right now. Just like in Prague, when it seemed like such a waste not to put my hands on her, my lips. It's easy to forget something so soft and beautiful is heartless.

I swipe off the glasses and toss them in front of her, not giving a shit about the ripple of tension spreading between us.

"The weight of the camera in the bridge will leave marks on the nose," I tell her. "Might want to think about that before we wear them. Make sure there aren't photoshoots or appearances scheduled after."

She nods and then finally lets her gaze fall to the table. "Right.

That's a … really good point." The last part comes out with a breath of air, either surprised I'd think of it or bothered she hadn't. "So, the mic pack."

When she turns with the black box in hand, her attention lowers to the bottom hem of my T-shirt. I get another flash of the discomfort she showed earlier, only this time I want more of it. I lazily lift my shirt, and a blush rises in her cheeks while her eyes skate over the ridges of my abs. They settle on the tattoo slightly dipping below the top of my jeans.

Restless.

"We don't have all day, sweetheart," I tell her in a bored tone.

Remi's gaze jerks to mine, and I point my chin to the mic pack still tightly clutched in her hand.

She releases an annoyed huff of air and starts hooking me up without another word. I watch her fingers brush my bare skin, my teeth clenching together with every second of contact. With her so close again, the same hint of jasmine from Prague floats through the air, something darker underneath.

I'd never admit it to a living soul, but I once sniffed my way through a perfume aisle, wondering which she'd use. A fragrance with flowers was my pick, but not dark. The memory of standing in the store like a creep surprises me. Especially when one side of my mouth turns up the slightest bit, remembering how much I didn't fucking care because it made me feel closer to her somehow.

The redness from her cheeks dips down her neck when she has to slip her hand farther up my shirt to attach the mic. "Lee said to keep the mics hidden as much as possible when filming," she says in a quiet rush. "God forbid we ruin the aesthetics with *too* much honesty."

I lean forward to give her less of a reach while she clips it on. "No one behind this wants honesty," I tell her. "They only want the profitable illusion of it."

"I want it." Green orbs flash to mine, then she's back to fucking with the battery pack on my waistband.

We've both kept our voices low, despite the room being empty. Maybe a shared habit of being around recording equipment. Yet some part of me says it has more to do with something more specific to us. A history of not wanting to be overheard by parents or roommates and to avoid aggravated stares from tourists in galleries and museums.

A section of her hair falls forward. She gives a slight shake of her head to move it, but it tumbles over her eye again. It's not until my fingers are brushing the strands away that I realize I've moved. The backs of my knuckles brush her forehead as I tuck the lock of hair behind her ear with the rest. The gesture stills her hands. Her lashes flutter along with her breath.

It takes a second for my arm to lower back down to my side. Remi looks up, and I have to look away before those eyes land on me.

"Basic mic pack. I think I got it," I tell her.

She takes a step back then and roughly swallows. My eyes wander up to find she's plastered on what I know is a fake smile. "Perfect. If you just want to finish hooking it up, then we can get this over with."

I nod, but my jaw tightens. "Yeah … about that." My fingers undo the microphone, and I snake it back down my shirt.

Remi shakes her head, the fake shit sliding right off her face until she's almost glaring at me. "What are you doing?"

"I realized I have somewhere else to be." I toss the pack next to the glasses.

"Oh really?" she says, the annoyance palpable in her tone. "And where might that be?"

"Anywhere but here." I give her a quick smirk and wink before I stroll off toward the elevator.

"And the interview?" she hollers after me.

I hit the button and swing my head toward her. She has her arms crossed, a hip popped out to the side in a sassy little display of the fire beneath the cool exterior.

"We have nearly four months together," I remind her. The

elevator opens, so I walk in, turning around at the back to face her again. "I'm sure I'll have time eventually."

She drops her arms, frustrated, our eyes staying locked while the doors close between us.

It's the last time I'll be able to get away from her for the next few months.

Fuck if I'm not going to take advantage.

Sure, it's a dick move. I know it. But that's what I was missing the first time around with her—the armor. Since she's the reason I forged it in the first place, it's only fair she gets the shiniest, most dickish parts.

7

FOSTER

Before...

THE TIP of my pen taps on the paper, leaving little dots and lines. Evidence I'm trying and failing to perfect these lyrics. The ones I've been working on the entire trip.

An entire month of scribbling shit words only to cross them out. The last few pages of my notebook have seen more ink than a tattoo artist.

Flinging the pen to the floor, I fall backward on the pillow. I'm prepared to stare at the ceiling for a while. Truly brood over my failed artistic endeavors.

I only get a few minutes, though, before my phone buzzes. I swipe it off the mattress and crack a smile.

SaintR has signed in.

I roll out of bed and grab my jacket off the floor. Pocketing my phone, I snag the black-rimmed glasses off the desk on my way out.

The room's technically an office with a mattress tucked in. Not that I'll complain. The fact we have a place to sleep that's not a park bench is more than enough for me while on this insane trip.

Reaching the kitchen, I'm unsurprised to see it's standing room only. People are piled on chairs around the table with extra stools and boxes dragged around for more seating. The group all has a glass in hand, drinking their way to drunk while playing poker.

I get a few raised glasses when I enter, a shouted "Foster," and a head turn. I nod in greeting, but it's the dude in the Cowboys jersey with a chick planted on his lap I slap on the shoulder.

Chase looks back with a buzzed gleam in his eyes and the girl's fingers in his dark hair. He gives me a cool once-over, noticing the jacket.

"Where are you going?" he drawls, hitting the Texan accent heavy.

"Where do you think?"

"Dude," he says.

"Dude."

"Brother," he tries.

"Brother." I give him a tight-lipped smile as I back away. "Someone has to pay for your ass to gallivant."

He glares at me as I reach the flat's door. Then my best friend dismisses me with a wave of his hand before using the same hand to grip the chick's ass, making her squeal.

The jackass makes a kissy face at me over her head while she slaps at him, and I wink back. A chorus of my name and byes follows me out, all cutting off when I shut the door behind me.

I shake my head on my way down the hall.

The last thing I expected when we ended up in Paris two weeks ago was crashing with a bunch of American college students. We ran into them the first day, and Chase latched onto the familiar.

In hindsight, his half-assed plan to take off first semester this year and randomly traipse around Europe was just as terrible as it sounded when he first came up with it. But once Chase gets an idea in his head, you either run away or hold the fuck on tight for the ride.

Plus, it pissed off the old man to hear the tuition he paid was nonrefundable.

Oops.

I grab a taxi and take it to one of my favorite places in the city. Small shops and galleries, a museum, and a park all within a few blocks of each other.

As I climb out of the car, I open the app and mark myself as available for a tour.

By the time I wound up in Paris, *Wanderer* already had permission to stream the exhibits in quite a few museums and galleries. They really know their shit and made sure to not only include the major tourist attractions but also more intimate places for tours. The quiet ones, where it feels like just you and the art.

Those are the places I take Remi.

I'm sliding on the glasses when the request comes through.

SaintR wants to wander!

She picked the little art gallery across the street, and I smirk. She always chooses something nearby as if she's afraid to be a bother. Which is why I waited to sign in until I got here.

Her profile might not give much away, but I have Remi Saint pegged as a college student in the Midwest. She's bored and looking for a little adventure she can't have. Adventure I can provide, thanks to the cash *Wanderer* pays per tour in their beta program.

The fall breeze kicks up around me. I breathe it in while crossing the street. It only takes until I walk through the door to the gallery for *Wanderer* to transfer funds onto my pay card, and I hand it to the guy behind the counter to swipe.

I lean on the counter and scan the large, open space. Empty. Perfect.

"Merci," he says, and I throw him a smile.

Then I press the button, flush against the frame of the glasses, and they connect to my phone seamlessly. The video pops up before dropping to just the corner of the screen, letting me see if chat lights up. Not that it does with her.

Not often anyway. I'll admit, though, I wasn't being very subtle about the brunette last week. Some art just deserves more screen time.

Since that day, we've been back to the silent tours we both seem to prefer. It's the main reason I catch as many with her as I can. She isn't constantly messaging, demanding to see something she saw on the website or complaining if I spend too much time on one piece.

It takes a few paintings before I pause, drawn in by the artwork. This one's different from the previous artists' works, something more delicate and thoughtful behind the strokes of the ballerina in front of me. She has her arms over her head, toe shoes pointed perfectly. But it's so much more.

It's the details that make the piece mark a small bit of the soul. The worn spot on the left shoe, her tights threadbare at the knee.

"She's crying," I say out loud, not even thinking.

I have no idea if the chick on the other end even has her sound on, but it needs to be said because I'm unsure if the well of tears in the girl's eyes will come across on the screen. And it's the most mesmerizing part, the slight uptilt of her mouth and the tears in her eyes. The rest of her life might be shit, but she's doing the one thing that makes her feel alive.

My phone buzzes. The chat bubble lights up, and I tap the screen.

SaintR: *It's perfect.*

"Yeah," I mumble. "She is."

A few minutes later, I'm circling a water feature set off to the side. Broken pieces of metal curved and shaped to have the water running from one piece to the next.

My phone goes off again, the chat icon with a red dot.

SaintR: *I can't see anything. The video is black.*

I take off the glasses, knowing I charged them last night, and turn them around, shoving my face at the camera like that will somehow fix the problem.

"See me?" I ask.

SaintR: *Nothing.*

I shut them off and hang them off the front of my shirt before switching to my phone camera. The box in the corner shows the framed portrait the camera's pointed at.

"Better?" I ask.

SaintR: *I'm still not seeing anything.*

"Shit."

SaintR: *I can hear you just fine though.*

"Good to know." I drag a hand through my hair and glance around, not even through the first room of the gallery. Such a waste.

The bubbles pop up to indicate she's typing.

SaintR: *They've been having trouble with video cutting out lately. I'll report it.*

SaintR: *Thanks anyway.*

"Wait." The word is out before I even think it through. "I'm already here and paid. Give me your number, and we'll finish the tour."

There's nothing for a while.

"Seriously. The exhibit in the next room is closing today. It would be a pity to miss it."

SaintR: *You want me to give my number to a stranger in another country?*

I walk over to a bench and drop down on it, stretching out my legs and leaning back against the wall behind me. "A stranger who had to pass a background check for this job. Plus, if you think I could find you with just a name and phone number, you're giving me far too much credit."

She types then stops, and I can't help but push a little.

"Come on, live a little. If it makes you feel better, I have no interest in anything but the cash and the art. Strictly business on my end."

SaintR: *Just art?*

"Just art," I agree. "You won't even see my face."

Another pause, then typing.

A number comes through.

I slip in my earbuds before I video chat her. Being a man of my word, I keep my phone down, and when she answers, I flip the camera around so the fountain shows. I break into a smile, seeing her camera pointed to a white ceiling.

"Beautiful view," I say.

The bubbles pop up on the chat, and I chuckle, not opening it when the dot appears.

"Nah, baby. Use your words."

A soft sigh comes over the line, and then, "Baby, huh? So much for strictly business."

Her voice is quiet and raspy, like she's keeping it between the two of us. I lower mine even though no one else is around me in the empty room.

"Maybe I'm a liar," I tell her.

She lets out a huff. "This was such a bad idea."

I get to my feet and move back to the fountain. "Right. Let's start over."

She's quiet on the other end. So quiet I almost fall into the silence before I hear her breathe again.

"Hey, Remi," I say, my lips turned up even though she can't see me.

A few more seconds pass. "Hey, Foster."

I smile the rest of the way.

8

REMI

Now…

I'VE ALWAYS DREAMED of being fully immersed in my work. Of shooting a documentary where I live, breathe, and sleep the subject. I just never really thought through the sleeping part until right now, awkwardly standing with my camera bag slipping off my shoulder in front of a luxury bus.

The band just finished kicking off the last leg of their tour with a show in LA. I've been filming with my handheld ever since they stampeded off the stage. Loving every second of the excitement of finally getting on the road. Even if it is mostly B-roll of cables being wound and bags flinging into storage beneath the buses. The power of adventure intoxicates.

At least it did until a few seconds ago when the coordinator directed me to a bus. The one without the band's faces on the side. The discreet one, lower profile for the higher-profile occupants.

Glory and Nate—my assistants for cam and audio— disappeared onto the other bus a few minutes ago with the rest of our equipment. The bus I should be on. I can easily film footage on the road by riding with the band a few hours here and there if that's what the label's worried about.

I'm hesitating outside the bus, about to go object when a hot body brushes by me. Foster's arm grazes mine, causing him to pause on the bus's steps and look over his shoulder. He quirks a brow, seeing me below. I can't help but take it as a challenge, and with a dismissive shake of his head, he makes up my mind for me.

I readjust my bag's strap and climb up behind him.

Christian's waiting at the top with a smile, even as he dodges Foster. I force something similar onto my face. I slip by him and stop to survey the lounge area. Two sweaty rock stars already cover one of the expansive couches lining each side. Plush and overstuffed with the worn-in throw pillows tossed out of the way.

Felix sinks deeper into the dark charcoal cushions. "Welcome home."

He slaps Dev on the chest with a flat palm, and the bassist throws me a smirk.

I scoped out the buses earlier today. I ran my fingers over the pristine leather of the couches, opened the microwave in the kitchenette for no reason. The four spacious bunks deeper on the bus are twice the size of the six on the other one. Worthy of rock gods in the making.

I'm flashing back to sleep-away camp and trying to recall which bunk is best when Colton appears from behind the drape that separates the back from the front. My brows slant together.

"You're sleeping on this one too?"

He stalls his steps. "Where else would I sleep?"

Four of these guys. Four bunks.

"Doing the math?" Christian asks, and I cut him a look. "Have no fear, gorgeous. I took care of you."

His eyes shift, and mine follow to carved-out footholds in the wall. I missed them earlier. They lead up to what looks like a loft space above the cabin.

"Roomiest digs on the bus," he says.

I question that but try another quick smile before taking the ladder. My head breaches first, and I stop. A queen mattress waits for me, fresh bedding and extra pillows. A small ledge borders three sides of the bed. A foot or so of space by the ladder already has my bags with more room to spare. I can't help the real smile that curves my lips.

I rush the rest of the way up and drop my camera bag with the others before I flop onto the bed. Flipping over, I blow out air and stare up through the skylight perfectly centered above me. Not much to see now, but I can already imagine the stars as we cross the country. Muted sounds filter up from below. A cushioned beat of bass. Someone laughs.

I close my eyes and listen in what feels like a room all to myself.

I ANGLE the camera to avoid any reflection as I shoot out the tinted window. The image through the viewfinder shows the road's shoulder across from us. Palm trees whip by as we meet cars on the highway.

"You ever stop with that?"

My eyes flick to Colton, his mouth lifted on one side.

The inside of the bus has been silent all morning. Other than the driver, I could forget anyone else existed until now.

We hit the road around two a.m. I slept better than I expected I would at first. The rocking motion as we escaped the city slowly morphed into a rhythm. Even so, I've been up for hours with my head spilling out everything I want to capture.

"Filming is kind of my job," I remind him.

He breaks into a full grin. "Cool. Mine is to keep these assholes safe. Doesn't mean I can never turn it off."

I pull my legs off the couch seconds before he drops onto them. Readjusting, I turn off the camera and set it on the floor beside me. Colton's studying me, I realize, glancing up, so I settle back and serve him a stare right back. He's wearing a tight black T-shirt again. His typical uniform from what I've seen.

After a second, he points his chin toward the side table behind me. "You've got my color."

Next thing I know, he's leaning over me for the red polish I used to repaint my nails. He drops the bottle onto my lap and tucks a foot under him to sit facing me. He holds a hand out, palm down.

His nails have the slightest remnants of polish lingering. I smile as I cautiously untwist the lid. I swipe the brush over one of his nails as he watches the color deposit. It's the most normal I've felt since this whirlwind began. The most included if I'm being honest.

Last night at the concert, especially, I felt like a documentarian trying to get a shot of a wild animal in its natural habitat. Being as invisible as possible and taking up minimal space—watching but never a part of it.

The thought has me warm, though, closer to my dad than I've felt in a long time. This was his day-to-day, on the move and having only seconds to capture an entire world in a frame. Although he was *actually* photographing wild animals. He would travel to the most incredible places and experience the world in a way so few have. I remember the stories he'd tell me, the promises to take me with him when I was older. How he'd show me the world.

I swallow down the tightness in my throat, re-dipping the brush. Colton sighs, and I glance up at him staring out the window with a content look on his face. His gaze darts over and then back to the scenery.

"Seems like a week ago, we were packed up in a sketchy van, driving this same road to an even sketchier bar gig. I think there were maybe six people standing on the concrete floor in front of the guys. The rest of the bar was regulars who didn't give a fuck if they were listening to live music or a jukebox. They sure as shit didn't remember the band's name by the time we started packing up the gear."

"And now?" I ask, curious of his take on all of this.

I've known since Prague that Colton's not just a security guard. I mean, he fully believed he could change the band's minds about bringing me onboard. Knowing he's been on the road with them since the beginning helps a piece fall into place.

"Now I can't think about it too hard because…" His eyes sweep over to meet mine before his attention falls to the brush as I finish up his pinky finger. "Because every second of this life feels so surreal."

"You talk like you're a member of the band," I say softly.

Colton whips out a grin made to destroy hearts and swaps hands. "Please. Adams wouldn't be able to compete with me. My sexiness would tear us all apart."

I roll my eyes, and he chuckles.

"Nah, I'd much rather experience the whirlwind from my perspective," he says. "I get to go along for the ride, being proud as fuck of my best friend, and not feel the weight of the world crushing down on me."

I nod, not needing to ask who he's talking about. Only one member of the band has that kind of heaviness in his eyes. The other two surely have their own stressors and fears of their sand castles coming crashing down. Anyone in their position would. But it's not them who look like they're drowning, fighting off the waves.

"You and Adams were friends before then?" The name tastes strange on my tongue now, as if Adams North disappeared in a wisp of smoke the second I heard his words coming out of Foster's mouth.

"*Adams* has been my brother since the beginning," Colton says, a sly little smirk forming—he doesn't realize I'm in on the joke. "He lived down the street when we were little. Our moms were close, so when his family moved to New York, they'd have these little 'video dates' for us. It kept us close until he moved back to Texas. And then…" He pauses, and for a split second, I catch his mouth twitch down on one side. Then he sniffs away whatever's bothering him and grabs the brush out of my hand. "Let's just say we've been through a lot of shit together. At some point, it became an unspoken understanding we'd go through the rest of it together too."

My thoughts immediately turn toward Foster's history with his father. The *shit* he put Foster through, the wounds he left him with to heal. Those are details Foster told Remi Saint in a completely different life, though. Something tells me he'd rather Remi Sinner not have access to those memories.

Even so, I can't help but wonder what new scars he carries, and the curiosity is burning. So much so I have to sit back against the arm of the couch and take a deep breath before I take a shovel to Foster's last five years.

I distract myself by watching Colton. He finishes his thumb before he tugs the bottle from my grip and screws the lid on tight. He holds it out for me, and as I reach for it, his eyes move over my head. My fingers graze the bottle while I glance over my shoulder, where my eyes collide with a whole lot of tattooed skin.

Dev's running a hand down his bare abs to the top of his gym shorts, his eyes half open and his hair a sleepy mess. Even in his drowsy state, he still manages to grin at me. "Morning."

I whip back around to Colton and his smirk. Right. Bus full of musicians. Skin is a part of the game.

Dev bangs around in cupboards in the kitchenette. He comes into the lounge with a mug of coffee, and then he's plucking the nail polish from my hand. With a wink, he drops onto the couch across from us. He balances the coffee on the cushion beside him while he opens the bottle.

"Help yourself," I mumble.

Colton chuckles. "Get used to it. These guys live like barbarians on the road. They see something they want, their brains go caveman. Chest-pounding, grunting, not washing their balls—"

"Hey, Colt," Dev says before he flips him off. "Get fucked. And for the record, my balls are licked clean regularly."

My nose scrunches. "Ew."

He gives a *not sorry* shrug and goes back to his nails with his lips quirked up. "Like you won't be privy to every pussy we hit, anyway."

"Preferably you won't be using my recording equipment while getting a blow job," I counter.

Colton stands and heads to the kitchenette. "Trust me, if it's going to happen, it'll be Felix's footage."

Dev snorts in agreement.

Now I know not to review Felix's footage around other people.

Colton returns with his own coffee and settles on the opposite end of the couch. He stretches his legs out on the cushions toward me. His socked feet sit a mere inch from my leg. In a weird way, it makes me feel included again.

Like he's accepted me as part of the herd.

He swipes the remote off the back of the couch and turns up the volume. The playlist from my phone pours out of the speakers lining this part of the bus.

Dev nods along with the song, seemingly approving of the punk anthem, while Colton drops his head back on the wooden cabinet behind him. His eyes close. His toes tap to the beat.

The moment has me leaning over for my camera off the floor. Colton cracks a lid when I move, his lips tipping up at what I'm doing.

"Never stop," he sighs out the words with a touch of disapproval.

I ignore him and hit record. The scene already unfolds in my head. An acoustic version of their song "Haunted" playing—if the label approves it—with cuts of their time on the road. Mostly on the bus. Candid moments like these. Ones like what I get by slowly panning from the landscape rushing by through the window to Dev on his couch. He has his head down in pure concentration, trying to paint the nails on his left hand. His profile is similar to how he appeared on stage last night, pouring every ounce of his focus into the finger movements of his bass.

From what I've learned, Dev's the dreamer of the group. He

told a story during our initial interview about the first time he performed—strumming a play guitar in front of his grandmother and her friends during one of their weekly get-togethers. Even while telling me about the sun shining through the windows and the rush he could feel over his skin, he appeared lost in the moment.

He's wanted exactly what they're doing now ever since: to change hearts with his music, repay his grandmother for every encouraging word she gave him growing up, to find a way to inspire the next generation to dream bigger than they can even imagine.

He glances up, breaking into a grin when he sees the camera, and with a shake of his head goes back to work. "Nothing is sacred now, huh?"

I zoom closer to draw attention to his profile—a snapshot of a little boy living his dream. Only now he has eyebrow rings and ink on his temple. This time he looks up to play-snarl at the camera, and I laugh.

After I get a little more footage of him, I ease the shot away to show the rest of the bus. The kitchenette, and then the heavy curtain to the hallway. Except the screen doesn't show the black fabric. I still when I land on tan skin stretched tight over carved pecs. Lower are hard abs, and then black ink disappears into sweatpants hanging off his hips, leaving only the top half of the word visible.

I figured it out when Foster pulled up his shirt for the mic pack. The word was like a spike in my chest, dragging the memory out of me regardless of how deep I tried to lock it away.

"You think you know me so well? Then describe me in one word."

Restless.

"I won't be once I get to you."

My eyes lift to a faded blue pair, watching me over my camera. Foster has a lazy look to him, effortlessly sexy in a state women would kill to see him in, with his hooded gaze all on me. My lips part as I draw in a breath, but I swear he drains the air from the entire bus, or at least the air that was feeding *my* lungs.

We haven't said a word to each other since he bailed on his interview at the label. I haven't even pushed to try again. Partly because the tour started up again and he's had zero downtime. Mostly because I can't be alone with him until I see him as Adams.

Given the way my chest fucking burns from not breathing right now, I'd definitely say I'm in a staredown with Foster West.

"Morning, sunshine," Colton says from behind me.

Foster's jaw clenches as his attention rises over my head to his best friend, but it lowers back to me before he rasps, "Hey."

His gravelly morning voice skates over my skin, rough and jarring enough I lower the camera, along with my eyes. Avoidance is the only escape I have right now.

While I set the camera on the cushion behind Colton's feet, Foster walks to the kitchenette. I'm fighting not to look again when Dev hisses, "Shit."

The bassist has already set his mug on a table. He flings himself off the couch to his knees, and then he walks on them to me. Stopping beside me with a defeated look, he holds out the bottle and his left hand.

Of all the experiences I've had in this industry, a musician basically pleading me with his eyes while on his knees for me to paint his nails is somehow one of the more surprising.

I take it without question, though. The guy already made a mess on the one nail he attempted on what's clearly his dominant hand.

I'm cleaning it up when Foster appears in my peripheral, sipping from a white mug that matches every other one on this bus. None of them used the brand-new espresso machine, all content with the drip coffee maker.

Foster crosses behind Dev and drops onto the other couch. I hold off as long as possible before I look over. A notebook balances on his knee, a pen in the hand not holding his coffee. He begins writing. The tension leaves his shoulders, his face relaxes. Even the air of annoyance he's constantly carried around me vanishes. His pen stills, and his eyes shut. He licks his plush lips, leaving them parted slightly. I swear I feel the words he whispers then.

I glance at my camera. The need to capture him like this is a living, breathing thing that pulls in my chest.

"Never stop." Colton leans forward and swipes up my camera.

He clicks his tongue at me but dutifully hits record and aims at Foster. While he films, I finish up Dev's nails, determined not to peek again.

I twist the lid on once finished and shoo the bassist away.

"Thanks, slugger. It would have looked like a murder scene if I kept going on my own." Dev gently knocks my jaw with his fist before returning to the other couch. "I knew you'd come in handy."

I sigh as he resettles. "Glad you've found a use for me."

Colton chuckles, and I jerk my camera out of his hand. He's completely unfazed and shifts to get comfortable, returning to his nap.

"So touchy," he mutters.

But his lips twitch.

I think he's adopted me.

Outside of the music, the lounge falls quiet. No movement, no distractions. It leaves me hyperaware of the presence on the opposite side. Not the chill one with freshly painted nails. The magnetic one. The space practically pulses around Foster, and I fight the urge to look up from my camera. To see if he's still lost in his notepad.

He's writing lyrics.

The words will be messy and scribbled. I've seen it before in a notebook he flipped through during a video chat. A chat where he could have switched the camera to his face at any time. He never did, though. I can't help wondering, what if he had? If he'd broken the only rule I gave him. Would it have changed anything?

I swallow back the sudden lump in my throat. My thoughts are drifting too far in a direction I refuse to go. I can't. Not now when I'm taking more risks than I have in over five years.

Distracted with ghosts, I forget not to and look up, only to lock eyes with Foster. His pen tip still touches the paper, but his entire focus hangs on me. All intensity like he's trying to solve a puzzle. My breaths start slipping, too short. The thrum of my pulse paces faster. I think about that damn lyric notebook. How I wrote his words on my bedroom wall, and now I know he wrote mine on his skin.

A few raw seconds pass before his jaw flexes, then his eyes fall away. Brick by brick, he lays a familiar cold wall of resentment between us. Like everything else to do with him, I slam into it heart first.

The pitiful thing clearly hasn't learned its lesson.

Gathering my camera and nail polish, I knock Colton's feet as I retreat to the only place I can. I drag myself up the ladder and collapse on my bed and fucking breathe.

I need the man down there to be Adams North. Not only for the documentary but my sanity. He can't be the wandering boy. He can't be that restless soul who's always echoed in mine. He can't be memories and constant reminders.

That man can't be Foster.

Because Foster hurts too much.

THE ATMOSPHERE BACKSTAGE ahead of a show is hypnotic, a drug direct in your veins.

At least it is with Of Men and Wolves.

People rush around, orders are given, and the air hums with an unidentifiable electricity. A mounting hype promised when the band takes the stage. It's hectic and fast-paced, but at the center of it all lies the eye of the storm.

Lounging in Dev's case.

His long limbs sprawl over the blue fabric couch in their dressing room. He has his eyes closed while his thumb strums invisible strings, his fingers stretched over an imaginary fretboard and his foot tapping. He's running through the entire setlist in his head. Every riff and interval.

It's his ritual.

They each have their own, I've noticed. It all starts and ends with shots as a band. Dev visualizes first. Then he'll jog in place, dispelling the building energy. He also has a tiny keychain shaped like Arizona. He'll kiss it and tuck it in his pocket. A gift from his grandma, he told me.

Felix takes a few extra shots and jerks off. A little less sentimental than a reminder of Grams. No one can deny the calmness and focus in him ahead of taking to the stage, though. All the chaos and crudeness step aside to let him do what he does best. Shockingly, that has nothing to do with pussy but sticks and a kick.

Adams, I haven't the slightest idea. He vanishes after the shot and returns in time for the other one. A buzz surrounds him then, and for the moment he seems to have tamed his demons.

Right before the final shot, the bandmates huddle together. The three of them form their own little world, foreheads pressed together and hands on each other's napes.

Then they go simultaneously devastate and enamor tens of thousands.

I check in with Glory and Nate to make sure they have everything they need. The tour has audio recording taken care of, so we can cover more ground with cameras. Glory will have one on the platform in the crowd, and Nate is at the front of the stage for closer shots. Christian has a pair of spy glasses ready for Felix. He won't get them until he goes onstage to avoid any "unnecessary" footage being caught beforehand.

Felix had grinned at that one, then grabbed his junk. "Everything about my cock's necessary. Vital, some might say."

With them all set, I grab my handheld from my bag and set off for a shot I've been desperate for since the first show. Several people flood through the hallway, but the closer I get to the stage, the quieter it becomes. Soon, though, a different sound begins to build. One that carries such an addictive quality, which makes even *my* blood pump a little harder.

By the time I stop at the steps leading to the stage, the noise of the crowd has taken over. Just like the previous nights, a slow chant starts somewhere deep in the arena, weak at first but growing until the words beat through the entire world.

Adams.

Adams.

Adams.

My heartbeat syncs to it.

A few renditions will continue until they roar for the opening band.

Wanting to be ready for the next one, I search for an angle. I move to the side of the stairs where a couple tall speaker stacks tower high. There's space behind them and a gap in the heavy curtains that otherwise block any view of the crowd. It creates a little hideaway, tucked right up beside the stage.

Dark, secluded, and the perfect place for my shot.

I turn sideways to wedge through a crack and hold my camera as high as I can to barely clear the top of the music equipment. Once I grunt my way in, the world below stage level vanishes. The overheads from the front barely reach through the gap, and the speakers block the dim backstage lighting. It bathes all of me in shadow except for eyes up, so I go slow and feel my way toward the stage. I step on a coil of cords, but mostly my path is clear.

Famous last words.

My shin slams into something hard and unmovable. I curse at the sharp pain that radiates and stumble. My hand flattens on top of whatever assaulted me and catches me. The addiction to obtaining the best shot immediately numbs everything when I push down. The coarse fuzz beneath my palm has no give.

I smile in the dark. "Perfect."

With one more test to see if it holds, I rest my knee on top of the equipment. It doesn't collapse right away, so I pull the other up to kneel. Between the curtains, I can see over top of the stage and lift the camera. The viewfinder catches some of the crowd, but something seems off. I adjust my position, walking on my knees sideways away from the stairs. My eyes flick between the digital image and the real one.

So fucking close.

I realize too late I've run out of fuzzy land. My knee misses the edge and keeps going. I gasp in a breath, losing my balance, and grab blindly for anything to save me. A warm hand clamps around my bare thigh to steady me just as I find something solid to hold onto. The solid moves ever so slightly. I realize it all in rapid fire. Soft fabric below my hand. A hard shoulder beneath that. Fingers flexing into my skin. My heart batters against my rib cage, but it turns into a full-on escape attempt when the hot palm slips higher.

Then it starts again.

The chant. The name.

A barely distinguishable shadow shifts off to the side of me. I can just make out a head rest back, the vagueness of someone sitting on who knows what below.

"Get your shot," Foster says, voice easy.

Foster. Despite what I said to myself and what an entire arena tells me now, it's not Adams.

Even with his touch branding me, the chant's so strong I can't keep myself from releasing his shoulder and bringing up the camera. I stretch in his direction, still not far enough over. Foster readjusts, sliding his grip to the back of my thigh to hold me stable. I take advantage and lean more, and then it happens.

An angle of the stage covers the bottom third of the frame, leaving the rest to show the crowd. Light shining off animated faces, fists pumping in the air. MARRY ME ADAMS signs, and a FELIX I'M PREGNANT.

Foster's thumb strokes over my skin, and I suck in air as goosebumps scatter up my thigh.

I stabilize the shot but look down into the shadows at the indistinct outline. It moves, and hot breath teases my naked skin. The sensation travels all the way to my clit.

"Foster," I breathe, asking a question.

His hand creeps higher, under the bottom of my skirt. And let's be honest, it's not that long.

"Keep filming," he rasps.

The words caress my thigh. I swallow and return my eyes to the viewfinder. Foster's other hand slides up my calf as I zoom in on a girl. She's beaming, balanced on a dude's shoulders, her arms down, his bent up, and their hands linked. I capture another couple, a guy's arm slung around another's waist, dragging him against his body.

All of them shout for Adams while Foster caresses higher. His calloused fingertips reach the curve of my ass. I stop breathing. Thank God I've already gotten what I wanted for the shot because every fiber of my being is focused on the slide of his palm.

He teases the lace edge of my panties before he starts to trail it back down. The camera lowers, and I close my eyes. My core is already throbbing, and he's barely touching me.

When he traces inward, I clench my thighs together. He bites the one closest to him, and I bite my lip to keep in a moan. It's all for nothing since I whimper the second Foster strokes over the drenched fabric covering my pussy. Featherlight the first time. Dragging the second. Then his thumb slips under the edge, and I shove my hand into his hair.

"Keep this area clear," a woman says.

I jump at her proximity, and Foster's hand falls from under my skirt, his hair slipping through my grasp. Realizing someone's by the stairs, I scramble backward off the fuzzy surface. I can't see shit once I'm down. I'm about to turn around but freeze when a hot body ghosts my back. His clothes brush mine. Touching but not touching. It makes my skin burn. A painful anticipation of more.

"Opening band is moving," a guy barks outside the speakers.

A strand of hair moves by my neck, the lightest of a sweep on my shoulder. Then the heat of him vanishes. Air moves behind me and stills. I turn around already knowing he won't be there.

My insides twist anyway, and I hate it.

I wish I could stop it. I want to promise myself it won't happen again.

But I'm already standing here alone. My breaths are still shallow, my panties soaked, and the dark feels darker. I just don't have it in me to lie to myself on top of it.

9

FOSTER

Not so long ago, I almost met my idol at a party. He stood on the opposite side of a room, both of us with drinks in hand. The musician talking to me casually offered to introduce us unprompted. In that moment, the stars had finally aligned. The fates wove the cosmic strings just right. My life had flipped so surreal, I fit seamlessly into his reality. He wouldn't even question if I strolled up to him. Fuck, he might even tell me he knew my music.

One of the final life-defining experiences I'd fought for waited for a head nod.

I threw my drink back and walked out.

They say to never meet your idols because they won't live up to the version of them you created. I think it's crueler than the bite of disappointment. Once you meet your idol, it's over and can never happen again. You've touched the star. Brushed your fingers over the string. The moment is capsuled, the exhilaration fades, and you're stuck chasing a high that can't be replicated. I wasn't ready for that to be gone.

Meeting your muse couldn't be more different. They've already been aligned and deeply woven into your tapestry. They're a part of the air you breathe, coloring every aspect of your world. Meeting your muse can never end because they feel like a piece that's been there all along. Something you always knew but never quite understood.

This makes losing your muse such a fucking tragedy.

She's suddenly everywhere and nowhere.

I can't see her, but I feel her in the dark.

And fuck her for feeling so damn perfect.

My eyes flick to the viewing area where Christian's on his phone on the other side of the soundproof glass wall. Today's our first day off since going back on the road, and the label booked us rehearsal space. A not-so-subtle nudge from Mac Records, reminding us they expect us to be in the studio a week after we wrap up in NYC.

We originally had more time between shows these last months of our tour, specifically so we could write. Then a performance of "Haunted" went nuclear at the start of it, and they crammed in stadiums for the last leg. We've been on a wild ride the past few years, but it still messes with my head how a rock icon reposted me singing and led to us playing the same stages she did a few months ago.

Sav Loveless—or more likely her team—altered our trajectory into the stratosphere with a fucking tag and *rock on* emoji.

Christian's pacing outside the glass, crossing back and forth in his rich-boy suit. Each time he passes, it flashes views of a messy auburn bun behind him. His legs and then a tease of a smooth one crossed over the other in an overstuffed chair. Him, then her. Him. Her. My focus shifts and turns his next passes into a dark blur, leaving me with just the fragments of Remi.

Always only pieces of her.

I smother a groan and drag my emo-ass attention back to the notebook open on the table. To my bandmates and my untouched acoustic at my feet. To the tick-tick of an invisible clock. The only shit I should be focused on.

I grab my guitar's neck to pull it up on the loveseat. The other two cover different parts of the sectional across from me, both in their own worlds. Felix beats away on a practice pad, and Dev's playing with a bass line.

None of us are committed right now. Maybe we *did* need the day off.

Slouching on the cushions, I will myself to create on demand. After a few seconds, my head rolls to the side. Christian's off his call, collapsed in a chair and not disrupting my view anymore. Remi flips through a magazine, looking beyond bored with her crossed leg swinging. Other than shooting through the glass, she can't do much until we leave. She filmed in here before we kicked everyone out. The dark flower scent of her still lingers. Every time it hits me, the world dissolves into thoughts of the other night when it surrounded me. Thoughts of silky skin beneath my palm, my thumb stroking wet lace.

My hands. Your body.

I breathed her in and felt my teeth dent her thigh.

Starving breaths on promise-covered skin.

Her whimper sent blood rushing to my cock, still trained to the sound.

My grip tightens on the fretboard while I watch her. I can't fucking stop watching her. And soon enough, I'm humming notes I've fought off for days. They've been spiraling. On the bus the other night before the San Francisco show. I succumb to them, finally listen. Then I feel for them on my guitar, my eyes on Remi the entire time. Once I match the first one, the others fall into place. I hit the end of the melody for a third time, but my fingers keep going, extending it a little longer before muting the strings with my palm.

"Play that again."

I swing my gaze to the sectional and realize I have Dev's rapt attention. Felix is sitting up, his sticks not moving anymore. Then he parrots Dev's, "Play that again."

I scrunch my face. "Nah."

"Play." Felix flings a stick, and I reluctantly slide back to the first note.

Halfway through this time, I actually hear what they do. I don't even bother looking up when finished, just shift straight back to the beginning. I hear more and feel my way through until the foundation settles. The riff develops naturally, like the entirety already existed and needed me to stop fucking around. Playing it over and over, I build and tweak.

The riff doubles. Dev's down an octave on his bass, deep and tonal. He varies the bass line as we jam, and I start to add chords.

"Fucking hell," Felix groans out. He hops off his ass and drops onto the cajón. "The muse is in the room."

Not quite.

I glance through the glass. Remi's at the edge of the chair, locked onto us in the rehearsal space. Even from here, I can see the rhythmic pulsing in my veins mirrored by the light in her green eyes. An unrelenting need claws at her to capture the rawness of us creating, the same way it tears music out of me.

With Felix drumming a beat on the box, the three of us sync in a way none of us try to explain. It's been this way since the beginning when we got together four years ago. A goddamn three-way soul read into an unstoppable creative flow. We work it for a while, shaping and harmonizing the initial melody.

It morphs into a chorus in my head at some point. I feel how the line will evolve for the verses. But I don't follow the chord progression yet. I'm chasing different notes, layered over what we're already playing. My lips start moving before sound follows. Mostly la-di-da shit to hear how vocals could fit.

Songs piece together differently with us. We have no code or formula. Sometimes I'll show up with every part breathing already. We'll work around lyrics on others. But not many have developed chorus first like "Echo" and "Haunted." Our wildfire and inferno. "Echo" set us ablaze, and "Haunted" engulfed the world in our flames.

The words aren't there yet, so I shrug when Felix asks *what* we have. Maybe the song goes nowhere. We could throw the whole thing out before we reach the studio.

I'm still flirting with a lyric melody as I walk down the corridor toward the kitchen. Dev's facedown on the floor in the viewing room, and Felix is getting high with Christian while we take a preventative "Colt break."

A couple years ago, the three of us sank into a writing bender —or bender in general. Three days of cigarettes, tequila, coke, and Maui Wowie. We ended with an album's worth of songs. Christian fell at our feet, money in the bank for him. Colton punched me in the face and took me to the emergency room for severe dehydration. Since then, we take breaks before Colt mandates them.

Bitch aims for the ribs now.

He has his back to the open archway when I enter the kitchen. I casually slap him in the head on my way by to the fridge. Colt curses as I swipe a glass bottle of water, and I smile, shutting the door. Only I sober once turned around. His massive frame blocked Remi on my way in. She has spy glasses pushed up into her hair. Her perky ass leans against a countertop, one bare foot on top of the other and arms crossed. The navy skirt hits her mid-thigh, and the R.E.M. shirt's ripped neckline dips low.

My hands. Your body.

"Write me a song, baby?" Colt asks.

I look down at my water and twist off the top, shaking my head. "You inspire me to get tested but not much else, my brother."

Colt rolls his eyes as Remi laughs. My lips twitch at the sound, and my gaze follows it.

Build the walls. Fight the siren's call.

"At least you're creative with the insults." Colt rotates to leave. "Channel that into something useful, and you might have a chance out there, kid." He condescendingly slaps my cheek while I drink and whispers, "Be nice, asshole," before he disappears around the corner.

Then it's just me and her. Alone for the first time since San

Francisco, when I lost the shred of control I have and had every intention of finger-fucking her by the stage.

Every second's a betrayal, every touch a threat.

Fuck, I need to find a way to survive this tour with her. Or at least try.

She lowers her arms and starts to follow Colt out, but I rip off a scab for the sake of my sanity the next few months.

"You went to Sound Clash." I spare myself the *two years ago* part. No intention of bleeding for her too.

When I spin around, Remi's frozen, still facing away. Her shoulders rise in a deep breath, and then she slowly turns around. She hesitates, likely wondering how long before this turns.

I couldn't tell her, but I'm fucking trying.

She steps closer when I wait expectantly, and the tension eases from her shoulders.

"I went to Sound Clash. A few years ago," she says, but it was *two*. "It was amazing—everything you said it would be."

I nod and repeat what I told her about the battle of the bands, "Wasted college kids, shitty riffs, and pure magic."

She laughs, nodding back. "The magic part's addicting. The atmosphere and crowd and … I don't think anyone can really understand without being there."

Without *truly* seeing it.

"You nailed it in your documentary. Maybe not as exhilarating as being on the stage yourself, but as close as you can get."

"I can't believe you watched it," she says.

I could tell her the band watched everything when the label brought her on. Tell her Dev and Felix loved it too. Instead, I drop the veil fully. I speak to Remi Sinner but ask Remi Saint what I've really wanted to know.

"How far into the park did you go?"

Remi slams me with the emerald eyes. The mask hiding the sadness in them slips, yet she has the tiniest upturn to her mouth.

I half-smile, question answered. "You saw the fountain."

"*Really* saw it," she almost whispers.

The amount of time that can span a few seconds of silence in the right circumstances is incredible. She searches my eyes, and I tip my head to the side, letting her. The broken girl and wandering boy are face-to-face for the first time. It's so hard not to fall into what we were. Who we were.

Who I *thought* she was.

I look away, and my armor's back in place when I return my gaze. "I'm glad something was real for you."

"Foster." She cringes using my name and checks over her shoulder to see if anyone's near us.

"What? Does my name make me too real?" I erase the space between us until she has to tilt her chin to look at me. "Was it easier in the dark, Remi? Not having to see me?" My thumb skims the skin between her shirt and skirt, her breath hitching. "I could finally touch you, and you could still pretend?" Her chest rises faster, my graze dipping under the top of her skirt and chasing more, and we both watch every pass lowering. "Maybe next time I play with your shadow, I make it come."

Her eyes flutter closed, lush lips parting on an inhale. I've seen parts of her this way more than once. Only now we're minus the phone screens, and the full view is even sexier.

I told her you never truly see something until it's right in front of you, and she's no exception. It's why I can't resist her in the dark. When I can't really see her, I can hide in the lies a little while.

My thumb stops, eyes trailing off while I chase the words instead of her skin.

"Foster?" Remi says, more hushed this time.

She touches my arm, near my wrist, and I look up at her.

The first line's right there.

I snag the black frames from her head, walking out with notes and syllables swimming. Christian stands by the door separating the viewing room and rehearsal space. I pass him while sliding the spy glasses on. I press the flush button without thinking. Muscle memory. Dev's on his bass on the sectional. I swipe the notebook and pen and barely hit the cushions across from him before ink hits the page. He stops playing, and all noise cuts out of the room after he shuts the door.

I write in fragments at first. Kill more lines than I save. I rework the same words three different ways, letting myself drift into the alternate reality that is creating—wrong builds to right and what fits perfect one time lacks the next. Then for no apparent reason at all, everything exists exactly as it should.

Everything flows in absolute harmony.

As Christian pounds on the door for a third time, demanding we get the fuck out, I drop back on the loveseat. I lazily launch my pen toward our manager. It *plinks* off the glass, but he gets my point.

It's been hours since we came back in here. My mind feels empty in a way that soothes the deepest parts of me. The paper's a mess of crossed-out words and circled ones. But what I want in the end remains mostly legible.

"You have enough lyrics to admit we wrote a chorus yet?" Felix asks.

I stare down at a chorus plus two possible verses and then smirk at him. "No, I might throw them all out."

"That's why I can't believe you recorded it," Dev says. "*You.* The dude who refuses to even let his *bandmates* in his notebook, and you just showed the entire doc crew."

"Only one of them," I mutter, sliding off the glasses and powering them down.

We take our time packing up, mostly to spiral Christian longer. He has his manager frown on when we come through the glass door. "We were supposed to be out of here two hours ago."

"You want an album or not," I counter.

Remi's dragging her camera bag onto her shoulder, and I hand off the glasses. I put on my shades and drag on the black baseball cap, jogging down the stairs and leaving the rest of them. Except for Colt, who's always a few inches from having his dick up my ass. There are worse things than being required to bring your best friend everywhere you go.

I walk outside into the same Seattle drizzle from earlier and the hum of Pike Place Market. Like a good boy, I stay on the cobblestone by the nondescript door.

The space is tucked in a little nook of the historic market but no less alive. No one on the sidewalk spares me a second glance with the sunglasses and hat. Everything else demands their attention, including the iconic neon Pike Place sign acting as a beacon in the distance. I have no issue leaning against the brick and being lost in the movement.

Colt's head is on a swivel, and I catch him glaring at a fishmonger farther down.

"Don't worry about him." I gesture to a flower vendor across the crowd. "If anyone's a pap, it's her."

"Ha. Ha," he says dryly, but he checks out the granny for a camera anyway. "You know I'd be less stressed if we took the alley exit. Or if the van wasn't parked in fucking Narnia."

A two-minute walk is hardly through a wardrobe, but I let him have it. Dev, Felix, and I might need additional security and disguises to breathe in public, but Colt's on the ride with us. He went from winding cables and drinking at our shows to holding back increasingly aggressive fans and coordinating with a security team.

The others flood out along with the other bodyguards, Anton and Henry. I push off the wall and grab my guitar case. We navigate through the throng of people. I've only been to Seattle for shows, never having a chance to explore. I'm tempted to check out every side street and dip into the coffee shops. Other than when I ditched Colt in Prague, I haven't gotten to wander for a while. I feel it now. The restlessness.

I glance at Remi up ahead, strap falling off her shoulder.

A street band blocks out the buzz of voices once we get to the corner. The music drowns out everything while we wait at the pedestrian light. Colt's scanning ahead, Christian is on his phone, and I almost miss the panicked, "*Hey*," right before Remi crashes into me.

I catch her as a guy in a denim jacket dashes between tourists with a camera bag. "Shit." Then I have to grab Remi again when she starts running after him. "What—"

She jerks around, and the absolute heartbreak on her face shreds deep, through the armor and into my marrow.

"My dad's card. Foster—"

I miss anything else, already dodging around her, case dropped, and forcing my way through the crowd.

People are fucking everywhere, shouts and laughs and more music. I weave around who I can and shoulder-check the rest, following glimpses of denim and the bag anytime he lifts it higher to squeeze through.

He clears a slight path by knocking bodies out of the way for me. I narrow his lead enough that I'm only a few seconds behind when he cuts a hard right. I breach the herd of tourists and sprint down a mostly empty alley after him.

The dude glances over his shoulder to check on me, and as he turns back, his foot slips on the wet cobblestone. It slides out from under him, and he barely saves his ass from hitting the ground before I catch up, gripping the collar of his jacket. I yank him toward the nearest wall and shove him against it, hand around his throat to keep him there.

"Wrong. Fucking. Bag," I bite out.

"No, no, no." His panicked gaze darts to the side at someone else running toward us. "Take the bag. Take it."

I rip it out of his hands, releasing him at the same time Colton pushes between us. The guy scrambles away, nearly falling again, and Colt turns on me, jaw hard and eyes murderous.

"What the actual fuck?" His nostrils flare, his breaths heightened like mine while he crowds me.

"Sorry," I say, distracted by the strap I have fisted.

"You're *sorry*?" Colt huffs an unamused laugh. "You tore off after a thief who could have fucking stabbed you or worse. All for a fucking *camera*?"

But that's not what I retrieved.

The racing of my heart lowers along with me to a crouch so I can unzip the camera bag. Colt sets off on a rant about how it would kill him if anything happens to me, but it barely registers.

My eyes scan inside. Black fabric and dividers, Remi's camera and cords and equipment. I drag the zipper across for the side pocket, then I let my fingers finish the search for me. The second they connect with velvet, I swallow and slowly pull out the dark red pouch. I can feel the hard plastic square through the fabric before I open the top of the bag. At the bottom lies the SD card.

A relic Remi cherishes above all else. Resentful dick or not, I'd never let her lose it without a fight.

Having it in my possession now, knowing without a doubt this part of us was true … it further disturbs our remains.

I have no idea if it changes anything or only intensifies the grief over what I lost.

10

REMI

Before…

A COOL BREEZE kisses my skin. Looking up at the orange and red leaves dancing in the trees above, I almost forget where I am. Finished wood presses into my palms, braced behind me while I lean back and stare skyward. It could belong to the top of a picnic table anywhere with an autumn. My legs could be dangling over the edge near a lake in Switzerland. The wind traversing Kyoto, Japan.

I blindly feel for my phone beside me, refusing to lose the view. I wait for the perfect moment. A gust wraps through the towering trees, and I snap a picture. I lie back the rest of the way, and shortly after, a text comes through. I bring my phone over my face to see the screen and smile at the picture.

An unfamiliar but similar sky peeks through branches covered in different oranges and reds.

The leaves floating toward me could be falling in Prague.

A video chat pops up. I close my eyes and bite down on my lower lip. All of me turns way too fluttery at Foster's name and the picture of his reflection in a shop window, phone in front of his face.

I fight it every time. Deny the warm tingle beneath my skin is anything other than a hormonal response to a sexy voice. Refuse to believe we share anything but a mutual appreciation of art. Ignore the uptick in my pulse at each *Wanderer* notification, and pretend every message outside the app and the video chats mean nothing more.

I just want to see the world, and he wants to share it.

The first text came a day after the video failed during our tour last month. He sent a picture of Le Mur in Oberkampf, where a street artist splatter-painted a neon lion on the wall. Then a video of people passing an outdoor café, his espresso in the corner while his fingers kept time on the cup. More followed, all a peek at the city. Of beautiful things. Right before leaving Paris, he returned to Le Mur, to the wide-eyed man panicked over a utility bill that covered the lion—the murals ever changing.

Since then, between *Wanderer* tours of museums and art, Foster's taken me all over Amsterdam, Brussels, and Vienna. A hidden medieval courtyard, the cat sanctuary floating on a canal, Jardin du Petit Sablon, a baroque library. Whenever he explores, he lets me see the world through his eyes.

Eyes I haven't even seen.

With about fifteen minutes left in my free period, I check to ensure no one's around before slipping in my earbuds. It kills the illusion of not being on a table in the high school's outdoor commons. At least I escaped for a little while.

I lower the phone from my face to answer and then flip the camera so I can show Foster mine while he shows me his. The dimming sky and trees in Prague obviously superior to everything in Ohio.

"Wait." Foster's camera dips from pretty leaves to his shadow on a worn walkway. "I want the first view back. The school uniform does it for me."

I roll my eyes. "I want the first view back too. Shouldn't it be the skirt you want to see, anyway? Not the white button-up?"

"Show me the skirt, then, Remi," he rasps into my ears.

The way his voice lowers on my name hits in far too many places. I take a deep breath, the October wind fully responsible for my nipples hardening. My next sentence sounds like the October wind is messing with it too.

"What did we say about the flirting, Foster?"

He shows me the sky again, growing pinker with sunset soon. "You asked if we could make it through a single interaction without it. I immediately told you no."

I sigh. "I liked you better when you followed other women's skirts and didn't talk to me."

"You're a beautiful liar, Remi." He's quiet for a second and then, "I haven't thought about you at all today," he says. "Now we can be liars together."

Warm tingles and all fluttery.

Foster's camera slowly descends from the trees to the park he's in and finally settles on worn-in dark jeans. He's sitting on a bench, a sneak of brown boots below. Then he waits, not saying a word but so loud.

He's kept his word about no faces since Paris. I've seen his shin so he could prove he ran into a bike rack because I distracted him. He caught his fingers a few times other than at the café, dragging them through wet paint at an interactive exhibit, thumbing through a guestbook spanning fifty years. The faceless reflection of him that shows up any time he calls.

My lashes flutter closed. I breathe. Without giving myself time to overthink, I sit up. The view I give him cascades down from the branches above to the rest of the commons until it lands on the green plaid of my skirt.

"Now…" He raises his phone, revealing more of his leg, more bench, more boot.

"You saw the skirt," I tell him.

"Not enough. I want to see you."

I am so screwed when it comes to him. I can't even fight it right now.

I lift my phone higher, exposing from the top of my skirt

where my white shirt tucks in all the way to the few inches of skin below the hem before the rest of my legs disappear over the table's edge.

Foster's silent long enough, I almost move the camera from feeling self-conscious over two inches of me. But then he audibly sighs. "Fuck, this was a bad idea," he whispers.

"Agreed. It's never happening again." I leave the phone in place, though.

"I never want it to, Remi." Foster not only meets my lie; he adds another one. "I have no desire to see every goddamn inch of you."

ONLY MY MAROON-PAINTED toes breach the surface of the pink rose-scented water. I wait until the rest stills around me in the tub, the surface glassy smooth and iridescent. After a final check that nothing else shows, I send the picture and then instantly close my eyes to hide from the guy more than an ocean away. Even after my phone vibrates, it takes me a moment to look at Foster's message.

> I might have a newly discovered fetish for toes.
> Unrelated to your text obviously.

I smile and sink deeper into the water, about to put my phone on the ledge when he sends another.

> Touching, licking, sucking. In case you wondered about my urges.

> ...biting.

> I regret everything. Stop talking.

> Not talking. I'm seducing. And why would I stop when you're naked for me?

Putting my phone face down on the ledge, I slide all the way into the water. I have to before I text my way into Foster's metaphorical bed. He's infected me. Ever since last week and the leaves and the two inches of skin, he's spread through my system like a fever, consuming my thoughts and smoldering in my veins. Every word from him, every pause and sigh intensify the heat.

He's scorching me from the inside out, and I can't cool down. I can't *slow* down. I can't use my head when it comes to Foster, and my other parts can't be trusted.

The bathroom door bangs open, and I jump up, sending the water sloshing around in the tub as I surface.

Ebony hair and an annoyed bestie face rush in.

"Boundaries," I tell Sage.

But it hardly slows her down.

She rolls her eyes so dramatically her head goes with them. Then she shuts herself in the bathroom with me.

"Please. I've seen you through all the cup sizes." She drops onto the rug, back against the porcelain. "Plus, you can see my tits anytime. What's mine is yours."

I laugh and flick water at her profile. "My tits are not your tits."

She hangs her head back to see me, her long black hair falling onto the tub's ledge. "Selfish, bitch. Be more of an only child, I dare you."

The world would be dark without Sage Teller lighting it on fire. She's fierce, albeit slightly unhinged, and no matter how far I might slip inside myself, she's either there to drag me out or waiting for me to find the way on my own.

"Is this a *you missed me* visit, or are we shooting someone up?" I ask.

She twists around and folds her arms on the tub. "I missed you. I always miss you ever since you fucking left me, but I am *dealing*." She sets her chin on her arm. "And maybe Miles didn't answer my text earlier, and I'm contemplating flying to California, and I need a talk down."

I push her hair away from her face. "There it is."

She wrinkles her nose at me. I grab my phone and find my texts with Miles, then I hand it to her after calling his number. Sage greedily grabs for it and turns on the speaker. The first call goes unanswered, so we go for a second. She's glaring at me because I'm the reason Miles isn't answering when he answers.

"Rem, is Sage okay?" he asks. As his greeting.

"She's perfect. The most calm and collected woman alive, like always." I give her a dry smile, right as he says, "I told you about my meeting, gorgeous. The one I just ran out of because Remi would never call me twice in a row without an emergency."

She bites her lips together, innocently looking at the ceiling. "I might have forgotten," she says.

I nudge her face away until she rotates fully. I get out as she moves to perch on the counter by the sink, tossing me a towel on her way, and I wrap in it before grabbing another.

"Are you mad at me?" she asks, pouting at me since he's not here.

I pout back in solidarity, toweling my hair.

Miles lets out a sigh that turns into a groan. "Nah. It was fucking boring in there. Give me five minutes to grab my shit, and then I want to listen to you come while I drive."

"Nope." I pluck the phone out of her hand. "Sage will call you in twenty from the comfort of her own room on her own phone."

She pretends not to hear me, checking her nails, but he chuckles.

"You good, Rem?" he asks. "Please spare me the *it's great* bullshit if it's all just shit."

Sage flits her eyes up to me, and I quickly force a smile at my best friend and tell her boyfriend, "No, it really is great bullshit."

"Everything still good with *Wanderer*? No more video issues? You've taken a few less tours lately. If you tell me it's because the app sucks, I will never forgive you."

"No, Miles. *Wanderer* is amazing. The tours are…" I grab for the doorknob, my mouth turning up on its own this time. "One of my favorite parts of the day. I've just been distracted with senior year and my escape plan."

And other things.

Sage shadows me out of my bathroom, the look in her eyes saying everything she's trying to bite back. She hates the escape plan. I think she worries she's part of what I'm escaping. In reality, she's one of the only reasons I'm still here. I love her too much to tell her all the reasons I desperately want to go.

The frumpy dress I wore earlier lies balled up on the floor, and I kick it under my bed on the way to my dresser. I'm done acting for the night. No need for reminders.

By the time I throw on sweats and a baggy tee, Miles is off the phone, and Sage traps me in a hug.

"I love you, bitch," she says, the term of endearment sweet as always. "I'll see you in a few days. I'm thinking we dress as slutty nuns or slutty sluts. I'm undecided."

I wince, pulling away. "Right. Halloween. Can't wait."

Dismissing the sarcasm, she heads to my window. I glance at the door and realize the pillows are still shoved up against the bottom.

"Why'd you come up the trellis?"

Lifting the window, she glances over her shoulder. "No one answered. I figured your mom and the chief were out."

My brow dips as she throws her leg through, but I school it. "Yeah, they must be."

Sage blows me a kiss before descending the trellis. I close the window behind her, leaving the latch undone as always. I feel too trapped with it locked.

I finish cleaning up from my bath and hit off the overhead lights. The LED strip around my headboard sends a blue glow bouncing off the walls and words written on them. I added new ones the other day after Foster and the leaves and our mutual lies.

The world's full of liars and the oblivious.

As I'm snatching my phone off the nightstand, ready to zone out in bed, a muted crash stops me. I stare at the pillows on the floor, unease washing over me while I wait. Another noise turns into a tightness in my chest. My shoulders. My jaw. My throat. Then the tear happens inside me. One part begs me to block the outside with more pillows. Or sit in the bathroom with the door closed again. The other demands I go out there. To fucking *try*. Even if it slowly destroys me every time.

Who am I kidding? Either choice chips away at my being.

When the screaming breaks through my barrier—muffled and so angry—I kick the pillows out of the way. The darkened hallway outside my room has an open banister where the living room opens up below. I look over on my way to the stairs to see what the fuck I'm running into. Like it will somehow matter. A destroyed lamp for sure and strewn fireplace tools.

The shouting only heightens once I reach the bottom of the stairs and see the rest. The entire dining table is upended, and every single plate, glass, and piece of silverware from dinner are scattered or shattered. Only an hour ago people occupied the knocked-over chairs. Soft music played.

The illusion tonight was a charming family unit. The doting wife who showed enough skin to feed her husband's need to be envied by everyone around him. An angsty—and "incredibly shy"—stepdaughter, so hard to love, but they do because who else would? And the solid oak providing the security and safety every family needs. A king on his throne at the head of the table, surrounded by sycophants and false walls of gold. No one is aware the real walls are filled with rot and the king's not wearing any clothes.

Or maybe they do know. They just don't care.

I only have a few seconds to survey the damage before my mother slams into my shoulder, passing me for the living room. While I bathed the night off of me, she's gone from seeming calm and agreeable to agitated and erratic. Pinpoint pupils now blown out. Pills to different pills or whatever else she's using. I used to keep track so I could...

Help.

"I tried, Daniel," she screeches. She whips around by the cold fireplace, thrusts her hands into her yellow hair, and pulls from the root. "I picked the dress you like. I only drank two glasses of wine at dinner."

She slurs it all, nothing about her stable at the moment.

I ease closer, ready to coax her upstairs—anywhere but here. "Mom, let's go—"

"I fuck you in that dress because you look like a whore, Rebecca." Daniel barrels through, and I draw back, wrapping my arms around my middle. I'm not sure if he's on something or just his usual raging, abusive fuck self.

"I told you to fucking be presentable and quiet tonight. Not pregame with a handful of painkillers and dress like you want Marlo to come on your tits at the dinner table."

My nails dig into my upper arms when she rips her head up, eyes wild. I hate it here. I hate every second.

"God, I wish he would have." She wobbles toward him, but I think she intends for a sexy sway of her hips. "I bet Marlo'll fuck me good. Better than your tiny dick—"

"Watch it, cunt." He rips his loosened tie over his head and fists the silk, forefinger pointed in her face. "I'll make sure you die in the fucking gutter where I found you if you pull this shit again."

She shoves him in the chest, and I flinch even before he grabs her by the jaw. I need her to stop.

"Mom," I say, stepping forward, but Daniel jerks toward me, face and eyes red. I stop. I look away. I can't move while being ripped in two different directions inside. A scared little girl, begging me to save her mommy like she always tried to, and the shredded remains from her failing every time, demanding I save what's left of us.

"Be grateful, Rebecca," he says, voice low and as much of a threat as his words. As his grip digging into her cheeks. "You're a pathetic junkie, thrown away by men once they figure out you're worth nothing but a quick fuck and regrets. Appreciate me for tolerating you and your fucking kid and be grateful I haven't traded in your gash for a better one."

My nails break the skin on my arms as he shoves her face, sending her stumbling backward. He storms away. I breathe in once he passes me, unsure the last time I exhaled, but my lungs were starved and my head swims.

But my mother doesn't wait for me to regain my bearings.

She rips at her hair and then screams, tearing through the living room. I lunge in front of her and barely catch her to keep her away from Daniel.

"Mom," I plead while she screeches and fights to get past me. "Please. Stop."

She shrieks so many insults, my ears ring, but it doesn't stop me from hearing Daniel shouting closer and closer behind me. The words don't even matter anymore. My eyes sting, and my heart beats out of my chest while crowded between them. His front presses against my back, and his pointed finger is right beside my face. The sensory overload causes me to throw all my weight against her. I move her a few feet in the safer direction until she twists away from me.

No.

I try to stop her. I try to lock around her middle when she dives at him. I *try.*

The little girl always tries, even though that's what broke her in the first place.

Daniel pushes her off, and she knocks into me, and then he throws her to the floor, following her down. Everything roars so loudly in my head, but I hear each word between his fists. "Fucking. Worthless. Bitch."

"Stop." But it's weak, my voice breaking. I rush toward a limp form forever burned behind my eyelids. "She's not moving."

He isn't stopping, though, and I shove his shoulder, trying to get to her, trying to get him off her. I land on my knees beside her, only to be ripped away in a split second, then the world's spinning out of control, and pain whips across my face as Daniel backhands me. My shoulder slams into the overturned table, a jagged piece of wine glass slicing into my forearm when I land on the floor. It hurts so fucking bad, but I grit through it, sharp inhales and exhales through my nose.

Daniel's already blown out of the room. I hear him swipe his badge and holster off the entry table and the quiet click of the front door behind him. His chief of police mask firmly in place while he hides the destruction behind an elegant door knocker.

I push myself up on shaky arms, the last sixty seconds replaying in flashes. Blood drips onto the white porcelain shards beneath my hand. I sit up against the table and wrap a cloth napkin around my arm, my eyes falling shut. They open to my mother crawling off the floor. She holds her ribs and grips a fallen chair for balance. And she starts for the stairs without even looking at me.

"Mom?" Every tear I refuse to cry strains the word.

She braces on the banister and slowly turns. Her face remains untouched as always even though mine throbs. After a second of her unfocused gaze on me, she shrugs. "Your own fucking fault."

I stare off at nothing once she disappears to their bedroom. Scar tissue scars differently, rougher and thicker and more noticeable than the original. Scarred scars tear easier. Each layer heals uglier and uglier, covering the previous but not with a neon lion or panicked man. They build on the last wound and embed its memory deeper.

While I clean and bandage my arm in the bathroom, I spare a glance in the mirror. The swelling and redness creep up from my cheekbone to my eye, no way of hiding it.

The need to escape builds to a point of overwhelm, and this time I get all the way to the window with my contingency bag. Only I pause for too long with my hands on the frame, think too much about the unknown.

I let the strap of my bag fall off my shoulder. It hits the floor, and I pull my headboard away from the wall. Lowering down, I run my fingers over the Sharpie words, smooth and tethering, even if his voice has faded from them.

You can always run to me, darlin'. Escape for a while and then weather your storm.

I unzip my contingency bag that I always keep hidden and ready for the worst. I pull the velvet pouch from the inside pocket, but I leave my dad's SD card inside—the only thing I have left of him. I took it from his camera after his funeral, and in seven years, I've never even looked at the pictures. It feels too final to see the last things he captured. Like there could be more, so long as I don't witness the end.

Like I can still run to him when it all becomes too much.

I pull my phone off the nightstand. Reality needs to fuck off until I can breathe again.

Even after calculating the time difference, I text my new favorite escape.

Show me something beautiful.

11

FOSTER

I CAST a glance at my phone's screen when it vibrates against the wrought-iron bistro table beside me. Rather uncommitted considering it's three in the morning, but then I see the name. Suddenly a lot of me feels committed.

Remi Saint has become an intrusive thought, nudging her way in where she doesn't belong. This woman hijacks my mind and steers me in directions I've never wanted to go, but I go every time.

Fucking siren, I swear. I haven't even seen her face or much of her at all. Her raspy voice, though, and the things she says with it. How she frames the world anytime she sends a video speaks to a part of me that wants to find the nuances and extraordinary in the mundane.

I'm an agreeable hostage at this point.

Of course the jackass on the other side of the table swipes my phone before I can.

"Remi, like tour Remi?" Chase lets out an *awww* without an answer. "Want me to handle this? Tell her how swell you are? Ten-inch cock on a tortured guitarist who saves puppies when he's not writing lyrics that will make her wet?"

I sigh and shake my head. "I'll miss you, Chase, but I will throw you off the balcony."

He passes off my phone when I hold out my hand. "You said that an hour ago, too. You're nothing but a tease."

"Fine. I'm a tease, and you're the worst wingman to ever wingman." He gasps, offended, so I remind him, "Anytime you offer to talk to a woman for someone, you end up dry fucking her in a corner."

"That happened twice," he says. "If anything, I'm doing too good of a job by sussing out the ones with wandering eyes."

"By wandering your hands all over them?"

Chase lowers his LED sunglasses on his nose to glare. "Ungrateful. See if I ever offer my services again."

He shoves them back on, and I chuckle, checking Remi's text.

Show me something beautiful.

Easy, given my view from our flat's balcony. Prague Castle's lit up in the distance with the city skyline surrounding it. I blew through what I planned to use for next semester's living expenses to rent this place. Ramen and walking everywhere will hardly kill me. The memory of doing this with Chase more than makes up for it. And now I can share it with my less and less intrusive thought.

"You never smile at me like that," Chase says.

I huff a laugh and sigh and run a hand through the back of my hair. When I look over, he nods with his lips pursed.

"Guess we like Tour Remi." Chase stands from his iron chair and crosses between me and the railing. "I'll tell her you're packing eleven inches then. I'm going out. Enjoy the sexting." He taps the bottom of his beer bottle against the top of mine, and I have to sit forward and suck up the foaming beer.

"The fucking worst," I call at him.

His laugh cuts off when he closes the double doors from

inside. I smile even though he's a dick. Hell, most of the time I smile because he's such a dick.

The first few days here, he moped around. I started to worry until he tossed glow sticks at me one night, informed me we were clubbing, and then dove on me to drive his point home. I finally dragged him out of the club at seven a.m. He had a massive grin on his face as we stumbled out into the morning sun.

I set my bottle on the table and skip the texting pretense. Remi accepts the call and shows me a familiar white ceiling. "I get a ceiling, and you get this?" I flip the camera and move so instead of showing the balcony above me, she has a panoramic view of Prague. The castle, and lights, and a few red roofs.

She's quiet even though my screen goes from white to a red wall and black words. I say them as I read, *"You can always run to me, darlin'. Escape for a while and then weather your storm."*

A breath comes through, and an exhale has never sounded so fucking sad. My brow lowers, but the silence feels too necessary to ask a pointless question. So I pan down and show her my world. Tree-lined cobblestone streets and the metal railing in front of me, even my beer on top of the intricately designed wrought iron, and my guitar leaned against the table leg.

"My dad used to tell me that," Remi says, and I return the lens to the skyline. "He photographed wildlife for magazines and commissions, traveling the world and experiencing moments most of us can't come close to." She sighs. "He lived his dream nine months out of the year, and I loved that for him so much. But it meant I lived with my mom most of the time, and she…"

The pause is achingly familiar, so much like mine anytime I hate the truth of the next words.

"She was your storm," I say.

"Yeah. Was. Is." Remi shifts, showing her bent knees at the bottom of the frame, and I fill in the blanks. She's on the floor, hugging her knees and looking at her dad's words. "I missed him constantly, so he bought me a phone when I was seven. He sent pictures of the animals or the landscape. And fountains. He loved them and always found one to share with me everywhere he went. He'd tell me if I needed him and he was unavailable on a shoot, I could find him there. I could always go to his pictures and pretend I was with him until everything became bearable again."

Now she has nowhere to run anymore.

"How old were you when he passed away?" I ask.

"Eleven," she whispers before she finds her voice again. "I looked at our messages every single day, but then my mom took the phone. She told me to grow up and get over it. I mean, it had been three months, so…"

"Fuck. I'm sorry, Remi. You deserved better." Then I add, "I have a feeling you still deserve better."

"He fell in the Scottish Highlands while there to photograph otters. He sent a picture of an adorable little fuzz ball, then he went to sleep with a brain bleed and didn't wake up." She adjusts again and gives me more, her arm wrapping around her knees. "I still have his last SD card in this red velvet bag. I used to carry it around like a security blanket without even knowing what's on it. Sometimes I still do, as embarrassing as that is to admit."

I snort. "We'll be embarrassing together." I swing the camera to the acoustic guitar again. "Meet my security blanket. I rented it our first day here, and I kid you not, I giggled after the first strum."

She hums. "And there goes the sexy persona."

"Pshh, I look hot as fuck playing. Plus, I sing. I couldn't lose the sexy persona if I tried." I show her the empty street, trees rustling in a breeze. "Be nice to me or I won't write a song for you."

A real laugh, even if it's short. "You gonna write me a song, Foster West?"

"Stick with me, baby, and I'll play your song on stage at Madison Square Garden."

"Bare a little soul to a guy, and he thinks he can call you baby," she says dryly.

The words are out of my mouth before I realize it. "What do I have to do to call you baby, then?"

I cringe. Fuck, I need an intervention for her.

But then she says, "Bare a little back, *baby*."

My mouth tips up, and I nod even though she can't see. I lay my arm out on my thigh and let her see the faded scar running down the inside of my wrist. "This is why I learned to play." My gaze traces the thin line. I can almost feel the boot tread if I let myself. "When *I* was seven, my old man gifted me a compound fracture to my wrist. Surgery fixed the break, but mobility was fucked all the way up into my hand. The physical therapist suggested guitar to help refine finger movement and working the tendons. A sweet old lady down the street named Alberta sold me a shitty acoustic for thirteen dollars." I fist my hand before releasing it and stretching my fingers. "Music pieced me back together—the fact I'm good is a plus. And while I want to live it and breathe it, it'll also be my ultimate *fuck you*. He tried to destroy me, so I'll make a life out of what saved me."

Then I'll be the one to destroy him, but I leave that part off.

"Poetic," Remi says.

"Wait until you hear your song."

"Hey, Foster?"

Goddamn, I love my name out of her mouth. "Hmm?"

"I'm sorry. You deserved better."

"Yeah…" I give her Prague Castle again. "We both really did, baby."

I slouch in my chair and brace a foot on the railing. She moves too. Auburn hair falls over the camera. A flash of skin. But it's not enough.

"I want to see you," I tell her. "Not just part of a skirt or your bitable toes." She huffs a laugh and gives a warning, *Foster* that I answer with, "Remi. We both know it stopped being about tours weeks ago."

She sits on her bed, knees folded in front of her on a midnight duvet. "Seeing your face will make it real. It makes *you* real."

"I *am* real."

"I need you not to be yet," she whispers. "I need you to be my escape from the real."

Remi sounds more heartbreaking than the exhale earlier.

I blow out a breath of my own and drag my hand through my hair. As much as I want to see her, to put a face to the broken girl on the other side of the screen, she's infiltrated deep enough, I'll be what she needs right now.

"You can always run to me, baby." I smirk at her soft sigh.

But she lets me call her baby a second time, and I'm not so sure I'm even a hostage anymore.

When it comes to Remi Saint, I think I've become a willing participant.

12

REMI

Now...

Fingers stroking shadows, it's so much easier in the dark.
No fear of us being real where the light can't touch.
We can hide in the lies without facing the truth.
I won't drown in you again with no visible proof.

FOSTER'S NOTEBOOK AND the lyrics he wrote have likely burned into my laptop's screen by now, they've been there so long. I've been dying to see the footage from the spy glasses he wore while writing the other day. A glimpse into his soul he willingly shared for the documentary.

Now I'm staring at the words.

And I've *been* staring at them. Unable to look away or unfreeze the video. He's forced me through time to a place I've desperately avoided for years. The real bathed in blinding light and inescapable like it was then.

Even when I ran to him.

They aren't necessarily things I've said, but a remix. I recognize the original song enough for it to sting.

A video call saves me from Foster's veiled message. I answer, only for my face to scrunch and my head to tilt. "What in the domestication are you doing?"

Heath looks over from where he's on his hands and knees, his glare cutting. "Clearly, I'm assembling a shrine to the gods. I need to beg forgiveness for whatever the fuck I did to deserve a life of throw pillows and wine coolers. Christ, Sinner. I'm building a crib."

I bite back a smile to prevent any more scathing responses.

Heath throws a package of screws and drops onto his ass. He lights a cigarette, inhales deeply, and blows out smoke and resignation. "Love crushes the soul as much as it completes it."

"A wise director once said, *'You know true love when you're desperate to live inside their skin while simultaneously wishing they'd forget you exist.'*"

"Sounds like a brilliant man—an actual philosopher." He does an *on with it* motion with the fingers holding his cigarette. "Report."

He's on the floor of his garage with his laptop since he's not allowed to smoke in the house. They renovated to add an apartment above for him to work in before they moved in. He agreed to kids and suburbia. His line was having to stay outside to smoke or get high.

It also protects any neighbors with poor judgment who might see him and mistake Heath Erickson for a *morning, how's the weather* type of dude.

I witnessed an unfortunate attempt at small talk with him once on set, and Heath threatened to blackball the guy from ever working in music again.

"Well, *sir*"—I throw him a wry smile when he flips me off—"we have about twenty hours of raw footage between all the cams. Plenty of concert takes, multiple angles and POVs from bass and drums. B-roll on the bus and backstage. The band has today and tomorrow off, so I'm hoping to get shots of them outside the tour space. Basically, we're on track."

"Then where the fuck is the Adams North interview?" Heath

lifts an eyebrow, and I look away. "Right. So we're going rogue and ignoring the label's very clear instructions to focus on him."

I glare at him for the reminder. The execs and their agent mentioned it plenty so long as the band was out of earshot. They want Adams North, but he's part of a nonnegotiable package deal.

"I have footage of him. And they're a *band*," I add. "It's a doc on Of Men and Wolves, and I refuse to make Dev or Felix feel like they're any less a part of this."

A corner of Heath's mouth perks up. "I didn't say I'm not onboard, Sinner. Only clarifying, so I can tell Mac to eat my dick if they push. But we do need interviews with Adams. You have a lot of one-on-ones with the others, but he only appears in groups or from afar. Is he intimidating you? Being an entitled fuck?"

"No." I say it quickly and then let out a settling breath. "Adams is the lead singer and guitarist for a band finishing their first world tour, writing their next studio album, and adjusting to an entire world's attention on them. He hardly sleeps from what I've seen, and there's little downtime with the additional shows. I'm not forcing a cam and mic on him anytime he's allowed to breathe."

The noise-canceling of my earbuds is highly unappreciated once I finish. The only sound is paper burning as Heath draws out a drag, studying me while I try like hell not to give him anything else. No need to accidentally mention with my eyes how *Adams* and I are allergic to anything one-on-one at the moment.

Foster's avoided me since Seattle, and I haven't exactly chased him down. He didn't even hesitate after I told him the SD card was in my bag. And asking about the fountain after so long. I didn't expect him to remember either, and it felt like I finally found him again. Now I have to remember what it's like to miss him.

Except he's everywhere.

Heath tosses his butt somewhere on the concrete of his garage. Away from the pieces of unassembled crib. His eyes bore into the camera and me and likely the rest of the bus behind me before he sighs and swipes up his phone. "Get the interviews."

Underneath the clipped tone, I latch onto the unspoken trust. We both know he'd be on a plane to Utah right now if I were anyone else.

"As you wish." I glance up when Colton comes up the bus's stairs and then return to Heath. "I'll send what we have from this week after I review it. Good luck finishing your shrine. Maybe try adding a pickleball racket."

He huffs and taps away on his screen. "Fuck off. I'm making Xander put this shit together."

Oh, my roommate will love that. Xander video-chatted me the other day, face down on our couch and begging for a reason as to why he agreed to be Heath's assistant while I'm gone. I rattled off a short list of the director's credits before he started fake sobbing. Crib duty might end in actual tears.

"Right." Heath drops his phone and sits forward, reaching toward the camera. "Don't fuck this up, Sinner."

The video blacks as he shuts his laptop, and then the call disconnects.

I smile and close my own computer. Even without Foster's— Adams's—interviews, a loose shape's forming for the documentary. I've rewritten and rearranged my original notecards a couple times, but more than a few feel solid. The key elements I'll fight for until the end. Those reveal more truth about Of Men and Wolves than any requests from Mac Records to further commercialize Adams North.

Black fabric rustles behind me when Colton comes through again. Tugging out my earbuds, I drag my feet closer before he lands on them. He has on his usual fit, except the tee has rips and holes. They show peeks of tan abs and a nipple piercing.

"Bear attack?" I ask, and he grins.

"I did not buy enough fake blood to pull that off." When I shrug at him, not understanding, he rolls his eyes. "Goddamn, you need to quit working. It's Halloween?"

"Halloween," I repeat.

As if summoned by saying the word twice, Felix bounds onto the bus decked out with leather chaps, a vest without a shirt underneath, a red bandana covering his face, and a cowboy hat. He points directly at me. "It's motherfucking Halloween, Cam Girl."

With a whoop, he gallops through, swinging an imaginary lasso and slapping his own ass. So he must be the horse too. A nice setup to ask someone to ride him, I'm sure.

The farther into the tour we go, the more antsy Dev and Felix become—especially Felix. He's become a bull in a chute the past week, ready to tear the place apart to get out. Even now, the chaotic energy pulses from him. These two days off might save us all.

Felix halts his horse beside me with a pull on the reins and tips his hat. "Howdy, partner. I dare reckon you'll need a mighty fine pair of chaps to boot scoot with us all on the Halloweeniest of all Halloweens this side the Mississippi."

I open my mouth to respond, but, "I have no words." My voice breaks at the end in a laugh.

Felix nods toward Colton. "I sounded just like you, right?"

Colton kicks him in the thigh. "I borderline hate you."

The drummer winks at him. "Love you too, sexy." He crashes on the other couch and yanks the bandana down so it hangs around his neck. "Seriously, though. We're going out tonight, and costumes are required with faces covered. For obvious reasons."

"For you three assholes," Colton says. "I'm adding guy-liner and enough blood to pass as a vampire. Remi, you can..." He considers me for a second and waves me off. "Throw on a skirt and be a yearbook photographer or some shit."

"Schoolgirl." Felix nods. "Very approved."

I wrinkle my nose at the costume suggestion. The idea intrigues me, though. "I don't know. Where are you going exactly?"

Colton smirks like I agreed already, but it's Felix who says, "I

C.G. BLAINE

grew up in a college town not far from here. One of the frats goes all out."

"You're letting them go to a house party?" I ask Colton, shock not at all hidden.

The security guard shrugs and nods toward Felix. "Have you seen this dude lately? Between him and Dev, it's more dangerous to *not* let them loose. I'll be with them, and Anton and Henry are dressing as mimes."

Ideas already swirl for POVs and an overhead shot. The schedule might not allow for any other chances to show the band out in the wild, so to speak. At least not until the break in Texas. It's not guaranteed all three of them will spend those two weeks together. Dev's mentioned more than once he plans to visit his grandmother, and I imagine they'll want to write.

"I'm bringing my camera."

Colton chuckles. "Sure, lioness. Bring your work along, but you're required to chill and keep me company."

"And take shots," Felix adds. "You and me are taking shots, Cam Girl." He glances out the window to the parking lot. "Rest of the party's here."

Figuring he's talking about Dev and Foster, I ask, "What are they going as?"

Before either answer, Dev climbs the stairs. He's wearing a black onesie—barely zipped because, of course, we need the obliques on display—with chicken feet. Then he flips up the hood to show me the red spiked ridge down the center.

He grins, holding up a beak. "I'm a cock."

I snort as he passes for the curtain.

"As for Adams, he's going as what he always does," Colton says.

I'm about to ask, but then Foster boards the bus, and I can't breathe. A deep V cuts down the middle of his black shirt with laces undone at the bottom, fitted ripped jeans, and a play sword hanging off a belt slung low on his hips. I don't need to see the black eye mask to know.

"A pirate," I breathe out while looking at a memory.

"A fucking pirate," the others echo.

Foster and I stare at each other for a beat too long before he swallows, turns around, and walks straight off the bus.

TURNS OUT, a frat in Utah is not too bad of a place for three rock stars to blend in for Halloween. In no time at all, Felix and Dev—or Cowboy and Chicken, since I refuse to call Dev *Cock* all night—are fully integrated into the frat party with no one even batting an eye.

The names are a Colton—Vampire—demand. Rather than chance someone overhearing all of the band's real ones and blowing their cover, everyone's going by their costumes for the night.

I'm walking through the crowd recording neck-down on the bodies because Colton's right. I never stop. But why waste a chance to catch these three merely existing? They can be a cowboy or a chicken or a pirate without the weight of who they are pressing down.

Cowboy ducks in close to my cam as I wander by him. He tugs down his bandana, revealing the Felix beneath, and then with a wink he pulls it back up and returns to the girls he's accumulated. Even without their status, they've managed to find a fan club.

Chicken has on a pair of spy glasses above his beak. Given how he's grinding on a bunny at the moment, I'll have to skip through the cleavage shots he's undoubtedly getting.

Students all play up the camera, too, but other than the overhead shot I managed from the stairs, I won't use it. Asking them all to sign a release form draws a little too much attention.

Once I've wandered enough to scratch the itch, I find a vampire where I left him on the outskirts of the room. Foster was with him when I left, but now he's alone and already shaking his head at me.

"Do I need to physically remove that from your person or are you going to fulfill the chilling requirement for the evening?"

"Hmm." I cock my head at Colton, hand-cam falling to my side. "Can it truly be considered chilling if it's required?"

He hands over my drink that he held like a gentleman. "One of these days, I'm forcing you to have fun, Catholic School Girl."

"No," I tell him. "You are not calling me Catholic School Girl. For one, it's a mouthful. Two, just … no."

"You have on a fucking plaid skirt and a button-up." He points at my legs. "*And* knee-highs. What do you expect me to call you?"

I'm about to say Remi because no one will tie me to shit, but before I can, a pirate materializes beside him.

"Call her Saint." Foster hands Colton a red cup, lasering in on me. "She acts like one."

"She's a sinner pretending to be a saint," Adams sings in "Haunted," *"crushing your soul while you kneel at her feet."*

A challenge lies in his eyes even beneath his mask. Except he's not the only one who can stab with our past.

"I've been told I'm a beautiful liar," I say to him while flashing a smile for Colton.

"Saint of the Beautiful Liars it is." Colton taps his cup to Foster's and then mine. "That should be a song."

Our gazes remain locked over the rims as Foster and I drink. Maybe it's the shots with Felix earlier that make me think his eyes heat when he looks down at my skirt. My school uniform was green instead of red and showed less thigh, but the way he lingers on the exposed skin above my black knee-highs, I don't think the color matters.

A lot of things have changed in five years. Foster West's preference for skirts and legs doesn't seem to be one of them.

He has a bandana covering his disheveled hair now, the dark red tails long. Between it and the mask, he doesn't look anything like Adams North tonight. But even disguised, I have no idea how I didn't recognize him that night in their dressing room. His full lips and ocean eyes. I fell for his voice and words before the rest avalanched, but his eyes I worried I wouldn't recover from months after I left him behind.

"Please tell me one of you has a joint," a blonde nurse says. She stops beside me out of necessity, although I'm not sure she notices with Colton and Foster in front of us. The length of her skirt puts mine to shame, and one wrong move with her top threatens a nip-slip.

Colton glances at Foster before he slides on the good ol' boy accent. "Sorry, kitten. All out."

"I'm sure you could make it up to me ... someway." She looks between the two of them, seemingly weighing her options. She moves closer once she's decided on the pirate. I hate how my grip tightens on my cup.

My gaze flits away, only the tug of Foster has it returning a second later. He's staring into his beer, free hand held out toward his best friend. Colton curses and fishes in his pocket, then he slaps cash into Foster's waiting palm and sighs at the nurse.

"You picked the wrong dude, kitten. He's not interested, and I'm petty. So as much as I need to fuck someone, it will not be you." He smiles at her, closed-lipped, and as he said, petty. Even his accent lightened.

"Whatever." She throws me an unnecessary mean-girl scowl before walking away.

"I hate you, Pirate," Colton says. Then he explains to me, "We have a continuing bet to see who gets more *fuck me* eyes. This douche canoe only wins because…" He shrugs and waves a hand for me to fill in the rest.

"Ah, but I'm just a pirate tonight." Foster pockets the money. "Time to admit defeat, lil bro."

Colton shakes his head. "Not a chance. Don't forget, I pull dick far better than you."

Foster smirks, about to take a drink. "I don't like dick."

"Eye-fucking is eye-fucking for the bet. You're the one paying me most of the time with dudes." He starts to drink, too, but then pulls his cup away at the last second. "You know what? I'm replacing you as my best friend." He nudges me. "You're in, kid."

I nod once. "Best friends for life, Vampire."

"I'll give her my half of the heart necklace," Foster deadpans, unfazed by the loss.

Colton tips his chin toward a guy by the window, wearing an open black robe and a rosary that hangs down his bare chest. "Wingman me, bestie. I'm going to fuck that hot priest."

Foster chuckles. "Not a phrase I ever expected you to say."

Colton licks his lips to hide a smile so he can pretend to ignore the pirate. "Seriously, let's go. I suddenly lost all interest in protecting a certain asshole."

"So you're going to bury your cock in one instead?" Foster asks.

Risking my new position, I laugh at that one.

"At least I share mine with the world," Colton mumbles before finally sipping his drink. "Unlike some pirate standing left of me has lately."

Foster's gaze bounces to me, and I look anywhere else. I blame the heat of everyone packed together for the flush creeping into my cheeks. It has nothing to do with Foster sharing his cock while dressed as a drool-worthy pirate. Or how he's watching me like he's not thinking the exact same thing.

Luckily, I'm saved a second later. An arm slings around my shoulders, and an amber shot appears in my face. This time it's not Felix, but Dev's arm and pouty, glassy eyes above his beak.

So, kind of lucky and kind of saved.

"You drank with Cowboy," he whines.

"Yeehaw, she did, Cock." Felix joins us along with two angels, a devil, a cat, and a firefighter. "Now she'll drink with you. Then me again. Then Pirate. Then Vampire. Then we're taking this show on the road."

I shake my head, accepting the plastic glass. "This counts as drinking with all of you, Cowboy."

"Boo," he jeers, and there's a repeat from the women.

Dev lifts his other hand, salt on his skin and a lime wedge ready. "We'll have to make this one count then."

"I have a perfectly good hand, you know?" I eye him, and he grins.

"You're holding a drink and your camera in it. Trust me, mine's better anyway. Lots of practice with my fingers."

He wiggles the wedge.

With a squint at him, I lean in and lick the salt before taking the tequila shot. I bite into the lime and then bat Dev away, grabbing it myself. He howls like a chicken-dog and hauls the cat to his side.

"You all saw it, boys," he says. "I got her tongue first."

I flip him off, which only earns me a wink. I drop the wedge and empty shot into my cup.

"You said what now about taking this show on the road?" Colton asks. "Because I remember this field trip having a singular destination."

Felix brings a half-full bottle of rum to his mouth, taking a swig. "It's not Halloween without a haunted house." He waggles his brows and then marches off with four girls in tow. Dev smirks and follows with the last girl. The two mimes who've been hanging back trail after them both.

"Fuck." Colton drains the last of his beer. "I'm not sure if it's worse to stop them or go with them."

Foster finishes his drink, too, and grabs all three of our cups—our fingers graze when he takes mine. Dev's words repeat in my head, only about a guitarist rather than a bass player.

He sets them on a side table and slaps Colton on the back. "It's Utah. Better to fuck around in the middle of nowhere. Otherwise, you'll be buying photos off random people of an impromptu orgy in a Starbucks bathroom."

He heads in the same direction as the others.

"Why do I think that's happened before?" I ask.

With a look of resignation, Colton grasps my shoulders and

points me toward the door. "Because you've spent more than a day with the band. They're cavemen, remember?"

Dev proves it once we step outside, and he's literally carrying one of the women over his shoulder.

It only takes three blocks before we reach our destination, walking while a mime follows with the van. Colton stops with his hands on his hips right in the middle of the street, and we stare up at the three-story Victorian together.

Felix immediately climbs the tire of the bulldozer parked on the dirt lawn and throws his arms out. "My fucking castle."

"It's not really haunted," one of the angels says, walking toward us. "Daddy's building condos. The owner of this dump finally died, so he's rushing demo. I don't even think they've cut the electricity yet."

Colton sighs, his entire body relaxing. "I can work with this."

By the time he finishes, Dev's already dashing up the cracked concrete steps to the deteriorating porch. Felix dismounts the demo equipment, chasing him in while the bodyguards gather up the fan club.

I'm stuck on the exterior, though. The cracked and peeling white paint over wooden siding, each side a direct mirror of the other. Bay windows and dormers and an oculus window high up beneath a gable.

"A beautiful thing." Foster steps beside me.

I nod, spellbound by the snapshot of time. "Art."

We stand there even after a flood of giggles rushes up the stairs. But not the entire fan club, apparently. The angel comes back to join us after a minute. Only she has her eyes set on a different piece of artwork, stopping in front of Foster. "Gross, right?"

Foster half-smiles at the house and says, "Not even close," before walking inside.

After he disappears through the door, Colton whistles and hooks his head from the porch. I step, and so does the angel.

"Are they really letting you bring that with you?" she asks with a point at my camera.

"What? Why—"

"Remi." Colton cuts me off once we reach the steps. The angel bats her lashes at him on her way up and goes with the mime detail into the house. He tips his head to maintain a view of her ass. "She already gave Adams the fuck-me eyes?"

"Oh, yeah." His comment registers, and I look up at him. "You used his name." And I remember, "You used *my* name."

He shrugs. "Not much of a point after the NDAs. We still confiscated their phones, though. We haven't fully made it past the orgy possibility of the night."

I blink. "I need to remove Dev's spy glasses."

We head inside, and he does me the solid of snagging Dev's glasses. Colton powers them down and hooks them in the collar of his torn shirt.

It takes about two seconds for me to hit record and pan around the gutted foyer. A dusty and precariously dangling pendant light above proves the angel right about power still being on. Toolboxes and broken pieces of plaster cover parts of the scratched hardwood. I pick my way around them to a stripped and partially torn-down wall. Through the hole, enough light shines in to see the massive brick fireplace. The mantel's long gone in what seems to be a forgotten parlor.

I scan the high ceilings, only checking the viewfinder to make sure it's capturing the crown molding. I want to see it all with my own eyes.

As I'm coming back, I film the grand staircase, spiraling up into darkness. The intricate carvings on the banisters break my heart. So much beauty to be destroyed.

"All right, ladies," Dev announces, and I swing around to see him and Felix in the center of the room. They've pulled down their beak and bandana, their grins downright salacious as they peruse the five women in front of them. "Whoever catches you keeps you for the night."

The women exchange quick glances, but none of them appear against the idea of being hunted down for what will likely end in sex. One is already slipping off her heels.

I stop recording and let the camera tip to the side. Any more footage will end up useless anyway. No chance the label wants the world to know about how the guys divvy up chicks for tonight.

Surprisingly, I've only stumbled in on rock star sex twice so far. Most wheres and whens to avoid are obvious, but Dev also informed me they're being gentlemanly for my sake.

Doggy-style on the bus's floor in front of the couches fits that definition in his case.

Colton's actually discreet, typically reappearing from between the buses after concerts with his chosen flavor of the night or re-zipping on their way out of the restrooms at venues. A wink when he sees me is more than enough confirmation.

I've dreaded walking in on Foster with anyone in any capacity. Women scream for him to fuck them or flash him their tits, and I have a physical response like with the nurse every single time. He hasn't visibly returned interest in any of them. I thought it was just good timing I haven't noticed, or he was that damn skilled at maintaining an untouchable persona.

More than one of the women blatantly stare at him right now where he props against a wall with seductive smiles and Adams North lust in their eyes. My jaw sets, and I slowly inhale, realizing my luck might have run out.

Felix chuckles, rubbing his hands together. "Should we give y'all a head start?"

There are some excited giggles and nods.

"Ten … nine … eight…" Dev starts counting down, the girls scattering in different directions—except two who stick together.

The numbers pause, his eyebrows rising at me. "You won't make it far with the camera."

I laugh, but it dies in my throat when he and Felix look at each other. "What?"

A wolfish grin forms, and Dev jerks his head over his shoulder at Foster and Colton behind them. "Four of us. Six of you. Sounds fair to me."

"You're joking."

"Not a joke at all, Cam Girl," Felix says. "Need me to repeat the rules? You want me to tell you *exactly* what's going to happen if one of us finds you?"

My gaze shifts to Foster against the wall. He lost the bandana and sword but has the mask on still, his focus on the hardwood. Colton's smirking off to the side of him, and he gives me a shrug.

"Run fast, lioness."

"Eight…"

Dev starts the countdown again, and Foster's staring at me now. So is Felix.

I scowl at them all, and my feet start moving as Dev hits six.

"Your music's trash," I call, rushing up the grand staircase and whipping out my phone for light.

Laughter follows me and my lie, along with Dev shouting, "One."

13

FOSTER

"No one touches, Remi." I kick off the wall and cross through the entry of the stripped house.

Felix goes maniacal with his laugh, throwing his head back and losing his cowboy hat. "Oh, come on. The way her eyes bulged was hilarious."

I walk to the winding staircase but don't respond. I can't without lying. It was funny. Then a blush spread over her cheeks —fuck, it brought on an onslaught of memories. Most of them about where else she's prettily pink. I need to stop before I'm roaming around with my dick hard. It's already been a challenge with her dressed in basically her old school uniform. The amount of times I jerked off to her in a plaid skirt borders on alarming.

"You know we wouldn't really fuck her," Dev says, equally amused. "Unless she begged, of course."

"Not even if she hits her knees for you."

I sweep my palm over the dusty banister to expose the designs etched into the wood before climbing the stairs. The dick and fake hick start their hunt with a yeehaw, and when I look, Colt's watching me, arms crossed. I flip him off for whatever he's thinking. His thoughts often earn him the finger, so I'm hedging my bets.

The shadows swallow me on the landing. The lights are off everywhere but the entry, and from what I've seen, a lot of busted bulbs are exposed. I consider going to the third floor, but a faint scuff of shoes above decides for me.

Even halfway to drunk, I have no desire to play Felix and Dev's game tonight. Colt needs to so he's less whiny. Here's to him finding the pair that scampered up here.

I break out the flashlight on my phone once the downstairs light runs out. The hallway's narrow given the monstrosity of a house. Far from a dump, even if it shows signs of neglect. The place deserves better than an excavator and condos erected on its grave. A lot of shit does, though.

Partway down, I catch movement inside a room without a door and pause. The brunette firefighter in a shiny skirt smiles as she steps out from behind an armoire, likely left because of its size. She tucks her hands behind her, bouncing on the balls of her feet.

"God, I suck at hiding." She laughs, aiming for self-deprecating, I'm guessing, but expectation flares in her eyes and smile. Like a sign blinks above me—step right up to fuck the rock star.

"Try harder." I stroll away and push through the door at the end of the hall before she thinks I mean try harder with *me*.

The hinges shockingly stay quiet, both opening and closing. I spin to shine the light around the bathroom. Dirty and cracked tile lines the bottom half of the dirtier walls, a pink toilet matches the mounted sink.

My attention snags on the sliding glass panels of the also pink tub. One closed and the other slid open. Considering my options, I weigh the grime-to-unwanted-attention ratio, and then I step over the side. Once I drop in, I wrench the glass door toward me. It grinds to a halt with a few inches to go. I sigh and let my head rest on the wall behind me, tapping off the flashlight.

Everything falls silent. No road noise or demands or the voice warning every second's fleeting. All the things I haven't been able to escape for months cease to exist. The only sound is my breath. I can't remember the last time I heard myself breathing. Something so simple. I missed it.

Slowly, snippets from the world find their way into my porcelain cocoon. Footsteps creak the floorboards above, a high-pitched squeal. Easy to ignore until the bathroom door eases open. I smother a groan, not in the mood to be rejecting these chicks all night. I want a few minutes of Foster before giving everyone Adams again.

But when I roll my head to the side, my face illuminates at the same time I see Remi's. She's so goddamn gorgeous, her hair in a clip, strands framing her face. She must not notice me in her rush for the tub, forcing the opposite glass door down the track. My lips twitch even before she freezes and jerks her head in my direction.

"Shit," she exhales.

Her attention switches to the door and the heavy footfalls coming down the corridor. I stay with my head tipped back and watch her struggle over the choice presented.

I'm an asshole for enjoying the panicked glances between me and the unknown. I'm fucking hopeless for my smile when she crawls into the tub in her chunky black boots.

I move a leg, bringing up my knee more to shift my own boot. She lowers beside the other. Metal scrapes metal as she drags the door into place, and she winces at the harsh noise. The glass on that one has more scratches. It's hazy and nearly opaque.

She kills the light a few seconds ahead of the door swinging inward.

Colt halts, staring at the broken mirror above the sink, then he rotates with his own phone's flashlight and blinds me.

"I have so many jokes about you being washed up," he says.

Remi's sunk down at the other end, trying to hide. I wonder if she realizes she's latched onto my leg. Resisting the urge to look at her, I nod at Colt.

"Can I top?" I ask him. "That was the point, right? Find me and fuck me?"

He snorts and shoulders the door shut. "Even if I bottomed, I'd still top you from down there."

My buddy saunters to the toilet and unzips. The grip tightens on my shin as his stream hits the dry bowl, and I lick my lips to suppress a smile. She has her eyes scrunched closed, knees tucked to the side in her attempts to blend into the shadows.

Once finished, Colt starts to reach for the handle before thinking it through. No water. Instead, he considerately closes the lid. While rotating for the door, his light sweeps over the glass, but he catches the doorknob, not mentioning the hunched form across from me.

Then he looks over. "Enjoy your bath, motherfucker."

He zeros in on Remi's exact location, a smirk forming on his way out. The latch clicks and plunges the room to black. The near silence returns, only this time with two sets of breaths.

Remi sighs, relaxing her grip even though the hand stays. I pick up my phone to turn on the light, and my eyes land on hers.

"Come here often?"

She fights a smile. "I visit when I can."

Returning my phone to the ledge, I set it so the light shines at the ceiling. Shadows cast sharp and harsh around us, only parts of her fully illuminated. A certain part gains my attention. My eyes lower as she readjusts her skirt to better cover her ass. Failing miserably. A pleading look comes my way, so I bend my other knee more, letting both fall open to rest on the sides of the tub. It allows her to find an angle that almost ruins my view, her legs folding before she gives up.

"I've seen a lot more of you than this," I remind her.

Her cheeks pink again, and she avoids my gaze.

"Why are you hiding, anyway?" She sets her camera between my legs in front of hers, and I pick it right up. My turn to avoid. I am hiding. Colt's jab about my celibacy streak holds more truth than I care to admit to myself, let alone her. She infiltrated before, and here I am again—knowing the damage she causes, yet I still can't *stop*.

I run my fingers over the matte black finish of her camera's body and down the navy shoulder strap she rarely uses.

"I can leave," she says when I don't answer her. "They've probably found the others by now. So, if you want to be alone—" She cuts off when I power on her camera, and I smirk at the apprehension creeping into her eyes. "What are you doing?"

I shrug a shoulder. "Fucking up your settings."

She lunges, and I jerk it out of her reach.

"Nope. Mine."

On a huff, she returns to her side of the tub, settled farther back on the porcelain, and the soles of her boots press against my ankle. I watch her through the viewfinder, studying all of her through the screen. Like in the dark, it transforms her into *my* Remi. Remi Saint. The broken girl who wrecked my world in the best way possible. Or it's the alcohol.

She crosses her arms, quite the glare aimed at me. Again, she asks, "What are you doing?"

I zoom in on her face, and her eyes shift from me to the lens' movement. "Observing my subject in a foreign habitat."

"You're a filmmaker now?" She cocks her head.

"Documentarian," I correct. "Up-and-coming. Turns out, there's no money in music."

She finally smiles all the way, shaking her head when she bites down on her lower lip. I move the camera over her, still zoomed to only show me the pieces. Auburn locks and a heated cheek. A mossy iris framed by fluttering lashes. Slender neck, partially in shadow.

The top two buttons of her shirt are open. I pause on her collarbone and flick my gaze over the top of the camera to hers. Her chest rises in a deep breath before she glances away.

"We need to do your interview still," she says.

As if a mention of work matters at all. Not when I'm still buzzed with her right in front of me.

I slowly roll my head side to side on the tiles in a headshake, and I *tsk* her. "I'm the one with the camera, which means we need to do *your* interview."

"Foster," she warns.

"Remi."

"You're not even recording."

I pan farther down, over her arm covering her middle. I pause where the plaid ends and skin begins on her outer thigh. The little red light blinks on that indicates I'm rolling, and her pouty mouth pops open. I hit stop and raise a brow in challenge. It earns me another glare, but then she sinks against the porcelain, adding her knees to the parts of her touching me.

"So, who are you hiding from?" I ask.

She hesitates, brows slanting. "What do you mean?"

I half-smile at the three seconds it took her to turn a question on me. "You ran in here to hide, right?"

"Wasn't that the game? Hide and Keep?" Her head tilts on another question before she finally uses a period. "I know they're messing with me about the sex part. I've been around long enough to know they like their women *enthusiastic*. But I wouldn't put it past Felix to *keep* me on the backhoe while he drives it directly into a police station or something."

Of course they were fucking with her—they would never cross those lines whether I said anything or not. She's not wrong about the last part, though. If he finds keys, the night will end with Felix driving the equipment. He'll go from back shot to backhoe.

"So, you're hiding from Felix?"

"All of them," she says like it's obvious.

"But not me?" I watch her through the screen as she stares through it to me. "You said all of them and not all of you."

A flush creeps up her cheeks, barely visible with the camera but there. She messes with the laces on her boot. "What about you? You never told me who you're hiding from."

"All of them," I say.

Before Now

She glances up at the repeat of her phrasing. A silent *but not me?* floats between us until I sigh and redirect like a champ.

"You're terrible at giving interviews. I'll hook you up with my publicist."

She snorts. "Great. They can teach me how to avoid them." After a not-so-subtle dig at me, she quits screwing with the shoestring, and her hand lands on my foot. "My talent lies in conducting interviews, which you wouldn't know." She's on a roll, and my lips twitch. "I'm not used to being on this side of the lens."

"Anymore."

Our eyes meet, and she softly echoes, "Anymore."

My free hand's close enough I skim my knuckles over her black knee-high above one boot. "You're just out of practice." The arm covering her middle falls to her side—her other hand landing on my other shoe. So, I flip my palm and let mine settle the same way. "With the right direction, I'm sure it'll come back to you."

She smiles and looks away, but like every other time, those hypnotic orbs return to me. "Direct me then."

Fuck, her raspy voice has no right to sound so sexy.

I drag my teeth over my bottom lip, switching to the viewfinder. "For starters, you need to relax."

"I am relaxed," she defends, but the tension remains in her shoulders and forehead.

"So relaxed." I adjust the lens to see more of her. "I think we can do better. Take down your hair."

After studying me for a second, Remi reaches up. My fingers flex around her leg as she removes the clip. Her dark red hair spills over her shoulders, the clip clattering into the soap tray screwed to the wall. She sets her phone down on the ledge by mine and repositions. Her lower body shifts even closer to me, her upper stretching out and reclining. Then she rests her head on the tiled wall behind her in a mirror to mine, the black ends of her hair splaying over her white shirt around the two open buttons.

Without thinking, I lean forward and tuck a lock behind her

129

ear. Her chest stalls when I touch her. As I sit back, my hand returns to her leg but higher. My thumb sweeps back and forth over the material. But I want her skin.

I want what I could only watch back then.

Remi licks her lips. "What are you thinking about?"

"I'm remembering how hot you look when you come," I tell her.

Her lashes flutter as she swallows. "Oh."

One side of my mouth lifts at what sounded more squeak than word. "Yeah, but..." I slide my foot closest to the doors forward, so she has to move her arm. Touch me or touch herself. She chooses me, resting it on my leg. "You were wearing a lot less clothes then."

I don't specify which time I'm talking about—I don't need to.

"Not at first," she says, and I look up.

"You were once I got you to strip out of your slutty fairy outfit."

We stare at each other, memories silently traded back and forth while her fingers grip my jeans. Mine slip between her knees for the warm skin I wanted. It only makes me crave more.

Remi must too because she follows my thoughts without me needing to lead. "So then, what do you want from me, director?"

The words go straight to my cock, and I lower my eyes to the viewfinder. "You know what I want, Remi."

She was standing in front of a full-length mirror before, face partially obscured with swirls of black and teal and silver. She's right in front of me now, all the pieces together.

"*Let me see*," I said before. Now I tell her, "Show me."

The hold on my jeans vanishes. Those same fingers start where her shirt tucks into her skirt. They ascend, button by button. My attention bounces between them and her teeth denting her bottom lip. Once she reaches the top, though, her other hand joins, and they gain my entire focus. She pops the third button while her thumb glides across her collarbone and dips beneath the fabric.

A fucking tease from when I couldn't touch her. She'd do the same damn thing when I could only watch.

As she works her way down, someone screeches from elsewhere in the house. Neither of us cares. My porcelain cocoon has become ours, the rest of the world separate from us. We're not even on the same timeline anymore.

Remi reaches the last button before her skirt. She doesn't untuck the shirt, letting the front create a V on her hand's slow drag back up. More and more smooth skin and then the swell of her breasts.

By the time the rest of the fabric falls open, her chest's rising faster. Pouty lips part as she tries to regulate her breathing. I'm struggling myself, having her right here and not touching. My pulse thrums, but lingering resolve keeps my eyes on the screen.

She dances her fingertips over the skin above her red bra. Glimpses of it through her white shirt tormented me all night. Remi appears more than pleased to pick up the taunting.

"You still like red, Foster?" she asks, toying with the top edge.

Fuck, my dick can't take her saying my name right now. It's pressing into my zipper hard enough to border on painful.

"Mmm. I do, but…" I rub the bare skin beneath my thumb. "I'll like it more if they match."

I gently lift her knee until she takes over, spreading her thighs to expose the tiny scrap of red fabric at the apex. Locking onto the wet spot in the center, I groan and am officially beyond not touching.

The camera hasn't even lowered when I surge forward and hook her around the waist. She gasps as I haul her across the tub. The camera lands by my leg, and she lands right where I fucking want her.

My body shifts enough she can straddle me while I tug her closer by her open shirt. I lick above her bra, right where she was touching, and then I suck hard. She whimpers, her hands on the sides of my neck but not stopping me even though she squirms.

The movement rubs her pussy over my jeans and hard cock beneath.

"Oh, fuck." Remi pushes her fingers into my hair. I owe the more-drunk version of me for losing the bandana.

I work my way up her chest and grab her ass in both hands, jerking her forward and flexing my hips. The friction sends her head back on a moan. My mouth moves over her throat, her pulse beating against my lips before I draw back.

A battle's waging over what part of me gets what part of her. But it's the first time I've touched her and seen her at the same time since the dim restroom in Prague. Fuck, do I want to see her while I touch her.

I look up and find her staring right back at me. She rips the mask off my eyes, dropping it behind her with the camera. We're face-to-face in a way we haven't been. So close her ragged breaths heat my skin, her tempting mouth an inch from mine. She doesn't try to kiss me and saves me from a worse internal fight. We'll leave the cocoon eventually. I need to keep something free of her for then.

Instead, she traces my jawline and down my neck while I rake my gaze over her. By now, her skirt's bunched up on her thighs, her cheeks flushed but not as red as the skin I tortured, marking her. I pull the rest of her shirt loose and urge her hips to move over me.

"So fucking sexy," I tell her, pushing the cup of her bra down on one side.

I draw her nipple into my mouth, soft with my tongue and then rough with my teeth. She pulls at my hair, and I thrust up harder.

"Foster," she breathes.

At first I think it's hearing *my* name that makes my cock throb. It's been a long time since I was between a set of legs and heard anything other than Adams. Then she repeats it, needy and desperate, and it has everything to do with *Remi* saying it. I'm losing my fucking mind over her—and not for the first time.

I yank down the other side of her bra, slipping under the back of her skirt to feel the soft skin beneath my palm at the same time. Switching to her other nipple, I tuck both cups under her breasts so I can let my thumb trail lower. Her hooded eyes follow it when I glance up, her lips parted and soft pants escaping. The sound fills the bathroom around us. The air pulses *more*.

Fabric coasts under my thumb once I hit the top of her skirt. I brush my lips up to her collarbone and squeeze her ass one more time before bringing my hand to wrap her rib cage to slow her movements. She stops, tracking the other's progress as it glides up her thigh.

"What else are you going to show me?" I ask, voice rough.

Lust-drunk eyes pop up to mine. This close, I catch the darker green flecks. "What do you want to see?"

Pushing her skirt up all the way, I lean her back a little and drop my attention between us. I ghost my thumb up her slit through the drenched red fabric. She whimpers as I reach her clit, her hand tangling in my hair.

"I want to see something hot and wet."

The sound of her breath cuts out the second I tuck my finger under the edge. I pull the material to the side, exposing her glistening pussy. Exactly what I wanted.

I groan. "You're fucking soaked for me, Rem."

With nothing between us, I swipe up the same path, and she sharply inhales, then she scoots back and braces a palm on my leg behind her to allow me more room.

I flick my eyes up to hers. "Are you making a request?"

"More like you fulfilling a promise." She draws a trail from my neck to my chest, but I catch her wrist and sweep my thumb over her pulse point.

"We might as well take care of a few then," I say, guiding her hand lower.

I use her fingers to drag her arousal up and press down on her clit. At the first hint of pressure, she lets out a sexy sound, and her lids crush closed.

"Not a chance," I tell her, and they flutter open, resettling on me. "Tell me where you're supposed to look, Remi."

"At you. Always at you." She rasps the words and circles her hips to grind her ass against my cock. I meet them with her hand as they come around.

"Good girl." I stroke her fingers all the way through one more time. They shine when I pull her wrist up and aim them to their true destination, slipping them between her parted lips. "Suck."

She moans, tasting herself, and I drop my hand back between her legs.

"Fuck, Foster."

Hers falls away from her mouth and clutches the front of my shirt while I rub her slick clit.

She rolls her hips for more, my cock aching every time she moves over it. I flex into her, only for Remi to grind down harder.

As stunning as the visual of her spread wide for me, I slide my other hand to her breast and follow with my tongue, massaging and licking and sucking. I feel her breath come faster. Feel her grip tighten on my jeans where she's braced on my leg. Feel the weight of her on me. The heat from her body. Her.

"What now, Remi?" I tug at her nipple right after asking, and she arches into me.

My fingers tease lower, circle her entrance, and retreat. It causes her to whimper, and she tilts her pelvis in an attempt to get them back. I hum, drifting lower again. I start to reverse, and she releases my shirt and grasps my wrist.

"You want me right here?" I ask, rubbing lightly.

"Yes," she breathes. "Please, Foster. I need to feel you."

Not the first time I've heard those words, but the first time I don't have to just say, "I know, baby."

She looks down, and I let her, my eyes staying on her face as I dip inside her. I thrust a few times before adding another, pumping in and out of her pussy, pressing my thumb to her clit.

"Oh God." She pushes into my hair, hips rocking.

I watch her mouth open on a silent gasp when I stretch her with a third.

Remi used to ask me to show her beautiful things—this was mine. I would have given anything to feel her while I made her come back then. I'm right there all over. And, if possible, I want it even more.

A *thud* breaches the walls from who the fuck knows what, and Remi flicks her gaze up, like she thinks I might stop, but I only thrust harder. "Fuck."

"Just like that, baby," I tell her, pinching her nipple and earning the sexiest sound. "Show me how this tight cunt drips down my hand when you come."

She tips her face up to the ceiling and gives me my name over and over. I speed up, feeling her thighs tighten, her pussy, her hold on my hair. My other hand slides up to the front of her neck, her pulse wild beneath my palm. Remi brings her head up on a moan, then she clenches around me, her eyes all mine as she comes with a muted cry. Fucking beautiful while she shatters to pieces for me instead of giving me ones of her like she used to.

I still once she relaxes, both of our breaths unsteady. Her forehead falls onto mine, and the hooded look she gives me is how I'll drown again.

We both ignore the buzz on porcelain from one of our phones. My fingers pull out of her, fucking soaked, and I drag hers down.

"See how good you did for me?" I swipe them through her pussy, making sure to graze her sensitive clit.

"Fuck," she breathes.

She grabs the back of my neck, lids fluttering when I suck them clean. I groan at how divine she tastes, releasing her wrist. Remi keeps her touch there, trailing across my lower lip, and I shove my hand into her hair.

The phone vibrates again. And again.

I glance at hers, screen up by mine and notifications rolling in.

She sighs and reaches for it. With her skin still pressed against mine, she unlocks it. The message thread opens as I look down.

Xander. The wannabe boyfriend I watched stake a claim on her outside her apartment building. I know that because his last message is a selfie. No shirt, tongue out, spiked hair, and holding up devil horns with a lightning bolt painted over an eye—*I'll be your rock god, baby.*

And the cocoon fucking disintegrates. We snap into our real timeline, and my jaw clenches. I sit back, my hands dropping away from her.

"He's my roommate," she says, dismissively.

"I know who he is, Remi." I slide her off me, back to the other end of the bathtub, and I stand up with my phone.

"Foster?" she says as I slide open the glass panel. "Where are you—"

"You were right. No one will touch you."

I don't look at her, stepping over the side, and I walk out without even wanting to.

Now she's the true Remi. Remi Sinner. The one who fucking destroyed everything.

14

FOSTER

Before…

THE THIRD SHOT in twenty minutes goes down, and I've barely swallowed when Chase sets another next to my beer.

"This is what we're doing?" I say over the club music. "Going the blackout route? Because I'd rather not—"

He blows fucking glitter at me from his palm. "Fairy God Pirate of Halloween says quit your bitching."

I hate everything about this moment, but I still crack a smile while glaring and shaking my head. "You are the fucking worst."

The asshole winks at me, shoves the shot to my lips, and starts tipping. I catch it before it ends up everywhere and throw it back. Chase nods, like he seriously accomplished something. He takes his own before returning the tricorn hat to his head. I've opted for a red bandana tonight and a black mask over my eyes rather than an eyepatch like him, but we both have on black billowy shirts with undone laces at the tops, black jeans, and cuffed boots.

A lot more chest on display than the original look. But we have a lot more to give.

The pirate costumes became a given a long time ago. We wore different versions three years straight as little kids for trick-or-treating. After that, it was a joke, and by this point, it's pirate or no costume at all. And Halloween in Prague with Chase requires a costume.

I get a reprieve from another shot when Chase plants a hand on the hilt of his fake sword and swaggers off into the crowd of monsters and skin. Fog covers the floor from machines and creeps up to our thighs, and I have to dodge a few LED spiderwebs. The DJ is decked out in a giant pumpkin head and currently playing the *Ghostbusters* theme blended with a techno beat.

I've pulled back on the nightlife the past few days. Shockingly, passing out every morning after drinking all night can lose its appeal to a twenty-one-year-old college dude. Not Chase—who almost seems to be going harder to make up for me. But I missed quiet. I missed exploring the city. I missed brooding over lyrics and strumming aimlessly, chasing what feels like magic.

It just so happens the spellwork lately includes auburn hair and a sexy voice and a restless desire to fill in the rest. The wandering often involves all that, too.

Tonight, though, I would have come out regardless of Chase threatening to knock me out and carry me out of the flat. Even if my pirate companion has twice now managed to find glitter somewhere.

I'm handed a green drink once we break through the throng of people. Chase is already downing his and on the move again toward three lifeguards, huddled off on the edge of the dance floor. He opens with an, "Arr, lasses, we're here to plunder yer booties," and maybe I needed one more shot.

The bikini-clad tourists fall for it hook, anchor, and cannonball, so he catches me around the neck and pulls me forward to join them. But rather than offering the chicks my sword, I'm playing up Chase tonight. Unlike him, I can fucking wingman.

"What's your favorite part of Prague?" one of the two brunettes yells at me.

A wolf howl breaks into a house mix of Monster Mash while I

tip my cup at my best friend. "Chase has taken me so many places. I can't pick."

She moves closer. To me. "Maybe you can show me a few."

"Nah." I scrunch up my face and clap Chase on the shoulder. "If you need a guide, he's the better man."

Chase chuckles, and then he slaps me on the back. "Foster's just being shy. This sexy man *loves* giving tours to hot women. Especially of our flat."

He adds a wink. I shoot him a look to knock it off, but he just pinches my cheek.

It switches after that to me constantly dodging. Suddenly, Chase is bound and determined to get me to fuck one of them—even pulling out the eleven-inch dick guitarist shit. The relentless pushing starts to piss me off. I told him before we threw on the costumes I'm not hunting for buried treasure tonight.

When they all empty their drinks, they decide we need shots. Chase throws an arm over my shoulders, bringing me along. We stop at one of the drink stations set up around the club. They have different themes, this one a vampire's lair. The bar top looks like a coffin with candelabras and skulls for decoration.

The lifeguards and Chase order two rounds of "bloodlust" shots, which end up being rum and raspberry syrup, but I wave off the second.

"I'm good," I tell him.

He rotates away from the lifeguards on his other side toward me. The redhead touches his arm and pouts, but he puts the shot down in front of him on the coffin, not paying attention. She realizes he doesn't care, so she returns to giggling with her friends.

By now, Chase is lasered in on me. "You finally come out and don't want to drink yourself into oblivion, and now you're cutting yourself off by midnight?" He drunkenly sighs and sets his hand on the back of my neck. "I love you, my little rock star, but you're killing the image of being one."

I shake my head. "I'm not your little anything. And

considering I barely have a band, I think it's safe to say I'm not a rock star either."

"Yet. You're not a rock star *yet*." Nudging the drink closer, he says, "But you fucking will be, Foster West, so you might as well start drinking like one now. Raw dog the life you want or some manifestation shit."

I snort. "Pretty sure that's exactly how the saying goes, brother." My irritation slips, and deciding fuck it, I raise the glass. "Carpe dick."

He grins as I take the shot. "There you go, buddy. The world is your Fleshlight."

"You're getting that on a pillow for Christmas." I smile, and he shakes me around until I shove him off.

Before we bro-spire the entire club, a panda and a witch pass behind us, talking about another DJ on the roof. I feel Chase refocus on me before I swing toward him.

"They have a roof," I say at the same time as he shouts, "A fucking roof?"

We have a thing that started when I moved back to Texas at fourteen. After all the shit surfaced with my dad in New York and the way it went down, I hated everything and everyone. So, Chase would force my ass up to the roof of his house. Nobody but us. No reason to hold it all in. I could tell the person I trust most in this world whatever I needed to get out.

It became our ritual. Something shitty happens, we find a rooftop—even if we had to pop a lock for access. Hell, we go on them without a reason anymore.

It's just what we do.

No surprise, he invites the lifeguards to go with us. Conveniently, they all have trench coats.

The closed stairwell up still has a throb of bass, but the tempo switches the closer we get to the top. Chase smirks at me before he throws the metal door open. And we walk out to a rooftop rave. Glowsticks and *boomsh-boomsh* and a strobe-lit dance floor under a canopy. People sprawl on glowing cubes, serving as furniture, and we might be the only ones not splattered with blacklight body paint.

Which seems like a top priority.

Chase already has a bundled-up lifeguard under each arm. "Let's paint, drink, and then we'll get you ladies out of here." He nods at the brunette he's been forcing on me all night. "Foster will give you that tour of flat surfaces in our flat with the flat of his tongue."

I let out an exasperated, "Dude," but don't finish because he walks off toward the stall set up for paint.

After another douche move, I'm seriously considering bailing, but the brunette grabs my bicep and hauls me in that direction. We stop behind the other three, people everywhere, close to a speaker. The last two shots are kicking in, which has everything developing a slight haze.

The brunette shouts up at me, laughing and hanging off my arm. Her hold slides all the way down, and she links our fingers. I look down at them, entwined, my eyebrows lowering. Her hand in mine, mine in hers. It scrapes at something inside me—and as she tries to tuck herself against my side, my mind finally catches up.

I can't detach myself fast enough. I actually have to hold her wrist to retrieve my hand. Then I walk away. From her. From the pounding music and the wasted crowd and the entire fucking scene.

None of it's what I want right now.

Maybe that should be a glaring reason to stay. The fact I have no interest in all the things I should want. Things I was interested in until a little red dot appeared on my screen in Paris. When Remi Saint told me to stop looking at women and show her beautiful things.

I make it all the way to the opposite side of the roof before I crash down on a wicker sofa. The air feels cooler, and the music doesn't take up all the space in my head anymore.

But someone fills in the gaps.

Digging my phone out of my pocket, I check out the view. One I haven't seen of the city. I know just who I want to share it with.

I unlock my screen but never make it to my camera. I smile. Remi beat me, sending a video twenty minutes ago.

With no one else around, I hit play and slouch deeper into the cushions. I squint at the screen, unsure what the hell I'm seeing. The shot is dim, random shapes and harsh shadows. An eerie scream plays in the background followed by the sound of chains clanking together.

It starts to come together once I catch the curve of shimmery black fabric and a slice of bare skin toward the bottom. Two things I excel at noticing—a skirt and legs. Another part of the screen shows the same but from a different angle. She must move then because it all shifts. Once it settles, the smooth line of her arm fractures across the screen, tilted in different directions.

Mirrors.

She's in a room of mirrors.

As if she'd timed how long I would take to figure it out, the shot pulls back, more of Remi visible until I have multiple reflections of her from the waist down. I have to piece them together for the full picture. Her fingers wrap around the back of a sparkly blue phone case, maroon nails to match the origination of my foot fetish. An upside-down fragment gives me the curves beneath a tight black dress. An angled view of the short skirt flares over her hips with the glimmer of iridescence in the fabric. Gorgeous legs disappear into boots with way too many straps.

"I want to try something," she says, and I sigh at her voice.

I might be slightly drunk now, but I am just as caught up in her sober. She wouldn't scrape. Not a chance in hell.

Everything morphs on my screen until only a close-up reflection of her shoulder and a thin black strap remain. I hear her exhale, and the mirror fogs over. A few seconds later, it starts dissipating. Then Remi's silhouette begins to fade in. More than a sexy curve or a flash of skin. All of her. Every fucking part.

"Remi," I mumble, a place inside me settling.

The video cuts off right before the mirror fully clears, and I groan, already typing out the message.

Why do you hurt me like this?

I blow out a breath and stand, bringing up my camera. The skyline glides across the screen while I turn a 360 to record. Not nearly as artistic, but she'll get what she gets after that bullshit.

"You can't be fucking serious."

Chase's annoyance announces him before I reach him in my rotation. I flick my eyes over to him. The colored lights from the rooftop rave swirl behind him, eye patch abandoned and his arms at his sides, lifeguardless.

Something below the surface has felt off with him all night. I've done my best to ignore it, chalking it up to drunk Chase. But now he's serving me more of a scowl than I did to him earlier. Like I'm the one being an asshole. The look alone has all the irritation returning. Mix it with the contempt in his tone, and I have no more patience for him at all.

"I don't know, Chase." I pocket my phone and face him. "After you trying to shove my dick down a chick's throat for the past hour, I'm not very giggly."

"One night," he says. "I thought I might get one *fucking* night with my best friend."

"You were getting it until you decided to ignore what I said about not wanting to screw anyone."

"Because you've wanted to screw anything lately? Or hell, even do anything at all?"

"It's been a few days," I remind him.

"Fuck off, Foster. It's been longer, and we both know the reason."

Running a hand over the bandana, I slide it off, scanning over the skyline before I come back to him. Outside of giving me shit, he's never had an issue with the tours or Remi. But since the tours help pay for him, I doubt the resentment is aimed at them.

"What's your point?"

"My point?" he asks, the words harsh. "We're supposed to be having the time of our lives on this trip. We *were* having the time of our lives." He shakes his head, stepping closer. "Now you ditch me to record the sky for some bitch you've never even met."

My head shakes, too, and I step. "Call her that again and see what happens."

Abysmal lighting aside, I catch his eye roll. "What are you going to do?" Step. "Kick my ass over pussy you won't ever touch?"

"You're fucking pushing it," I grind out.

"And you're fucking pathetic if you think anything between you two is real."

He strikes an exposed nerve with that one, and we both step, less than a foot between us.

In all the years I've known him, all the times he's been a prick, I've never been close to hitting him until this moment. He appears just as close to unloading on me. His fist clenches at his side and then relaxes and then tightens again, the rest of him equally tense.

We've never gotten here before. Nearing a point of not being able to take shit back. I can't figure out why he's pushed us here now, but I move the rest of the way to him. Chest to fucking chest.

"I don't know what the hell your problem is, Chase," I say, my tone low but even. "Or where any of this is coming from, but I'm over it. I'm over you, and I'm over this entire fucking trip."

I stare him down while he seethes right back.

"Maybe you should leave then," he bites at me.

"That's the first thing we agree on all night." Then I step again, around him, walking away.

He curses and knocks something over behind me and shouts for me to stop.

I don't, unwilling to give him the fight he clearly wants.

Chase is my brother. Nothing could ever change it. But right now, his bullshit is on the list of things I have no interest in.

On my way down the stairwell, I order a ride, and once outside the club, I cut off the end of the video.

I send the rest to Remi.

15

REMI

Slutty fairies.

Black mini dresses with a corset top, see-through front panels, a sparkly tulle over the skirt, and of course, silver wings. My heeled boots have straps and buckles and stop mid-calf, which means plenty of skin. The costumes are sexy. Attention-grabbing.

And fucking freezing.

Even with the arm warmers I insisted on wearing, covering wrists to elbows, I can't pretend we are anywhere except Ashfield, Ohio, in late October. As much as I'd rather be anywhere else.

The Halloween carnival my town puts on every year loses its appeal after about an hour. Not that it had much to begin with— outside the room of mirrors. That was by far the most fun I've had all night.

Dimitri Sinner might have made his living photographing wildlife, but he completed a series out of college involving mirrors. Some kids read bedtime stories with their dads, mine told me about shoots, showing me the prints. He went into detail about his processes, how he framed each photo. With the amount of information I absorbed simply from falling asleep as he talked, it would be shocking if I went into anything other than visual media.

Specifically film studies.

He captured stills of the world, and I want to capture it spinning.

Document all the beautiful things.

It just so happens, I found someone interested in seeing all those things, too.

As I wait for Sage to come out of the lovely portable toilet she avoided for as long as possible, I tug my black arm warmers higher. I tug one anyway. For the left one, I carefully ease the fabric back up to my elbow to avoid pulling at the wrap farther down on my forearm. Other than tonight, I've gotten away with long sleeves to cover the bandage.

But, slutty fairies required some improvising.

"Bitch"—Sage bounds over and grabs my hand—"it's trick-or-treat time."

She drags me behind a booth for pumpkin carving, but then keeps ahold of me, sidling right up beside me while she bends over to dig in her boot.

"You won't be cold tonight, huh?" I ask.

Sage tosses my hand away from her, fishes in *my* boot, and holds her chin a little higher when she straightens. "I'm not cold. I was just trying to show you affection. Sor-ry."

I let her have it, even if she goes rigid, fighting off a shiver through the attitude.

She swaps the two matching flasks she retrieved back and forth before she wiggles them for me to pick. I reach, but she pulls them away, giving me a look.

"Trick or treat," I say through my teeth.

A smug smile appears on her shimmery black lips, and I grab one of the flasks. We tap them together and drink. My entire face feels the lemon vodka. My eyes water, and I breathe through my mouth, loathing whoever gave her this idea. Her lips twitch. The Fireball truly is a *treat* compared to the *trick* flask I've gotten twice in a row.

"I feel warm again." She snags my flask and tucks it in my boot, then she slips the other in hers.

I head back toward the midway before someone notices us.

"Now," she says, catching up, "do we bail? I mean, there's not shit to do other than that house party that chick in your class is throwing. Oh." Sage grasps my arm, right over the bandage, and I flinch. She doesn't notice, though, releasing me just as fast. "If we go, you can show me which football players you've banged."

"I have never once said I've banged a football player."

"Right, because you don't tell me the juicy shit—as we've discussed. Regardless, lame party or stay." She links her arm through my other one. "Those are the only two options."

"I might have a third," a deep voice says from behind us.

We both stop, me calmly and Sage stumbling. Then we both smile, hers a little manic and mine wide because Miles and I successfully pulled off his surprise visit. As soon as she turns around, she launches herself at him.

He catches her with a grunt and grins at me over her shoulder. "Hey, Rem."

Once her feet hit the ground, she pushes her hands into his sandy hair and drags his face down to hers.

"Hi, Miles. How was your flight?" I ask.

"Good," he mumbles with a thumbs-up beside Sage's head.

She detaches, and he swipes over his mouth in case her black lipstick transferred while she spins on me. "You bitch. Is this why you whined about girls only tonight when I wanted to call him?"

I shrug, not admitting to anything. Now that I know it works, I might need to use it again in the future.

"This is hot." Miles thumbs her bottom lip and then glances over to me. "Pretty swirls, Remi. Very slutty fairy."

"The face paint mask was necessary." Sage slides her arms into the front of his jacket, *not cold*. "Nothing else was going to cover the black eye she's rocking."

His brows pull in, gaze jerking to me. "Who the fuck gave you a black eye?"

Before I can even open my mouth to lie, Sage answers, "She got it having wild car sex."

I force a laugh, his eyes still on me, and I shake my head. "I got elbowed by a girl in gym, but that's boring, so..."

One side of his mouth lifts, but the undercurrent's sad. Like Miles knows I don't take gym class.

The look vanishes a second later, and he shrugs off his coat and drapes it over Sage. "Let's take a lap, and then we'll get out of here."

She latches onto my hand and cuddles against his side, and we wander the midway with her as if the exchange never happened.

But I want it that way.

When Sage and I were nine, my mom went to rehab. I lived with my dad full-time until she came back. I have no idea how long she stayed clean, but I got a real mom for a few weeks. Sage didn't understand why I was so sad after she relapsed. If rehab fixed everything, I just needed to tell my mom to go again. It was simple. After she smiled and hugged me, so excited we solved the problem, I stopped telling her the bad if I could help it.

Sometimes I wish she'd see it, though. Like tonight when I told her I got elbowed in my nonexistent gym class. We were on the floor in my room by the mirror, pillows against the door. She gave a *psshh* and accused me of not sharing the *juicy shit*. I stared at her while she painted a picture about hot car sex, simultaneously painting swirls of black and silver and teal on my face, burying the truth I desperately wished she would notice.

Except Sage doesn't even know what to look for.

The worst thing in her life is dealing with a long-distance relationship with a boyfriend who adores her. Mr. and Mrs. Teller love her, praise her, and support her. They've been happily married since they graduated college and have a fund for Sage's tuition set up—whatever she decides to do with her life. Her mom gets tipsy on wine once a week at her book club. Her dad still drags her to father-daughter dances. She lives in a stable home. A safe one. My best friend gets to not know the bad because she doesn't have to survive it.

I want it all to stay simple for her for as long as possible before the world inevitably turns on her.

Miles wins her a big pink skeleton stuffy at a ring toss booth. She beams, names it Pigeon, and then he plays again to win me one too. I get a wink as he hands it off.

We've circled back on the midway, reaching the carnival's entrance when Foster texts back about the video I sent him of the mirrors.

Why do you hurt me like this?

I bite down on my smile, staring at the words like they're the actual man. At this point, the fever of him burns hot enough that I quit trying to cool it. The delirium feels too incredible.

Feeling the stare, I rotate to face Sage a few feet away, likely trying to read my mind. Miles went for his car in the parking lot, offering to pick us up to save a heels-and-gravel situation. The man gets shit.

Sage tips her chin up and flits her gaze everywhere but at me, clearly uninterested in what's on my phone.

I sigh.

"His name is Foster," I tell her, and her grin spreads.

"And he is…" She raises her eyebrows, waiting for me to finish the sentence.

I shrug. "He's Foster, the wandering boy."

That earns me a squint, but I don't know what Foster is. I just know I want him to be.

"So, just some guy you're lamely talking to? Ugh. I thought maybe he was the car ho, but I do applaud you for keeping them lined up."

Before I can remind her there was no car sex, we hear a deep, "Remington Sinner" behind us.

I spin, catching the black police uniform first. The spike of anxiety only lasts a second because above it waits possibly my favorite smile in existence.

"Are you a stripper cop tonight?" Sage asks Roman as he stops in front of us. "Because there is an ATM..."

His expression changes to the one he always gives her—like he wishes she'd find a filter. "I am a normal cop, like always, and no, I don't want to know what you're dressed as, Sage Teller."

"Slutty fairies," I supply, punctuating with a bratty smile.

Roman runs a hand over his face. "Christ."

"Oh, come on, Officer Moore." Sage pops a hip toward me. "We're both eighteen now. You get to enjoy the view without being pervy."

I press my lips together, suppressing a laugh at the absolute regret on his face. He gives me a look and then nods behind us. "And there's the boyfriend with wonderful timing."

We both glance over our shoulders to see Miles pull up. He's from Ashfield, so he's seen Roman around over the years, patrolling streets and events, and he gives the cop an easy nod back.

When I swing my head around, Roman smiles at me again, a slight tip to his head. I smile, too. It's been weeks since I've seen him. Even longer since hearing his voice.

Sage sighs. "As much as I love being a third wheel, I have my own wheel to mount." She zeros in on Roman. "You taking my girl home in your sexy cruiser or what?"

I shake my head. "You don't have to. Miles is perfectly capable of—"

"He is, but so is Roman," she interjects. "I imagine you two don't get nearly as much time together as you'd like." She waggles her brows, causing Roman to close his eyes.

He opens them, narrows them at me in question. Enough of an affirmative for Sage, apparently.

"Perfect." She bumps the popped hip against mine and winks. "Love you, bitch."

"Love you," I say as she walks toward the car.

Miles must piece it together because he rolls down his window. "It was great to conspire with you, Rem. Be safe for me, yeah?"

His eyebrows slant with the last part, and I nod, my mouth hitching up.

"He means no more black eyes." Sage cocks her head, swinging open the passenger door. "So, use the back seat. There's more room." And because she is Sage Teller, she slips in, "You drive a spacious SUV, right, Officer Hottie?"

Before my glare fully lands, she ducks into the car. They drive away as I turn, and Roman's already staring down at me.

"You have no idea how glad I am she's only minimally rubbed off on you."

I laugh and fall into step with him when he heads down the sidewalk to his police-issued SUV parked at the curb. "She still has time, *Officer Hottie.*"

He chuckles, and I crawl in, smashing my poor wings against the seat.

Roman Moore is handsome, though. Dark brown skin and strong features that don't go unnoticed, his beard trimmed short, and wavy hair in a low fade. And his eyes—deep brown and warm. They've always been so gentle. What you'd want to see in a crisis, which is why he says his grandma wanted him to become an officer. It took a while for life to get him there, but he made it.

Even when I first met him, he could make me feel safe. That was when I was eight, and he was a strung-out twenty-two-year-old, fucking my mom. I fully ignore the last part in my mind. I think he does too. Especially after Daniel married her and became Roman's chief.

He'd been clean for years by then, got out of Hunts for a fresh start. I remember how bad it got for him before that. Before he told me he had to leave, and he was so sorry, and I didn't see him for a long time.

By the time my mom and I moved to Ashfield, he'd been working here as a cop for a few years. The chief at the time thought his recovery and commitment to sobriety showed resilience. Too bad the man retired. From what I've witnessed, Roman's one of the few cops under Daniel that stays clean.

As we pull out of the parking lot, Roman flips on the heat for me. He shakes his head when he looks over at my skirt, illuminated in a streetlight. But then his lips turn up, and he reaches over, squeezing my shoulder.

"I missed you," he says.

"I'm pretty damn missable."

He nods. "That you are. How have things been since the last time I snuck you away?"

"Nothing all that exciting," I tell him, infusing it with pep. "It's senior year, so everyone's choosing colleges and hunting down scholarships and filling out—"

The words stop when he hits the brakes, pulling into an alley behind the library that sits off our town's square. He throws the cruiser in park and shuts off the headlights but keeps it running for the heat.

Then he unbuckles and twists toward me, gripping the back of my seat. He studies me in the dim light, and I swallow.

"Remi," he says quietly.

My lids fall closed when he grasps my chin, but I still know when the dome light turns on. Tears sting the backs of my eyes. I wait until it stops before I open them, Roman's gaze hard. His jaw's even harder, his focus on the sliver under my eye not covered by face paint—where the bruising shows.

"What's the lie you're going to tell me?" he asks.

I half-smile. "Some chick elbowed me in gym class."

The words are weak, little effort behind them since he already called me on it.

Then he looks down at my arm warmers, and my chest constricts.

"And what did she do to your arms?" After a second of me not answering, he lets his hand fall from my face. He slowly reaches for the top of my right arm warmer. He gives me every chance to stop him. Instead, I exhale and carefully draw down the left one and show him the bandage over the underside of my forearm.

"I landed on a broken wine glass," I whisper the truth.

Roman's nostrils flare, his head shaking. I can tell he wants to unleash on something, his fists clenched. He forces a slow inhale, hands loosening. "Is this the first time he's hit you?" His voice sounds strained, the calm surface level.

My entire body hurts, and I can't bring myself to say it aloud.

When no answer answers him, he laughs without humor. "Of fucking course it's not."

"It's not normally bad for me. He usually…" I swallow and have to push the words out, "I got in the w—"

"Finish that sentence, and I'll lose my fucking shit." He swings his gaze to mine, his eyes safe to me even when he's seething. "The only way to get in the way is if it's happening. If it's happening, not a goddamn part of it is an accident."

I nod because what else can I do? Disagree? Daniel accidentally gets loaded and fights with his pilled-up wife, and then unintentionally beats her? And me when I try to help too much?

The little girl always tries to help.

As I put the fabric back in place, I glance down.

Roman touches my other cheek, and I look up. I look up, and I *see* the tear inside him.

"I would kill him if I could. Fuck, I'd report it if it would do a damn thing besides make it worse." His thumb sweeps back and forth before his hand returns to the back of my seat.

"I don't have that long left," I say, putting more behind it now. "I got approved to graduate early."

I haven't told anyone since Sage will doom about me leaving her. But when his lips twitch the tiniest bit, I feel less alone in it.

We still lived in Hunts when I started taking extra classes freshman year. My mom pissed off a boyfriend before locking down a new one, which meant nowhere to go after he kicked her out.

Us out.

At four in the morning, lying on my back on a merry-go-round, staring at the sky for another night, I needed a reason. Coming up with a way out that kept me from having to sleep on playground equipment or hold my pee to avoid cracked-out creeps near the park's restrooms served the purpose. Graduating early became the first item on what developed into the escape plan.

"So," I tell Roman, "I only need to last in the step-house for a little over a month. After that I won't have to worry about finishing school without a place to live."

"You don't have to worry now if you move in with me."

I sigh. "Because harboring the chief's teenage stepdaughter would turn out well for you? I'm eighteen, so Daniel can't have you arrested, but I have a feeling he'd fire you without hesitating."

Roman snorts and gives me a *I dare him to try* look. "I'm one of two officers in that department who isn't white. He won't fire me without a legit cause—just like he hasn't tried to kick me for being his wife's ex. He can't even have the other guys give me shit, given how much of it Martinez and I already put up with every shift."

Another reason to hate it here. But I'm so fucking close, and despite what he says, we both know it could get worse for him. They'd probably target Martinez, too, for being his partner. So incredibly convenient the only Latino man on the force was partnered with the only Black man.

"It would make sense for me to move in if we finally got married." One side of my mouth curves, and I sink into the seat. "I asked you to marry me *years* ago, so…"

He smirks, but it turns soft. "I'm going to steal you away more then, and you're going to text me more."

Once I nod, he blows out a defeated breath. His gaze sweeps over me one last time, then he turns off the light and drives.

I adjust the arm warmers once we're close. This time less to hide anything but because I'll need them in a second. Roman eases to a stop by the curb a few blocks from the step-house. My throat's actually tight as I climb out, and his jaw's clenched again.

"You're too pretty to not smile, officer," I say.

He gives me one. "Same goes for you, pretty girl."

I give him one, too. "Thanks for the ride."

"Anytime." His brow furrows. "Do you want to maybe—"

A flash of headlights has his eyes darting to the side mirror. Without another word, I quickly shut the door, heading to the sidewalk while he drives away.

I don't recognize the car that passes, and my muscles relax, even though I'm freezing within thirty seconds. Thank God it only takes a few minutes before I'm rounding the corner to the house. But all that tension returns with a vengeance when I see the chief's unmarked car in the driveway.

The trellis it is, then.

Except, the front door opens, and Daniel charges out in uniform. His head jerks up, destroying any hope I have of him not noticing me. He halts by the hood of the sleek BMW—better known as most of last year's department budget.

I have every intention of ignoring him on my way inside, but he has other plans.

"You went out looking like that?" he spits at me.

With a sigh, I stop closer than I prefer to be to him. "I went to the carnival."

But the tracker app he installed on my phone likely already told him that. Other than location, it doesn't give him anything, so I haven't bothered fighting him over it. It's not like I go many places but school anymore. I have more important shit to worry about, and if the need does ever arise, I can set it to Airplane Mode.

"You went to the carnival," he repeats. "With half the town there to see you dressed like a slut?"

I look away, my lips twitching. I can't argue with that one. Even if we have different connotations of the word.

"Is that funny?" The step he takes twists in my belly, but it stops at one. Because we're in the goddamn front yard. The mask can't come off out here where anyone could see the ugliness it hides. His voice does lower, though. "You and your pathetic mother are wearing on my patience. When you leave my house, you're representing me. Be fucking respectful and stop begging for it."

My jaw locks as I hold his glare with one of my own until someone drives by. He breaks into a smile, waving at the minivan. The expression harshens once they're a safe distance away.

"I know the need for men's attention is bred into you"— Daniel jerks open the car door, his words only as loud as they need to be—"and the man who should have taught you to keep your legs together is long dead, but you won't leave my house looking like that again. Not without consequences."

I bite the inside of my cheek, nails buried deep in my palms.

"I have plenty of my guys ready to treat you like the whore you clearly want to be, so just give me a reason." The chief, sworn to serve and protect, drops into the driver's seat. "Clean up the fucking mess inside."

No part of me moves until he's backed out of the drive and disappeared around the corner.

And then I walk to the front door. I pretend he didn't just threaten to have men rape me if he doesn't approve of the way I dress. I remind myself I'm so fucking close.

I go inside and clean up the mess.

16

REMI

"Mom," I call out.

I swoop down for a throw pillow, tossing it onto the armchair as I pass through the living room, which is otherwise intact.

A groan leads me to the stairs. She's sprawled out on her back like she started crawling up them and gave up. Her head's lulled away from me when I crouch beside her.

"Let's go." I nudge her shoulder and then sigh, trying one more time. The chances of me getting her to her bedroom on my own are laughable if she's dead weight. "Mom," I say louder, shorter. "Rebecca."

"What," she grunts.

"I need you to get up."

She slowly brings her face toward me and licks her lips. But they're not just dry. The bottom one's busted open. It matches the swelling and split skin on her brow bone.

"He hits you in the face now."

Not a question. No shock. Just a fact.

As far back as I remember, all but two men she brought into our lives hit her. Roman being one, and the other an Army vet we crashed with for a few months. My dad didn't either, but they weren't together by the time I was born. She'd been a functional addict then—she's even bragged about barely using while pregnant. She was functional when she met Daniel, too, working for an insurance company and buying us essentials before her fix. But like every other time, it didn't last.

Just like him being careful not to hit her in the face didn't last.

I help her up, and she clutches the banister. The redness on the inside of her elbow catches my eye, fueling my suspicions she's spiraled past only pills.

We make it to the top before I'm hauling most of her weight into their room. She does what she couldn't on the stairs and crawls into bed.

"I'm going to grab what I need to try and clean this up," I tell her.

The light's still off, and on my way to flip the switch, she says, "Remi?"

"Yeah, Mom?" I glance at the lump on the comforter.

"Get the fuck out."

I huff a laugh, no more surprised than I was over her face. "Right."

But I still toss a blanket at her and then shut the door behind me. Honestly, she saved me from stumbling onto her stash and going from knowing to seeing.

Ready to block out the world, I secure the pillows at the bottom of my bedroom door and lock it. A text came through while I was with Roman. I didn't need to check to know the sender. I toss my pink skeleton on the dresser, smiling at the notification with Foster's name.

> Here. It's the sky. Not that you deserve it.

I laugh and play the video of him panning across the Prague skyline from high up. He doesn't say anything, but a soft bass beat plays in the background while he shows me a new perspective of the city, twinkling below and beyond. He must spin in a circle because the view's interrupted by a dark rooftop. A few pieces of wicker furniture sit empty, and what looks like a bar that's not being used.

The video ends before his rotation finishes. I wonder if it's payback for cutting the end of mine.

When he asked to see me the other night, I couldn't with my eye swelling. But I think I would have told him the same thing regardless. I need him to be my escape for a while longer, the place I can run.

Then he can be real.

I set the LED lights so my room glows red and then reply to him.

> What do I deserve then?

I'm ready to shed my wings. The whole costume, really. But then my mouth kicks up, and I open my messages again.

Since I plan to leave Ashfield and never look back, I haven't exactly prioritized meaningful relationships with anyone here. Which means I don't have to scroll too far to find the ones with *R* even though our last texts were over two weeks ago. I send Roman a fairy emoji, and then I add a black heart. He answers with one and a jack-o'-lantern as I'm slipping off the wings.

Another text pops up as I take off my boots.

FOSTER

Where are you?

I toss my wings on the bed and snap a picture of them on my comforter with a corner of pillow. He calls a few seconds later, and I grab my earbuds off the nightstand. I answer with the camera low before I flip it around, showing him the flimsy wings again.

His camera stays unmoved, the view spiking my pulse. The top of his black shirt hangs open, the video focused on a defined tan chest underneath. Laces are undone below that, and part of a tattoo peeks through on one side.

"The world," Foster tells me, his low voice coating my skin. "You deserve the fucking world, Remi."

I smile and touch the edge of a wing. "Straight to the flirting, I see. Or was that meant to seduce me?"

The bass beat from his video is absent now, and he has far better lighting. "Nah, baby. It's a truth. Flirting is saying I want to give you the world."

"And if you were seducing me?" I shouldn't ask, but I do, all fluttery even before he answers.

"I tell you that every goddamn second since I heard your voice, you've been becoming mine."

Yeah, it's starting to feel like Foster West is going to be *very* real when I let him be.

The guy isn't even fighting fairly at this point. He's using hard pecs, tattoos, a sexy voice, and even better words as weapons. All I have for defense is pretending that not seeing his face would make me miss it all less if he disappeared.

"I'd also have the camera aimed at my chest when you answer," he adds. "Now what was your Halloween costume, so I know what winged creature I can expect to be hot for in the future."

"A slutty fairy."

He groans, and I laugh, sitting beside the rest of my costume.

"I'm even more devastated you didn't let me see it all." His camera shifts to expose the base of his throat, then it looks like he stands up. The view flips as he moves down a hallway.

"Where are you taking me?"

"My bed." He walks into a dark room and switches on a lamp, bathing a white comforter in the soft light.

"Here I've been settling for your balcony view," I say.

"Mmm. Is that what you want? Because I had something else in mind." He rounds the bed, the camera staying on a dark, shaggy rug. "Can I show you, Remi?"

He hits my name low and gravelly and in a way that has me saying, "Yes," without a thought.

I have no idea what I'm expecting, but my mouth curves up when he lifts his phone a little to a thick black belt on the rug with what looks like a fake sword and red bandana. Then he keeps going up, and my heart stutters. The feet of a free-standing mirror appear, fitted black jeans reflecting with the bed behind him.

"What are you doing?" I whisper.

"I'm showing you my costume." His black shirt is loosely tucked, and those open laces dip below his sternum. He has his elbows bent, both hands holding his phone. It blocks most of the exposed part of his chest, but I'll take the flexed forearms and broad shoulders as a trade. He stops there with almost all of him on the screen.

"You're a pirate." I'm breathing faster, more focused on the parts of him than the costume.

"A sexy pirate," he corrects.

The image starts creeping higher again until his Adam's apple comes into view. The tiniest bit of a sharp jaw appears at the top of the screen. My fingers tighten on my phone as he pauses.

"And unlike you, I'm going to use the mirror the right way."

It's my only warning before he flicks the rest of the way up, and even with a mask over his eyes and almost half his face concealed, I don't stand a fucking chance against him. Dark hair unruly in the way it falls. He has unfair lashes framing light eyes that cut through the screen.

"I'm not really breaking the no-face rule if you can't see all of mine, am I?"

"I guess you're not."

Foster smirks with plush lips, causing my entire body to react.

And the fever of him consumes me.

I can't even blame the trick flask and shots of lemon vodka when I stand up. My skin has a beat beneath it as I walk to the other side of my bed, his view of the cream carpet under my feet. I stop by the edge of the mattress in front of the full-length mirror leaning against the wall a few feet away. A sliver of reflection hovers at the top of the shot.

Foster's throat bobs with a swallow. "What are you doing, Remi?" His voice remains a velvety rasp, enough grit in there to feel it.

"I'm using the mirror the right way."

I slowly tilt my phone, his jaw tightening the higher I go until I reach the face paint mask.

The silence from him doesn't make me self-conscious this time. Not when he licks his lips and the heat in his gaze sears through his reflection and phone screen.

"Shit," he breathes after another second.

"Does the slutty fairy outfit do it for you like the school uniform?" I cock my head, and he glances up into his mirror, like he's staring right at me.

"Screw the clothes. It's you that does it for me." His attention lowers to me again. "But you are beyond fuckable in that dress."

My nipples pebble at the roughness surrounding his words, and I look at my own reflection. The red glow in my room absorbs into the black of my dress while bouncing off my skin, twisting highlights through the waves in my hair that fall over my shoulders.

"You said you're supposed to be a slutty fairy," he drawls, my attention returning to him. "Both parts of my sexy pirate are right here for your viewing pleasure. So far, I've only gotten hot fairy from you." He steps closer to the mirror, cool eyes dragging me under. "Tell me, baby, have you been slutty?"

The last word drips with sin. Not at all the same out of his mouth as when it was spat as an insult earlier but pumped full of desire. Foster wants it, encourages it.

I slowly shake my head. "Not yet."

Foster runs his thumb over his bottom lip. "Lucky for you, I'm here to help then." He grabs a handful of the back of his shirt and tugs it off. His reflection stabilizes, assaulting me with smooth skin, ridges of muscles, and a curation of black ink.

Then he waits, his eyes locked on me without a word. He showed me his, and now it's my turn. Not that I think he'd care if

I didn't. If I laughed or rolled my eyes, he'd probably smirk and show me the city from his balcony.

It's why I sweep my fingertips over my collarbone, wanting to show him mine. I catch a tightening in his jaw when I dip lower and trace the corset top of my dress. By the time I reach for the zipper at the side, the hungry look he's giving me smolders, and I don't even have the full effect with half of his face under the mask. But it's more than enough to have me grasping the tiny metal pull.

"Like this, Foster?"

I drag the zipper down, pulse racing. I'm not entirely sure if it's from what I'm doing or the way he's watching me while I do it.

"You're a natural, Remi." He winds through my veins, taking over. The material goes slack, ready to fall after I slip the thin straps off my shoulders, but the hand gripping my phone braces the front, holding it to my chest.

"Let me see," he says.

I move my hand, dropping the rest. Cool air coasts over my bare breasts and exposed skin, and Foster curses as I wiggle the dress off my hips. It hits the floor at my feet, leaving me in black panties. Other than those and what hides behind the swirly mask and under the arm warmers, I let him see all of me. I expect him to mention the last one, but he seems distracted.

"Another fucking bad idea," he mutters.

"Agreed." But I move the phone and angle it toward the mirror so he has an unobstructed view.

Foster flicks open the button on his jeans, causing a stutter in my already pounding heart. "I couldn't possibly have a worse one." He unzips but then stops, a tease of dark fabric visible underneath. "Say no, and we stop right now, Remi."

"I know," I say, not a doubt in my mind. "Now tell me what happens after I say yes."

His mouth hooks up at my wording. "You're going to make

yourself come for me while I get off, wishing like hell my cock could be buried in your cunt."

My core clenches, a blush spreading over more than my face-paint-covered cheeks.

I nod but receive a lazy shake of his head.

"Nah, I need an answer from those pouty lips, baby."

"These lips?" I ask before biting my bottom one.

My fingers trail over the curve of my breast and nipple and then drift lower until they skim the top of my panties. I run them all the way across, teasing just below the hem and drawing out the delicious tension. It becomes a living thing between us, a vibration tingling against my skin and him appearing closer and closer to losing control.

Heady and addicting.

"Remi…" he warns.

"Yes. I want you to watch me come for you, Foster."

He groans and sinks his hand into his open jeans, gripping his dick over his boxer briefs. "Lose the fucking panties," he demands. "You're going to spread your sweet thighs for me in front of the mirror."

I draw the fabric down on one side before moving to the other. Foster nearly growls at the first glimpse of skin beneath, and then my panties are on the floor, and he's pushing his jeans down.

Snatching the last pillow off my bed, I drop it on the floor. Nerves free-for-all inside me, but I ease myself down, eyes set on the erection straining beneath his boxers. I already feel wetness on my thighs as I fold my legs in front of me. And I earn another head shake from Foster.

"Let me see."

Leaning against the side of my bed, I draw my knees up, centered in the mirror. Then I slowly part my thighs, skimming a hand up the inside of one as I go, every breath infused with anticipation.

"Fuck." Foster keeps his eyes trained on the phone. "Just like that, Remi."

My mouth dries even more when he shoves down his briefs, clit throbbing at the sight of his bare cock. He kicks them away with his jeans and palms his thick shaft.

I reach the top of my thigh, legs open and reflection showing him *everything* between them.

"The immoral things I'd do to touch you right now. To feel how wet you are and spread that tight pussy around my cock." Foster gives himself a hard stroke, and I shiver, fingertips creeping inward. His lids droop, hand gliding up and down. "Touch yourself before I lose my mind."

I drag my fingers through my slick core, all the way up to my clit. The contact alone makes me whimper, but knowing he's chasing the movement with his starving gaze has me dizzy.

"Fuck, Foster," I breathe, not even sure he hears but needing to say his name as I rub my clit. I'm a little rougher than I would be on my own—how I think he'd touch me. How I *want* him to be with me.

"Christ, you might be the ultimate beautiful thing." He licks his bottom lip, muscles flexing while he strokes himself. "Look at you, soaked and on display, desperate to be fucked."

I moan, my head falling back and eyes clamping shut.

"Eyes on me," he commands, and mine flutter open, connecting with the screen. "Keep them right fucking here. They're mine. You understand?"

"Yes."

"Fuck yourself for me, baby. Hard and deep like I'd fuck you right now."

I swear, the voice and words are enough. The visual of him fucking his hand almost makes it too much.

My fingers drift lower, to my dripping entrance. I push two inside, and I immediately clench around them when Foster groans, the sound pure lust.

"More," he says. "Show me how your cunt will look stretched around me."

I withdraw, adding a third before driving back in. It fills me, but he'd still fill me more. My hips lift to grind against my palm while I thrust, obsessed with the way Foster's watching. He jerks his dick faster, and I match his pace.

"God, I want it to be you inside me," I admit.

I want him touching me. His hands and lips and tongue.

His eyes flick up to the mirror from under his mask—the sensation of him staring straight into mine a lash of pleasure all on its own. "You have no goddamn idea." Then he looks down to see me about to break into pieces on my bedroom floor, fingers pumping hard and deep like he told me. "You gonna come for me?"

I dig my teeth into my bottom lip, barely capable of nodding. The pleasure is twisting along the edges, so close but a breath out of reach. Part of me wants it to stay there and leave me at the precipice so I can stay lost in my favorite escape. In him.

"Foster." And then because it feels so fucking right, I repeat it twice more.

He all but growls, "*Come*, Remi."

I bite back a cry as the climax slams into me, like he jerked it by the leash. My legs shake, heavy-lidded gaze staying on him through the quiet moans.

"Fuck, I need that on my cock," he says while my pussy continues to pulse around my fingers. He tips his head back, and his abs tighten. "Shit. *Fuck.*"

He works his fist up and down his shaft faster until he groans, cum shooting out as he finds his release. Muscles rippling, lips parted, his hard chest heaving.

Foster said I was a beautiful thing, but he's a work of art. Watching him is its own brand of pleasure.

We're both panting when he gives one last slow stroke. I can still feel my orgasm lazily sinking into my bones. No one in the actual flesh has made me come so hard. Left me so utterly wrecked.

And he never even touched me.

I slide my fingers out and drop onto the plush carpet beside me. Foster must fall backward onto his bed because my view goes from his incredible body to the ceiling. Fair, since I'm giving him the floor and a dresser.

"Eyes," he says before flipping his camera around.

His appear on my phone, still through the mask. Up close, I can finally tell the color's an icy pale blue, darker around the edge. They fit the rest of him—unfair in how they captivate me.

I smile and bring the pillow with me onto my own bed. I flop down and switch modes on my phone, showing him the same. With the red light and sharp shadows, the bruising is lost in the silver and teal and black that swirls around my eyes.

He sighs, his gaze flitting over the screen, like he's studying me. Memorizing.

It feels almost more intimate, looking at only his eyes and the sea of black surrounding them.

"You were wrong," I tell him, lying naked aside from the arm warmers. "This was a worse idea."

"Hmm, was it now?" I can hear the smirk.

I nod, study, memorize. "Nothing like this is ever happening again."

Foster chuckles—staring right at me. "Whatever you say, my beautiful liar."

17

REMI

Now...

"Here's next week's scene list."

I copy it from the notes on my phone and send it to Glory and Nate in our group chat. "The key one will be the meet and greet. We'll go over specifics that morning, but I want all of us on cams, getting as much footage as possible since we haven't snagged much fan interaction."

Thanks to Mac Records for that one.

Felix mentioned they had more time with fans up until this leg of the tour. From what I can guess, it was the easiest cut to make to account for the extra shows, other than days off for the band.

Who cares about the artists and fans so long as the former performs and the latter buys, buys, buys?

Of Men and Wolves are feeling the effects of their tightened schedule. They won't admit it, but the entire point of me being here is to see them. Audible sighs when climbing on the bus without downtime after a show. Ducking the cameras more often to do what I assume is coke. Even with it, Dev and Felix crashed during their writing session yesterday.

All of us could use a breather. I want to sleep while standing still. A shower not shared with four dudes. Maybe even a break from toting my camera around—a short one. Like a day.

"Who's the best bet for spy glasses there?" Glory asks.

She slips on her own glasses so she can scan over what I sent. Nate's doing the same, the third side to our little triangle in the parking lot by the buses. I'm sure they're feeling the bars on the cage, too. Which is why I opted to meet out here rather than on their bus like we have been.

I worked with the two of them a few times last year on different shoots with Heath. When the label and band came back with the requirement for minimal crew, I easily decided on them. Glory has a similar instinct to me for grabbing a camera to capture what others might overlook. Nate's quick to learn and mimic different styles.

Heath calls them the twins even though they are in no way related. In fact, they didn't even meet until he started throwing together his original crew. But their hair might be a shade of dirty blonde apart. Nate has had his glasses on since coming off the bus, and both have dimples in their chins.

"Adams would be ideal," Nate answers absentmindedly. He looks up fast, panicked he overstepped. "I'm sorry."

A symptom from working under Heath. We're still working it out of my crew's systems.

"Don't be. You're right." I toss in a smile, hoping it comes across as encouraging. "Adams would be perfect. He knows how to work the glasses best to frame a shot."

Almost like he's experienced—or the reason I started using them in the first place.

All the sprinkles of Foster's influence along my path are glaringly obvious from the glasses to the damn industry I work in the most. Fortunately, he's the only one who can play connections with it all. Unfortunate, too, considering he might very well hate me.

"We'll plan on him wearing a pair," I tell them, checking to see if we need to cover anything else ahead of time.

Since I might change my mind by the day of, I keep it vague most of the time. They'll get an equipment list each morning, but nothing's ever set. It's one of the alluring parts of filming unscripted, realizing you have *the* shot halfway through it.

"When is the group interview?" Nate asks, so cautiously it almost hurts. I think his hand even trembles. "It's the last scene on here, but without a date or time."

"Call that one wishful thinking on my part. I want to try to get them as a band before the break in Texas next week, but Christian won't commit to anything yet. Depending on how much time he can find us and how much of a heads-up he gives me, we'll figure out the logistics."

"And the one-on-ones will be when we're back on the road?" Glory finally looks up from her screen.

"Either then or during the break since they'll be easier to coordinate."

She nods. Nate nods. Then the not-twins-twin energy really kicks in when they share a furtive glance before Nate throws my smile from earlier back at me, his equally supportive.

I'm not sure what exactly I need supported until he clears his throat, staring at our circle of feet.

"The, uh … Adams interview."

A half-second of silence from me sets them both into a panic.

"Sorry," Nate blurts.

"He's only asking because of the second round of one-on-ones," Glory rushes out with a squeak. "We can totally get away with editing one interview to look like two, if that's what you want. Or three, if you want to wait until the end of the tour. Whatever you decide, Remi."

"Breathe," I say.

She actually inhales through her nose and exhales through her mouth. Maybe when this is all over, I'll give these two a crash course in how to survive Heath Erickson. The man scents weakness on the wind and feeds on doubt. No need to let him binge. Then again, he'd get a snack out of me right now.

"I'm working on the Adams interview." Not really, I'm avoiding him after being abandoned tits-out in a dingy bathtub. "But we'll edit around it if we need to. Plan?"

Double nods. "Okay," they say in unison.

My lips twitch as my phone goes off in my hand. "I'll press Christian on the group interview." I back away toward my own bus. "You guys are doing amazing. Maybe you should go do something fun this afternoon before the concert."

I catch Nate's brows dip before turning around, so I'll assume Glory's do too.

Seeing Xander's scrunched face on my screen, I answer on my way past the venue's security and the metal barricades set up, providing a straight path from our bus to the building's exit. The video connects, and the same face is shoved into one of our couch pillows.

"I'm glad things are going better for you," I say dryly, boarding the bus.

His muffled groan reminds me of my first month with the director. Xander can handle him, though, playing cool until he can scream into cushions.

I left my earbuds up in the loft, but everyone already went inside the venue. Of Men and Wolves did a photoshoot this morning, and the magazine sent someone for the interview that will pair with it. So, I take advantage of the silence and empty lounge area, settling onto one of the couches.

Then I have to smother a flare of annoyance over Adams North being at an interview while still dodging all attempts at mine.

I sit against the cushioned arm and stretch my legs down the cushions. "Tell me more."

Xander rolls his head to the side, near-defeat in his pretty hazel eyes. "He's openly torturing me at this point. I'm convinced he's acting out because you're not here, so really, you're the problem."

"Clearly," I laugh out. "I'm sorry he's still putting you through it, but remember, it's his love language."

He squints. "Heath Erickson would explode into dust before he felt enough emotion to love."

"The prophecies do say it's the only way to vanquish him."

He cracks a grin and drags the pillow down, hooking an arm around it. "I have twenty minutes before I have to go help plan a baby sprinkle for Jasmine—whatever the fuck that is. Soothe me with tales from the road. How's the tour going?"

I search to find out what he's in for with Heath's wife. "Great. Some of the shots we've gotten—God, Xan. This has so much potential if the label will let it happen. The band will be unstoppable if Mac would get out of the way."

"And you'll be a part of it."

I half-smile, tapping to bring him full-screen again. "*If* the label lets it happen."

"They'll have to once they see what you're putting together. The footage I've seen come through with your notes is gold. I can always tell when you're behind the lens. The entire vibe is set and direction clear." He huffs. "Heath can't even find shit to bitch about." His gaze lifts as he weighs that a little. "Other than the missing Adams interview. You need to get that locked down, or I might be the one who suffers."

I wince. "Yeah, I know."

With it mentioned a second time in less than half an hour, my time for avoiding the one-on-one with Foster has run out. Whether either of us likes it.

The thing is, I want his answers to the questions. I've heard Dev's version of the band's origin story. Of his drummer not showing for a gig, and Felix subbing in, improvising most of the set. How they saw Foster play that same night at an open mic when they went out to drink after the show. Felix told me the heavens opened the first time they jammed all three of them. He said he never truly understood what it meant to belong until they started writing their first song.

But it feels incomplete without hearing Foster's experience. Besides the interview questions, I want him to tell me how he became Adams North. If he's experienced his *fuck you* moment with his dad yet, or if that happens when they play their last show on the tour at Madison Square Garden.

"Are you sure everything's okay?" he asks. "It seems like something else is going on with this."

A thought of confiding in him flits through. Maybe I give enough about *Adams* I could at least talk to someone.

Xander and I've been bonded in the flames as far as work, and we even spent last Christmas together. But I still want the rest to stay locked away, where it belongs. The only way it can happen is to keep the past vague and the truth smudged.

I shrug it off. "It's just rock stars being rock stars."

"We both know what that can mean." His expression softens. "Is everyone treating you right?"

"Of course they are, Xander."

"No one's making you uncomfortable or pushing shit too far—"

"No," I tell him, and then I repeat it to make sure he hears me. "No. I just…"

Foster bounces up the steps, roughing up his dark hair. He has on low-slung sweats and a sleeveless shirt despite the chill outside. I've detached from the world, even before he looks up and pauses. Suddenly it's all noise and blurry edges, other than the path between us.

Outside of a mic pack handoff and the required words for filming, we barely even exchanged glances since last week. We definitely haven't been alone. For good reason since two seconds in and all I can think about is coming on his hand. How right it felt with him looking at me like he did once upon a time.

What happened after creeps in then. The coldness in his eyes and dead tone when he walked out, leaving me with his pirate mask and emotional whiplash.

"Rem? You good?" Xander asks.

The sound of his voice has the iciness seeping into Foster again, his nostrils flaring.

"Yeah," I say, experiencing a chilling of my own.

I jerk my gaze back to my phone, forcing it to stay there when Foster storms past.

Xander sighs. "You have no idea how much I miss you."

He smiles and drags his teeth over his bottom lip. It reminds me of the last night we went out and the next morning when I was the goal.

My attention shifts to the picture-in-picture, where I can see Foster stopped behind me, gripping the curtain, then he disappears through it.

"I need to go." I flash a smile at Xander, but it falls flat. "A baby sprinkle's like a shower but less about necessities. Pick some mocktails you can make baby puns with and always choose the most bougie option. Jasmine will love it, and you'll earn an extra toleration point with Heath. Good luck."

I end the call before he can respond, tossing my phone next to my camera at the end of the couch. I'm on my feet by the time the curtain rips back a second later. Foster comes out, but I block his path to the exit, forcing him to a stop.

"Move," he grits out.

"Not until we talk."

His eyes remain locked with mine. "It seems to me you already have someone to talk to. The wannabe boyfriend, right? Your *rock god*."

Heat rushes to my cheeks as he refers to Xander's text from Halloween.

I can be your rock god, baby.

My gaze lowers to the floor. "He's not … Xander's my roommate." When he doesn't answer, I glance up. "He was making a joke about the half-built baby crib behind him. Heath made him bail on a party to put it together since he's covering for me while I'm here."

Foster shakes his head like he doesn't believe me.

"Is that the reason you shut me out that night? Because you saw his texts?"

"It doesn't matter," he says dismissively. "None of this matters."

My embarrassment flares along with the hurt. "It fucking matters if that's the reason you left me there."

I glare at him, but Foster's scathing look puts my indignation to shame.

"Why? Did it feel shitty to have someone abandon you?" The air thins as he steps toward me, readying words tipped in the worst type of venom—the truth. "For someone to disappear with no warning. To have them there and then not?"

Tears sting my eyes, the past deafening and raging. "Foster—"

"Come on, Remi. Let's compare notes. Tell me how much it fucking hurts to believe everything you have with someone is real only to find out it never was."

The last part cuts me as deep as it appears to slice him. I open my mouth, but nothing comes out.

Foster's expression fills with disgust, and he backs away. "Great fucking talk," he mutters.

Then he whips around, leaving me reeling and wanting to scream at him to stop. Only he pushes through the curtain without me moving or finding my voice.

Because my Foster scar's been ripped wide open, the edges jagged and raw. One wrong move, and all the others twisted with it tear open too.

The threat immobilizes me. But then the curtain falls between us. I can't see him anymore, and for a shaky breath, it feels like he might not even be on the other side at all.

Somehow the possibility of him being gone again frightens me more.

18

FOSTER

ALL I WANTED WAS an hour of sleep before switching it on tonight. Instead, nothing feels safe as I break through the curtain to the bunks.

The air's laced with her, and my chest throbs and burns. It accompanies my thoughts as they play a game of what-ifs in my personal brand of torture.

And I just fucking trapped myself at the back of the bus.

Not that I had much choice unless I wanted to physically move her.

I couldn't trust myself to touch her.

The space has never felt smaller, with nowhere to go and nothing but a thick, velvety fabric separating me from what I need to stay away from most.

"Fuck." I'm forced to a stop by the bathroom door, a closet closing in on each side of me. "Fuck."

I scrape both hands through my hair, willing myself to distance from the deluge of emotions clawing toward the surface. They're so mixed up, tangled worse than ever. I'm the closest I've been to dredging up the corpse for a postmortem. I have this pounding desire to set it all ablaze, reduce it to ashes and ask her every single *why* that holds me prisoner.

Why lie? Why not just end it? Why cut me in the one way she knew would bleed me out?

Why not me?

I close my eyes, thinking the last one, knowing I can't ask any of them. The questions threaten more than I can risk. It already aches to be around her. My armor's scuffed and bent from the battle of having her on tour. Hearing any of those answers from Remi could be the sword that slips through my ribs.

Then everyone suffers.

Again.

Blowing out a breath, I spin around and find the cruelest mercy in the doorway. Remi hugs herself around the middle, standing barely inside the curtain like maybe she doesn't want to be.

I don't want her to be either, but I also don't want her anywhere else. Two assholes struggle inside me, one needing to exist in misery for the other to have any chance at peace.

"What," I say, not hiding the harshness in my tone. "You can't do enough damage from out there?"

As I stalk down the aisle between the bunks, she swallows, but she holds her ground in her black-and-white striped mini skirt and tight black top. We set up for the same impasse as out there. Except we're getting a different ending.

"I will move you, Remi." The warning curls between us, and I don't stop until I'm towering over her. She tilts her chin up to hold my stare. I'm beyond pissed I have to fight through the glint of sadness always lurking in hers.

Her breath picks up. Mine saws in and out.

She breaks the stalemate right before I follow through.

"You really think it wasn't real between us?" She studies me when I don't answer, and then her arms fall to her sides. She forces a lifeless attempt at a smile. "Right. I'm sorry I even asked."

She backs into the curtain, and I clench my jaw, refusing the words. But when she moves to leave, I say them anyway.

"Was it real?"

She stops, casting her emerald eyes up to me. "*Of course* we were."

The sad morphs to something more akin to heartbreak as she starts to turn, and I step, wrapping my hand around the front of her neck and tugging her back to me. My mouth crashes down on hers. The damage is instantaneous. Her warm lips against mine and the feel of her sharp intake of air are all it takes before I need more. I plunge my tongue into her mouth, demanding it.

Fuck if ruin doesn't taste sweet.

Remi claws at my shirt, and I groan as I push her against the doorway.

"Foster," she breathes, my lips skating across her jaw, and because it's us, I answer, "Remi."

I kiss down the side of her neck, breaking away to rip off my shirt when she shoves it up. My lips capture hers again, and she latches onto the back of my neck. I grab her ass and press into her. Her moan makes my cock throb. I hike her up so she locks her legs around me, and I can grind right against her clit.

"Oh, God." Her nails dig into my scalp, only making me rock harder. "We should—"

"Not stop." I bite her jaw before scraping my teeth lower and then nipping right above her collarbone.

She gasps when I suck the same spot, only letting up once I guarantee a lasting mark. She'll have to work to cover it, but the need to see me on her borders on obsessive. I didn't get the satisfaction from the one on Halloween. I'm not taking the chance on my new one.

The angriest jerk-off session of my life happened that night. Furious with myself because the memory of my fingers pumping into her pussy played on repeat. The way she tasted infused on my tongue. But no matter how much I hate wanting her, I. Can't. Stop.

Remi's hands glide down my chest and torso. Her feet hit the floor, so I can drag her top over her head. I toss it aside and pin her to the doorway with my hips, bracing my forearm above her. Our hard breaths twist together, and she shivers at my fingers drawing up her ribs. Then she teases hers down my abs to the top of my sweatpants with a long sweep over my tattoo.

My gaze drops to where her teeth sink into her lower lip. I pull it free and skim my thumb across it.

"I want this," I tell her, voice rough as hell. "Your pretty little mouth on my cock."

She stares up at me, a mirror to my desire. Her lids fall heavy as I push my thumb between her lips. She sucks and strokes with her tongue, eliciting a low sound from the back of my throat. I've officially depleted all reserves of self-control with her.

Before I lose it entirely, Remi slides off my thumb, and then she sinks to her knees in front of me.

Our gazes hold while she tugs down my sweatpants, but hers quickly redirects to my dick. She wraps her hand around my shaft and drags her tongue up the underside.

"Fuck." I fist her hair and tip my head back, ready for a sweet death as she teases the crown.

"Eyes." She echoes the command I've given her.

I smirk even before I look down to see hers waiting for me. Sultry but edged in a challenge.

Then I issue my own demand.

"Mouth."

With my hold, I ease her forward, her sexy gaze on me when I push between her parted lips. She seals them around me and sinks down my cock. Her cheeks hollow as she starts to suck, pumping with her hand. The pleasure overrides any lingering sanity. I groan and tighten my grip in her auburn locks, thrusting into her and guiding her to meet me. Remi hums in response to me taking control and lets me fuck her mouth.

"Fucking phenomenal. I knew you'd be perfection on your knees." I drive deeper and bump the back of her throat. "Take more of me, baby."

I thrust farther in each time until she starts gagging on my cock. She moans when I withdraw, and I give her a second before I fill her throat again. Her thighs press together, her tear-stained lashes fluttering up at me while I drag in and out. The sight alone makes my balls draw up. Then she swallows around me, feeling too fucking incredible.

"Jesus, Rem. You're a goddamn vision with my cock in your throat," I tell her, bobbing her faster. "You'll look even better painted with my cum, though."

Her eyes flare at what she should consider a promise.

Bracing on the wall, I smirk down at her. "You like th—"

I cut off at a muffled voice.

Remi pops off my dick and scrambles off the floor, wiping her mouth with a panicked gaze locking onto mine. A moment passes of me not giving a shit if one of the guys catches her sucking me off. None of us ever remotely care outside of maybe getting our own dick wet.

But Remi's not a groupie or random. She's Remi—in her bra, a gorgeous flush all over, and sexy lips swollen. Fuck all the complications between us and with the doc, no one's seeing her like this.

At the first sound of someone boarding the bus, I trap my hard-as-fuck cock away and am already nudging her toward my bunk, swiping our shirts off the floor. I'm crawling in and dragging her with me at the same time when Christian laughs up front.

More pounding on the stairs precedes a "Fuck you" from Felix.

I drop onto the mattress and yank Remi against me. Her back hits my chest while I ease the bunk's heavy blackout drape closed.

And I'm officially hiding on my own tour bus mid-blow job.

The material settles a heartbeat ahead of the other curtain rustling. One of the two jackasses walks through it. Easy guess is Felix, since he stops at his bunk above mine, meaning he stands right on the other side of the fabric. Directly in front of Remi.

Her nails dig into the arm I have wrapped around her, and she presses closer to me. Which translates to her ass rubbing all over my raging erection.

I grit my teeth and bite back a groan.

Felix fucks around in his bunk, Christian staying up front. Before I ditched at the end of our interview, I dutifully reported to Colton I was coming in here to sleep, but I have no idea if he shared with the group.

A zipper pulls above us, and then Christian audibly groans in the lounge.

"Yeah," he snaps, likely answering his phone.

His voice bounces in distance, so he must have started pacing. The distraction plastered to my front holds most of my attention, though. My thumb sweeps over Remi's bare skin below her shoulder. I breathe her in while, from what I can tell, she's barely breathing.

Felix sighs like the weight of the world just left him. The big curtain swishes, but he stays on this side of it. "Here."

Christian stops talking and comes closer. "You really need to hide in the fucking bathroom? The film crew's certainly not in here shooting. Remi's not even on the bus."

Fuck.

Realizing what's happening, I sigh. A different feeling behind it than Felix but over the same baggie of coke.

"As my fucking manager, do you want me to chance a camera stumbling in with me nose deep in a line?" he asks. A beat passes without a response. "That's what I thought. Now snort your shit like a good boy and let me get high in peace." He takes a step and calls back, "The rest of that goes to Dev, so don't be a selfish prick."

After he passes, Christian returns to his phone call. Felix disappears into the bathroom, closing the door.

A hot puff of air washes over my forearm, and Remi's body sinks farther into me. Like she wishes she missed that entire exchange.

No one thinks she and the doc crew are oblivious to the drugs floating around on tour. Felix and Dev sure as fuck haven't let up. But we struck a deal back in LA to be somewhat discreet while filming the documentary by not openly using with the cameras around.

In my mind the cameras equaled Remi.

I'm unsure if her reaction stems from overhearing what Felix clearly didn't mean for her or because this forces her to bear responsibility in knowing without a doubt why people keep disappearing on her sans reason. I can't help with either. But at least I guaranteed no one gets fucked up right in front of her.

Reckoning we won't escape until they leave, I slide my arm under Remi. She rests her cheek on my bicep, and my thumb trails over her skin again. Dark flowers swim through my senses, and I drift lower, tracing the swell of her breasts. I slip under the black lace bra. Her breath hitches, my fingers grazing her pebbled nipple before I slide the rest of my hand in to cup her breast.

"He's on tour—he doesn't have time for that shit."

She arches, pushing against my palm. And while I might not care about whatever Christian's droning on about in his manager voice, my still hard dick's *very* interested in the way her movement makes her ass press back. It twitches, still wanting the release that was excruciatingly close.

"*Fuck*," I exhale, flexing my hips into her.

I catch her chin with my thumb and finger and twist it toward me, so when I push up, my face hovers over hers. My eyes instantly drop to her lips. "You drive me fucking insane."

I cover her mouth with mine, my hand already shoving under the front of her skirt. Her gasp stays trapped between us, but then I kiss down to her neck and slide under the top of her panties, and a soft whimper escapes.

"Foster…" she says, barely audible, and my hand stills.

I press my forehead against her temple. "Do you want me to stop?"

A slight hesitation makes me start to remove my hand. She

catches my wrist, keeping me there until she guides me lower, between her thighs. Drenched fabric rests on the backs of my knuckles, her pussy so wet I almost groan.

"Good girl," I rasp, lips at her ear. "My cock's not done with you yet."

With the first swipe of my fingers through her slick center, a shiver works its way through her. I rub circles on her clit and adjust my arm that's under her so I can palm her breast, barring her against my chest. She latches onto my arm and reaches back to grasp my hip. Her ass grinds on my erection through my sweatpants, and I mentally note to cockblock Felix and Christian from here to eternity.

I can't take not feeling her skin on skin anymore.

I run my hand around between us and push her panties down her thighs and then work my sweats down to free my aching cock. A rough stroke smears precum and her wetness on my fingers over my shaft.

The need to fuck her is mind-numbing, but I don't have any condoms in my bunk. It's entirely her fault. She's a witch with the magical ability of locking down my dick. Since she recast her spell, the only thing I've fucked is my hand. Can't say I expected it to change with her sleeping on my bus.

On the edge of reason, I drag the head down the crack of her ass until I reach her thighs and push between them. She's soaked, making it easy to glide through her pussy. Remi gasps, and her head lulls back when a different one connects with her clit. Nails sink into my flesh. A mark for a mark, I guess.

I draw back and thrust forward, earning another set of crescents dug into my forearm. They deepen while I slide back and forth, a grip on her hip. She makes a mess on my cock, allowing me to move smoothly without friction. Each stroke ends with me rubbing over her clit.

Her thighs clench when I tease her nipple, and a desperate sound spills out of her. My hand flies up and clasps over her mouth in time to catch another one.

Impeccable timing.

The bathroom door jerks open. Remi freezes, tensing at Felix's footsteps coming down the aisle. I slow my hips, barely moving, but I don't quit, continuing to fuck between her thighs and against her hot cunt at an excruciating pace.

He stops at his bunk to put away his coke. Inches from where her unsteady breaths heat the back of my hand. And I feel her pussy flooding my cock while he stands there. Fucking Christ.

While he unzips the inner pocket of the duffel he uses as his stash, my fingers loosen on her hip. I smooth my palm over the curve to her front, nudging my way between her clamped thighs until I brush her clit.

She squeezes the fuck out of my hand and dick as I start to rub, a low growl almost breaking out of my chest.

Another zip sounds, and then Felix walks away and through the curtain.

Thank. Fuck.

I thrust forward and add pressure with my fingers, pressing my mouth to her ear. "You're fucking dripping, Rem. Did you want him to rip back the curtain? To catch you being a slut for me?" I rub faster, her hips rolling against me for more, and the vibration of a whimper kisses my palm. "That's what you are, aren't you? My little slut, in my bunk and about to come while I use your hot, sopping pussy to get off."

She nods, panting through her nose.

"Dude," Felix says not far from the big curtain.

Christian pauses his phone call to tell him, "You have the patience of a toddler."

My teeth tug at her earlobe, making her shudder. "Come with them right there, baby. Show me how much you love it."

Remi grasps my wrist for an anchor and shatters in my arms, so fucking breathtaking, succumbing to the pleasure. I can feel her fluttering over my shaft, and I'm desperate to cant my hips. To drive into her. Fuck her while she comes apart.

My palm muffles her moan while hopefully the curtain blocking us drowns the rest.

Her orgasm has a direct line to my balls, and the second her body goes lax, I pull my hand from between her legs and slip free, drenched in her cum. I stroke hard and fast, then smother a groan when my cock pulses in my fist. The first rope of cum decorates her ass. She whimpers into my palm while I paint the backs of her thighs with the rest. I was right about how incredible she'd look. I come harder watching my release drip down her skin than when I fuck anyone else.

When I have nothing left, my hand falls from her mouth. Our labored breaths quietly fill the bunk, but we're the only sound. No talking. No walking. No audible signs of assholes anywhere to be found.

"Fuck," I grunt, crashing my forehead onto her shoulder.

I only stay there a second. I grasp the side of Remi's face, pulling her around, and kiss her. She tangles her fingers in my hair on a sigh, and my tongue finds hers as she lures me down, down, down. It stays hard and slow, hot and sweet.

Drawing back, I tuck my still semi-hard dick away and snag my shirt. I have to force myself to wipe the streaks of cum off my canvas.

New obsession unlocked.

After I toss it down, she rolls to her back, propping on her elbows. I crawl over her to get out but pause, hovering above her, and I lower my head so my nose touches to hers. "See how chivalrous I am? I ruined perfectly good art."

She doesn't risk talking yet but smiles. I kiss it before ducking through the curtain. I draw the other one to the side with the back of my hand, verifying the bus is empty.

"We won hide-and-seek."

"Reigning champs," she replies.

When I peel back the bunk's curtain, she's sprawled on my bed with a kick at the corner of her mouth. I look down at her. Her face flushed, hair covering my pillow, meadowy eyes more sated than sad. I keep looking but can't see a difference between her and my Remi. I can't feel the difference either.

It's been overwhelming, to say the least, ripping between needing more of what I've missed and despising reminders of how I lost it. But staying on one side is somehow worse.

And it fucks with me. It really fucks with me.

I swallow, blinking out of a goddamn trance. "I need to go before anyone else traps us in here."

Remi sits up, swinging her legs out of the bunk as I grab a clean shirt. Hers landed at the end of the bed earlier, and she reaches for it.

"You're good?" I ask, pulling mine on.

A close-lipped smile flashes at me. "Yeah."

The expression drops fast, and her eyes even faster. A tension takes over the space, both of us waiting for the switch to flip between us. But instead I shock us both and bend down, catching the side of her face. I set my forehead on hers.

"I'll make sure no one hangs around the bus, so you can escape."

She nods against me. "Thank you."

A memory trickles in, the emotions that go with it close behind. Too close.

My thumb strokes her jaw before I straighten. Then I walk through the curtain. Off the bus. Into the sun.

And she still feels like my Remi—my perfect girl who looked like heartache and dissolved into a dream. Not callous and cold or capable of not caring about the pain she leaves behind. She feels like I want to believe her about us being real. The possibility bears down on me. Maybe I've been wrong this entire time.

I head back inside, security barricades lining the short path and two security guards flanking the venue's exit. Already set up for the concert. Colt's in the hallway, posted against a wall. He pushes off with his foot when I walk in.

"Sorry if they woke you up. I didn't know they were out there until they came back in."

"I wasn't sleeping," I tell him.

I hook my head, passing him, and he follows as the heavy door bangs shut behind us. It sounds like something cracks, but I ignore it. Probably just that armor I'm fucked without.

19

FOSTER

Before...

WALKING through the flat's door, I toss the single key on a dinky ring on the kitchen counter. I pause, noticing the other single key on a matching dinky ring, and try to determine if it's moved since last night. When I left this morning, I barely paid attention. Now I'm overanalyzing, searching for something that isn't there.

There's a simple way to find the answer. I just need to ask the keeper of the key. Except Chase has barely spoken to me since Halloween. A grunt here and there. An irritated whatever.

Four fucking days.

We talked more when I lived halfway across the country than we are sharing the same thousand square feet.

At first, after I stopped being pissed at him, I over-cheered the shit out of everything to be a dick. He'd scowl. I'd grin. He ignored me asking if he wanted to grab food. I praised him on his commitment to finishing the entirety of the trash show he was watching in a single binge session.

Then he switched to avoiding me, and I decided fuck it and stopped trying to break him out of his tantrum.

I still have no idea what it's even about. The Remi hate came out of nowhere. The day before our fight, he ran around the couch, pumping his fist and chanting #TeamFomi. I'm the one who told him to chill—it's not that serious. Chase responded with, *"You're so cute when you're full of shit. Like a baby kitten."* He scratched the air, using his hands as claws. Ten minutes later, he was blaring audio of an entire litter meowing.

Since the sun's down and it's peak avoidance time, I expected him to be out for the night already.

I unhook the tour glasses, dangling from the neck of my shirt, and toss them on the counter with the keys and then add my wallet.

After a shower, I grab my guitar and notebook, unsettled beneath my skin in a way I can't explain. It happens a lot. The only way it seems to calm is working on music or wandering around. Not aimlessly, per se, but similar to when I'm writing a song. I don't know where it's going, but I know when it gets there. I'm where I wanted to be once I'm there. Until then, I follow different melodies, see if a path leads the right way.

It's why *Wanderer* screamed at my soul. And now they've incorporated more lax tour options for these final weeks of the beta testing. Which means if someone wants to see what it's like to cross the Charles Bridge or poke around outside of museums and art exhibits, I can get paid for simply walking around.

As I pass Chase's room, the door's cracked ajar. I sigh, stopping in the hallway outside of it. My fuck it seems to reverse itself.

"Have you graduated from the mime program yet?" I call.

Shockingly, he doesn't answer, so I nudge the door farther open. Light spills in, and he's scrolling on his phone in bed. He acknowledges me with a tic in his jaw.

"Is this your newest tactic to avoid me? Sitting in the dark? Or are you taking up spelunking next and want to acclimate to cave-dwelling?"

Nothing.

"Dude, what do you want from me?" I ask, the entire ordeal

exhausting. "You were mad I wasn't going out with you enough, but that can't change if you won't even be in the same room as me."

The blue glow off his screen catches the irritated shake of his head.

"You're acting like I don't get it, but I don't even know what the fuck *it* is, Chase."

We're supposed to be above this petty bullshit. Beyond holding grudges and expecting the other to flail around until they land on the correct answer. Instead, he's icing me out and acting like I'm not even here.

"You're pissing me off with the silent treatment. So, by all means, continue on in your one-sided fight. But I'm not leaving you alone until you talk."

Another round of no response, and I step into the room and flip on the light. That earns a reaction, his glare snapping up. We sit in it, and I just want him to say something. But then he scoffs and refocuses on his phone.

"Chase—"

"Weren't you fucking leaving?" he spits, not looking up. "I'd say *weren't you going home*, but…" He lets a shrug finish for him, knowing the rest already landed.

It's my fault. I wanted him to talk. I never specified I wanted to like what he said.

I shake my head, turning for the door. "Let me know when you want to apologize for that."

"Shut the light off."

"My pleasure," I reply.

My fingers land on the switch, flipping it down. Then I catch it again on the way up, popping the overhead back on.

He never specified to leave it off.

With that glorious moment of bonding over, I step out on the balcony. I drop my notebook on the table and slouch into the metal chair, guitar coming with me. No one's complained yet about me playing out here, so I doubt they'll start tonight.

But it all seems off, and I end up staring at the sky, fingering chords on the fret even though I'm not strumming.

I have a place to live. A dorm room at school in Texas with a Cali-boy surfer for a roommate. I also have places to stay when not at school, Chase's parents' one. A home, though? I haven't had one of those in a long time.

Not in the permanent residence definition or the one you feel in your heart and bones.

Chase simply used my truth as a weapon.

Still stings, though.

I pull out my phone, my other hand never leaving the guitar's neck while I check for this month's deposit. The money sits in my account, pulsing and festering. It's an infection I keep contained because cutting it out would only negatively impact the other parts of my life. I'm using the money to get where I need to be as fast as possible. A calculated way to set myself up so nothing will stop me from being on a stage, playing my songs and singing my words.

The second that path clears, I'm going to blow up his entire life.

For kicks, I read his bullshit memo: Invoice 1229. I blink at it a few times before I laugh. Un-fucking-real. The motherfucker used my mom's birthday.

Moments like this eradicate the twist in my gut over Andrew West's hush money. They make me want to bleed him dry instead of only taking what I need to survive while focusing on music and school. Or snag a plane ticket to Europe, knowing he can't get a tuition refund for the semester.

I finally pick out a melody I've tweaked a few dozen times already, working it some more until my phone lights up. The video shows a busy coffee shop, people buzzing, and a random bark of laughter. In the center of the shot, Remi's fingers tap against the side of a white mug. A nod to one of the first videos I sent her.

Except now it links to another memory of when I watched her

driving those fingers into her perfect pussy. Another two memories, after last night. I got a show from her point of view, looking down her body while she lay on her bed, legs splayed. No face but fucking hot all the same.

Seeing her come really had been a worse idea, the worst one I've had yet when it involves her. I thought she'd infiltrated before, but she proved me wrong. The more of her I get, the more I need. I'm starting to think that wouldn't change even if she gave me all of her. And I'd be a smitten, little, shit-filled kitten if I said the idea of having all of her isn't feeling like it would be my best one.

Glancing at my guitar in my lap, I half-smile and text her.

> You want better background music?

A shattered image of the bottom half of a slutty fairy appears in response. I angle my chair more toward the table, and I answer, already setting my phone up. I lean it against the rectangular planter of succulents, so she'll only see the middle of my guitar.

Her hand curls around her mug as I relax in the chair. "*You're* the better background music?"

"I am," I tell her. I lazily strum the open strings a few times and then switch to something I started in Paris. It stayed in my head until we got here, and I practically sprinted to rent an acoustic.

When I hit the last note of what I have, I slide down the strings, causing them to squeak. The effect sounds right, how the song should end.

"I think I like you serenading me with your guitar," she says softly—an admission.

"I think I like you," I reply, but it's *know*. "Be warned, though. Once I add lyrics, you'll be throwing your panties at me."

"Hmm." The shot dips, and she picks a backpack off the floor, offering a peek at the plaid skirt with a leading role in my jerk-off fantasies—sharing the spotlight since Halloween. "You think you can seduce me with songs now?"

"Are you asking me to prove I can?"

She shows me the world in front of her as she leaves the coffee shop. Across the street is a town square with trees and benches. "Weren't you supposed to be writing me one, by the way?"

I smile at her bratty tone. "Maybe this is your song. I just haven't told you yet."

She crosses to the square and passes shrubs, bare until spring. "Tell me the lyrics, then."

My hand adjusts on the neck, and I play the first few notes again while staring at the notebook beside my phone. I've filled pages these past weeks, a common theme developing in the lyrics. Words I've never used before like darlin' and maroon. Lines about my hands and her body and her devastating siren call.

"Nah, baby. Not until I sing it for you." I look back to the screen. "This is a switch-up. Where are you taking me on our tour?"

She laughs as she passes a sign stabbed in the ground for the Ashfield PTA bake sale. "I'm about to show you the best my town has to offer." She swings to a dead-for-winter flower bed with equal parts faded mulch and cigarette butts.

"I really appreciate how the artist incorporated that plastic cup into the neutral color palette."

"A masterpiece, truly," she deadpans. Then she swipes the cup and tosses it in a trash can. "I'm going to the house. I only have so much tolerance for this uniform and need it off."

Despite an easy opening to suggest she strip for me, my eyebrows draw together. Maybe I'm more sensitive to it because of Chase being a dick, but I ask, "Not your house? Not home?"

"It's my stepdad's house. I live there, for a little while longer anyway, but it's definitely not mine." She proceeds to pierce me straight through my goddamn heart, adding, "My dad was my home. I lost it when I lost him."

I huff a breath. The fucking timing. The universe must be

bored, playing matchmaker with broken pieces, and ours just aligned.

"I don't have a home either."

She's quiet for a second. "Will you tell me why sometime?"

"Yeah." My lips tilt up, and I start strumming again. "You showed me yours, so…"

"Can I tell you something?" she asks, more light to her. I hum in response, and she wanders to a tree, spinning when she reaches it, giving a different view of the scenery. "I got approved to graduate early. I finish school in December at the end of the semester."

"Look at you. Then what?"

"I leave and never come back. At least that's the next step in the plan. Save every penny, graduate early, and move anywhere else until I start NYU next fall."

I mute the strings with my palm. "I've got you covered. There's more than one place for you to sleep in my dorm when I get back to Texas."

"More than one, huh?" she says, amused. "Are they all in your bed?"

"Beside me, on top of me, under me…"

She laughs. "So many options. How's a girl to resist?"

A deep "Remington" barely picks up on her mic. The guy's walking toward her on the sidewalk, coming from the direction of the coffee shop. Dark gray winter coat unzipped with a lighter shirt underneath. Tall, short beard, and a wide-ass smile aimed her way.

"Roman." A softness in her tone wraps his name, and fuck, that feels like jealousy nudging at my chest. "Uh, I've got to go talk to someone." She tacks on, "He's a friend."

"Yeah," I force out, watching him stop a few feet away to wait for her.

And yeah, I am jealous. Not necessarily of the guy—although it does feel like he's grinning at *my* girl—but because I want to be that close to her. Closer.

"Night, Remi." I lean forward for my phone.

"Hey, Foster?" Mine's wrapped in something else, warm and raspy. The camera lowers to the sidewalk. "Thank you."

"For what?" I ask.

"For being."

One side of my mouth lifts, and I decide the way she says my name is better. "Anytime. Feel free to show me when you get out of your skirt."

She sighs, ending the call. But by the time I drop back in the chair with my phone, she sends a text.

Maybe I will.

Jesus, how am I supposed to *not* trip over this girl? I never planned to bail on Chase, but right now, I wouldn't mind standing on a sidewalk somewhere else.

Trying to distract myself from ... everything at this point, I fuck around with the song from earlier for a bit. My heart's not in it, though, so I trudge inside, more unsettled beneath the surface than when I went out.

I snag a beer and stand against the counter in the kitchen, figuring out my next move. Where in the city I haven't explored that might do the trick. Or even somewhere I have but will look different at night.

Mid-sip, my gaze lands on the keys. Both are still there. Sighing, I shake my head and take a longer swig. Chase stays in after starting a war with me over it. Up until last week, I would point it out. Up until last week, we wouldn't have gotten here either. Something's going on with him. I just have to wait for him to be willing to tell me what it is. Otherwise I need to go roof shopping. He wouldn't dare tarnish the sanctity of a roof. But I guess he kind of already did.

I finish my beer and sort through the drawers until I find one with office supplies. At first I grab the sticky notes, but they cover a better option. Walking down the hall, I see Chase kept his door open after shutting off the light I left on. An invitation. Not that I need one.

Sure enough, he's passed out. One thing never-changing about my best friend, my brother, is his ability to sleep through almost anything. We used to screw with him all the time but over the years matured. Given our current circumstances, I think a little throwback is in order.

I pop the top off the permanent marker on my way in to leave a love note that doubles as a *fuck you*. A sentiment from me to him that says, who needs a home when I have a douchebag like him? And to make sure he sees it, I scrawl it right across his bare chest.

Bro is where the heart is.

Although, if I want to avoid more kitten allegations, I might need to admit a bit of mine might be in Ohio, too.

20

REMI

"Here I thought I'd have to wait until the weekend to see you."

I trap my phone in my skirt's hem, narrowing my eyes at Roman. "Were you planning on kidnapping me?"

"It would be abduction, but we both know you'd come willingly." He gets a shrug while I shove my earbuds in my bag. He's right. "I did plan to track you down, though."

"Mysterious and intriguing," I tease.

A lady leads her dog by us on the sidewalk, not paying attention, but I still scan for anyone else. Roman's in street clothes, clearly off-duty. Nothing about us talking in the town square should translate into anything, but a moment passes between us. He hooks his head in the direction he was going. We walk to his car not too far away.

"Silly," I say, sliding into the passenger seat.

He holds the doorframe, a scowl aimed at me. "If you're about to make fun of my car again, maybe you should keep walking."

I press my lips together while he closes my door, muttering under his breath.

His car isn't silly. A black two-door classic something he loves more than life. What's silly is watching him fold himself into it because he won't give it up.

As he contorts to fit in the driver's seat, I look out the window and suppress a laugh. I might have taken my sweet time in the square to talk to Foster longer, but I'm near shivering under my coat, and a warm ride from Roman beats the cold any day.

"So, are you no longer satisfied with our emoji-only conversations?" I tilt my head at him as he pulls from the curb. "The paper, paper, weary face, pen, repeat, steam coming out the nose text was great."

He chuckles, one hand rubbing his jaw and the other turning us away from the square. "It would be far faster to tell you I'm sick of never-ending paperwork."

"I thought you meant you were exhausted from folding so much origami." I smile when he side-eyes me.

The emojis started long ago, so long I'd need to scroll for a while to stumble upon anything else. We play it as a game, a challenge to keep it going. Although, deep down, it doubles as another contingency. Like my hidden bag. Like his contact name *R*. Like us right now in his car.

We use it as a way to protect each other from the potential fallout.

And texting my mom's ex in his police chief's house sets up for all kinds.

"You could give up, you know? Admit defeat."

"Never," he says.

Roman pulls into a tiny lot of gravel near the playground equipment at the park. Somewhere for parents to marginally supervise from their car. My urge to grab my phone and capture the emptiness of the jungle gym surges. The abandoned slides and monkey bars missing life. Long dead leaves twirling across the bridge in the cold breeze. Everything exists in a state of waiting until the noise of laughter and life return.

"I love when you do that."

I swing around to Roman studying me while I imagine the shot. "When I completely space the real world for one I'm framing in my head?"

"When you lose yourself, finding so much in the real world no one else cares to notice."

My dad would say everyone experiences the pulse of the world around them, but only the rare eye sees through to its heart.

I slump in the seat, playing with a button on my coat. "Maybe I see it because I'm one of those things that go overlooked."

Sometimes even by the man I loved more than anything.

The thought brings on a familiar onslaught of guilt. After my dad died and my mom got rid of the phone he'd given me—along with everything else I inherited—my anger turned on him too. He left me with her while he lived his dream, and his dream is ultimately how he left me forever. But then I realized it wasn't fair to him.

The world shows us everything up front, and whether we look is on us. I learned young to hide what people don't like to see— spare them the burden. I can't blame my dad for believing I wouldn't. He thought I missed him, not that I needed him to stay too.

A beat passes before Roman reaches in front of me to open the glove box. He places two fingers on a soft pink envelope and slides it straight out and into my lap. I squint at him, picking it up while he closes the compartment.

"Writing me love letters, Roman Moore?"

He pulls a face, clearly offended by the thought. "If I come across as someone who writes love letters, I need to reevaluate my shit." He tips his chin to the envelope. "Open it."

I unceremoniously tear through the flap, ripping the top. My head tilts, eyebrows slanting at the card inside. "What…?"

"It might be a little early, but you mentioned it the other day. I didn't want you to think I didn't hear you."

A greeting card.

"I'm outta here." I read the sparkly font on the front, arching over a black graduation cap and matching tassel sitting side by side in a convertible and driving into the sunset.

My throat tightens, lashes violently trying to stop the burning in my eyes. The well of emotions is something I immediately want to escape. I fight to shove them down so I don't fall prey to any others they may unleash.

"Congrats, graduate." Roman rubs my cheek with the backs of his knuckles, and I swallow, battling still. He plucks the card from my hand and returns it to the envelope. "Read the rest later. When I'm not there."

I laugh through the threat of tears. "So it *is* a love letter then if you don't want me to read it in front of you."

He holds it up between two fingers for me to take with a look, and I cut the defense mechanism, giving a halfhearted smile.

"Thank you." I tuck it in my bag as my phone goes off. One quick pulse that makes my eyes clamp shut for a second.

Not needing me to say anything, Roman sobers. The air in the car tenses along with him. "You need to go?"

I check the message from Daniel, ordering me to the house. "Yep. The king's holding court tonight."

The reminder of dinner tonight writhes in my stomach. I'll wear a dress chosen by him, my performance required to uphold all the smoke and mirrors. Sit, eat, and if I can't speak without being a "disrespectful cunt," remain silent.

I almost never talk.

"Do you want to run away with me?" I ask Roman, cocking my head.

"Tempting." He lightens up enough one side of his mouth hooks. Not my favorite smile, but I like this one too. "But if you stopped showing up to classes now, I'd have to take the card back."

Fair enough.

The sun's starting to set when he drops me off to walk the last two blocks. I'm already over it, considering a revisit to the abduction strat again. But conflict swims in Roman's eyes, so I grab the door handle.

"Promise I'll see you soon?"

"Yeah," he says, solemn, resigned. "See you soon, Remington."

Slipping my strap over my shoulder, I walk to the sidewalk. I draw out the trek by stopping to fish my earbuds from the bottom of my bag.

"Remi, wait." Roman's car door shuts behind me.

When I rotate, he's rounding the trunk on his way toward me. Before I can ask why, his strides close in. He hasn't even stopped yet when he pulls me into a hug. His arms encircle me, one hand on the back of my head and my face pressed into his shirt through his unzipped coat.

"I'm fucking looking at you, pretty girl. You're not unnoticed. I see you."

Suddenly it hurts. Everything hurts so much. A silent sob works up my throat as I throw my arms around his middle. I sink into him and close my eyes, trying to absorb every bit I can of the moment. The warmth, the touch of skin on mine, the pressure as he crushes me tighter.

Without another word, Roman lets go, leaves me on the sidewalk, and drives away.

I feel cold again, missing all the things. Other than Sage, no one's hugged me for a long time. I kind of wish he hadn't now, so I wouldn't have to realize it. But I'm really glad he did.

Since I've been summoned, I can't sneak in through my window and chance my emergency escape hatch being bolted shut. Daniel nor my mom has noticed my lack of coming and going through doors, but they'll be paying attention tonight. Every move and breath stand trial during these dinners.

I'm so close to never enduring another one again.

The chief puts these on whenever he needs the minions to swarm around and reinforce the power and control he holds over everyone. Those invited bow at his feet, and anyone who feels slighted kicks up the ass-kissing a notch.

He has his favorites who come most often. I hate both of them.

I'm almost to the house when one rolls up on me. Elvin makes the air taste acidic. I can't think of a much better way to describe being in the presence of his shaved head, boxy build, and wildly inflated sense of self-importance. Especially when he drops his voice real low and talks to me like we share a secret. I fear the toxin getting in my mouth, lungs, and on my skin.

He creeps along in his cruiser while I act oblivious with my earbuds in. It works out until I need to cross the street. Elvin accelerates to beat me and turns onto the cross street, stopping and blocking the path. He hangs out his window, and I begrudgingly pop out an earbud.

"It's cold," he says. "Get in. I'll take you the rest of the way."

I want to point out he has to turn around now, which will take longer than if I walk. Not that I'd ever willingly get in a car with him. Instead, I bite back half the snark and simply say, "No."

"I thought you'd appreciate the ride." Low. A secret. "Come on, Remi."

"No," I repeat. Slow. A fuck off.

I dismiss him with a once-over and dodge around the rear of his car.

If I have my way, I'll speak nothing else until after dinner.

I HAVE MY WAY. Maybe not in the blue floral dress hung on my doorknob when I went upstairs. Certainly not by ending up squeezed between the favorites at the table. But I don't utter a single syllable the entire time.

No one even bats an eye, thanks to my mom's hazy smile, her dropping her water glass mid-drink, and the apology she stutters out in slow-mode. Not that anyone dared bat a speculative eye at any of that either.

"Migraine," Daniel explains. "Rebecca's been suffering with one all week, and the effects on her…That's what happened here." He brushes his thumb over the split above her eye, covered in foundation. "A dizzy spell got the best of her."

One of the wife's fucking *awww* while bile breaches my throat.

His hand finds my mom's, bringing it onto the table,

displaying his devout affection for his poor love to the audience. "Why don't you go lie down, honey?"

She's pliant as he helps her from the table and to the stairs, which she manages to disappear up without crawling. I stare at my plate, not eating after the performance.

With Mrs. Kane safely stowed out of sight, Daniel catches my wrist after dinner before I can escape to my bedroom.

"Help clean up, won't you?" His grip tightens enough to warn but not enough to show.

I jerk my arm down, breaking his hold and meeting his stare while I grab a plate. He moves everyone to the den for drinks. I swipe my mom's surprisingly untouched wine glass, gulping most of the red down on my way to the kitchen. Then I empty the rest of the bottle and polish it off too.

Completing my task, I fold over the top of the kitchen island and hide my face in the crook of my arm. I need a minute to just be. But I should know better.

"Such a good little wife you'll make."

His voice lands on my skin like pellets of acidic rain. I straighten, rotating to Elvin slithering his way in from the hallway. My lip curls at the comment, but I continue my wordless streak as I move for the other doorway. He slides in front of me with a smirk.

"What the fuck is your problem," I spit out.

His gaze drops to my chest, so I cross my arms over it. "Chief's told me a lot about you. What you get up to."

I huff a derisive breath and maneuver around him, only for another body to swing around the corner. The other favorite, Marlo, fills the doorway. He plays the part of a golden retriever. He looks it too with bouncy blond hair and a quick smile. But his actions come off forced, as if right below the surface waits teeth and the instinct to attack without warrant.

"Hey, Remi," he says. His eyes bounce from me to Elvin and back. "Did I interrupt something?"

"Nope." I step, but he stays anchored, and when I feel Elvin shift closer behind me, I dig my nails into my palms.

"I was just about to tell her how nice she looks tonight," he says.

"Ah." Marlo nods. "The chief has said how much you like to express yourself with your outfits."

The shudder happens even before Elvin's finger draws down my back, over the dress's fabric that covers it entirely. "Like this one, right, Marlo? What does it say to you?" Another finger runs down the sleeve to where it stops halfway down my arm.

"Let. Me. Leave," I grit out. My breaths shallow, throat constricting from the acid and bared teeth caging me in. "You are both fucking disgusting." I try to turn for the hallway, but Marlo presses closer. I shove him in the chest, gaining nothing other than another grin of misdirection.

"Now, Remi, that's not very ladylike. Then again, you're not a lady from what I hear." His gaze lifts to Elvin behind me. "You saw how she pushed me. You think she likes it rough?"

I'm light-headed, the kitchen tilting as I struggle to inhale. My chest's about to crack open from the beating it takes from my heart.

"I wouldn't be surprised." Elvin toys with a strand of my hair from behind, and I feel his face right over my shoulder. "She dresses up for us, practically begs for a hard fuck. She checks all the boxes for a hot little slam piece."

I throw all my weight back into Elvin, catching him off guard and forcing him back a step. Marlo backs off too, chuckling while giving me an up-down. Then he just leaves. I whip around, already putting distance between me and Elvin. He smiles, tilts his head.

"Next time you need a ride, call me." His voice lowers, the hush returning, but this time it matches his words. "I can keep a secret too."

I blink after him as he waltzes away. Suddenly I'm alone in the kitchen. I don't stay, not tempting a replay of whatever the fuck just happened. I steel myself and rush upstairs. By the time I lock my bedroom door and secure every pillow at the bottom, I've surfed the waves through terrified to numb to confused to fucking livid.

The seams of the dress rip as I tear it off of me, and I smash it down into the trashcan in my bathroom.

I crank on the shower, setting the water near scalding before stepping under the spray. My lower lip trembles while my skin burns. No other way to cleanse a memory like that from your soul other than scorching it off.

By the time I finish, my whole body has tinted pink. I return to my bedroom in only a thong. I crash down on my bed, rolling onto my back and staring at the coffered ceiling without putting anything else on. There isn't a point. They just proved the clothes never mattered.

21

FOSTER

I END up on the streets of Prague at two in the morning.

After fucking with Chase—I add an adorable heart border to my message because he only deserves the best—I need a full reset.

Most of the times I've walked around this late while in Europe have centered around a bar or club or party. None of them allowed me a chance to notice the contrasts, but the city doesn't disappoint. Shadows cast by streetlights rather than the sun are softer around the edges. The sounds that are typically masked with voices and bustling emerge.

When I get to Wenceslas Square, the foot traffic picks up, but nowhere near how it was during the day. A couple pubs remain open, and a few muffled bass beats mix together from the clubs. I dodge people spilling out of one, drunk and happy. I follow a flicker of flames to a food vendor, taking advantage of the nightlife. The fire's behind glass while a spit rotates above it to bake *trdelník*. The chimney cakes spin, and the scent of caramelized sugar brings people leaving the clubs in.

I sign into *Wanderer* before I head toward Old Town in the off chance I can get paid for my little excursion. They announced the updated options for tours yesterday with a pop-up. I had a bite during the day. Lydia Song in Oregon wanted to see Lennon Wall. I laughed when I pieced that near-rhyme together mid-tour.

The buzz beneath my skin has somewhat settled by the time I get to the square. I'm not far from the vague destination I thought of when leaving the flat, though, so I keep going.

It only takes about ten minutes for Charles Bridge to come into view. I smile. Exactly what I wanted. Not a damn soul is on the bridge when I walk to the middle and stop. It almost feels eerie, like no one else exists.

Except someone does, and as I watch the water, my favorite *Wanderer* notification hits my phone.

SaintR wants to wander!

The only one I'll willingly share my bridge with.

She requested right where I am. I accept the tour, then I lean back against the railing and show her the view.

Our tours together have only changed in how they feel. The connection between us has a heartbeat now as I let her explore the world through my eyes. But we still rarely use the messages, and I stay quiet so she can hear what she would if she were standing next to me.

Most of the time.

"Hi," I say, panning the abandoned bridge.

A red dot appears seconds later.

SAINTR: *Hey.*

That's it. I stand in the center and return to watching the water, shifting her view every so often. After a while, I finish crossing the river. She ends the tour, and I snag my earbuds out of my hoodie pocket. I slip them in as she calls. When I answer, I flip the camera from the Longhorns logo on my chest to the cobblestone street.

And I get the immaculate view of her tits. I close my eyes and exhale through my nose, fucking tormented I can't suck those pretty pink nipples into my mouth.

"I hate you."

"Now who's the liar?" she rasps. "Is this better?"

I peek an eye open and groan. "Fuck you, Remi. And fuck that mouth."

One side of that mouth hitches. It's all I see other than part of her jaw pressed against a pillow. "Why are you giving tours in the middle of the night?"

"Why are you taking them when it's the middle of the night in Europe?"

"One of my favorite guides signed on, so—"

"Baby, don't make me track down everyone in the beta program when I get back to America. Try again. Tell me which guide signed on."

"*My favorite*," she mouths, over-enunciating. Such a fucking tease.

I lean against a building near the bridge, in no hurry to return to the tense bubble waiting for me. "I can't stand being still for too long. Music usually helps, but I needed to move tonight. Explore." My head rests back on the stone facade. "Plus, Chase is mad at me, and I don't know why. Being in the flat with him acting like I don't exist is getting to me. It added to me wanting to be anywhere else."

She knows the trip originated thanks to my best friend's impulsiveness. I know I have hers, Sage, to thank for the Halloween costume.

"I'm sorry." Her mouth downturns, and she sighs. "I requested the tour because I want to be anywhere else right now, too. And my favorite guide is also my favorite escape."

Fuck, I like that way too much. Being her favorite, her escape —her anything. This woman took me hostage, turned me into the one seeking her out, and now I might very well become a beggar at her feet. All without letting me see her face in its entirety.

"Do you want to talk about it?" I ask.

She bites her lip like she's unsure. I won't push. I know what it's like to have shit in your life that feels worse to talk about than dealing with it in silence. Chase dragged me onto their roof half a dozen times before I said much more than, "*I fucking hate him,*" or some variation. But after a second, her teeth slide off her lip.

"If I tell you, can we pretend I didn't?"

"Whatever you need, Remi." I say it before I realize I mean it.

She takes one of her sad breaths. "My mom's an addict. She's used most of my life. Pills almost constantly, and then she cycles to heroin or meth or whatever else she can get her hands on. Her husband's a complete piece of shit. He's the chief of police, and yet he..." She trails off, and an even sadder smile appears for a second before the expression falls flat. "Everyone treats him like a king when his crown's made of deceit."

I clench my jaw to avoid telling her how sorry I am. I want to tell her she deserves better, like when she talked about losing her dad. Her home.

Then I remember something she said, and I push off the wall.

"My dad was an abusive prick to me when I was a kid." I show her the baroque architecture as I start to walk, a new destination in mind. "Other than my wrist, he also fractured my orbital socket when I was ten. Those are the injuries I was treated for anyway. I got tackled playing soccer a while ago and needed X-rays. The doctor asked if I knew I'd had four healed rib fractures because I didn't put it on the forms."

"That's terrible," she says. "What about your mom?"

I laugh once. "He never touched her. He never needed to because she was subservient. My mom was perfectly happy being submissive, which means she didn't dare intervene on my behalf."

My screen darkens, Remi covering her lens. I'm about to complain when she reappears—her eye, gorgeous dark lashes, and part of a sculpted brow, that is. She has devastating eyes. Mossy irises, enough sorrow deepening them to make me want to take whatever hurts her away.

I am so over my head when it comes to Remi Saint. I can barely make out shapes on the surface anymore.

"We moved from Texas before he fucked up my wrist. He was a management consultant. His firm had transferred their headquarters to New York two years earlier, and he'd been bouncing between there and Texas, more frequently at the end. He still traveled every couple days but claimed it was easier staying in the tri-state area."

"Is that why you don't have much of an accent?" she asks.

"I don't have an accent at all anymore." I switch hands with my phone. The first goes in my hoodie pocket. I'm colder than I'll admit, but I'll survive.

Her eyebrow lifts, a spark in her eye. "You did last night when you told me to come."

I scrunch my face. "Fine. I have a little bit of an accent when I'm hard as hell and watching you finger-fuck yourself."

Eyelid flutters shut. "You moved to New York," she says, moving us along.

I wait until it opens. "We lived in a suburb at first, which is where he fucked up my hand. I'd deal with Andrew West two days on, two days off. My mom would dutifully wait for his return." We're getting close, so I slow my steps, taking it to a leisurely stroll. "After three years, we moved to a town not far away. A nice neighborhood, great for kids. It had a wonderful medical staff for when he broke my face."

More sadness in her eye, maybe an apology in there too.

"He quit messing with me after I shot up at thirteen and hit back." My lips twitch, remembering how goddamn good it felt the first time my fist connected with his jaw. "As a freshman, I tutored as an excuse to not be there when he was. I went to three houses twice a week. My favorite, Landon, was nine and only a twelve-minute bike ride."

The bronze statues come into view, so I stop. I do the same as Remi. I cover my lens to adhere to her rule, flip the mode, and then move to show her my eye.

"Hi, Foster," she says, and I smile and reply, "Hey, Remi."

Then I breathe for a moment, disconnect as much as I can. "Landon's mom pushed our session later one day. Andrew left that morning, so I almost canceled to stay home and play my guitar. But she offered extra for the *inconvenience*. I rode my bike over, sat at their kitchen table like I had the past six weeks, and didn't even glance when his mom squealed at the garage door opening."

I look skyward, hating I still feel it after everything. Betrayal fucking annihilates under the right circumstances, though. And then it leaves you constantly in fear of it happening again.

"Landon's dad was home from a business trip. The kid mentioned once his parents weren't married. His mom added it's why she gave Landon her name, so Drew would finally *put a ring on it* one day if he wanted to carry on his legacy."

She gasps. "No."

"Yeah," I say, drawing out the word. "She came back under Andrew West's arm. He tucked Landon under the other when the kid jumped up to hug him. I sat there, watching their happy family reunion until he locked onto me. I don't remember leaving or getting on my bike. All I recall is thinking about Landon never having so much as a bruise on him. His genuine excitement at seeing the man who beat me most of my life." I chuckle. "It's fucked, right? He cheated on my mom, moved both families to the same place to make it easier on himself, I guess. He lied, deceived, and all these reasons to hate him. But I was most furious he fucked me up but loved another son."

Remi's eyebrow draws in, her head shaking. "I'm sorry. I hate him for it too. What happened with your mom?"

I smile, half-amused and half still disbelieving. "She blinked at me for a solid minute, then calmly told me we'd talk about it when my father got home. That's the moment I stopped having one. He showed up hours later, walked by me like I didn't exist, and pulled my mom into their bedroom. I heard most of it, muffled, but clear enough. They came out a united force, and I was to forget everything I saw and never mention it again to anyone."

"What? She was…"

"Subservient," I remind her.

A similar disbelief swims in her gaze.

"But me? I kicked the living shit out of him until—here's the best part—my mom pulled a knife on me."

Remi whispers, "What the fuck?"

"She claimed it was to protect both of us, scared I'd kill him. I might have. We'll never know. He threatened me more, but I held all the power. I could tell his second family about the first. So, they shipped me back to Texas, and he gives me money to live off every month and pays for school to keep me away. I feel like a piece of shit for it, but it got me away from them. Once I graduate and have my future set, I'll fuck up his life in every way I can."

"I understand it," she says. "I'd probably do the same, honestly."

"No one's hurting right now because of it. My mom's happy, her depressing version of it anyway. She even willingly divorced the bastard five years ago so he could marry the other chick. Which means his new wife got what she wanted, making her and the kid happy."

Remi laughs once, and then I laugh too. It's all so absurd. My mom freely went from wife to mistress, becoming another fake bank memo when he sends her money out of the accounts he shares with his now wife. Everyone's either delusional or ignorant, and both are better than the fucking reality. Sometimes I wonder if I'm not doing the kid a solid by letting him grow up in bliss before he feels the same damaging betrayal I did.

I glance up ahead to check the bronze statues aren't on a timer, lucking out when the light catches as they move. But I look down, and Remi has her brow lowered again.

"Fuck, I made you sadder." I walk the last of the way to the Kafka Museum.

"No. I hate that it happened to you, but I like that you told me." She pauses. "I might even be less sad because of you."

I stop at our destination. "Not enough. I'm shooting for barely sad. And what I'm about to show you will either hit the mark or backfire horrendously, and you'll be all the way sad again."

Her eye narrows, and I think I can read her with only one by now. But I want something else for this.

"I want to see your mouth again."

More of a squint before the lens pulls away, and then I see her pouty lips and soft jaw. "Are you going to tell me why?"

"No." No one's around, so I take out my earbuds, letting her hear the trickle of water. "But I'll show you."

I switch to front-facing mode. She sucks in a sharp breath, her mouth falling open at the fountain of two guys pissing. Their hips move, along with their dicks, and the pool's shaped like the Czech Republic.

"Well?" I ask. "I hope this isn't the type of fountain your dad would send you, but it's one I would."

"Foster, this is..." She breaks into a pure smile and laughs, and I'm unnerved by the way it melds with my soul but settled all the same. "I can't believe I'm about to say this, but it almost feels a little like home."

"Not a sentence probably spoken about the Piss Sculpture before." I circle the fountain, giving her a full view of what these dudes have to offer. "What was your favorite fountain he sent?"

"Hmm. He photographed raptors in Pennsylvania not long before he died. He sent a video from a park in the small town he stayed in. Three tiers of chipped concrete, but he focused on the etched designs and explained why he found the fountain beautiful. I watched it so many times, listening to his voice and the melody of the water. There was distant music, too. He said there was a band competition—"

"Are you talking about Pleasant Park?" I ask, lips turning up. "Benches on three sides of the fountain and trees everywhere?"

"Yeah. I couldn't remember until you said it. How did you know?"

"I went there last summer. They host a battle of the bands called Sound Clash. A lot of agents circle around, so I wanted to get a feel for what it was like. The stages are on the east end, but dead center of the park is the fountain."

Her smile softens. "Now that I know, maybe I'll go."

"You should. It's wasted college kids, shitty riffs, and pure magic. Once I have a band, I want to enter. A lot of managers find opening acts there, too." Then I add, "When we go, I'll show you your dad's fountain, and we'll watch the bands."

"Oh," she says, the brat back in her tone. "You think we're going together? Who said I want to share my dad's fountain with you?"

I smirk as I round the fountain once more. "No one yet. But you're about to."

She bites her lip like she might not but then releases it. "I think I'd like you taking me to Sound Clash."

Walking to the sign posted near the fountain, I focus on the number. "If you text it, they'll write your message in the water."

Her phone moves, telling me she's sending one, so I tap out and write my own. Neither of us asks what the other texts, and I'm fucking grateful she doesn't, so I won't have to lie.

I'd more than like taking her. I'd more than like a lot of things when it comes to her. And I'm already thinking how I can make every single one of them happen.

It should worry me how sideways she's turned me. How my direction suddenly seems pointed straight toward her. I'm not one to let others have access to the organ in my chest in the way she's demanding. I let it beat for music and experiences. People don't take enough care to not crush something as delicate as a heart. I know this, and yet, not only has she taken part of it, but right now, the *thud* of mine sure is starting to sound a lot like *Remi*.

22

REMI

Now...

It's different.

When I meet Foster's gaze as I enter the dressing room, seeing him for the first time since he left me in his bunk, he rakes it over me. The smirk that follows reignites tingles and a fluttery sensation he used to always elicit. Only now they accompany thoughts of him kissing me and touching me. Memories of his gorgeous face and heavy-lidded eyes staring down at me while he fucked my mouth.

The space between us hasn't lost a fraction of the tension, but *it's different.*

My pulse picks up as he projects an all-out erotic replay of us on the bus from across the room. The back of my neck heats, and I break eye contact before everyone else notices the blush spreading over my cheeks. But seriously, it's indecent how he's looking at me.

I set my equipment off to the side, near where the guys tossed their own bags. The next time I glance, he's still eye-fucking me from the armchair, but his smirk's more amused.

Asshole.

But I never want him to stop.

"Who's got the glasses tonight, Cam Girl?" Felix grins, man-spreading on the sofa.

I ignore the twist in my gut, the same one from earlier when I overheard him and Christian. I knew about the coke. But I didn't want to *know*.

Drugs are unavoidable in most of the music industry. Even on a sober video shoot I worked on last summer for an artist in recovery, her manager was zooted by the time Heath wrapped.

Being around it rarely affects me, other than a tug on the web of memories I have to shake off. Felix using more often is bothering me, though. Likely because he's not a random musician on a set.

Before I can answer him, Foster says, "I got the glasses."

He basically causes a record scratch in the room.

My brows slant. Colton has a V form between his. Christian looks up from his phone. Dev blinks rapidly like he misheard. Felix drops his head back to see Foster upside down.

"You get high before shows now?" Felix whisper-yells.

Foster ignores the shocked responses and stands. He comes over, slipping the spy glasses from my hair, and he slides them into his. His visual assault continues but closer, then he stalls on the high neckline of my sheer black top. It has white suns and moons and shows my strapless top beneath it. What it doesn't show is the brazen mark he left below where my shoulder meets my neck.

"What is this aesthetic?" He's between me and the rest of the room. Music plays, but he still keeps his voice low. "Mystical goth?"

"Yes. Is that a problem?" I ask, suspecting it's not.

He shakes his head, confirming, and flicks his eyes up to mine. "No. I very much approve. And now I know to bite higher to accommodate."

My mouth almost falls open as he retreats to take the first shot with his band.

He disappears not long after, and the other two dig into their own rituals. Felix ups his extra shot to gulps straight from the bottle of whiskey. I hate that I notice, but I'm not the only one. Colton props on the wall beside my equipment.

"He's stressed."

I nod and force a small smile. "Yeah. They all are."

He sighs and tips his head back. "It's when he stops trying to hide it we'll worry, okay? Then he's not putting the doc and band first anymore."

The connected strings pull tighter, but I won't acknowledge them. "Hopefully it doesn't happen during the two-week break."

His lips purse. "Hopefully."

Glory and Nate check in with me before Of Men and Wolves take the stage. Once they verify they're set and we breathe through the panic after Glory shares an opinion, I wait in the hall for the band to walk.

I'm trying to provide space where I can, so the guys won't feel suffocated by me at least. I refuse to add to the stress any more than I have to.

Christian swings the door open and winks on his way past. "Always a pleasure to see those legs, Sinner."

"One day I'm going to cut off your man bun," I call after him.

He throws his head back on a chuckle, and I smile with the weightless threat. When the band's sequestered for writing sessions, which are most of their days off, he's not the worst company. He even remembers my coffee order now.

Dev's backing out of the dressing room as I turn around, and we collide. He catches my arm to save my balance and grins down at me. "There are better ways to get my attention, you know?"

I roll my eyes in time for Felix to exit. "You can always have my attention." He gives an up-down with his eyebrows and then adds, "Get my good side tonight, sweetness."

Foster's next with Colton right behind, the first's lips twitching and the second's in a full smile. By the time they've all vacated,

I've dismissed the concerns of them feeling crowded by me. I might even have my own place in the pack.

I go in to swap batteries, but I only make it a few steps before the door clicks shut behind me. I spin and barely process Foster before his hand slides into my hair and his mouth ravages mine.

Fast cars have nothing on my pulse, calm to rapid in a breath.

He claims my tongue with his, grasping my ass and yanking me against him while my fingers tangle in his shirt. I always knew I never stood a chance against him, but he's proving it anyway. I'm entranced by him, surrounded by cedar and leather like in his bunk. His pillow I shamelessly buried my nose in after he left.

When his palm settles against the front of my neck, he nips at my bottom lip and presses his forehead to mine.

"What..." I trail off as he kisses me again, only gently. Soft and deep, a flash of everything Foster and I were supposed to be. Should have been.

He shrugs at my unfinished question and backs away. "I wondered what it's like to kiss you before I go on stage. Next time I'm going to tongue your cunt so I taste you when I'm up there."

I smile, all tingles and flutters in a very specific place as he waltzes out the door.

Next time.

Foster said *next time.*

THE BAND'S mood shifts for the better once the bus crosses the Texas border. They still have three shows before the break in Austin, but it revives them. A light at the end of the tunnel, so to speak.

If only the light was an adorable lantern, hanging as a welcome to a peaceful garden, and not a bullet train ready to annihilate.

During their day off between the Dallas and Houston shows, Christian's rented a bungalow not far from the arena for the guys to work. He usually hangs around with me and Colt, but the manager ducks out shortly after we arrive.

I'm mostly company for Colton at this point since I rarely have anything to shoot. They stay on the upper floor while we fight over movies on the main. I fold and let him pick to avoid the pettiness he's ready to engage in. But after the band takes a break three hours in, Foster pauses on his way to the open stairway.

"Grab your handheld," he says to me. I cock my head in question, and he angles his back. His mouth lifts, eyes soft. "The space is a beautiful thing."

I frantically grab my cam and follow him up.

The two of us haven't been remotely alone since he kissed me in the dressing room two shows ago. We have these intense moments where we watch each other. Maybe because we spent so much time not being able to.

As we reach the top of the stairs, his fingers skim across my back, slipping under the top of my jeans. Skin on skin.

"I owe you an interview," he says, voice hushed. He leads me across a catwalk, overlooking the living room. "We should do it tonight."

I smile over at him but stay suspicious. "Really? Have you run out of ways to avoid it?"

"Mmm. Not even close. But it gets me alone with you before I say fuck it and carry you off. So, it's in everyone's best interests."

We stop outside a dark wooden door at the end. He looks over, my mouth his focus. He licks his lips, drags his teeth over the bottom one. But then his eyes flick up, and he studies me, growing serious.

"Then we can talk," he says, pushing down on the handle, "about everything."

He misses me flinching. Inside. Outside. Hell, even the aura around me jolts at what he's asking of me. Because everything's not the weather. It's about everything *before*. The reason I disappeared on him.

The answer comes out ragged when I reply, "Yeah."

But I'm already wishing for a way out of it.

All the anxiety dissipates as I follow him in and see the rehearsal space and studio. Lush purple velvet chairs and tufted sofas. Deep mahogany slat floors, covered in a massive ornate rug. The wood makes up the walls as well, but built-in shelves filled with books line two of them. The lighting is moody and sensual, and the overall effect carries a brothel sort of vibe.

Dev looks up from his bass then at Felix pouring a drink at the bar off to one side. They exchange a glance.

"Adams has officially lost it?" Felix asks.

Dev nods. "It's officially time to shop for a new member."

"Officially fuck off." Foster tips his chin toward the bar. "Artists who've used this space etch their names in the bar top. I thought you'd want a shot of us adding ours."

"Yes." I finish at the same time as him.

His mouth hooks up. "You can stick around a bit after if you want any footage while we jam."

I blink at him, and Felix barks out a laugh, landing on a barstool with his drink.

Dev snorts. "You either broke her or made her come."

Foster grins then and walks toward the bar. "I might have done both."

I would glare or comment back, but the scene's staging in my head. I figure out the angle then have a flash of another once I move close enough to see the grooves in the wood. Rich with history and talent.

The guys switch off wearing the spy glasses I had hooked on my shirt's neck, so I get their faces and them carving without compromising either. Then I become a piece of furniture, afraid if I breathe wrong, I'll lose access to them while they create.

I imagined this scene a hundred times and then said a painful goodbye when they said no filming during these sessions.

About fifteen minutes in, the door flies open. Christian doesn't even wait for the band to quit playing.

"We're leaving."

Between the barked tone and the muscles of his jaw rippling beneath the skin, not a damn person in the room attempts to argue. He steps out onto the catwalk, giving me a wide berth to pass, and then I cross to the stairs. Colton's in an arms-crossed stance by the front door. He shrugs when my eyes ask, *What the hell?*

"He barreled in, demanded to know where you were, and then sprinted up there."

Me? A harsh knot solidifies in my chest.

Our twenty-minute return ride to the buses remains silent other than road noise. Foster's arm brushes mine after I crawl out of the van, and my lips turn up when his do.

"Miss Sinner." Christian's monotone, adjusting the cuffs of his baby blue dress shirt. "I need to have a word."

Dev *ooo*s like I've been called to the principal's office, and with the *Miss Sinner*, I feel like I was. Christian Vero's nearly exclusively called me Sinner with a handful of Remi's tossed in through the entirety of our relationship. The only *Miss* I recall was when he dismissed me in Prague after the band said no to working with me.

"Yeah, of course," I tell him.

"We'll talk on the band's bus." Then he adds, "Would you be more comfortable if someone is present with us?"

His question takes me aback, and I realize he hasn't looked at me once since the bungalow.

"What's going on?" Foster asks, stepping beside me.

Christian looks up at him, face of stone. "Adams."

Nothing else audible passes between them, but Foster seems to understand perfectly and nods before tossing a concerned glance at me. I give one in return, the knot twisting and growing exponentially.

"Miss Sinner, would you like someone with us on the bus?" the manager asks again.

I shake my head. "No. We can talk alone."

He turns on his heel and strides away. "Take them somewhere,

Colton."

After a mixture of confused mutters, the band loads back into the van, driving off by the time I board the bus. He stands at the far end of the aisle with the black drape at his back, and now he's locked on to me. Not an ounce of emotion tells on his face, and yet his eyes convey a myriad.

But the most striking is hurt, which only throws me off more.

"Christian, what's going on? You're actually scaring me." I drop onto one of the couches and pull a throw pillow onto my lap. The one with the frayed tag from me messing with it so much the past several weeks.

"There's nothing to be scared of Miss Sinner. Not me nor the band nor anyone else employed on this tour should make you feel otherwise. I'm deeply sorry if anyone's comments or actions, including my own, have made you feel uncomfortable."

My skin numbs at an apology I fail to understand. "Why are you telling me this?"

"You have my word," he continues, voice slightly strained, "as well as that of Mac Records, any unfavorable behavior will be dealt with immediately. If you wish to speak to legal counsel or the label's HR, I encourage you to do so. I'll gladly get you in touch with them."

As his implication hits me, my eyes bulge. "You think the guys are making me uncomfortable?"

He flexes his hands, and then a disturbingly vacant smile appears. "I'm not here to speculate, Miss Sinner. I'm here to guarantee you feel safe on this tour and can complete your work without being subjected to comments or behaviors that are unwelcome. To help facilitate this, the label and Mr. Erickson have requested an addition to your crew as well." Directed pause. "In case you're uncomfortable with me handling it."

"Heath's involved?" I squeak it. My thoughts are spinning, my head shaking. None of what he says makes sense. "Christian, what the fuck is going on?"

He has a moment of hesitation, an almost imperceptible

tightening in his forehead before a return to distant, disconnected. "Mr. Erickson brought concerns to the label and myself after speaking with you and others. He recommended bringing in an assistant to … ensure everything stays aboveboard from here on out. The label has agreed. You'll be moved to the other bus once we resume the tour. Unless you prefer different sleeping arrangements immediately? If so, we'll provide a hotel."

"No," I say. And I mean more than the goddamn hotel. "None of it's necessary. Nothing has happened to warrant any of this."

His gaze darts out the window to the parking lot, nostrils flaring. "Your assistant has arrived." Attention flicks to me. "Thank you for allowing me to attempt to make things right for you, Miss Sinner. Please don't hesitate to bring any concerns to me so I have an opportunity to act."

The last part has a bite. A slip of the hurt. He believes I went to Heath and the label behind his back about being—what? Sexually harassed? I've never considered anything as such, and I'm certain if I'd displayed the slightest bit of unease, whatever had been said wouldn't be said again.

Christian marches past me and leaves without another word.

I'm not far behind him, wanting to fix whatever the fuck is going on. But when I step off the bus, my assistant waits for me. Pink hair and pretty amber eyes I've seen nearly every day for the past year.

Xander's smile tells me before he says it. "God, I missed you."

23

REMI

Before...

THE VISUAL MEDIA lab in my high school remains abandoned all but a few hours a day, so I take advantage when the temperature drops too low to hang outside in the commons. I rarely use the room for anything but a spot to disappear in the quiet since my needs have moved beyond the ancient software and outdated equipment. My phone has higher quality video, and apps offer better editing programs.

Having limited resources and tools helped hard-sell my skills and passion on my college applications. Raw, focused, and heavy in the story, which fits my style anyway. I may avoid the realities of my life as much as possible, but I expose it on film every chance I get.

I leave the lights off and settle in my usual corner by a window. The ledge has enough space to perch on, and I rest my temple against the cold glass. My breath fogs over a patch, and I go all gooey, watching it dissipate. Like the mirror on Halloween.

By now, most everything ties to Foster in one way or another. Even worse, I miss him during the in-betweens. I worry the fountain sealed my fate.

I check the message he sent earlier while I was in class. Raindrops cover a windowpane in the picture, the gray sky, the iron railing of his balcony, and everything else beyond out of focus.

He hasn't signed into *Wanderer* today, so taking a chance he's staying at his flat because of the weather, I pause the song playing through my earbuds. Foster apologized for not educating me sooner and started sending me playlists after Halloween. He mixes genres in some; others stick to a theme. I've never used music outside of a way to check out, but the songs he's been selecting are like a creative hit. Now I hear them when I film or they inspire me to seek out a shot to fit.

My video chat goes unanswered, but I haven't even restarted my music when he returns the call.

"No tours in the rain?" I say, camera on the school emblem on my uniform sweatshirt. I flip it, giving him a view of the empty media lab while his stays on what looks like a jersey. "Not what I expected out of my favorite guide."

"Oh, I'll guide the fuck out for a voice like yours," a guy drawls, catching me off guard. "Tell me what you wanna see, and I'll provide in the absence of Daddy Foster."

After pushing past the shock of not-Foster talking, I quickly identify the owner of the Texan accent. "Are you claiming Foster's my daddy or yours, Chase?"

Foster's best friend hums for a second, tipping the phone back and forth as one would their head. "If I say yours, will you start calling him daddy?"

I laugh. "I'll consider it."

"Wait. Why the fuck am I hiding *my* face?" He brings the camera up and purses his lips before perfecting his dark hair in the picture-in-picture. Square jaw, deep espresso eyes with a promise of the unexpected behind them. Chase is a wildcard, and I'm willing to admit I like him. "Now, I'm sure you're wondering, where is the sexy beast with a voice like honey who charms my panties off daily?"

"Exactly the wording I would have used," I say dryly. "Are you sure he's not your daddy, Chase?"

He winks and straightens, his white backdrop ending up a wall. An open doorway appears behind him after he walks through, and then the video washes out from him turning on a light. It rebalances as he switches modes, and a muscular back appears. Tan skin and tattoos and a white sheet draped low on his hip, the band of his boxer briefs visible. Foster's asleep in his bed with a pillow over his head and a bicep on top, pinning it in place.

"He woke up long enough to blame me for his hangover and curse at the rain that's been falling since we got in this morning."

And send me a picture of the damn rain.

My eyes trace the lines of his body from a new angle until Chase returns my view to him. "I take it you're not mad at him anymore if you went out together?"

He screws up his face as he sits on the mattress, the pillow and arm visible behind him. "I haven't been mad at Foster a day in my life." His mouth hitches, despite him sounding all business. Then his head jerks over his shoulder when the arm shifts. "Our time together might be over, Tour Remi."

A deep groan transforms into a, "Dude. What the fuck?"

I cover my mouth to silence a laugh as Chase jumps up, spinning around to get away from Foster.

"For the record, she called me." He winces through a smile and appears to duck. "That only hurt the pillow."

"Give me the phone," Foster demands, deep and growly from sleep. He sounds almost as hot as when he issues commands to me in a very different scenario.

"We haven't even gotten to the discussion of how she's going to provide for you." Chase ducks again, and a pillow hits the wall behind him. "Fine. Ruin all the fun." He looks ready to relinquish me and the phone, but then he lowers his gaze to the screen, and a devious smirk curves his lips. "But first, can I see your face?"

I expect to say no, but the conspiratorial look from Chase causes me to reconsider. "Why?"

"Obviously to hold it over Foster's head," he says, moving quickly, and then he's slamming a door to another room and leaning back against it.

"You're the fucking worst." Foster's muffled voice sounds mostly annoyed but holds a bit of amusement.

"What's in it for me?" I ask.

Chase answers without thought, "I'll pledge my lifelong allegiance to Team Fomi and send you a hundred bucks."

I mull it over for a second. "Deal."

He chuckles, and a quiet, "Fuck," comes through the wood. I switch modes and am face-to-face with Chase through the screen.

"Goddamn." His head shakes, grin wide. "A pleasure to meet you, Tour Remi."

"You too, Chase."

"Treat my boy right, yeah?" He straightens as I lower my phone, then the video darkens, the sound of the door. "Brother, you. Are. Screwed."

"So much for not fucking the boat." Foster sighs, and the picture flashes before I'm staring at a familiar chest. "I can't believe you'd break my heart like that."

"What can I say? I like him better."

Foster's jaw comes into view, a hand running over the stubble. "Liar." The view fades, and when it returns, I have his ocean-blue eye and part of a white pillow. "Now I'll balance with a truth. I decided some stuff last night."

"Before or after getting drunk?"

"Before. Then I really decided while drunk."

I maneuver the shot to focus on my eye and cheekbone. "What about?"

"Us."

God, I am not anticipating the full-body reaction to two letters. A flutter in my stomach, a stumble of my heart, every inch of skin growing hot at the delivery.

"And what did you decide?" I ask, raspy and quiet.

"There is one."

My mouth turns up. "I might like an us."

A smile enters his eye. "Good. Because I also decided I'm coming for you."

I want him to, so much it terrifies me.

"I'm making you mine," he tells me, my pulse thundering. "I'm going to make you fall in love with me."

"Yeah?" I say, but it sounds more like *promise?*

"Yeah, baby." He seems as lost in me as I feel in him. "I am."

The chimes dismissing classes sound, and I glance away before I decide to stay. "I have a class. Maybe we can wander later?" I look back as he nods. I'm about to end the call, but I stop. "Foster?"

"Hmm?"

"I think I might like all the other stuff you decided, too."

But it's another lie. There's no thinking anymore when it involves Foster West. I want him, and I *need* him to be real, and I could already love him. All of those, and I've never really met him. Not in the smell him, touch him, breathe the same air sense. I haven't even seen him all at once.

The other day, he said you can never truly see something until it's right in front of you. He was referring to art and everything he's shown me—at the time, the Žižkov Television Tower with giant crawling baby sculptures on it. But it applies here, too.

I haven't truly seen him, and he hasn't truly seen me.

Foster just told me he plans to remedy the truly part. Maybe we don't wait until then for the rest.

I PLAY with the idea of showing Foster my face over and over again for the next week. But I always change my mind at the last second.

The hesitation has nothing to do with Foster being real—he's so real it hurts. He always has been, even when I pretended otherwise, but the missing him part remains. It will only amplify if I see all of him. All I'll want to do is *see* all of him. A problem considering he won't return to the states for another fifteen days, so as much as I want to, I decide to wait until then.

Although I won't be surprised if I fold at any point over the next two weeks.

The guy's still a fever, primed to take over without warning.

Part of me hopes he will.

With only three weeks left in the semester, I feel lighter. I'm in far too decent of a mood to walk in the front door of the step-house after classes. So I follow the stone path around the side of the house. I secure my bag's strap on my shoulder and start up the trellis. Only movement through the window freezes me. I duck to avoid being caught and take a quick sweep of the scene inside.

And what I see sends me scaling down—fucking furious.

I leap to the ground and tear around the house through the front door. It slams behind me, and I thunder up the stairs. The one to my room sits wide open when I reach it. My dresser's yanked from the wall, drawers dismantled and on the floor, the trash from my bathroom scattered, the contents of my closet strewn.

And in the center of it all is my mom.

"Get the fuck out!" I shout.

She doesn't hesitate, let alone acknowledge me storming in. All my anger and resentment toward this goddamn woman hits at once, and I shriek it this time.

"Get out!"

I rush to my stripped bed, dragged to the middle of my bedroom, where she's trying to search under my mattress. My hand latches onto her arm, and I jerk her around before she rips away from me. Her momentum flings her against the bed, but she recovers fast.

"How fucking dare you," she hisses, charging at me.

A side-step dodges her. She nearly stumbles into the hall before whipping around, which puts me between her and the destruction. Hot tears cloud my vision, every muscle tense and ready to fight if she tries to come closer. She has a fresh bruise on her cheek, a hand clamping over her side near her kidney.

"Pills?" I ask, voice shaky even on the single syllable. So much rage floods through me I need to scream, but I refuse to break for her. "Is that what you want?"

"What I want is to have never had you." A disgusted twist in her expression accompanies the hate. "And now that I know what you've been up to, I'm looking for what else you're hiding."

I cross my arms, fists clenched. "Oh, do tell. What is it I'm doing, Mom?"

"Sneaking around with Roman Moore."

Shock radiates through me, and I swallow, shaking my head. "I don't know what you're talking about."

She chokes out a laugh. "Fucking liar. Elvin saw you in his car. He saw you all over each other, too."

Everything from the other night closes in on me, from Elvin stopping me outside to what he said leaving the kitchen.

"Next time you need a ride, call me. I can keep a secret too."

I chalked up the encounter to Daniel trying to scare me— sicking his favorites on me. But Elvin knew I'd been with Roman.

"You act like you're so much better than me." She picks at the bottom of her sweater. "But here you are, down at the bottom, fucking my junkie reject."

My lungs struggle for air, and I speak through my teeth. "You have no idea what you're talking about."

"He told ya he's clean, right?" She has a sway to her stance and follows it a half-step forward. "He's not, *honey.*" The last word's so condescending I almost lose it on her. "He's used the same act for years. Plays the good guy until he gets what he wants. If you fell for it, you're stupider than I thought."

I force myself to ignore the ill feeling creeping through me. She's wrong. She's lying. She's an addict grasping at sand. "Forgive me if I don't believe the actual junkie he left when he got sober. Maybe if you covered your track marks, you'd be more convincing."

Her lip curls as she yanks down the sleeve pushed up on one side. "Stay away from him, or Daniel will deal with it, you ungrateful whore." She pauses before crossing the only remaining line I have with her. "Dimitri was smart, dying to get away from you."

"Leave," I demand, moments from unleashing on her. "Stay the fuck away, and don't you ever say his name again."

She snorts and turns. "Hate to break it to you, *darlin'*, but he was a piece of shit, too. Always begged not to take you. He hated y—"

I drive forward and thrust her into the hallway. She knocks into the banister, grabbing it for balance as I back into my room. I look her over, the same pathetic woman who's repeatedly destroyed pieces of me along with herself. At least I have a few left. I'll be damned if she ruins them too.

Gripping the door, I huff a breath. "You better hope Daniel's there and feeling generous the next time you OD. Because I sure as fuck won't be." I slam it, lock it, and cover the bottom with pillows.

But it's not enough. Not with my insides shredding. Her words are poison I thought I'd built an immunity to. Right now, they're too much. Everything's too fucking much. Tears streak down my cheeks, blood pounding in my ears so rapidly I'm shocked I haven't passed out.

My dad loved me. He wanted me. Roman's safe. He cares.

I scan around my room, the only place I've considered mine in so long. I have no clue how long she was in here. What she might have taken. My heart lurches, and I spin for my closet. Dresses thrown, boxes gone through.

"Please, please, please."

I drop to my knees and dig through the mess. A surge of relief fills me when I uncover my contingency bag in the corner. Right there but completely missed. I still yank on the zipper and then check the side pocket. A sob breaks out of me when I pull out the red velvet pouch. Feel the SD card. I also find the pink envelope I stowed away at the bottom, needing to keep it secure, too.

Then I scramble to my feet, gripping the strap while I tuck the pouch away. I grab my school bag off the floor before pulling out my phone.

Months ago, I asked Roman why he stays. Why he continues to be treated like shit when he deserves so much more. He answered by asking me the same thing. I blinked as tears pooled and had to look away from him to stop them from falling like they are now.

My go-to is I'm terrified of the unknown. Of finding myself in a worse situation than the one I'm surviving now. Or I could end up in one I don't.

It's not a lie but not the all-encompassing truth. Even though she's broken me in ways I likely won't ever completely heal from. Even if every emotional scar, she's had some hand in. Deep down, my mom's always been part of why I've stayed. Guilt or responsibility or love for the woman I wish she could be.

I never told Roman any reasons, but I didn't need to. He knew. And there's a card in an envelope in my bag where he told me his.

When I open my messages, I pause at the window. The overwhelm hits, the doubts and fears and what-ifs, but I find *R* and text him anyway. I'm not sure my reasons are enough anymore—if they can keep me here another second. If that's the case, then at least one of Roman's won't matter either.

24

FOSTER

Now...

NO ONE HAS SPOKEN a word since Christian burst in, cut off the music, and demanded Felix sit.

He wasn't even wearing his manager brows or using the tone as he cursed his way through a recap of the call from the label. He looked rocked, telling us about the concerns for Remi's safety. Worries about the conditions she's working under with us. The insinuations we've been harassing her. Ones that are worse. A mention of what might happen to her alone with us on the bus. And the straight-out reprehensible question of whether Mac Records needs to *"clean up any messes."*

All of it burns on the way down—but the last one's a blue flame right to the fucking chest.

Christian eventually stops his pacing at the front of our private, soundproofed room. He leans back against the karaoke machine, under the shiny fucking disco ball reflecting shimmering color over us.

"I told you to take them somewhere," he spat at Colton on his way in, "and you picked the stupidest place."

Honestly, it was a great time until he started hurling the verbal equivalent of knives at all of us.

I stare at the egregious lime green pattern on the blue carpet while Dev shifts on the couch beside me like he might say something. But Colt beats him, finally breaking the screaming silence inside the walls.

"Hold the hell up." He stays against the wall, his arms crossed. "They're claiming she might be sexually ass—"

"Uh-uh," Christian chides without hiding his annoyance. "We're not to use possibly 'harmful words,' only dance around them like they did. God forbid anyone call forth the boogeyman."

The bite in Colt's tone is sharp when he continues, "Fine. They claim Remi might be *unsafe* on the bus as the only woman, worried the four of us can't keep our *sunshine sticks* away from her, so they sent the fucking wannabe to protect her? The dude was practically humping her leg when we picked her up in New York, trying to big dog us."

"Make it make sense," Dev mutters.

I grind my teeth together, about to snap at the mere mention of our tour's new addition. Xander, the wannabe boyfriend she's clearly fucked. Her roommate who misses her. Her new assistant.

Every thought and feeling bombarding me on the bus before I kissed Remi has resurfaced. Why I can never trust her. Now I remember it all. I remember him.

A friend by any other name.

No excuses, though. I reread the book, expecting a different story.

Christian groans up front. "Christ. Okay." He groans again, even more exasperated. "Shit. I don't even want to ask this."

"I'll do it then," Colton says. "Did anyone cross a line with Remi? Say something, do something?"

Dev sighs and tips his face up. "She's never acted like we got close to any line. Even on Halloween, she bit right back at us and joked around. If she ever felt..." He audibly exhales. "Fuck. I don't know."

"Well, we know Christian's talked to her legs from the beginning. You had her licking you for a shot." Colton kicks off the wall. "Foster's been a prick since moment one. Felix is Felix."

I glance at our drummer, slumped in a chair and looking at nothing. Other than his thumb tapping his thigh, he hasn't moved. Damn, I bet his demons are circle-dancing around the flames right now.

"Anyone touch her?" Christian hates the implication of the question. I hear it in his tone, but he needs to ask.

"No," Dev says, and Felix slowly moves his head side to side, gaze remaining unfocused.

"Foster."

My eyes shift to Colton, my jaw about to crack and knee bouncing. When I give him nothing else, his eyes close, head falling forward.

"The bathtub." Not a question. He saw her attempting to hide. "It was consensual." Another statement, but I nod when his head lifts because it needs answered. It deserves an answer, even if we've been ordered not to use the words sexual harassment and assault. Two of the other three focus on me, then he says, "Any other times?"

I nod once.

"The bruise she's been covering up is from you?" This from Christian, referencing the mark they've all caught glimpses of but no one's called out.

A nod.

"Oh, shit." Dev shoots me a concerned look.

"My advice is we not do any of it anymore." Christian directs it toward everyone but looks straight at me. We all know if I'm the only one who's touched her, the likelihood of whatever the fuck is happening involving me skyrockets. "Regardless of who and what caused this, we're all responsible moving forward. We need to remember Remi's not one of us. She's here for Mac and Erickson, and now they've sent the wannabe. Anticipate him jumping on anything he views as inappropriate and running to them. To cover all our bases, assume his definition includes everything he considers a threat to what he wants."

Colton pops his neck, a mask in place when he locks eyes with me. The stare reiterates the warning about Remi and Xander. I nod, having been force-fed what I already knew and, for some fucking reason, tried to ignore.

THE TENSION LOOMS over all of us, the darkening sky serving as a dark cloud as we return to the bus. Christian's already on his phone, wandering off, when Colt charges ahead to board first. He's in security mode, reappearing before I reach the stairs with a nod.

"You're good," he tells me.

But I'm not because I realize it's Remi. He's protecting me from *her*.

I halt at the door, which forces Felix and Dev to a stop. I need to breathe, a second away from everything. Shaking my head, I change direction, following the length of the bus. Dev curses behind me. Not Felix, though. He still hasn't said a word, and a gut check says he won't until he's high.

Clasping my hands on the back of my neck, I round the end of the bus into shadows. As soon as I'm out of sight, I let in what I've staved off since the karaoke room. The anger and fear and doubt, and then the heartbreak and ache and guilt. The bitter taste of betrayal returns, and all the way at the bottom of the Remi box, the hate.

And it's as potent as ever.

I drop my hands, followed by my forehead onto the cold metal. The situation feels wrong, like a piece has been forced in where it doesn't belong. But I can't be fooled by the faulty wiring inside of me when it comes to the sad, broken girl—my beautiful liar. Only two of those words have ever been true. Remi was never my anything. She was never mine.

In need of a distraction, I push off the bus and spin, leaning against it. I fish out my phone to shoot off a text. I intend to ignore all the notifications until one snags my attention. The same number called three times since yesterday. Without it in my contacts, I would usually ignore it, but this one's also in my messages. At the top and from less than a minute ago. When they text again, a bunch of question marks show in the preview.

Aggressive.

Every now and then a fan gets ahold of my number, or someone sends a woman my way. Uninterested in entertaining either, I tap the thread open to block the person. But they text again before I can, my thumb hovering over the screen.

UNKNOWN

Two minutes is all I need. I'll even prove it's me.

I scroll up to their first message from yesterday where they admonish me for not checking my DMs. I snort, but all humor and thoughts vanish when I read the next one. The name's as much a shockwave as the first time it appeared on my screen. Before I have a chance to doubt, the proof auto-scrolls me to the newest message from her.

In the selfie, Sav Loveless holds a phone, today's date on the lock screen, the time on it the same as mine when adjusted for a time zone difference.

Then the number calls again.

I answer, and any lingering disbelief disintegrates.

"Finally," she sighs out. "You, Adams North, are nearly impossible to get ahold of."

"By design," I say. "But I'd think Sav Loveless would have an easier time than most."

The lead singer of The Hometown Heartless laughs. "You'd think, but your team sucks. From your label to agent, they gave my coordinator the runaround. And when she finally got ahold of your manager, he shut her down."

"Christian?" I ask.

"He told her you're on tour and have no time for what I'm calling to ask. Which I understand, but I also know there's a break in your schedule coming up."

My desire to punch my manager in the face returns. "He never said anything."

"I'm not surprised. I have a feeling your label doesn't want me anywhere near you." Then she doubles down on her text. "This would have been a lot easier if you answered DMs. I messaged you last week."

"I haven't checked anything lately." Between shows and writing, I haven't done more than random posts. "Trust me, I'd have replied to you, busy or not. What did Christian shut down?"

She hesitates. "Well, it was always shorter notice, but there's a benefit concert for the families and people displaced by the hurricane that hit the Carolinas. Almost all the money is going toward rebuilding the communities. Bringing awareness can encourage people to volunteer on top of donating, and six of the hottest bands and artists on the same stage draws a *lot* of attention. Six acts, so long as I convince Adams North to play."

Holy shit. Sav Loveless called to ask me to perform. I thought hearing a stadium of people chant for me was surreal.

"You're behind the benefit?" I ask, knowing I'll say yes.

"I am. I have an in with the owner for one of the construction companies coordinating the rebuild project, and the area's near where I grew up, so it's close to home." She adds, "Which is why the rest of the money is going to a program set up to match the families and people with hosts for the holidays. They already lost their houses. By being welcomed into someone else's, they might at least have a chance to feel a sense of home."

And she nails my soft spot—as if I hadn't already decided.

"Sold," I tell her. "Can the entire band perform, though? If Felix and Dev can't make it, I'm down to perform solo. But I wouldn't feel right not trying to include them."

"Yes. Please. With the time constraint, I didn't want to push my luck, but the spot was intended for Of Men and Wolves. Speaking of, you agreed before knowing *how* short notice this is."

I chuckle. "I imagine very since it seems to line up with our break, which starts in three days."

"It's next Saturday," she says, and I hear the wince.

Close call. Only one day would have me saying no, and it's next Sunday. I need to be in Texas. Nonnegotiable.

"I'll be there. I'll ask Felix and Dev if they're available as soon as we're done here."

She sighs. "Thank you. I owe you, Adams. There are donation goals and incentives for reaching them, and adding you or the band will let us aim higher."

She owes me nothing. Even after this, I owe her for life. "No problem, Sav."

"Okay, then. The marketing team has slow-dripped the artist reveals on social media, so they can announce whoever still. You and Heartless will be the last ones. There are more details, but I'll send the number for the woman in charge," she says. "And I'll send it to you directly, so I know you receive it."

"Message me who to talk to, and I'll make sure it gets handled. I'm sorry about all the assholes. If you ever need anything else, skip them and let me know. Directly."

She laughs. "Deal. You can make it up to me by playing an unplugged 'Haunted' for an incentive."

I can't help a hint of a smile at the request. "I can make that happen."

We say goodbye, and Sav sends me the coordinator's info as I swing around the corner of the bus. But I barely shove the phone in my pocket, let alone track down Felix and Dev, before reality crashes in. Remi steps off the other bus, turns, and we immediately lock onto each other.

Fuck.

She looks exactly the same as when I saw her earlier. Right here in the parking lot. Except nothing feels the same, like a filter flickered out, revealing what it covered. I clearly see again. My armor's been reforged and reinforced.

I stride toward the front of the bus, her steps erasing the rest of the concrete until she's right in front of me, both of us in front of the open door.

"Can we talk?" she asks, eyes flicking inside.

I shrug. "Does it have to do with filming?"

She shakes her head. "No. Did Christian tell you what happened? Foster—"

"Adams," I interject.

Remi jerks back like I slapped her. "What?" When I don't respond, she blinks up at me. "You can't be serious. You think I complained to the label about you guys? You know me. I'd never..." She trails off when my gaze lifts, and she glances over her shoulder to Xander, grinning like a douche as he exits the other bus.

"Your assistant looks like he might need you. Maybe you guys can talk about how much he missed you." Before he reaches us, I add, "So we're clear, I *don't* know you—not anymore or ever. And you chose to not know me. It's time we both remember it."

Sad, sad eyes, but I can't bring myself to care anymore. If she didn't complain herself, I can guess who did on her behalf. The guy who steps beside her, looking down at her, then up at me.

"Holy shit, you're Adams North," he says. "You have no idea how stoked I am to meet you. I'm Xander Salvatore." He sticks out his hand for me to shake, and I stare at him until he withdraws it. "I, uh... The fact I get to work on this project with you and the band is insane. I really lucked out."

I huff a disbelieving laugh, returning my eyes to Remi as she shifts uncomfortably. "The luckiest man, I'm sure."

"Especially getting to work side by side with Rem again." He edges closer to her, her arm overlapping his now. Another clear message from the wannabe. And she doesn't move away.

On a slow inhale, I tick through all the reasons not to break his face. But it might happen if I don't get the fuck away from them.

"Speaking of work, Rem." He glances down with a smile. "We decided to grab dinner while you all catch me up."

His skin brushes hers, and I bite out, "Is there anything else, Sinner?" I cock my head at her, and after a few seconds of studying me, searching my eyes for something she won't find, she shakes hers.

I board the bus without another word to either of them. Without another look. Because it doesn't matter who he is or what she says he is to her. It doesn't matter how many times she casts her sad eyes up at me or drags unwanted memories out of me.

The lies stay lies. Our past remains.

What broke is still broken.

I won't let myself forget again.

Because the truth is, I fell in love with Remi Saint and emerged loathing Remi Sinner. She can't be both, and I should thank her for reminding me which one's on my tour. It's not the one who ended up being an illusion. Now I wait it out until she disappears from my life again. Only I'm not going after her this time. I learned my lessons the hard way.

25

FOSTER

Before...

"If we miss our flight, I will push you into traffic."

Chase chuckles and winks. "I love it when you talk dirty to me."

I sigh, forehead meeting my arm on top of the airport bar while he orders a final round. We took up residence on the stools, waiting for our connecting flight to London.

Which started boarding five minutes ago.

The bartender stops in front of us, and I raise my head as she pours four shots. I nod a thanks and hand over my card. Chase splits the glasses, sliding two over for me, and he lifts one, elbows on the bar.

"This is it," he says. "Almost three months ago, we started in London."

I half-smile. "No better place for us to end."

He claps his free hand on my shoulder. "We never end, brother. Our trip ends. Your dick's freedom ends once a sexy little redhead gets her hands on you. School will end. And in ninety-seven years, life ends. But not us."

I swipe up a shot. "Here's to ninety-seven more years of you being a freeloader, then."

We grin at each other and drink, his hand gripping my shoulder tighter.

It took another two days after I drew on his chest in permanent marker for my best friend to come back. But when he did, it was in true Chase fashion. I was on the balcony, playing my guitar, when he appeared and nonchalantly set off a confetti cannon.

"*There's no place like bro,*" he said. "*Now come get fucked up with me.*"

I let my eyes fall closed, silver foil hearts raining down on me. Then I went and got fucked up with him. Our first stop was a rooftop bar and an apology from him.

"*I was out of line, Foster.*" He shook his head, drinking his beer.

"*I just want to understand what happened, man. We were fine, and then we weren't. You were relentless about the lifeguard and flipped on me about Remi.*" I studied him as he looked at me with regret in his eyes. But I didn't want his regret. I wanted to finally talk it out with him.

"*I'm sorry for all of it. You weren't the problem. It was all me. Registering for next semester's classes hit harder than I expected.*"

We'd signed up the day before Halloween, hours after the #TeamFomi chanting and my start as a shit-filled kitten. We grabbed dinner, and then he went out while I worked on my song.

Chase scrubs a hand over his face. "*We have a year before life comes for us. I'm not like you, Foster. I have nothing waiting for me on the other side.*"

I frowned as he continued, "*I kept thinking how little time we had left. How we needed to fit everything in now because we won't have another chance. Not like this. Not before everything changes.*" His gaze drops to his beer bottle, and he starts peeling the label. "*I took it personally when you stopped coming out. It's stupid, but I felt like you were already moving on without me. You talking to Remi was something to blame it on and made her an easy target. Then I said that shit about you not having a home."* Chase exhales, his forehead creasing. *"Hurt people hurt people, but it's not an excuse. My head was fucked up, and I hate it took me this long to sort it out."*

I sat forward, bracing my forearms on my thighs. *"I'm glad it's sorted, so I can tell you what a fucking idiot you are. You have something waiting, Chase. You have me. On this side, the other side, I'm on every one of your sides."*

His mouth hitched, the most familiar eyes on the planet meeting mine. *"I know. I just got twisted up for a bit."*

"You're my brother. No matter what, we stay family. No way out for either of us," I told him. I needed him to hear me, let it sink in, and be permanently marked deep inside his chest instead of permanent marker on it. *"I have no sides without you."*

Chase nodded, groaning in annoyance when he wiped his eyes. Then I knocked my bottle to the top of his, sending him forward to catch the foaming beer with his mouth for once.

Since then, we've celebrated his birthday, I've dragged him to exhibits and attractions, we gave a salute to *Wanderer* at the end of the beta program, and he's tormented me about seeing Remi's face.

And now they're calling for us to board. Again.

My impatient gaze swings to Chase. His lips twitch, confirming he's doing this to fuck with me.

"You're the fucking worst," I say.

But I smile as we throw back our last shots, bidding a *na shledanou* to Prague.

Until we meet again.

Catching the strap for my bag as I stand, I palm my phone. I told Remi to let me know once she's out of classes, which should be soon since she finishes early on Fridays.

I told her I'm coming for her, and I am. Remi Saint will be mine—it feels like she always has been, and fuck knows, she's been claiming parts of me since the beginning. And I have this crushing feeling the moment I see her, I'll willingly hand over the rest.

The past two weeks have turned torturous where she's concerned. She's seemed sad less and less and reminded me every day how long until only land separates us instead of an ocean. I've played for her more and shown her lyrics in my notebook. She begs me to flip the page when I stop because the rest are about her. For her.

I send playlists when she demands them. She says she fell in love with music because of me. I think I figured out what love is because of her. Then there are all the promises of what we'll do to each other once we're finally in the same place. Soon. I'll do every single dirty thing I've imagined to her soon.

But not soon enough.

She texts as we rush in the direction of our gate, and I stop dead in my tracks. People flow around me while I put in my earbuds, and she voice calls before I have the chance.

"How long?" I ask at the same time she says, "Hours."

Remi laughs. "Remember when you doubted how well I know you?"

I do. And I'll never forget.

Last week she was claiming to know me so well, so I told her to describe me in one word.

"*Restless*," she said in her raspy voice.

"*I won't be once I get to you.*"

A truth. Remi settles me more than anything.

Chase circles back and hooks me around the neck, pulling me along while he grins.

"We're almost at our gate," I tell Remi. "I didn't want to hear your unsexy voice before we boarded."

"Same. I left my last class late, hoping I missed you."

We reach the gate, the window view of the plane and the dark night sky. "Mmm, tell me one more lie, baby."

Chase rolls his eyes, tugging me into the short line. "Christ, the future rock star persona is dying a violent death right now."

Remi stays quiet long enough, I worry something's wrong. But then my beautiful liar says, "Here's three. I didn't just take a picture with my face in it. I'm not sending it to you. I couldn't care less if you send yours back."

I smile, not moving ahead with everyone else. "Show me yours, and I'll show you mine."

"You sure that's not a lie?" she asks, a matching smile in her voice.

"It's a promise." I hesitate, the line gone and Chase waiting. "I'll see you soon, Remi."

A beat passes, and I feel her more than ever. "I'll see you too, Foster."

Her text comes through as I step onto the plane. As soon as I land in my seat beside Chase, I knock his knee with mine for more room. Before I check her message, I open my camera. The asshole beside me jerks me over by the sleeve, elbowing me while shoving his arm around my neck.

I side-eye him when he snags my phone.

"What?" Chase says. "It's not like she'll get confused by the extra sexiness. She's already seen my face." He settles in next to me, ready for a selfie. "Now, hit her with that broody thing you do."

"Dude."

"Fine. Look like shit for her," he bites out. "One, two, three, Foster fucking sucks."

My lips tip up at the last part, and he smirks, capturing the heart-warming moment.

He tosses my phone back and starts scrolling on his, slumping in his seat and pretending not to watch me open my messages.

My pulse races, heart thundering as I tap on hers. Then Remi appears on my screen. All of her. No swirly mask, no fog obscuring the details. The skirt and sexy legs, slender neck, and devastating eyes. High cheekbones set below them and rosebud lips I need to taste. She gives me it all, what I memorized and what I've been missing.

I sigh, well aware I am fucked beyond reason, and yet I've never wanted anything more.

She's perfect, the ultimate beautiful thing. She feels like everything.

I send the picture Chase took, keeping my promise to her.

And then it all vanishes like it never happened. Remi Saint never responds.

26

REMI

Now...

After Foster disappears onto the bus, I spin on Xander, grabbing his hand and hauling him with me. I march all the way to the front of Glory and Nate's bus for some semblance of privacy. We've been around them since he arrived, but I'm not waiting any longer to find out what he knows.

I release him and cross my arms. The sun has set, the temp dropping. Most of the light bouncing off of us belongs to the light poles scattered through the parking lot.

"Why are you here?" I ask.

"Damn, Rem," he says, a touch of rejection in his eyes. "You really know how to make a guy feel welcome. Have you held that in this whole time?"

I soften my expression as much as I can, my face grateful for somewhat of a reprieve from the tensed state since talking with Christian. "I'm sorry. I meant why did the label and Heath send you? You must know something. Tell me what the hell is going on, Xan. Christian was terrified to be alone with me. He apologized for inappropriate conduct and offered for me to talk to legal."

He rakes a hand through his hair, hanging onto the back of his neck after. "Heath and I were worried."

"I'm sorry, what?" My eyes bounce between his. "You had something to do with all this? Why? What the fuck, Xander?"

He nails me with an incredulous look. "Yeah, I had something to do with this. And what the fuck is, I haven't seen you cagey once in the two years we've known each other, then the second Adams walked onto the bus the other day, you shut down."

Unbelievable.

"So, you what?" I quiet my voice, but I want to yell at him. "Decided the band—*Adams*—was sexually harassing me and ran to Heath? I told you nothing was happening." I shake my head, not hiding my annoyance in the least. "What am I supposed to do now, Xander? The band thinks I made accusations against them. They aren't going to trust me anymore, and I don't know how to fix it."

The band thinks I betrayed them, and it feels like Xander betrayed me. Given the reactions from Christian and Foster, I'm unsure they'll even believe me if I try to explain. And then I'm only passing blame to Xander, who's expected to finish the tour with my crew. A clusterfuck of its own with how Foster acted minutes ago. Everything's always so delicate between us, and someone just took a hammer to it all.

"Rem," Xander starts, tone lowering to pacify me, mouth turning down at the corners.

But I'm too upset.

"I can't talk to you right now." I back away, arms dropping to my sides. "I'll see where Glory and Nate want to go for dinner. We'll fill you in on our process for concerts. We can redistribute the work for tomorrow's and cover the shot list for the meet and greet in the afternoon."

His head falls back between his shoulder blades, but I leave him there. I shiver and wrap my arms around myself as I walk away, not even hoping for the best. Only bracing for the worst.

And I'm right to.

After dinner, I board the bus as Felix and Dev are coming through the curtain into the lounge, both carrying their duffel bags. Dev's jaw sets, Felix immediately lowering his gaze to the floor as soon as they see me.

"I swear I didn't say anything to the label," I tell them again. I tried before leaving, but I cut Xander off without the entire story, so I'm missing details. "There was nothing to say. Something got twisted along the way, and I think—"

"Can we get by?" Dev asks, closing in on me.

Part of me wants to refuse. Block them in and make them listen. But with the callousness aimed at me, they won't hear me. The trust is gone, shattered, like I feared. As much as I hate it, force won't repair the damage. Not without breaking something elsewhere.

I swallow the sting and move aside. Dev turns his body, inching past like I'm poisonous spikes to avoid. The next blow hits even harder.

Felix follows suit, side-stepping to maintain as much distance as possible between his front and mine. "Excuse me, Remi," he mumbles.

I'm Remi now. Not Cam Girl.

They stomp down the stairs, and my eyes crush closed.

In a handful of hours, I went from part of the pack to a pariah.

None of the guys will talk to me.

None of them sleep on the bus.

The band, Christian, even Colton—they want nothing to do with me.

ALL THE STRESS CARRIES OVER, ready and waiting for the awkwardness of filming together the next afternoon. We need shots of the meet and greet and fan interactions, and regardless of if they hate me, the documentary needs to stay the priority.

I arrive at the music store with the crew instead of the band. A drastic change from the rest of the tour. Yesterday morning, I watched Felix and Colton bicker over nonsense, ending with Felix leaning over and licking Colton's pancakes. Now when they walk through the alley entrance and see me in the storeroom, they fall silent. All five faces stoic and eyes avoidant.

Within three minutes, I wish for outright animosity rather than the indifference and professionalism surrounding me. I'm a suit. Even Foster plucks the spy glasses from my hand with utter disinterest.

I exit the storeroom ahead of the others, following the corridor to where it opens up to the front. Despite the shop windows and the music playing from speakers in one corner, the hum of voices reaches me. A sea of people wait on the sidewalk, and then a contained line snakes down the closed street, kept orderly with crowd barricades.

Hands wave and fans shout as I walk each side of the locked, guarded door, filming over the displays of guitars and amps. I swing through the shop for B-roll of keyboards, drums, and the little section of woodwinds. The place holds a vintage vibe behind the modern equipment. Records on the walls, autographed pictures framed. A nook intended for testing instruments even has an orange shag carpet on the walls for dampening sound.

I understand the draw for Of Men and Wolves in wanting the event held here.

At the rear of the store, they set up a charcoal backdrop for pictures. I land off to the side, near the alcove and close to where Nate set up his audio equipment. The angle allows a focus on the band but guarantees to capture every interaction. Glory and Xander will float to get the shots we discussed while Nate monitors mics.

They appear a handful of minutes ahead of the start time. Xander catches my eye and offers a small smile. My return one fails to stick. Along with everything else I haven't figured out, our dynamic on tour earns a spot on the list. I need to de-ice enough to talk to him first.

Colton walks out with Christian. The latter folds his arms over his chest and leans by the doorway. But it's Colton who surprises me. He heads toward me, scanning the place. Then he stands next to me.

I want to say something, but he stares at the hallway where the band will emerge any second and crosses his arms. We're not keeping each other company. We both need the same proximity to the action.

Screams and shouting breach the walls and windows when the band appears. I immediately home in on Foster. He's not wearing the frames I gave him. Felix is. It feels personal.

The noise grows louder once they open the doors to let the first wave inside. Felix and Dev kick up the charm as the line begins cycling through. Like they needed any more between the effortless swagger and smooth grins.

But nothing compares to the magnetism of Adams North. The hunter green tee stretches over his chest and around his biceps, and he's wearing black ripped jeans. Every inch of him pulls you in, his charisma a force of its own. He flashes irresistible smiles to balance the seductive angst always skimming his surface. All confidence and sex and a magic I can't describe.

I've witnessed him hypnotize a packed stadium over and over, but the man is dangerous in an intimate setting. The entirety of his attention is not for the weak of heart. I would know. Mine's felt pretty beaten into submission by Foster plenty of times.

All three seem at ease as the people and groups rush for their pictures and hugs, where the guys never actually touch the fans. I'm unsure the fans notice, but the band's hands and arms always hover, not quite making contact with anyone outside of handshakes.

The screams resume after the last group finishes and the guys wave on their way to the back through the doorway. Felix shouts a, "We love you," and I flinch at the decibel level spike.

"Fuck," Nate hisses behind me, and when I glance over my shoulder, he's shaking his head.

If the other moments of cries and screeching didn't peak the audio, that one certainly did.

I expect the band to be gone already by the time I help Nate break down audio, but they're still in the storeroom. Foster, Felix, and Dev are signing autographs for two store employees by the exit and posing for more pictures. Christian's scowling, not at me, but it matches the glower on Colton.

"We need to go before it gets worse," the security guard says. He swings his gaze to me and gestures toward the door with his chin. "One of the event security fucked up, and people flooded the alley. We've cleared space to our van, but the one you brought is in front. Safest bet is to drive out together."

I nod. "Yeah. No problem."

"Anton will take you back." He glances at my crew. "Unless whoever drove here wants to avoid all the moving bodies?"

Nate shakes his head violently. "Fuck, no."

His eyes dart to me, checking he answered correctly, and I subtly nod. The relief that flashes in his eyes—Glory pats him on the shoulder.

"We'll load your crew, then the band," Colton says, all business but not in the cold way from earlier. He's just serious. "Your van has less room around it, but they shouldn't cause an issue once they see who we're bringing out."

I nod again, and Colton asks Nate for keys to hand off to Anton, who must already be outside. The band's posted against the wall by the door, dutifully waiting, no concern showing when we move to leave. Xander respects my space and hangs back behind the other two while I end up in front of the door with Colton. It puts me between him and Foster, leaning beside me. My eyes flit to him as always, and he has his head rolled in our direction.

The animosity I wished for earlier swims in his eyes now. Disdain paints his expression, similar to the look he gave me on the bus when he claimed what we had before wasn't real. I blink, redirecting to the gray metal door in front of me, the push bar across it. But I still feel him. Forever tugging.

"You're with me, Remi." Colton grasps the strap to my camera bag, and I let him take it off my shoulder, smiling at him in thanks.

Foster lets out a derisive breath. "They brought the wannabe in to protect you, yet it's my security doing the job, first out there and now here."

I take in a steeling breath to counter his. "Interesting you would say that, considering I handed you the spy glasses for shots of the event, but Felix wore them."

He refuses to hear me out. It doesn't mean he can treat me like shit without pushback.

I look over. Our eyes meet, his cold, cold, cold. The tension's different again, and not back to the way we were before the bus. It's a new one, missing the heated base notes present since Prague. No glances at my mouth or lower. No warmth at all. Foster might actually hate me.

Colton's doing a final check when Foster smirks, not in challenge, but in warning. I fight off a shiver.

"I'll tell you what, director." He tips his head back on the wall, closes his eyes. "I'll do my job once he does his."

THE DRIVERS MOVED the buses to the venue while we were gone, so the vans take us there.

Colton called it. The fans showed no interest in the crew. Of Men and Wolves walked out, and they lost their shit. I watched out the back window while security moved the barriers to let us leave, and people surrounded the other van. It took the event detail walking in front so Colton could safely get them out of there.

Christian's already on the phone when we cross paths in the parking lot, upping security for future appearances and shows.

They need to adjust for the band's ever-climbing popularity and reactions to them. Mac Records might have all but taken over the tour from him, but Christian remains the one looking out for the guys in the end.

Keeping up with the cold shoulder, the band and associates go straight inside to their dressing room. I need to time it right if I want to try to explain I had nothing to do with the label and Heath. With Xander. Hours ahead of a concert is far from right.

Plus, I still have nothing to explain until I talk to my *assistant*.

And when I walk into the lounge after showering and getting ready, that time has come, apparently.

Xander shoots up from being sprawled on the couch where he slept on last night. "You can't avoid me forever, Rem."

I shrug. "That has yet to be determined." But then I sigh and gesture to the front of the bus. "Ready to carry stuff inside?"

His lips quirk up, and he nods. "Absolutely, boss."

I roll my eyes and nudge him out of the way. I climb to the loft and snag my camera bag.

We work as light as possible during concerts, just our bags and anything specific shots might require. Both Glory and Xander will need extra equipment tonight, so we gather his from the other bus's storage.

I also keep a duffel of backups with me—along with a couple of my favorite lenses. A filter or two. Maybe a recorder for ambient noise. And the projector for a shot I'm dying to get of old band footage playing on a wall or curtain as the guys walk in front to the stage.

All vital shit, really.

Xander snatches the duffel from me, slinging the strap over his shoulder on our way inside. He tosses me a grin. I narrow my eyes in return, and he groans, exasperated as security opens the door for us.

I check the handy venue map on my phone for the band's dressing room. Christian sent them for every show so I could plan logistics and scenes. They save me more often than I care to admit.

Xander catches my arm as we cross the backstage area. "Can we please talk this out? I hate you being mad at me. And I really hate you acting like I'm a bad guy in your movie."

"The misdirection would work so well, though. The pretty face, close proximity as my roommate, the friends-to-hookup-to-friends threaded into the storyline. You're perfect for the villain."

I flash a wry smile but then take pity on him. I drag him with me, backing out of the way from the stage. We stop beside an empty dolly and spare amps, and I face him, chin tipped to glare at him properly.

"Go ahead. Tell me why you're accusing people of sexual misconduct. Or, with how Christian was acting, was it assault?"

Xander jerks back and then ducks closer, his voice hushed. "Jesus fuck, Remi. I didn't do either. You think I'd baselessly cry assault on someone? The thought might have crossed my mind, but I never voiced it."

I believe him, the shock from him seeming genuine, the hurt too. "Well, you clearly voiced something."

"Yeah," he says. "Concern. I told Heath you were acting off. Which he agreed. The subject shifts to Adams, and the vibe changes with you. In all the time we've worked together, not once have you missed a deadline. Hell, Heath wanted to come himself to scorch earth based on those things alone. The interviews with Adams are essential, whether you're giving the middle finger to Mac Records or not. It's a scene you, of all people, should be salivating over. But you're putting it off and giving flimsy excuses."

The fight leaves me because he's right. Even though I've refused to focus solely on Adams from the beginning, before Prague, a day-one nonnegotiable shot was his interview.

I look away, suddenly feeling responsible for the mess. Maybe not directly, but I fed them every reason to go down the path. "So, Heath went to the label?"

"After checking with Glory and Nate if they noticed anything, yeah. Well, I checked with them. Can you imagine if Heath called those two, demanding answers? Can you imagine Heath not losing it on everyone when it comes to you? His heart might not beat, but whatever powers him is protective as fuck of you."

"The lifeblood of innocents, mostly."

He huffs a laugh, and I return my gaze to him, his still serious. "I have no idea what was said to their manager. They wanted someone on tour, and I offered. Heath threatened every facet of my life and bought me a ticket here."

"Sounds like him," I whisper.

Xander studies me before a half-shrug. "Tell me what you would have done, Rem. With everything you've experienced around this industry, I know the answer isn't pretend to not notice."

I can't disagree from his perspective, but I own the full story as to why I acted differently about Adams. Because Adams is Foster. And Foster is a direct link to what I've spent so long avoiding at all costs. Even now, the tightness creeps into my chest, my muscles bunching, mind bucking against the possibility of going there.

But Foster's also where I want to be. He makes me wonder if I can say the bad aloud and tell him why I left the way I did. All the regrets and stupid decisions and the weight of them.

I almost attempted to on the bus when I couldn't stand the idea of him not being on the other side of the curtain. Then I choked on the words, and he kissed me.

"Adams has his reasons for avoiding the interview, and I'm being respectful. If I thought it was truly detrimental to the documentary, I would go to Christian. Like you said, I've experienced a lot on sets. I know what makes me uncomfortable and when my lines have been crossed, Xander. I understand you and Heath were trying to protect me, but I didn't need it. Now…" I lift a hand only for it to drop. "Now," I say, letting it encompass the mess in its entirety.

Xander blows out air. "I'm sorry if I overstepped, but I won't apologize for worrying about you. I won't stop either. Not only because I care about you, but because I promised to watch out for you."

I manage a small smile at the welcome reminder. "You also promised to keep your hands off me. We both know that didn't happen."

"Nope. Not before and not after."

"But none of that matters. Sex was always whatever with us. You need to talk to me the next time you're worried—and I mean really talk to me—because we're *friends* above all else, Xan. First and always, right?"

The question pulls double duty. No one's motives are pure. Humans are too inherently selfish for entirely selfless acts. Xander's concern I believe, but I also think he inserted himself to guarantee nothing sexual happens in regard to me. Consensual included.

"Right. First and always," he says, a little too enthusiastic, but I'm confident we're on the same page. "I really am here to help, Remi, not just play bodyguard. Your mentor's mine too. Heath just likes you more. Unless it comes to torture, then I'm his favorite."

I nod, emphasizing my agreement. "I'm sure wiggling out of Heath duty was devastating for you. Please tell me you found a fill for his assistant. He will be insufferable if not."

"I found one, but we both know he'll be insufferable regardless."

I almost laugh. I would if the world didn't feel so heavy. Xander gives an *aww* when I frown, and he wraps an arm around me, hugging me to his side. It only lasts a second before I step back and his arm falls, but in that two-blink period, Foster emerges from the dark shadows near the stage, homed in on us.

My heart plummets, more damage occurring between us in real time.

He shakes his head as he walks away, a smile spreading, but it's cruel and pointed. He disappears down the hallway for the dressing room, and I toss a fake smile at Xander.

"I'll see you after the show." I take my bag so he can go to the front of house. "Let me know if you need anything."

Then I head for the same hallway. It's empty when I round the corner, the angry rock star already inside where the cold professionalism will no doubt continue from everyone. Even knowing all the details, I'm unsure of my next step.

I pause at the door, looking up and preparing myself for whatever happens on the other side. But when I push down on the handle, it doesn't budge. No give at all.

They locked me out. The band fucking locked me out.

Or at least the last person to walk in did.

I throw the door open to the band's dressing room after the concert. The handle on the other side bangs into the wall behind it as I charge in.

I never come in post-show, always grabbing my bags before the tits and dicks are on display, but not tonight. Also, there aren't any tits or dicks since Felix and Dev passed me like I didn't exist on their way to the exit.

An asshole sits on the tan leather couch, though.

Foster's eyes lift long enough to slash me with a glare, then lower again. "I thought you'd take the hint you're not welcome in here, director," he says, voice rough from performing. "Get out before I call security to take care of it."

"Take care of it?" I spit back. "I'm filming a documentary about *your* band, and you locked me out. We had shots planned..."

My attention dives to the guitar case on the coffee table in front of him. The coke he's cutting on top of the smooth surface.

"What the fuck, Foster?" I glance over my shoulder to the door, realizing anyone could walk by. He might not care, but I do. I close it and come back, his head shaking in annoyance I'm still here.

He can fucking deal.

"I get you're mad at me, but messing with filming over it? None of this works if you cut off my access to you. To all of you."

Foster tosses aside the keycard and looks up, giving a careless shrug. "I told you I'd do my job when your wannabe boyfriend does his."

I swallow down the urge to scream at him for being such a dick. "Xander filmed the merch table and entrance line tonight. He did his job."

"Nah, I mean his real one. Tell me which of us he's protected you from. Or is him feeling you up backstage part of his plan? If he's doing it, no one else can? Fucking genius, honestly." A harsh smirk forms, and I drop my gaze because he's getting to me. "Maybe he'll earn a raise for fucking you."

I whip my eyes back to him. "It was a hug." I clip the words, fists at my sides. "Xander's a friend. Yes, we've slept together, but nothing since before Prague and never again. I don't want him, Foster. I didn't go to the label or Heath or ask for any of this, so stop fucking punishing me for it."

Foster dips down and snorts through a line like he has a point to prove, and I feel it like he intends.

He stays forward, forearms braced on his thighs, and he nods at the door behind me. "If you're done..."

"You know what? Fine." I hold his stare, my frustration meeting his anger head-on. "Hate me. Despise me. Loathe me. Act like an ass and try to hurt me. But you won't ruin the documentary. I won't let you, and not just because of what it means for me. Because of what it means for Felix and Dev, for how fucking proud Colton looks of you when we're filming." I blink back a rush of tears, but they reach my voice anyway. "And for you—not Adams—you, Foster. I won't let you stand in your own way, no matter how you feel about me now."

He surges to his feet, anger to fury. "Don't act like you care about me. You never fucking cared," he grinds out. "The only true thing between us was that you were a liar, so save the bullshit. I won't fuck up the doc because people I love need this. They need me to show up, and I will. Over and over again. And I'll do it for me. I'll turn it on and be everything I need to be in spite of you, Remi. Because I already lost enough to you when you fucked off out of my life the first time. No way in hell you're taking anything else from me before you're out of it permanently."

My heart pounds in my chest, his heaving while the words linger. They tug at strings attached to anchors of pain buried in the muddy deep. Except the water level seems to have dropped, and what I've always wanted to say to him is right there.

The door swings open, and Colton strides in.

"Oh," Colton says. A divot forms between his brows at the sight of us, Foster seething and me struggling to stand, three lines of coke on the case in the middle. "You good, Adams?"

Foster gives me a harsh once-over, then looks to his security guard, tone dead when he tells him, "Take out the trash before I do it myself." He walks away, slamming the door to the bathroom behind him.

I swipe the tears away as the truth sinks back into the depths.

I never thought I could be sad about that.

27

FOSTER

Before...

I WASN'T LYING when I said Remi gave me too much credit if she thought I could track her down with a name and phone number. But I have a hell of a lot more than I need in the end.

The end comes almost two weeks after I land in Texas with Chase. Remi sent her picture, and then nothing. No texts or calls. I've struggled over the stalker aspect of looking for her, showing up where I last knew she was. But none of this makes sense. Remi vanishing without a word is wrong, and the hollow feeling in my gut wins out.

Ashfield, Ohio. A café with a town square across the street. The house almost too easy to find.

No, it is too easy. When I pay for my coffee, the police chief's address is written on a pink piece of paper and taped to the counter. Chief Kane.

I fish my phone out as I return to the rental car. The picture of Chase kissing his bicep like a total douche covers my screen with the incoming call. He's texted a dozen times over the past hour, but my head hasn't been in the right place. I tuck it away without reading the messages, still not there.

The last two days, he's been on another level. He's wanted to go climbing, bungee jumping, and to the bars every night. I think he's trying to cheer me up or distract me. But nothing will work until I find her. I can't let it go. I can't let her go.

I park on the street in front of a two-story, white with black accents. My breaths shallow when I spot a trellis against the side of the house, barely visible through hedges and tree branches. She mentioned it once, how she sneaks in and out. Seeing it in person unsettles me because where the fuck is Remi?

Less and less sure about this, I climb out of my car. A black BMW sits in the driveway. Extra antennae, lights on the side mirrors, and a radio inside when I walk by it tell me it's an unmarked police car. I step up to the door, look at the brass knocker. Fuck, my pulse is thundering in my neck, chest weighing me down.

I skip the knocker and rap my knuckles on the door.

After a few seconds, a middle-aged man answers. "Can I help you?"

The piece of shit stepdad. He has a hardness to him, light brown hair, jeans, and a gray button-down.

"Uh, yeah," I say, the doubt seeping through my pores, but the wrongness overpowers. "I'm looking for Remi."

His forehead barely creases before returning to neutral, eyes quickly scanning me. "You know Remi?" I nod, and he steps back, opening the door wider. "Come in out of the cold, son."

I hesitate for a moment, then step inside. I only go far enough he can shut the door behind me. Two vases of flowers sit on a table in the entryway. An archway off to the side leads to what I guess is a living room. I only get a glimpse from here of a table with more flowers by the window. A woman waits beside it, hands folded in front of her. The blonde's probably in her forties, a kindness to her face but something commanding underneath.

Remi said her mom's an addict, but nothing tells me one way or another with this woman. Not that appearances always matter in that regard. If the chief of police's wife is using, it makes sense she'd hide it well.

The door shuts behind me, and her stepdad slips around me. "Give me just a second." He approaches the woman, touching her elbow as if to turn her. Whatever he says makes her eyes flash to me, and then she nods before the two of them walk farther into the house, out of sight.

Blowing out a breath, my head falls forward for a second. Fuck. I have no idea what the hell I'm doing here. Actually, in need of the distraction, I decide to check Chase's messages. And I instantly regret it.

> Happy dude-bro day, my dude-bro.
>
> We have a busy agenda. Then we're re-releasing your dick into the wild tonight.
>
> Fuck that chick. She's hot but not worth the trouble.
>
> I bet she's completely different in person. We'll find you better in a heartbeat.

The opposite of helpful. I shove my phone away without finishing them and pace the space. I scrape a hand through my hair and grab the back of my neck, turning around. On a sigh, my arm drops to my side, and I glance down at the table with the vases. A roar fills my ears, the floor dropping out from under my feet. My eyes jerk from the paper program to the flowers. Both have white cards tucked in plastic holders.

I go back toward the door and step into the archway to the living room. Other than the flowers by the window, I notice more on the end tables. Arrangements line the mantel of the fireplace. They cover the stone hearth.

With a rough swallow, I stride to the entry table and snatch up the program. The woman on the front has golden hair and a too-soft smile—Rebecca Kane is printed beneath her picture along with a birthdate. And her death date.

What the fuck?

My brows draw in as I flip open the funeral program for Remi's mom. The first page has her obituary but only says she died unexpectedly in her home. It gives the same date as the front, a match to the last time I heard from Remi. As I scan through the rest, my attention snags at the bottom.

Rebecca is survived by her husband, Daniel, and daughter, Remi Sinner.

Sinner. Sinner. Sinner.

Not Saint, but Remi Sinner. The name cinches my chest tight, thoughts racing.

"Please let us know what we can do, Chief," the woman says. My head jerks up as she and Remi's stepdad reappear. "We're all here for you, whatever you need."

He nods. "Thank you, Julie. I'll be back next week." He gestures to the vases. "Take a bouquet for the front desk, would you? They posted my address at the coffee shop, and people keep stopping by with food and flowers. Rebecca would have wanted them to be enjoyed."

"Yes, sir." Her mouth tilts in apology, and then she gives me the same look as she grabs flowers from beside me.

With a sigh, he shuts the door behind her and turns his attention on me, noting the program still in my hand.

"Is Remi okay?" I clear my throat, swallow through the dryness and anxiety curling through me. "I haven't heard from her since the day her mom died. Is she here?"

The man's jaw tics. "She's not here." *She's not.* "I was kinda hoping you'd know something about where she went." *Where she went.* "I'm Daniel, by the way."

"Foster."

I shake his hand on autopilot when he offers it, his grip firmer than necessary. Then he continues, "My wife and her daughter weren't the closest, but I never thought Remi was capable..." His head shakes when he pauses, and I need him to fucking finish. "You seem like a good kid, Foster, so I'm just going to lay it out for you. Remi took off the day Rebecca passed with a man named Roman Moore. No one's heard from her since."

Roman. Her friend. The guy from the town square.

My insides twist, not only jealousy driving into me, but a biting sensation I've only felt twice in my life shoots beneath my skin. Once when my old man hugged the son he loved in front of me, and again when my mom pulled a knife on the son he didn't.

"Took off." I breathe, refusing to jump to conclusions, but it aches already. "What does that mean?"

"She'd been acting out for a while," he says, "growing more disrespectful. We had a hunch she was hanging around this man as a way to hurt her mother." When I stay silent, Daniel tells me, "Rebecca dated him years ago, and it affected me as well with him on the force. Christ, I worried he was taking advantage of her, but she was eighteen, so my hands were tied. Rebecca tried to talk to Remi, warn her away from him. But Remi wouldn't hear it."

I blink at him, hearing him but struggling to process more and more. "She was seeing her mom's ex and ran off with him?"

They were together—that's the part tripping me up. She listened to me about my dad and his secrets and cheating and betrayal. Now, I'm supposed to believe she was with another guy the entire time. Now she's just done with me, no word or warning.

He nods, sticking his hands in his pockets. "After she found out about Rebecca, she bolted, and no one's seen either of them since." He shakes his head again with a shrug. "Her mother passed away, and the first thing Remi did was skip town with her ex. She'd been more secretive and lying all the time. But I never thought she was capable of such a selfish act. To not even grieve or attend the funeral?" His eyes close as he pauses. "She left all of us behind to worry, too."

A numbness that started in my chest reverses. The concern in his tone sounds manipulated, and then his eyes open, locking on me the second his lids clear. Like he's gauging my reaction.

Him being a piece of shit wasn't the only thing Remi told me about him.

"Everyone treats him like a king when his crown's made of deceit."

"And you know they're together?" I ask, studying him more closely.

"Roman called in his resignation the same day. No one's seen him come or go from his house, windows always dark. I worried he might have abducted her," Daniel adds, "but her friend, Sage, confirmed they'd been sneaking around."

I try to match my Remi and the one he's describing. Saint or Sinner. Not using her actual last name on an app means nothing in the grand scheme. Plenty of reasons exist for it.

But I saw Roman myself—heard her say his name and hurry off to talk to him. Her best friend would know better what was happening, being here in the flesh, than I ever could through a screen and not really seeing a damn thing.

It still feels like I'm missing something, though. I get cutting me off if she ran off with another guy—if she would really hurt me in the worst possible way. But why would she abandon Sage?

"You said no one has heard from her? Not even Sage?"

A head shake. "She's heartbroken Remi abandoned her without saying goodbye, but she said Remi had been talking about leaving for a while, so ... I guess she meant leaving everyone behind too."

Her escape plan. Graduating early and never coming back. She hasn't called or texted once since she left.

Suddenly not telling me her last name feels more important. A lot of shit suddenly looks a hell of a lot different. Like someone switched on the light.

"She hurt a lot of us, Foster..." Daniel keeps talking, but I stop listening.

I can't with everything crashing over me at once. Realizations and truths. Him and her—not her and me. The lies and pretending and saying I'm not real. Maybe I was the only one not lying and who was never pretending. Maybe Remi Saint was the one who was never real—we were never real.

Chase was right. I was so fucking stupid, letting myself believe we were.

I'm unsure who to blame for the crack in my chest. For carelessly handing someone my heart to crush. Who played me harder. Who was a more beautiful liar all along. I'm unsure who's betrayed me worse.

Remi Sinner or myself.

28

FOSTER

Now...

"I HATE YOU."

Colton slaps the cash into my hand and then serves the poor chick at the hotel's reception desk one hell of a glare. I chuckle and stuff the five in my pocket.

"We can stop any time," I remind him.

But he scans the lobby and then smacks me in the chest. "No fucking way. Put your shades on so you quit cheating."

I slide them on, and we both wait for the chick crossing toward us, a bellhop following with her bags. Once she's close enough, Colt coughs. She gives an annoyed glance at first, only to change her mind. She scans us both before smiling on her way by, attention staying on him.

"Fuck, yes." He forgets her and holds out his palm, his smile smug.

"I never stood a chance against you." I return the cash.

Neither of us would carry any if not for the bet. For a long time, we traded the same bill back and forth, almost like a marker. The scales tipped in my favor once people started recognizing me in public.

Or when I started cheating, according to Colt.

"You aren't closing with her?" I ask.

He shrugs, his expression mimicking it. "Those who do not carry bags do so because of their baggage."

"Preach."

Christian winks at the other receptionist, tapping the cards on the counter before he spins. "Third floor is ours. Keycard access only for the elevator, which also goes down to the private gym, pool, movie theater, and whatever else she said." He waves a hand toward the desk and then passes out keycards, rattling the room numbers as he goes.

My eyes move to Wannabe—Xander's official name now—when his room winds up on the opposite end of the hall from Remi. His head shakes the tiniest bit, and I catch Christian's lips twitch. He might be a pompous ass, but he's our pompous ass. Turned out damn good at music management, too. He and his business major were corporate bound until he pivoted to act as our manager. With the way he adapted, navigating the industry and growing with us, the temporary part of the gig extended to indefinite.

I'm dragging, walking off the elevator. One more show tonight and then three days to write before we fly to San Diego, followed right up by the benefit concert.

Just like I expected, the guys agreed to play. Dev pushed his trip to Arizona, and Felix planned on hanging around the hotel anyway. Then we looked into the situation more, the way formal relief has fallen off and the continuing effects on those the disaster displaced, and I'm convinced they would have made it work regardless.

I sent Lee a singing telegram to her office to *thank her* for bringing it to us. She then signed us to the San Diego appearance since we "clearly have the energy." Our agent dodged giving a reason, making me wonder if Sav's right. Mac Records wants to keep us away from her. Lee needs to remember who she works for. And it's not them.

As for Christian, Felix promised to piss on his designer watch collection if he ducks another opportunity he knows we'd jump on. He's excellent at his job but forgets goodwill exists. It's time he realigned his vision and the rest of our team with what we want for ourselves.

Colton stops at his room, one before mine. "Later, ass-face."

I chuckle, impressed by his maturity as always. When I reach mine, I glance over, but he's disappearing inside, which has me looking straight at Remi, coming down the hall. She adjusts the strap for her messenger bag and lowers her eyes to avoid mine, cheeks flushing.

It reminds me of the day at the label. How uncomfortable I made her. I've earned it now.

More than earned it after the other day. But the dam broke watching her and Wannabe backstage before the concert. Instead of calming while listening to the crowd, my thoughts tangled, past, present. He hugged her, and I couldn't stop seeing Roman in his place. The guy she chose over me.

They say hurt people hurt people, and the day I went after her broke me. I almost lost a part of myself.

I face my door, feeling her pass behind me. Tapping my card, I look down the hall again. And all the way at the end, Wannabe hesitates in front of his own door, watching her. Or us.

I CRASH for a few hours but wake up unsettled. I put on a sweatshirt and step onto the balcony, notebook in hand. The second I look down at the courtyard below, blocked off for privacy, I tip my face to the sky.

"Fucking kidding me."

Turning right around, I retreat, shut the door, and erase the fountain from my memory.

I retreat to the oversized sofa. It takes ten minutes of tapping the pen on the page before I throw it across the room.

Goddamn.

Giving up, I sprawl out on my back with my phone, replying to Christian's text and another. Then I scroll down, down, down. My thoughts keep drifting in this direction, so I might as well.

I go through the same mental gymnastics as every time I call, a hollowness inside me when she answers.

"Hey, Mama." The last bit of Texas lingering in me slips out at the end. No matter how long it has been since the rest of my accent faded, that one word holds on for dear life.

"Foster, baby," she says softly. "I've been thinking about you."

"You should have called." I'm rolling my eyes at her response before it comes through the speaker.

"Well … you know how it is."

My eyes close, the bite beneath my skin still there after all this time. "Yeah. Are you good? Taking care of yourself?"

"We've been good. Your brother decided to not come home for the holidays—"

"Please don't call him that," I sigh out. I can't stand when she talks about his family like she's a part of it. But I gave up trying to change it. Change her. All I can do is ask she not force me into the dysfunction.

"Right," she almost whispers. "Landon's staying at school for Thanksgiving, possibly Christmas. Your daddy and Rose aren't too happy about it. He's been distancing himself lately. It hurts your daddy to see it. I wish I could do more."

I silently snort, looking at the decorative swirls on the ceiling. "I think you've done plenty." I leave off that the fucker deserves the pain.

Cheers to the kid. Might be hope for him yet.

"Tell me how your music thing is going. I hear you've been busy."

Music thing. My hobby, as far as she's concerned. "It's going well, Mama. We're back on tour, writing our next album, filming a documentary our record label set up."

"Sounds wonderful, baby. I remember when you got your first

guitar. How happy you were to sit and play every day. It warmed my heart."

I nearly break my teeth, grinding them. "I had to play every day, Mama. Remember? I was in physical therapy after wrist surgery."

The rest I bite back. If I reminded her my old man threw me down and stomped on my wrist because I reached for water and spilled it on his paperwork, she'd excuse it or act like I'm the confused one.

Denial is one hell of a drug. In my mom's case, it protects her from the shit. Suppressing memories or manipulating them into a less upsetting narrative.

Her remaining friend in Texas got her mental health license a couple years ago. She stays in touch to keep my mom from being completely isolated in their fucked-up world. She says gentle coaxing is best, but to back off when meeting resistance. And resistance I meet.

"Well," she says, dismissively. "I'd love to hear you play again sometime. Maybe you could send me another message to listen to."

"Yeah, Mama. I'll send one. Or you could come to a concert and see me on stage. We'll be in New York close to your birthday. I could set you up in the VIP tent."

"Oh, that's not necessary. But listen, baby, I've got to go. Your daddy's home. He…" She hesitates while I brace for whatever she's gearing up to say. "Your daddy … Foster, he worries you'll try to upset Rose and Landon again. He thinks it's in our best interests to keep some distance."

Again. Because it worked so well the first time.

Two years ago, I sent a letter informing the current Mrs. West of her dedicated husband's infidelity. Little good it did since his ex-wife-turned-mistress helped cover his trail. I'm uncertain of the details of how he convinced his wife it was bullshit, but a PI discovered his house with my mom is in her name—well,

Meredith Glaser's name. She apparently went back to her maiden name, at the behest of the bastard no doubt.

She changed her name for him, and I use a stage name because of him.

Neither of us want to be associated with Andrew West, but for completely different reasons.

Mine will be linked eventually. Maybe I'll see what else the PI discovered and blow up his shit then.

Right now, I'm too exhausted by it all to bother.

"Okay," I tell her. "Think about—"

"Bye."

She ends the call, and I toss the phone onto the floor. I scrub my hands over my face, groaning out the past few minutes. Then I roll to my feet, grabbing my notebook and pen off the floor. I close the balcony door behind me before lifting the entire fucking bench and setting it down facing the opposite way. Looking at myself in the reflecting privacy glass.

What fountain?

If only I could *what* everything as easily.

But duty calls. As much as we'd like to avoid Remi and Wannabe, we agreed to the group interview after the concert. Christian sent the location to our group chat.

I write for a bit before I scroll up through the vulgar combinations of emojis, seeing it's on the limited access floor with the gym, pool, and whatever else the chick at the desk said.

Playing rebel, I head down without bothering Colt to explore. It's the best I'll get for a while. I step off the elevator and into an open space with couches and lounge chairs, sitting areas scattered. Doorways surrounding the common area lead to the different amenities, and glass separates the gym. Off to one side, the documentary crew has left their equipment to set up in preparation for tonight.

I might have dodged solo interviews, but we've filmed two group ones. Remi always has instruments in the background, today no exception. I catch the neck of the acoustic and use the hotel's piano in the corner to tune it before dropping onto an oversized couch.

My eyes are closed while I play, just following the notes. I haven't been at it long when I hear a, "Uh, Adams."

I internally sigh and then look at Remi. She's near the set where her other two crew, Glory and Nate, are starting to assemble lights.

"I just wanted you to know we're here," she says.

Despite the audience, I stay. Her gaze flits to me more than once, and I feel the craving building inside her. The next time she looks, I'm waiting. I hook my head, and she doesn't hesitate to grab her camera. She settles on the side of the L-shaped couch.

I continue wandering through whatever feels right while she films without audio. It slowly starts to morph until it sounds familiar. I'm unsure what it even is at first, but then I shift down on the fretboard. As soon as I change keys, muscle memory kicks in.

Remi moves off to the side, and when I glance over, she's lowered her camera.

Sad eyes stay on me while I play an unfinished song. A song I've played for her before. I squeak the strings at the end and set the guitar on a cushion between us.

"You get what you want?" I ask.

She nods. "It was perfect."

I nod back, standing, walking away before I say what I'm thinking—she was.

OVER THE NEXT THREE DAYS, Felix, Dev, and I spend more time in the common area than on our own floor. The place has been a ghost town. Perfect for us to slap on our metaphorical scuba tanks and dive down into the creative depths.

"Colt Breaks" included. He checks, so we comply.

We will leave on Friday for San Diego, benefit on Saturday,

and by the time we finish packing up Thursday, I truly believe we can pull off an album by tour's end. I'll work on an idea swimming in my head while Dev's in Arizona. I won't be surprised if he has something of his own when he gets back. The guy's best ideas have come from him raw-dogging a flight. Just him and his thoughts.

And it might shock people to their cores, but the piano in the corner will call to Felix. He's classically trained. If we write lyrics first, he can rework a melody a dozen different ways until they sync. So long as no one watches. He's a bashful little thing.

While they go to dinner with Christian, all of them needing a few hours out of the hotel, Colton and I go to the gym. He hooks up his phone to the speakers and blares what I've dubbed his high-schooler weightlifting playlist.

My lips twitch as he turns around, and he flips me off. We go hard on the weights for about half an hour before he shoves me toward the treadmills. He hops on the one to my right and immediately sets it higher than mine. So, I kick it up because it's what we do.

We'd end up at a dead sprint if the door didn't open. The mirror in front of us shows Remi walking in behind us. She and I haven't spoken directly since I played for her before our last show. It seems we've fallen into a wordless truce around one another. Not that I've seen much of anyone outside the main dickheads, but when she has popped up, she films me, and I let her.

Like now. Our eyes meet in the reflection, and spotting the camera in her hand, I nod. Her mouth perks up instantly. "I only need a few minutes."

Colton and I settle on a sustainable speed until she finishes. My eyes flick to her in the mirror within seconds, but then everyone's attention shifts to the door. I scoff as Wannabe waltzes in, dressed for a workout. He flashes a surprise grin—the surprise part utter bullshit—toward Remi.

"I was curious where you'd wandered off to," he says.

She forces a small smile. "I wanted to take advantage before everyone leaves tomorrow."

With the short notice, we're not bringing the crew. I prefer it. For obvious reasons.

Xander lowers the volume on our music, and Colton serves me side-eye for it.

"The plan still to play catch-up the next few days?" he asks her, walking toward us.

She nods. "I fell behind on reviewing footage, and Heath and I have a call."

The second Xander steps on the treadmill beside me, I'm out. I slap mine off and cross toward the fridge of waters. The same competitive look appears on Colt's face as earlier, spotting new competition.

"Are you staying in Austin for Thanksgiving or going home?" Xander asks.

Our gazes catch for a second across the room as I open the glass door for a bottle, but I look away, unscrewing the lid.

"No, I'm staying here," she says.

"What about Christmas?" He pants but not enough to shut him up. "My mom's already bugging me about my plans. I told her it depends on if we're doing like last year with your dad coming to our place."

I almost choke on the water, jerking the bottle away and locking onto Remi.

Straight panic floods her eyes. No fucking clue what pours from mine when they meet, but nothing makes sense. "Your dad?"

The words aren't even audible, but her face pales at them. She rips her head toward Xander. "I don't know," she rushes out. "I'll see you later."

Remi almost runs out of the room, avoiding looking at me as she pushes out the door. I blink after her for a moment, fight through the dissonance ricocheting through me. And then I'm setting down my water, already moving, doing what I said I'd never do again. I'm going after her.

"Remi," I call once out the door. She ignores me, walking fast to the elevator, but I chase her down. "Remi." I beat her to the button, planting myself between it and her. "What the fuck?"

"I…" Her head shakes, tiny, quick movements, while she stares up at me.

My focus lifts over her head toward the gym before I tug her by the hand through the doorway to the movie theater and around the corner. I let her go behind the back row of luxury chairs. The dim lighting's enough to see her, chest rising and falling faster.

I walk to the wall, jaw clenching. My pulse races, mind a goddamn mess. She wraps her arms around her middle on my way back, and I duck in close to her.

"Your dad's alive?" I ask, voice low but steeped in disbelief. "Why the *fuck* would you lie about that?"

"No." She takes a half-step toward me but stops, brows knitting together. "I didn't lie, Foster. I swear."

"Then what, Remi? Because right now, I have no idea if anything you've ever said was true."

"It was."

"Make me believe it then. Tell me why Xander claims to have met your dad."

Her hands fall to her sides, fists tight, gaze imploring me.

"Tell me," I repeat.

She closes her eyes. "I can't do this now. I'm sorry."

Then she turns to leave. But I can't let her. I can't fucking stop. I can't keep it buried anymore, everything swirling in the air around us, hot and stifling.

"I know your mom's dead, Remi."

She freezes, and I step in front of her again, waiting until she looks up at me. Light reflects off the tears welling in her eyes as they bounce between mine. I stare down into them.

"When you stopped answering, I went after you. I tracked

down your stepdad's house," I tell her. "I know you ran off with that guy. Your mom's ex. Your friend." I swallow past the bite, and now I'm imploring her. "I need to understand, Remi. I saw the SD card in your camera bag, but … why is Xander talking about your dad spending Christmas with you?"

Her chest rises slowly, inhale shaky, and she lowers her gaze. "My dad died when I was eleven. Xander was talking about Roman."

I stare at her, silence encasing us while I struggle with her words. The past rearranges between us, certainties vanish, and doubts reemerge.

"Remi," I say, fucking lost. But she looks it too, sad eyes, panicked eyes, the broken girl. It all feels wrong again. Like when I stood in the house that wasn't her home.

"I need the truth—from you." I step closer. Of all the *why*s I've wanted to ask, this wasn't one. I didn't need to ask because I knew. But now, I need to *really* know. "Why did you disappear on me?"

She blinks up at me, right before changing everything. "Because he killed her."

29

REMI

Before...

THE THRUM of my pulse intensifies as I hit send on the picture to Foster. The all-of-me picture.

And he promised to send his back.

I smile, clutching my phone and closing my eyes.

Yeah, it's over for me. I'm done for him.

The flutters and tingles carry me up the trellis. I toss my bag by the bed, strip off my coat, and fall back on the mattress. While waiting for his reply, I scroll through our messages as a distraction. One stands out from the rest.

FOSTER

You're dangerous, Remi Saint.

Shit. He still thinks it's Saint and not Sinner. I blame him, though. It's his own fault for distracting me with everything him the past few weeks. I could forget the whole world with how he takes over my mind.

Returning to my picture at the bottom, I consider whether to clear it up now or wait for his text. Before I decide, I hear a noise from downstairs. My gaze trains on the door as I wait for another.

Shouting breaches the pillows.

My gut twists, overshadowing the Foster high, and I sit up, listening for more. Only nothing else breaks through.

The tear inside me happens anyway, forcing me to make the choice all over again. Little girl or me.

I keep waiting for another sound. At least a few minutes pass before I get up. My screen's dark. Foster hasn't responded yet. I hope he doesn't for a little longer, so his real doesn't tangle with this reality.

A reality I'm a week from escaping.

Tucking my phone into my skirt, I kick the pillows out of the way, tired of not knowing. I ease the door open and quietly step into the hall, to the banister. As I grip the wooden railing, I scan the living room below. It looks like it often does—a lamp knocked over, picture frame on the floor, the fireplace tools scattered like they were thrown.

Except one thing doesn't match all the other times.

My mother's unmoving on the floor in front of the fireplace. She's wrong, though. Blood runs from her nose and a gash to her forehead, but it also soaks her top and covers her exposed skin. It absorbs into the rug from what has pooled on the hardwood around her.

"Mom," I shout, already running down the stairs.

I land on my knees beside her body. Because that's what I'm looking at—my mom's body.

Fuck, fuck, fuck. I check for a pulse. But I already know, blinking rapidly at the puncture wound on the other side of her chest just above the neckline of her sweater.

Then I see the blood on the fireplace's hearth. The poker lying on its side, pointed tip wet and darkened with more.

I look down again, and my hand falls away from where her pulse used to be. A sob bursts out of me, my stomach roiling.

"…take care of it."

My head jerks toward the kitchen—to the muffled voice.

Daniel appears from around the corner, on the phone. He stops when he sees me, surveying me on the floor, kneeling in blood. "Make sure Marlo's the unit they send to the house." He ends his call, and I can't breathe as he holds out a hand, gesturing to the body—the body. "I heard a crash on my way in from the garage. Someone was running out the front door, and … she was already gone."

I scramble to my feet as he steps forward, my skin throbbing with every pound of my heart.

"She was already gone," Daniel repeats, tone steady. So fucking steady while my body's near convulsing.

My eyes fall to the literal blood on his hands. "I tried to find the source of the blood and resuscitate her, Remi. The intruder attacked her. She must have fallen on the fireplace poker and punctured an artery."

My phone vibrates. Foster's text. His picture.

"The intruder," I say, voice weak and not steady, "who ran out the front door?"

He nods and comes closer, but I side-step the body and then back up to keep the distance between us. I dart my gaze over him —no holster, no gun. The next step he takes, I run for the front door.

I have to open it.

I have to open the door because no one else has run out of it or they'd have left it open like I do. No one else was in the house. Daniel never came in from the garage. He *never* comes through the garage.

Every other word is likely true. The attack. Mom landing on the fireplace poker and becoming the body.

But it was him.

Daniel shouts after me as I run down the street. I run until my lungs heave and my legs ache. But it's more. All of me gives out once I reach the town square. I bend over and empty the contents of my stomach. I continue to heave, even when nothing else comes up, like my body thinks it can purge what just happened.

My mom's dead. And Daniel killed her.

THEY PUT me in a room at the police station. An interrogation room with the two-way mirror and a camera in the corner. There's even a metal arch on top of a table where handcuffs attach. I have no idea how long it's been since the female officer, Julie, with the apologetic eyes, draped me in a blanket and left me alone.

She found me mid-panic attack on the freezing ground in the square. I was hyperventilating and violently shivering, and she helped me breathe, then helped me to her car. My mind felt as numb as my fingers when I stupidly let her put me in the passenger seat. Then she brought me here. To the one place I should have been going after finding my mom murdered. After seeing the body.

Except she hand-delivered me to the king's personal court. The gilded walls equally as rotten beneath as the ones I've wanted to escape. I can't escape.

And the longer I sit here—the more my body warms and my mind emerges from the fog—the sicker I feel again.

The door finally opens, and I'm not even surprised when toxins invade the air.

Elvin.

Julie reappears behind him, but she stays by the wall, letting him approach me.

He repeats what I stuttered to her through my useless breaths in the square. Only he phrases my convictions as questions, doubt veiling the words.

When Elvin stoops down in front of me, I recoil in the chair. But he takes my hands anyway. I close my eyes, tears spilling down my cheeks as he apologizes for what I witnessed.

"...it can't be easy to process ... our minds like to play tricks on us."

I struggle to breathe while he continues to try to convince me of what I know is a lie.

He knows it too. He just doesn't care.

The next time the door opens, I don't need to look as the footsteps enter, slow, steady, threatening.

"Are you okay, Remi?" Daniel asks, tone soft now. "I tried to go after you, but I ... I couldn't just leave her—"

An award-worthy sob leaves him. I draw in poisoned air before opening my eyes. Fresh clothes. Clean hands. At least that's what everyone else sees. Everyone except Elvin. And then Marlo when he walks in a second later, his hidden teeth showing in the once-over he gives me.

Julie shuts the door behind him, trapping us with the danger. The concern she aims at me seems genuine, but my gaze lowers to the tile floor.

"I found enough at the scene to bring the son-of-a-bitch in," Marlo states.

"Did you hear him, Remi?" When I don't answer, Daniel continues, "They've already caught the bastard who did this. Some addict piece of shit who terrorizes people for money. My guys spotted him only blocks from our house, tweaked out of his mind and talking to himself."

I didn't think my heart could hurt more, but it further breaks for the man.

They continue telling me the man's history of mental illness. A previous B&E charge.

Nothing worthy of this.

Tears are streaking again when Daniel grasps my arm, helping me to my feet. His fingers dig in enough to hurt before he gently rests his hand on my shoulder.

"I'm going to take her home—" His voice actually breaks, an audible inhale following. "I'm sorry she was so confused when she got here. I can't imagine the damage this caused." He squeezes while they talk around me.

Marlo steps in front of me as close as the night in the kitchen as he stares down at me. "You might want to have her talk to someone."

"I've already called Dr. Sood."

"A psych eval?" Julie asks sharply.

My eyes jerk up. "What?" They flash between everyone in the room, but Julie's the only one reacting. The others are part of the choreography and all hitting their marks.

"We'll see how she's feeling when we get out of here," Daniel says. "Hopefully, now that she understands what really happened, she can begin processing. We'll keep our options open. Whatever's best for my Remi."

I swallow against the acid churning in my stomach, feeling utterly helpless against his performance.

"It'll help when the trash is off the streets and behind bars." Elvin shakes his head off to the side, but his gaze shows the lie in his disgusted expression. "It'll help both of you, Chief."

My heart hammers harder as Daniel escorts me out of the room, handing Julie the blanket on the way. We walk through the precinct, officers lining the corridor in respect for their grieving chief. He guides me through the lobby. Out the door. The favorites trail right behind us.

Then Marlo opens the door to Daniel's cruiser, and I stop existing for a second.

"In you go, Remi," he says with a nudge.

My teeth chatter, but I force myself into the car. Marlo ducks in, reaching for the seat belt, so I grab it first, not wanting him touching me. He closes me in as Daniel slides behind the wheel. He gives a nod to the two officers and turns the engine over.

As we pull out of the lot, all the adrenaline from earlier assaults me at once. No one will know the truth—at least no one who isn't loyal. He'll get away with it. So long as he takes care of me.

"Do I need to take you to Dr. Sood?" Daniel asks, far colder without an audience. "Or are you going to accept what really happened?"

I don't answer. I can't answer. My mind races through scenarios, and all I know for certain is Daniel killed her. And the worst thing that can happen now is going back to the step-house with him.

Daniel's still talking, retelling me the story he created, trying to gaslight me when what I saw is brutally branded on my soul. I frantically scan out the windows. I need to run. I need to get out of this car and away from him.

I slowly sneak my phone out of the hem of my skirt, but Daniel pulls up to a red light and glances over.

He sighs. "I think it's best if you give me that, Remi. You're clearly not in your right mind, and I'd hate for you to embarrass yourself more than you already have."

My breaths grow flimsy, the surge of adrenaline somehow spiking higher.

It all happens at once. I swing at Daniel's face, hitting as hard as I can with my phone and unbuckling at the same time. The impact catches him off guard, so I have time to throw open the door. I scramble out of the car, a cry wrenching from me when I fumble the phone to the ground.

But I don't have time to grab it—even if I did, he has the tracker on, and I need to run, not mess with settings.

Daniel's cursing and shouting and out of the car. All I can do is sprint toward the park.

Going to the right place this time.

I cut through the park, and the sound of Daniel raging fades. My lungs ache by the time I reach the other side, finally letting myself check behind me.

Nothing.

He's nowhere in sight as I tear down the street.

Icy wind seeps into my bones as I run, and then I see the police SUV parked up ahead and push harder. Even his unit panics me, but I dash up the sidewalk past it. I pound on the door, shivering and shaking. It jerks open. Hot tears flood my eyes, searing down my face.

Roman's nostrils flare, his jaw grinding when he grabs for me. "Fuck, Rem," he says, pulling me inside.

The door slams, and my face is already buried in his chest, fists clenching the back of his shirt. I hold on to him for dear life.

"He … Daniel, he—"

"I know. I knew the second I heard the call go out, but I couldn't find you."

I don't even think it's a sob that rips out of me this time. It's more painful. A splintering rather than a tear inside. Like half of me has no purpose anymore, and the rest is more broken than ever.

"You're safe now. I've got you." Roman's chin rests on top of my head, arms locked around me. "I've fucking got you, pretty girl. He'll never touch you again."

30

REMI

Now...

I said the words aloud.

Sad maybe, but I've only cried them out, body racked in sobs. Words I've never calmly uttered, even to Roman, I gave to Foster.

I almost hyperventilated, ran away, and wretched in the toilet when I reached my room, but I said them. And I have a lot more I'll need to give him.

It's why I'm hiding on my balcony, curled up on the bench and wrapped in the bed's comforter. I cried for a while on the bathroom floor before brushing my teeth and then sat under the hot spray of water in the shower for a long time. I need to simply exist for a bit, feeling the feelings of all the scars torn open at once.

Because just like why I still avoid looking at my dad's SD card, admitting what happened to my mom makes it final. Even after all this time.

At least it was Foster.

The city of Austin stretches below me through the glass, extending for what looks like forever. I sit long enough my hair's only damp when I fully return, both mind and body, and check my phone. I want the time but end up with something else.

Something better or worse, or both.

> Hey, Remi.

Better.

My eyes close at the text from twenty minutes ago, the number unknown but not the sender. I respond the only way I can.

> Hi, Foster.

His next message reminds me how Foster West rarely fights fair. I see part of his arm at the bottom of the picture, resting on top of the glass surrounding his balcony, and a gorgeous fountain in the lit courtyard below. A small smile forms while the sadness recedes a little. Like the last time he showed me a fountain.

I show him my view and then wait. When he calls, I can almost see his reflection in the window, phone in front of his face. I answer with the camera pointed at the comforter, then flip it to the cityscape. His goes from the gray of his shirt to the fountain.

He doesn't say anything. He doesn't push. He's just here. And eventually, I blow out a breath.

"I'm sorry. I'm so sorry, Foster. I should have told you when I saw you again in Prague. Or at the label before we left. I let you think I wanted to…" My gaze falls, like by not looking at the screen, I'm not looking at him. "What happened really fucked me up. At some point, I started forcing myself to not think about it so it wouldn't eat away at me all the time. Then I refused to remember and hid from it. I needed to try and erase it to get my life back."

"I'm sorry, Remi," he says, soft and deep. "I didn't know how she died, only that it was sudden. I hate you went through any of it. And you don't owe me anything. When I—" He cuts off but then, "I'm just fucking sorry."

I swallow, finding myself wanting to talk when I expected a need to retreat. "I found her after sending you my picture but before you replied. Daniel was already orchestrating to cover it up, and no one would believe me. Hell, half of the cops in that town likely helped pin it on the poor homeless guy they were setting up."

I tug at the corner of the comforter and mess with the tag. "I have no idea what he would have done if I stayed. I dropped my phone, getting away from him. Probably for the best. He had a tracker app installed and might have caught me if I tried shutting it off while running." My eyebrows dip, a wave of guilt crashing over me. "Not that it mattered in the end."

"What do you mean?"

I almost have more trouble with these words than the others. This memory of why I almost didn't go to NYU. Why I barely left my dorm room until I became Heath's TA. Why I still panic anytime I see my name in credits or anywhere for that matter.

"You don't have to tell me anything. I meant what I said, you owe me nothing. We can stop talking about it if you want."

"I know," I say, snuggling deeper into the blanket.

It's why I want to try.

"Roman's friend had a house outside of Columbus where he got sober way back when. Bea still let Roman use it whenever. We figured Daniel would be looking, so he took out cash on our way, then he avoided credit cards and drove hours to different ATMs anytime he needed more. He even sold his car and paid cash for one in Bea's name. All these precautions to protect me."

Shockingly, I have more tears left, but I blink them away. What happened was my fault. My guilt to carry.

"The first week, I cried and slept. But by the second, I was so fucking angry, Foster. He stole everything from me without consequence. My mom was dead, and I'd never see my dad's SD card. I missed Sage and you. God, I missed you."

He moves, the angle lowering as he sits down, but I still see the fountain.

"I was too scared to even log in to anything since he had my phone. Then one day I broke. Roman mostly only left for groceries or cash—even then I'd freak out until he came back. But he went to lunch with Bea, and I took the car, going back to Ashfield."

"I was there twelve days after I last heard from you," Foster says.

My heart aches when I tell him, "I was there thirteen after."

"*Fuck*. If I'd have known—" He sighs, not finishing the thought. But I'm betting he would have been there a day later because I would have gone a day earlier if it meant seeing him.

"I made sure Daniel wasn't there. His car was at an officer's house who helped him. So, I parked several blocks away and climbed up the trellis. The window was still unlocked, my room untouched. I only wanted the SD card and to find my phone. I could delete the app or at least get your and Sage's numbers, but it wasn't there." I shake my head. "I couldn't bring myself to leave my room to look anywhere else. The only thing keeping me from talking to you again, and I couldn't fucking open the door. Knowing I'd walk into the hall and see where…"

I said the words once, but I avoid them.

Foster shifts. "There's no shame in that, Remi. I can't imagine what it must have been like. You'd already been through so much. It was brave to even go back inside that house."

"Yeah, and it ruined everything." I pause, enduring the guilt. "I thought I was careful, but Daniel must have followed me because three days later, two of his guys showed up."

The favorites. Elvin and Marlo. He let them off their leashes, both more terrifying than I gave credit for.

"What happened?" He strives for calm, but concern seeps in, something else too. "Did they hurt you?"

"No." I find the tag again, ready to rip it to shreds. "I was in my bedroom when they broke through the window. There was a covered access panel in my closet. Bea said it was for utilities, and I crawled inside to hide—essentially between the closet wall and the living room's. They searched the house, but it sat off the floor, and with the random clothes hanging, they must have missed the cover."

"Fuck."

"They hurt Roman, though," I admit. "They beat him, calling him the most heinous shit, telling him what they'd do when they found me. I was literally on the other side of the drywall. I heard them and Roman and when they cocked the gun." I stop, needing a second, and Foster stays quiet.

The memories don't even feel like mine. I'm watching the terrified girl, hand covering her mouth to keep from making noise, tears rolling over the back of her hand.

"One of them tore through the house again. They kept trying to force Roman to tell them where I was, but eventually, they called Daniel. I guess killing only one of us would make it harder to cover their tracks. They put him on speaker and let him personally threaten Roman. Warned if he so much as heard whispers of either of our names again, he'd go after Sage and Roman's parents. He also swore to make it worse for me and make Roman watch before he killed us."

"Remi." It's all he says, silence floating between us for a second.

"I was so stupid, Foster. I avoided him tracking my phone, I never accessed accounts, Roman went through so much to steer clear of a paper trail. And then I led them straight there to nearly kill him. I don't know how. I was so paranoid driving back and constantly checking behind me."

"It's not your fault," he rasps, and the sadness in his voice hurts me too.

Roman said the same thing, and I didn't believe him either.

"Either way, I couldn't put his life at risk like that again. The chance of them going after anyone because of me terrified me. I barely existed for a long time, having panic attacks all the time. Even after Roman moved us to New York, registered me for classes at NYU, and forced me to attend. Then I took Heath's class, and he gave me no choice but to be out in the world." I half-smile, remembering the hell he put me through, but I'm so grateful for the man. "I still had panic attacks when he first booked a flight with my name or when he credited me in a video. Eventually they stopped. And I let myself look for the beautiful things again."

He stays quiet long enough I wonder if I dumped too much. I don't think I would have if it were anyone else. I don't think I could have, but with Foster ... he's him.

"I'm sorry you lost so much. I'm sorry anyone made you feel like you had to make such an unfair choice. I'm sorry—fuck. I'm just sorry."

I watch the fountain, the water cascading, the light and shadow.

"I would have hidden with you."

"I wouldn't have let you," I whisper.

He sighs, standing up. "Yeah, but I wouldn't have cared."

I know.

After he walks into his room, he shuts the sliding glass door. "I need to go. I have something to do."

I fight the dip in my stomach. "Okay. Night, Foster."

The call ends, and I lift my face to the sky, feeling less raw. Not better enough to run and tell the world and plaster my name on billboards with my coordinates, but a little more healed with him knowing I didn't want to leave him behind.

I gather the comforter, staying wrapped as I go inside. I haven't even reached the doorway to the bedroom when Foster texts.

Fuck, I missed that. Missed him.

The video shows a carpet matching mine, gliding over it until Foster opens a door, steps into the hall, then he walks down it, turns to stop at another door.

"Let me in, Remi."

Flutters. Tingles. A reemerging fever.

When I swing it open, Foster looks up, his forearm braced on the doorframe. He straightens and steps over the threshold until he's right in front of me. His fingers hook under my chin, tipping it up, and his lips lower to mine.

A relieved breath escapes me, and he kisses me harder in response. Like he's been as desperate for this as me.

Because nothing feels different about us this time. Instead, we're how we were always meant to be.

He shoves his hand into my hair, backing me farther into the room. The door slams shut behind him as his tongue dives into my mouth. I let the comforter spill to our feet so I can run up his chest to the back of his hair, pulling him deeper.

His chest vibrates in a husky groan, and he frames my face with his hands. Cool blue eyes draw me in even more when Foster rests his forehead on mine, his body pressing closer. Skin hot against me.

"I need to make sure you understand how sorry I am, Remi. I've acted like a dick, and you haven't deserved any of it."

"I thought you hated me," I say softly.

"I thought so, too, before."

"Before what?"

"Before hearing your name again. Before I looked offstage and saw you. Before I touched you, kissed you, breathed you. Before now, when I can finally admit to both of us what a fucking liar I've been every second since I lost you. The truth is, I've been wrecked over you all along."

He kisses me again, swiping the fresh tears away with a sweep of his thumbs.

"Christ, I missed you," he mumbles against my mouth. "I knew something was missing. It was you. It was always you."

Then his tongue's dominating mine, and I slide up his shirt. He rips it over his head and crushes his lips back to mine long enough to grasp the bottom of my top. He breaks away while he pulls it off.

His hungry gaze rakes over me. He grips my sides, brushing the pads of his thumbs over my peaked nipples, and my eyelids flutter closed.

Foster's mouth drags up the column of my neck, and his teeth graze my earlobe. "Say no, and we—"

"Yes." I tangle my fingers in the back of his hair. "The answer's yes to everything. Yes, yes, *yes*," I hiss the last one as he pinches both nipples.

"That's a dangerous game, baby." He skims his lips over my skin until they ghost mine, palms sliding to my waist. His pupils have blown wide, the sea of black inside the blue. "I just might ask for everything."

I think the answer would be yes anyway.

My breaths shallow as he walks me backward through the room until the cool wall beside the glass balcony door presses to my bare back. He squeezes my ass as he grinds into me, then he's kissing over my jaw and working his way down.

When he trails across my breasts and sucks my nipple between his lips, a whimper escapes me. He switches to the other, using his teeth, while pushing my sweatpants off my hips. He lowers with them to his knees, and his hands already glide up the fronts of my thighs to my panties. Eyes on me, he drags the flat of his tongue over the fabric. Slow and hot.

Cursing, I thread my fingers through his hair. The tips on the other squeak over the glass beside me as his hot breath continues to tease through the material. His thumbs slip under the edge, and he guides them down my legs.

I barely step out of them before his arm hooks under my thigh, draping it over his shoulder.

"Fucking finally."

He licks through my wet pussy to my clit and latches on. He sucks hard, causing me to moan. I drop my head against the wall, both hands tight in his hair.

"Foster," I breathe out.

He groans and shifts me higher. It pushes me onto my toes, spreading me wider for him. He rolls his thumb over my clit as he thrusts his tongue inside me.

"Oh my God."

He hums against me. "Nah, baby. I got the praying handled. I'm already on my knees, worshipping your heavenly cunt."

My eyes roll skyward anyway as his mouth returns to my clit. He grazes it with his teeth, causing me to clench around the finger he slides into my pussy. I moan and rock my hips, but his arm bars over my pelvis to halt my movements.

I whimper, desperate to grind against his face and tugging at his hair.

"Words." Stubble scrapes my inner thigh before he bites hard enough to sting, and I gasp. "You want something, you ask for it."

"More," I rush out. "I want more of your fingers fucking me."

His lips curve up, his eyes on me. "Such a good girl." He drives in another, pumping in and out while his tongue swipes over my clit. Then he stretches me with a third, and a broken sound tears out of me.

And all I can do is feel every lick and suck and stroke. The sensations twirl together, mixing with the sight of him watching my face from between my legs.

Foster's rough, demanding control, but he looks at me with such reverence. In a way that's always been right.

"You want to come?" he asks.

I nod. "*God yes.*"

"Ride my face and fingers." He moves his arm, switching to his palm flexing on my thigh. "I want you running down my chin while you scream for me, Rem."

His mouth seals over me, and my eyes roll back.

"Fuck, Foster."

I writhe against him, not even needing to chase the pleasure. He sends it shooting through me, white, hot. My back arches off the wall as I come. But Foster's relentless, sucking on my pulsing clit until I give him what he wants and cry out for him.

Shudders rack my body, and just as it becomes too much, he lets up.

"Holy shit."

I fight for breath, fingers still dug into his hair while his withdraw. Foster licks through my pussy and groans and drags his tongue over me again for more.

When my leg slides off his shoulder, he kisses up my body, and then his hips pin me there.

His mouth crashes into mine. My lips eagerly part so I can taste myself on his tongue, and I moan, feeling his erection pressed into me. Skimming my hands from his neck, down his chest, and over his abs, I palm him through the fabric.

Foster growls and hauls me with him away from the wall. He spins us, steering me backward to the bedroom with his hand sliding up to my throat. My legs bump into the bed.

"Fuck me," I plead.

I push his sweats and boxer briefs down, freeing his cock.

I lick my lips, remembering how it felt thrusting between them.

It's always looked intimidating. Except, through a screen, I could easily convince myself his size wouldn't be a problem—just a dick.

Having him fill my throat on the bus changed the game. But I loved it. I'm more than willing to let him split me open.

Foster groans as I stroke up and down his shaft. "Tell me you have a condom."

I shake my head. "I wasn't going to sleep with anyone while on tour with you. And I didn't think…"

"Me either." He skates his lips down my neck and sucks on my collarbone, thrusting into my hand. "I can go for one, though."

"Or not," I say. "I'm on birth control."

His cock jerks in my palm. "Fuck, Remi. Ask me. Ask me to fuck you bare."

I've never had sex without a condom, never considered it, but with him it's not even a question.

"I want you inside me, skin on skin."

Barely letting me finish, he lifts me and climbs onto the bed. My back hits the mattress, legs already locking around his waist as he comes down over me.

The head of his cock pushes between my pussy lips and nudges at my soaked entrance.

We're both panting, his denim eyes dancing over my face.

He flexes his hips, only pressing inside me enough for a taste of how his cock will break me open, then he retreats.

"Yes to everything," he rasps, teasing with another shallow thrust that leaves me aching for all of him. "So tell me, is this dripping cunt mine, baby?"

I clasp the back of his neck, hips rising in a chase for his. "Yes. Yes, now claim it."

A low growl rumbles from his chest, and he drives all the way in.

I cry out, stretched and filled by every inch, nothing between us. Nothing but everything. Face-to-face, flesh on flesh. Every nerve alights as my body yields to his.

Foster groans and slowly drags out before slamming back in. "Fuck."

With a rough grasp on my thigh, he starts pumping into me, so, *so* deep as he bottoms out. I'm already hooked on the sensation radiating through me each time, clawing at the rippling muscles in his back for more.

"Christ, you feel perfect wrapped around my cock. Tight and hot and taking it like such a good girl." He scrapes his teeth over my jaw before he grasps it, his forehead pressing to mine. "You're fucking ruinous, Rem."

His kiss is ravenous. Teeth and tongue and *him*.

He fucks me harder, his thrusts merciless while I meet every one.

It's all-consuming, the two of us finally sating the only craving we couldn't back then.

And it still doesn't feel like enough.

When Foster dips down to nip my breast, he pulls out and rolls us. My knees hit the mattress on either side of his hips. One of his palms roams up my thigh while his other hand's in my hair, our panted breaths mingling.

"I want the full view when you come on my cock. Show me. Use me."

He tugs at my bottom lip with his teeth, and I plant my palms on his chest. Sitting up, I grasp his thick shaft and drag his head through my wet center. He roughly grips my hips, fingers tightening as I sink down onto him. All. The. Way.

"God, Foster," I choke out, feeling him in my stomach.

"There we go, baby." He thrusts up and hits a spot that sends my head back.

I moan as I begin to move. Foster flexes into me, a greedy gaze on my body while I ride him. Mine traverses the contours of his torso and up his chest. His abs contract as he guides my hips.

"Fuck, you look good spread around my cock." He watches where we're connected. "I knew you would, but *fuck*."

With his palm flat, he runs it up my stomach until he cups my breast. The bliss is ready to crest even before he pinches my nipple. Heat sparks in my core, and I arch my back, nails scraping over his pecs.

He brings his thumb to my swollen clit.

"Let me feel you strangle my cock while you come. Come, Remi."

The pleasure coils tighter and tighter as he adds pressure, then he thrusts into me hard, and I career over the edge.

"Yes," I cry out. "Yes, yes."

The word turns into an airy chant, all I have left with my mind fracturing. Foster growls as my pussy pulses around him. He grabs my ass and drags me up and down his cock, fucking me through every second. His thumb demands even more until I'm writhing and whimpering, utterly undone.

"So fucking good."

Then Foster flips me onto my back and drives back into me. His lips bruise mine, punishing and delicious. He moves me how he wants. He pins my wrists above my head and hooks my leg with his arm. It pushes my thigh to my chest, his thrusts deep and rippling through me.

My gaze traces the hard-cut lines of him, and then his nose

brushes mine, mouth not touching mine, but I feel every word nonetheless.

"You need to know, if I come inside you, I might never leave."

"I never want you to."

He kisses me hard, upping his pace.

His mouth presses to my neck, breath hot as his guttural groan works through my skin. The grip on my wrists tightens, and his cock pulses with his release.

Foster's hips slow, and he sinks all the way in one more time. He stays there and grinds against my sensitive clit. My hips jerk in response, and he lowers my leg, only to grind again, causing me to shudder.

"Foster," I sigh his name as he tortures me, tightening both legs around his waist.

"Mmm, Remi."

I hear the smile.

After freeing my hands, he brings his head up. Our chests rise together, heart-stopping blue eyes stare down at me.

My fingers follow his sculpted jawline until he pulls them to his lips and kisses them.

"You remember all those bad ideas I used to have because of you?" He drags my knuckles back and forth.

I nod. "You had so many."

"Yeah, well, this one is on you."

I narrow my eyes. "What was that?"

"Fucking you without a condom." Lowering my hand, he shifts, reminding me he's still inside me. Still hard enough to draw a soft moan from me when he gently thrusts. "Because filling you with my cum just became an obsession."

That should not sound as hot as it does.

Foster groans as he pulls out and then crashes onto his side next to me, bracing on a forearm. He traps a piece of my hair between his knuckles, slowly gliding down to the black ends. He studies them.

"I like this," he says, low and soft.

The strands fall as he trails down. His knuckles drag over my chest and breast and graze my nipple. He skims to the other.

"I really like these." He captures it and tugs. A whimper slips from between my lips, but he's already drawing a line from my sternum to my navel. The light touch sweeps back and forth, dipping a little every time.

"Anything else you like?" My pulse picks up again while he teases lower still.

The palm flattens over my pelvis, spanning all the way across. "Yeah."

His lips twitch, clear in his intent not to tell me.

When he looks up, I lick mine to shield a smile. His gaze moves from there, covering every inch of my face. Like he's finally letting himself look at me. And I trace my fingertips over the back of his hand and run the others over his bicep, touching him because I finally can. I can catalog each tattoo and ridge of him. He can lean down and taste me with his tongue.

For the first time, Foster and I have all the parts at once. We're truly together in the same place.

I'm living and breathing him after thinking I'd lost any chance. And there's nothing left to take it away again.

31

FOSTER

I was wrong.

Not a first, but by far the worst.

And as I stare at a dark ceiling, arms around Remi, her head and breaths on my chest, I'm trying to figure out how long I can keep her. How after all this time it was me who fucked everything. Me alone.

The one thing I could hold on to of her for all these years was sharing the blame.

Not anymore. Not ever.

Guilt's still there, though—and now I have even more to carry.

When my screen lights up, I reach for my phone on the nightstand. Our flight to San Diego leaves sooner than I want. Which is at all. The timing couldn't be less ideal.

I finally have her and need to go.

In the message Christian sent our group chat, he threatens to drag us out of our rooms if we aren't by the elevator in twenty minutes.

To avoid running into anyone in the hall, I need to get back to my room now. Until she and I talk, I don't want anyone else pushing or prying. A lot changed last night, but we still have jagged pieces to sort out.

At some point over the next two days, I need to bring the guys back to Remi's side. Even without the details, I know she's not responsible for what happened with the label. I likely called it with Wannabe.

Another piece.

I carefully shift out from under Remi and scrub a hand over my face, standing up. I redress and tap out a text to her while I return to the bed. If I wake her, I'll fuck her. As tempting as it might be, I hit send. Her phone lights as I lean down and kiss the top of her head. I straighten, stare down at her, and I'll find a way to keep her.

I can't let Remi go again.

Even if it means keeping the rest buried away for a little while. Just until I figure out a way to make her stay once she knows the truth. The whole truth.

VERY LITTLE COMPETES with performing for an amped-up crowd. The stage grows and the seats multiply, but the heart remains unwavering. I lived for it then, now, always.

Playing the benefit concert isn't any less potent of a high.

Between the crowd and those watching the live stream, they blow through all of our incentives for donating—they have all night. We started by playing behind a white curtain hung from the ceiling with lights behind us, casting our shadows for the crowd. It only fell after they hit the first goal. For the others, we each answered an audience member's question, only kept playing so long as they met secret mini-goals for a song, and matched everything raised through another.

Then they unlocked the stripped version of "Haunted" to finish out our set, and the donations are still pouring in as we walk off stage. Felix claps both hands on my shoulders from behind on our way down the stairs, but Dev jumps on his back, so I duck from under them.

They and Colt are planning some epic night I have no intentions of joining. I need to shower, and after coming down off the high, I want to try for at least a few hours of sleep before our early morning flight back to Texas.

We stop for photos with the fans who won chances to be backstage and interact with the camera streaming online for extra behind-the-scenes shots.

We're heading to our dressing room when someone shouts down the hallway. Sav Loveless comes bounding toward us, fucking beaming and ready for The Hometown Heartless to close out the show.

She slows once we turn around, walking the rest of the way. "I wanted to thank you again for helping last minute. You guys killed it."

"The way your team put this together is incredible," I tell her. "We should be thanking you for letting us be a part of it."

"Like it was even a question given the year you've had." She glances over her shoulder as a guy saunters up behind her. "Did you get 'Haunted'?"

He nods to her, then at us.

"This is Levi," she says. "He was on camera duty. I've wanted to hear an acoustic 'Haunted' since I saw the video of your Toronto show. I almost demanded it in my post. The song hits different—raw and moving. Mac Records should have been begging you for the unplugged version. Clearly, they're idiots—"

"Savannah."

She flits her gaze toward Levi. "Tell me I'm wrong."

His lips twitch, and she's back to us.

"We wrote it to be acoustic," Dev says, and Felix adds, "We wanted to release the original as a bonus track, but they shut it down, wanting to wait to maximize profits or some shit."

Sav throws a look at Levi that screams, *told you so*. But I'm stuck on what she said before.

"You were the one who posted the video and tagged us? Not your team?"

She nods, a smirk forming. "And I'm going to post this performance with a middle finger emoji, tagging Mac."

"She's not," Levi interjects.

Sav shrugs. "I should."

I chuckle. "Won't be mad if you do."

She smiles like she really might, and out of all the rumors about Sav Loveless, one is definitely true. She's a force.

"Savvy."

She and Levi both half-turn to Torren King down the hall. The bassist raises his arms and drops them.

"I think they want you, rock star," Levi says.

Sav's lips perk up, a familiar spark surrounding her. I bet the exact feeling courses through her as the one racing beneath my skin every time I'm about to go on stage.

We exchange goodbyes with Levi before he heads toward the rest of The Hometown Heartless.

"Enjoy the end of your tour." Sav starts backing away. "Whenever you're ready to stick it to Mac Records, you have my number."

"We do," I mumble as she turns around.

Her silver hair swings behind her as she jogs back to her band, and Felix slaps me in the chest, grabbing the front of my shirt.

"Did that just fucking happen?" he asks.

"No chance." Dev sighs and hangs his head. "It has to be group hysteria."

But I smile and knock Felix's hand away. "Nah, we're lucid. But you're right. It didn't just fucking happen." I spin and slap a grinning Colt on the shoulder on my way past him. "We made it fucking happen."

32

REMI

"Sinner."

I narrow my gaze at the meddling director glaring back at me through my laptop screen. "Heath."

The stare down continues until I consider the possibility of the call having frozen. But before I break first to check, Heath releases a pent-up sigh and relaxes into his office chair, finger to temple.

"So, you're still upset."

Still refers to the three-paragraph text I sent after talking to Xander about what went down with Heath and the label. I told him he was wildly off base, and if he'd bothered talking to me first, he could have saved himself the trouble of caring. He replied with: *I'll call Sunday. Be over it by then.*

"Yeah, I am." I sit back on my bed, pulling the computer onto my lap and leaning against the headboard. "You took into consideration everyone's input on me, my safety, and my working conditions *except* for mine."

He looks like he has plenty to say, so it surprises me when he says, "You're right."

I blink at him. "Wh-what? Is this a trap?"

"For fuck's sake." He rubs his temple like I'm giving him a

headache. "No, it's called introspection, Sinner. After twenty years in an industry full of abusive man-babies who think breathing is consent, you morally bottom out and act oblivious, or you assume everyone is a duck all the time. I made a call based on experiences with too many terrible fucking people. But you're right. I should have talked to you before anyone."

Twice he said I'm right, and twice I've feared someone might have a gun to his head. "Um … thank you?"

His gaze darts to the side and appears further annoyed once it returns. "Text me another essay, and I guarantee you'll never have another director credit in your life."

"He's lying," Jasmine calls from off screen.

I press my lips together to school my expression as his face tips to the ceiling.

"And that's why," he mumbles.

His gorgeous wife pops her blonde head in from beside him long enough to wink at me and kiss his cheek. Turns out, the director did have a metaphorical gun to his head this entire time.

Once she and her baby belly have gone, the unholy glare Heath unleashes on me is a warning, a threat, and possibly a curse on my soul if I say a word about it. But I wouldn't dare. The man slipped, showing he cares for me by overstepping with the label. He was dangerously close to humanity with an almost-apology. Buried deep in there might have even been a near admission of respect.

The tiniest push and he may implode.

"I'll be sure to make my point succinctly in the future."

"Great. Fan-fucking-tastic. Now, do I need to hold your hand to get the Adams interview or can you do us both a favor and fucking nail it down?"

"There will be three Adams interviews by the end of the tour. The only hand you need to hold is Jasmine's in the delivery room. Who else will scowl and terrorize the birthing center staff if not you?"

I tack on a grin he ignores completely.

"The first two better not take until then," he says. "After you get those and the last of your main shots once the break is over, you don't need to stay on the road. With Xander there, your crew can finish up and send you the footage."

The comment catches me off guard, the plan being I remain on tour until the very end. "I can't leave before New York. I need to conduct the third solo interviews after their last concert."

"So, you meet the band in New York for the wrap interviews or fly out to LA." Heath grabs his phone, his interest waning.

I shake my head. "I'll probably stay. Who knows what shot we might miss."

"I don't care what you do, Sinner. Just don't fuck it up." Without looking, he reaches forward to end the call, but he stops and glances up. My mentor's jaw appears ready to crack until he forces out, "I'm glad I was wrong. Tell me if it changes."

The video blacks out before I manage words. Probably a good thing because I can deal with heartless prick with a god complex Heath Erickson all day long. But I am ill-equipped for whoever I talked to just now.

I return to reviewing footage, nearly caught up. Heath was technically right. Other than three key shots and a handful of self-indulgent ones—I still haven't used the projector—Glory, Nate, and Xander could complete shooting for the last month of the tour. It would clear me up to start assembling raw footage and structure the story.

But I have two reasons to stay. Foster is obvious. The other is a vibes thing I can't explain. When I worked on the documentary for Sound Clash, I went in with a solid plan. I left with a completely different one because of moments I couldn't have anticipated.

The all-girl punk band I ended up centering the experience around, I bumped into while the first band played. They were neon colors and feathers and giggles. I fell in love with them.

I only asked the guitarist to wear the spy glasses during their set, but they continued swapping them off all weekend. What they captured changed the story I wanted to tell. All the way down to the final minutes.

You never know when a tiny detail can shift a perspective. Leaving the tour early, I might miss one.

Needing more than the same two rooms and a balcony, I pack up and move down to the hotel's lobby.

The band flew in this morning, and the private floor is a prime spot for them to hang and write. If they want to avoid me, I won't force myself on them.

I have no idea if anything changes now. Things with Foster still feel fragile, but more in a *what comes next* sort of way. We haven't talked about what anything from the other night means. He left before I woke up the other day, and outside of a few texts, I haven't heard from him. Understandable with their stop in California, followed up with the benefit concert.

His last text said he had a few things he needed to do today, but tonight, I was all his. I'm trying to not fall too hard over it, even if it feels like I'll succumb to the Foster-induced fever faster the second time around.

I set up with my laptop, sinking into a cozy armchair in a tiny nook near the elevators.

After an hour, a shadow falls over me. Then a disappointed sigh.

"Have you left the fucking hotel since we got here?" Colton asks.

"I don't stop, remember?"

When I look up, he half-smiles. "Adams told us you weren't behind the shit the label pulled."

I shake my head. "It was a misunderstanding that got out of control. No one's come close to crossing my boundaries. If they did, I'd have said something, and I know it wouldn't have happened again. You guys are all your own levels of douches, not creeps."

Colton nods, then squints. "On the douche hierarchy, where am I? Specifically in regard to Adams. More douchey or less?" He breaks into a full grin when I glare and dips his chin toward my laptop. "You're done working. It's time for some mandated chill time."

"What are we doing?" I ask, realizing how much I missed him. The easiness.

He shrugs and walks to the elevator. "Put your shit away and find out."

FOR THE FIRST time since leaving LA, I ride in the front seat of a car rather than the back of a van or Uber.

Colton drives us to a different part of Austin in the flashy little coupe he rented. Much more residential with the cozy neighborhood vibe. Kids even dart out of the street to let us through, kicking a soccer ball to the middle again once we pass.

When he pulls into a cul-de-sac, he parks in front of the gorgeous Mediterranean house nestled at the end. Shrubs line the walk, a balcony on each side, and it even has a turret. I climb out, already seeking out the details before shutting the door.

"And this is why you left the camera." Colton steps on the curb and turns back, hands on his hips. "Can you drool over the arches on the inside at least? Maybe if you're really good, I'll let you foam at the mouth over the rooftop patio later."

I toss him a look on our way up the drive. "I have a feeling I'll like your brother more than you."

He snorts. "Insulting, honestly. I'll remember you said that."

A metal gate leads to an outdoor entry. On one side sits a smaller structure, but I follow him through the double doors into the main house on the other side. We step into an airy kitchen, opening to the living room. A brunette glances over her shoulder from the couch and grins.

"My favorite of the brothers," she says.

The elbow to my arm is *not* subtle, Colton nearly knocking me down.

She rounds the end of the couch with a smile, sneaking a side hug that ends with a hard smack to his stomach that makes him grunt. "I saw your gift, asshole." She nails him with a look and then swings to me. "It's a lamp shaped like a woman's ass that you turn on and off by slapping it."

"Oh, come on, Val. You can't be jealous of a lamp." He grins, very proud, and then he tips his head my way. "This is Remi. Remi, Valeria. My brother's hostage."

She rolls her eyes before melting into a smile. "Hi, Remi. Feel free to escape back in here when you need wine." She darts her gaze to the double doors. "The birthday boy is *out there*." Her nose scrunches in mock disgust, and I like her. "The cake will be here in twenty, along with your parents."

Colton nudges me the way we came, and we cross to the other set of doors. They bring us into another kitchen space, smaller with an adjacent sitting area, but he keeps going through the large archway.

We walk down a short ramp into a den-like room. The mounted TV takes up most of a wall, and a sectional lines the other two on that side of the room. It's covered in throw pillows, all with cross-stitched phrases.

"*Boning up the wrong tree*," I read off one.

Colton snorts. "I lean more toward, *When it comes, it pours*."

"*Better late than pregnant*?" I ask.

"Careful. Too much bro-spiration at once is dangerous."

I spin to a guy by the pool table on the other side of the room. He has short dark hair and a familiar look to him—a similar bone structure to Colton and something else.

"My brother," he says, tossing his stick on the felt.

"Happy birthday, dickhead." Colton meets him halfway and leans down to give him a hug in his wheelchair. The exchange includes very aggressive backslaps on both parts.

"Now move. She's hotter than you."

Colton shakes his head but steps aside, and his brother rolls over. He stops in front of me, brows dipping and eyes narrowing.

"This is Remi." Colton stops beside him. "She's directing the band's documentary."

His brother's features smooth out and morph into a grin, almost conspiratorial and tug, tug, tugging. "She's fucking Remi. And she's shooting the documentary."

He says my name like he knows it. I swear I know the way he says it too. Wait…

"Glad you can retain simple sentences," Colton mutters, then he tells me, "Meet my older brother, Chase."

Chase smirks as the realization plows into me. My mouth opens, but nothing comes out, so I close it. My lips turn up instead. "Chase."

"It's an absolute pleasure to meet you, Remi," he says. Then his eyebrow perks up as a door opens off to the side of us. "Look who Colt brought for cake, my brother."

Foster stops mid-step, our eyes locking. My stomach swoops at seeing him and flips again when his gaze lowers over me.

"Shit." Colton winces. "Sorry, Adams. I thought you weren't sticking around long."

Foster stays on me another second, then switches to the others and moves to grab a beer bottle off the pool table's ledge. "I wanted to see your parents before I leave."

Chase glances between us with a curious squint and nudges his brother. "Val hides Christmas gifts in the garage attic. My money's on the ass lamp being there if you want to check."

Foster shoulder-checks Colton on his way toward the ramp, knocking him in that direction. They both walk up it as Colton chuckles.

"I'll be right back, lioness," he calls on his way out.

The door barely closes before Foster reappears with a second beer. His sight is set on me, and my pulse spikes, his heated stare consuming me while he strides over.

He holds out the extra beer for me. I take it once he's close enough. Then he's grasping the side of my neck, pulling my lips to his. They part when his tongue demands it, diving in to stroke mine, and a satisfied sound vibrates in his throat.

Foster claims my mouth like he needed it. I needed it too, a promise everything from the other night is real.

His thumb brushes over my jaw, breath hot on my skin. "Hi."

"Hey." I smile, and he kisses me again.

"You never greet me like that," Chase says.

Foster's hand falls away, a sudden rigidness to him, and he turns to his friend. "Taste like her, and I'll start."

My cheeks heat at the grin spreading on Chase's face, and I take a swig.

"So." He crosses his arms but still points a finger between us. "You kiss her like that in front of me. Yet Colt called you Adams in front of her…" He lets out a surprised chuckle. "Little bro don't know?"

"No." Foster steps forward. "Keep it that way, asshole. It's complicated." He slaps Chase's palm, telling him, "If I don't catch your parents on the way out, tell them I'll stop by the house this week."

Chase nods. "See you in the morning for fishing."

"Can't wait to throw you off the boat." Foster smacks him in the back of the head. He ducks in to kiss my cheek, a noticeable dip in his mood. His fingers skim over my hand, lips still on my skin. "I'll see you later."

A shiver flits down my spine, and I flash a small smile. My gaze trails after him as he walks away.

Chase sighs. "I'm suddenly remembering how disgusting you two were."

I tilt my head at him and squint. "And I'm suddenly remembering you owe me a hundred bucks."

He shrugs, pushing backward and spinning around to the pool table. "I'll play you for it."

While he racks the balls, Colton returns—blue ass lamp in hand. Fitting since Chase proceeds to hand me my ass in pool.

"You were right," I tell Colton.

He spares a glance, pulling into the hotel's parking garage. "I already know this is a setup, so go ahead."

I shrug as he parks. "I didn't like Chase more than you." When he starts to smile, I open my door. "Valeria's so superior, neither of you even rank anymore."

The driver door shuts, and his eye roll is still going.

But I'm serious. Val rescued me from the bro-holes—her words, but they feel accurate. We went up to the rooftop patio, drank wine, and talked about all the things the guys never would. She's already texted me a list of spas and demanded I pick one for us to visit before we go back on the road.

Spending time with her was easy, even when we dipped into heavier topics. Nothing too deep, which I appreciated, but enough to remind me how lonely it gets sometimes.

I've always avoided the deeper connections. The ones where you share the bad and dark places. My last close-close friend was Sage, and I still kept a lot from her.

Foster's the only person who has it all.

Maybe telling him what happened back then is the next step forward I needed in reclaiming my life. Maybe it leads to pushing through the lingering fears. Maybe I'll tell someone else. Right now the idea of either has my skin crawling, a ball of anxiety lodging in my chest.

But I've conquered a lot the last two years. So, I'll take maybe one day as a win.

After wine, we caked. Several other people showed up to help Chase celebrate. I can't help but wonder if Foster left earlier to avoid a group. If he thought he needed to because of who he is to most of them.

When I met Chase and Colton's parents, they beamed over Adams. But the name didn't sound nearly as familiar from them as it should, given the subject lived with them as a teenager, which makes sense. They probably see Foster in private far more often than in public and don't use the stage name much.

Knowing him, he didn't want them to stress over it with other people around. Or draw attention from Chase. I just wish I could shake the feeling of his unease before he left having to do with me.

As I lean back against the elevator wall, Colton scans his card and presses the button for the private lounge floor.

"You're coming down, right?"

"I guess I am now." I hesitate. "Are Dev and Felix still mad at me? You said Adams cleared it up."

He rolls his head toward me. "We're all on the same page. We were assholes, but I hope you can see it from the band's point of view. Out of nowhere, they were told you felt sexually harassed. The label even made it sound like you were scared to be on the bus with us alone."

"I hate they did that. And I do understand. I wish you guys would have trusted me more, but I understand why you wouldn't. You thought I was a threat, so you circled the wagons to protect what the band has built."

Colton sighs and faces forward. "We circled the wagons, and I'm sorry it meant locking you on the outside. The entire thing hit a tender spot—especially for Felix."

Our gazes connect, the conversation we had about the drummer lingering between us. "Is he okay?"

"He'll be better when the outside world lays off for a minute. It's been almost two years of a nonstop push, and now he's having to fight his demons while under a spotlight."

"Demons made worse by the sexual harassment accusation?" I ask.

I'm fishing from a human place. Not a storytelling one.

"Them implying we would assault you," Colton says, looking over at me.

I nod and let it drop as the elevator doors slide open. The man in question's head tips back so he can see us coming from over the couch before dropping it down again. Dev's sprawled on a giant ottoman. His shirt's riding up, and he has a can of beer balanced on his exposed lower torso.

"You can only be here if you brought snacks," Dev calls.

He raises his brows, still reclined, and I round the end of the massive sectional. "I brought Colton. Does that count? He's delusional enough to think he's a snack."

Dev grins. Felix chuckles. And Colton barrels into me on his way by, swearing at us under his breath about being a whole damn meal.

Dev eyes me, and I can see the words working through him. But Felix is the one who stands, his jaw locked. He leaves his drink on the cushion, stopping in front of me.

"Adams said we're good, but I need to hear it from you." He has a softness in his voice he hasn't had before. At least not that I've heard. It extends to his expression, forehead tense and eyes searching mine for reassurance.

"We can be better than good if you want, Felix."

I half-smile, but he's still stoic.

"You swear to put us in our fucking places if you do ever feel like we're disrespecting you? Because we never want you to feel unsafe. Around us or in general."

"I swear." I hear the relief in his exhale as he nods. "And I want you to feel safe being your authentic self around me. So can you please go back to being a crass and obnoxious man-child?"

He smirks, his chin tipped up while he stares down at me, cocky and the Felix I know. "Who said I haven't been holding back this entire time, Cam Girl?"

I laugh, and he swipes up his drink before crashing onto the couch with it.

"What about me?" Grabbing his beer, Dev sits up and pushes his unstyled hair off his forehead.

"No," I say fast. "I can't stand the real you."

He squints, feigning offense with a huff. "Fine. I never liked you anyway."

His lips turn up on one side, and he winks.

Just like that, I'm accepted back into the pack and feel settled again. The only thing that could make it better is the wolf who's missing.

33

FOSTER

THE FOUNTAIN in the courtyard holds me in a trance.

My forearms rest on the glass surrounding my balcony, my head buzzing from the weed and bourbon. It's enough to help counteract the turbulence in there.

My truth shifted under my feet when Remi told me hers.

Mine shaped me. Molded me into who I am. Hers tears it all down, and now the painting I created has been scraped away, revealing one of contrasting colors underneath.

I'm replaying conversations and interactions. Doubting every move I made.

I finish the remaining bourbon and then take one more hit, holding it in until I straighten up. I drop the roach in the ashtray on the outdoor coffee table and abandon the balcony.

Dropping onto the couch, I swipe my phone from where I tossed it earlier. Chase texted me mid-introspection.

if Director = (fucking + Tour Remi), then Foster = (best friend - vital info)^(You Suck) + Asshole

I'm uncertain if his math is right, but he gets his point across regardless.

The reality is, I didn't plan on mentioning Remi to Chase at all —or Chase to Remi. Then the other night happened, and everything changed, and I haven't even finished figuring out what it means.

But fuck, if seeing her at Chase and Val's didn't make one thing abundantly clear.

Remi Sinner is absolute.

And exactly like I thought, I was wandering until I got to where I'm supposed to be. It's her. My endpoint has always been her.

> Like I said, it's complicated.

The response won't buy me much time, but I'll take what I can get.

I've no more than hit send when Remi sends a picture. A close-up of a door, part of the card scanner visible on the bottom right and two digits in the opposite corner. The last two in my room number.

I smile, shaking my head as I leave my phone and go to my door. When it opens, her eyes pop up, but mine detour down to her sage top. The straps meet behind her neck, and lace edges the low V in front. Add the bow tied right below her tits, and she's a gift in need of unwrapping.

My gaze returns to hers. "Eventually one of us is going to knock."

She hums, stepping closer until she has to tip her chin up, and I have to look down. "And ruin our streak?"

A smile plays at the corners of her mouth. I capture her around the waist, dragging her inside. She laughs, but my mouth connects with hers, and it morphs into a soft, sexy sound.

As ragged as the last three days have run me, kissing her surges me back to life.

I drop into one of the oversized accent chairs, cream to match the sofa, and she's already crawling into my lap to straddle me. My hands flex against the front of her thighs once she settles.

Her lips brush mine. "You taste like bourbon."

"Give me a few minutes, and I'll taste like you," I tell her.

She bites her bottom lip and looks down to where she's playing with the front of my shirt, but then the tiniest scrunch appears between her eyes. I free her lip with my thumb, stroke across it.

"What just happened? What thought did you have?"

"You seemed bothered earlier before you left."

When she flicks her gaze up, I read it easily. She thinks it's because of her.

"Not because of you, Rem." As much as I'd love to leave it there, doubt still lingers in her eyes. Mine lower. "A lot has changed since I last had you and Chase both in my life. The two of you meeting in person … You knew him before his accident. Seeing you together made me think about it."

My head falls onto the chair back, jaw tightening.

She softly says, "I'm sorry."

"I'm not." I run my knuckles down her arm. "I'll never be sorry to see you." I follow the bend up to her wrist and sweep over her pulse point. "I just fucking hate thinking about his accident. He fell and almost died. It still messes with me a little."

More than a little, but it's not her problem. I won't let it be.

The scrunch between her eyes returns, curiosity swimming as she studies me, and I worry how deeply she'll dissect. Through my flesh and muscle, down to the bone.

Before she has me cut open and exposed, I sit forward, clutching the back of her neck. "I also couldn't stay there and not touch you."

My thumb teases the denim over her pussy, and her lids fall heavy.

"Fuck," she whispers, and her chest rises faster.

"I couldn't not kiss you." I press my lips to hers and tease them open.

Remi grasps my hair as I thrust my tongue into her mouth. She moans into mine and ignites herself in my veins.

Starved for her skin, I strip off her top and bra, going straight for her perfect tits. I palm her breasts, kissing and sucking through her desperate whimpers. Her hips rock against my hardening cock, causing me to groan.

"Do you get it yet, Remi?" I ask, already working open her jeans and reveling in every sexy pant escaping her. "I can't be near you without having you every goddamn way."

She crashes back into me, kissing me like she understands perfectly.

I scoop her up and move her onto the chair before tugging off my shirt. And then I'm dropping to my knees in front of her, slipping my fingers into the waistband of her jeans. I peel them and her panties off and hook my arms around the backs of her thighs, her pretty pink pussy calling to me.

Remi gasps as I drag her to the edge of the cushion. "Foster— *fuck*."

My tongue parts her lips, licks from bottom to top, and then I devour her.

She tangles her fingers in my hair while I drag against her clit, and she moans. I coax another from her when I suck it into my mouth. A shudder racks through her, nails scraping my scalp.

I groan against her. "Jesus, you taste good."

I've wanted exactly this since I left her hotel room. Thought about having my face buried between her legs countless times.

She's already so fucking wet when I tease her entrance, and I hum in approval.

"Such an eager cunt, Remi." I dip two fingers inside her, causing her lips to part, her face to tip up.

I pump in and out and use the tip of my tongue to make tight circles on her clit.

"God, yes," she says on a ragged breath.

The desperate sound she makes next jerks my cock. When my eyes lift, she's biting her lip, hooded gaze on me without command. I've only been possessive over a fucking look when it comes to hers. But it fuels a primal desire to claim.

Remi whimpers at a light graze of my teeth. She moves her hips, the pulling at my hair rougher as she rubs against me.

"There you go, baby. Make yourself come."

She rides my face, taking, demanding, and I give, letting her, loving every second. I thrust faster, swiping and sucking on her clit. Her back arches off the chair, her pussy floods my hand as her climax hits. And her face is goddamn ethereal.

She melts onto the chair, and I kiss her trembling inner thigh before straightening. Even more of a flush appears in her cheeks while she watches me lick my fingers clean. So I drag it out. Make it obscene.

The color spreads, and she draws her legs up, the intention to close them.

"Not a chance." I catch her foot. My thumb runs along her instep, and I lean in, hooking her leg around me as I draw a peaked nipple between my lips.

"Fuck," she hisses, clutching onto the back of my neck.

She wraps her other leg around my waist, and her drenched pussy drags over my abs. I groan, my dick rock-hard and aching to sink into her.

"Turn around." I stand, flicking open the button on my jeans. "On your knees."

As she moves to her knees on the cushion, I shove down my jeans with my boxers and step out of them. My eyes eat up every curve of her form, and I fist my shaft.

She looks over her shoulder. Her gaze flits to my hand then back to mine, and she licks her lips. Grabbing the back of the chair, she arches so her ass pushes out in offering, batting her lashes. "You want me like this, Foster?"

My lips twitch, and I move behind her, tapping the inside of her thigh so she widens them. "Careful with the teasing, baby. It's not a good idea."

"No?" she asks, arching more when she faces forward. "And why's that?"

"Because you're mine, Remi." I palm her ass before spreading her open. "Teasing me makes me think you don't remember."

"Am I yours?"

She sucks in a shaky inhale when the head of my cock drags through her soaked pussy.

"Mhmm. And I already want to fuck you until you're swollen and dripping with my cum. So don't tempt me to make sure you never forget it."

I line up and push inside her, grasping her hips. Fuck, she's perfection, squeezing me within an inch of my life and gasping as I fill her. I slide all the way out and drive back in on a groan. Nirvana.

"Holy fuck." Remi shoves her ass back on my next thrust, and I pump into her faster, watching her take every inch.

"Christ, your cunt swallowing my cock is a beautiful thing."

The sound of flesh slapping flesh mixes with her whimpers each time I bottom out. It makes me fuck her harder, chasing her breathy moans.

When I glance at movement off to the side, my attention catches on the sliding door. While outside, the glass reflects for privacy, but whatever they used enhances the reflection inside too. With the lights, the door's like a dim mirror, showing me her tits bouncing with my thrusts.

I grasp Remi's jaw and turn her face so she can witness me pound into her from behind. "See? Look at how fucking perfect you look on my cock."

She clenches around me while my hand slides down her neck and tight body.

"Now watch yourself come on it. Eyes right there, baby."

I find her clit, and she cries out as I slam deep.

"Fuck, don't stop, Foster. Don't. Stop."

I don't stop. I haven't been able to. I doubt I ever will.

Everything about this woman threatens to consume me whole.

The way my name falls from her lips while she pushes back against me and contracts around my cock. All of it could sustain or obliterate me. Right now, I don't even care which one takes.

"*Jesus fuck, Rem,*" I growl as she strangles my dick.

She clamps down, coming hard, and my hold tightens on her hip. I thrust into her, cum pulsing deep inside her pussy with my own release.

I drop my head onto her back and slow the roll of my hips, dragging in and out a few more times, loving the way it makes her shiver and clench again.

She's still trembling when I kiss her neck and her shoulder. Then she sighs as I slide out and looks back at me with eyes like a meadow. My lips press to hers, and she pulls me closer, drags me down, down, down.

I realize it's both. Always has been when it comes to Remi. She sustains me and obliterates me, and I'll still be begging for more.

It takes a second to peel open my eyes. Another to recognize the pounding from the other room.

I mentally groan to avoid waking Remi. She's snuggled against my side, so I'm careful while I get up. She's also gloriously naked. And once I deal with whoever the fuck is still beating on my door, she'll be full of my cock.

After throwing on a pair of sweatpants, I go to deal, shutting the bedroom door behind me. The knocking is familiar enough, I already know what to expect when I swing open the suite's door.

Colt stands on the other side, looking as unamused as I feel. He has a keycard in hand I safely assume is to my room.

"Can we not do whatever this is right now?" I ask, bracing on the doorframe.

He snorts. "If you'd have answered anyone's texts and calls since last night, we wouldn't need to do this at all."

Shit. I leave him there and stroll to the sofa, swiping my phone from where I set it after seeing Remi's message last night. He follows me in, the door loud when it shuts behind him.

Everything shifted to Remi after I carried her into the shower. I let her wash my cum from between her legs and then fucked her against the tile. I warned her it was a new obsession. Then I put her in my bed, and we stayed there.

Scrolling through the messages, I let my annoyance cool. No emergencies, but plenty of variations of *what the fuck, dude*. Fair, considering I haven't responded to a soul in over ten hours. No one's had any visual sightings either since I came back from Chase and Val's and holed up in my room.

He texted too, unsurprisingly, responding to my *it's complicated* about me and Remi.

CHASE

> Then include a flowchart so I can keep up. Make it a whole presentation if you want. I'm not letting you vague your way out of this, bro.

"Are those…?"

I glance up as Colton trails off. He's in the middle of the room, hands planted on his hips. He has a smug grin that typically earns him the finger, zeroed in on Remi's clothes still on the floor. Along with mine.

Colton shifts his focus to me.

"Don't," I say.

"Don't what?" he counters. "Don't mention the top you definitely can't fit in? Or the jeans that are all wrong for your body type?"

"Yeah. Both."

"Right, right." He tips his head toward the bedroom. "So you *really* prefer I not call out the odd quirk you've developed for shutting your suite's bedroom door when you're not in there, huh?"

I sigh, raking a hand through the back of my hair.

There's no point in denying. He already knows Remi and I

hooked up before Wannabe joined the fray. Hell, I admitted to it happening more than once while under a disco ball. Add in my sudden *be nice to Remi* speech from the other day, and he wouldn't believe me if I tried.

"Are you fucking done?" I ask. He shrugs like an asshole, and I shake my head, returning to the bedroom. "I'm alive. You've verified. Let yourself out."

Then he says, "Fishing."

And I stop. Crush my eyes closed. "*Fuck.*"

Anything else I'd blow off for the sexy redhead in my bed. Any*one* else.

I check the time on my phone and grab the handle. "Give me ten minutes. Without you in my suite," I add.

He chuckles as I slip through the door.

Enough light leaks in around the heavy shades that I can track back to the bed. I crawl in and kiss Remi's bare shoulder, then her neck, then I ease her onto her back. She grabs my bicep as my lips sink lower, and she makes the sweetest sound. So sweet I need to quit now or I won't.

As if pulling back has ever been my strong point in regard to her.

While cupping her breast, I brush my thumb over her pointed nipple, teasing the other with my tongue. She pushes against my palm and mouth. Adding a scrape of my teeth has her wrapping her legs around my waist.

"Shit." I ease away, avoiding a temptation I'll never pass up. "If your pussy comes anywhere near my cock, I'll have you face down, ass up."

I drop onto my side next to her, propping on my arm.

"Hmm, and how is that a bad thing?" she asks.

My hand follows the curves of her body. "Colt's waiting on me to go meet Chase for fishing. We haven't seen him since this leg of the tour started, so we planned some things while we're here."

Not even working on the new album trumps time with Chase. He took the week off from his cushy job as a product manager at a tech company in downtown Austin for the same reason.

By now, my vision has adjusted so I can distinguish Remi's features, minus details. But I know them anyway.

I've thought about waking up beside this woman more times than I can count. Even dreamed about it one time. I was furious when I opened my eyes. Partly because it wasn't real—a harsh taunting of what I would never have—but also a reminder of why it wouldn't happen and the pain it caused. I clung onto the latter. I refused to acknowledge the heartache of missing her.

I had to remember she was the reason it all fell apart.

Except she wasn't.

And now she's here. In my bed and arms. In my life.

It's why I need to do this right with her. I'm not risking it turning to ash or being another dream.

Remi's quiet, but the craving coiling beneath the filmmaker's skin is not. That hunger to capture.

"We booked a place for axe throwing on Wednesday," I say. "They're shutting it down for us, and there's a bar and rage room where you break shit. Dev will be in Arizona, but Felix is coming, and probably Christian."

"Why are you torturing me?" She has an adorable pout to her tone.

"Hmm, is it torture if I'm asking you to come with your camera?"

She lights up even in the semi-darkness when she smiles. "I guess not."

Far too close to losing all willpower, I haul my ass out of the bed to get dressed. On my way out of the bathroom, I stop. The bedside lamp Remi switched on washes a soft glow over her. Auburn and black hair contrast the white linens. Her soft lips contrast her hard hold on me.

Detouring, I grab another shirt from my bag. She pushes up onto her elbow, watching me as I walk over.

I toss it at her. "Put it on."

She looks at it and then at me, but when I cock a brow, she complies.

With a smirk, I duck down and kiss her. "Good girl."

"You don't want me to leave?" she asks.

"Never." I stop at the door, hand on the handle. "Tell me you're mine, Remi Sinner."

"I'm yours." She says it without hesitation, and I swear nothing has ever felt so right, settled me more. Not until she asks, "Are you mine, Foster West?"

"Always," I answer, needing that to be true for both of us. "Everywhere and every second."

When I walk out, I roll my eyes. Colt's still in the center of the room, arms now crossed. He shakes his head, his focus on Remi through the open doorway as I gather my keycard and sunglasses.

"No one called this," he deadpans. Then, "Seriously, lioness. We can find you someone better to hook up with than Adams."

"She knows my real name, little bro." I give him a condescending tap to the cheek as I pass and look in at Remi. "I'll see you when I get back, baby."

The tint in her cheeks is visible from out here, but her lips press together, fighting off a smile when I wink. I snag Colton by the front of his sweatshirt and haul him to the door; his face confused the entire time.

And I walk out with a smile I haven't smiled since wandering Prague. Well aware of how fast it snowballs from here.

Remi never relinquished all of my heart. No matter how much I denied it. It'll take no time at all for her to reclaim the rest. Either by stealing it again or me offering it while at her feet.

34

REMI

OUR UBER DRIVES OFF, leaving us in a small parking lot outside of Your Next Axe.

The building looks distressed, thanks to the paint technique. Strategically placed sheets of metal appear rusted along the edges and slapped on the front. Even the sign itself hangs slightly askew.

Valeria sighs beside me, not quite as sold. "I specifically remember saying spa day, Remi. Spa. Day."

I adjust the camera bag's strap on my shoulder and shrug. "We got our nails done. And this is like a dude spa, right?"

"Sure. We'll go with that," she says. "Come on, let's go watch our guys share a brain cell."

She smiles and brings me with her toward the door. A normal one, which mismatches with the rest of the building, so it oddly fits in perfectly.

I went from a fan of Val to attached over the course of lunch. She grew up in Austin and danced for a ballet company. A stress fracture put her out of commission last year, so now she runs an online boutique and makes jewelry. She effortlessly matches Chase's energy with sarcasm and doesn't take shit, but she always has an underlying kindness and genuineness shining through.

She already knew about me and Foster when we met up. A certain version anyway. Chase apparently couldn't even wait until Colton and I left their curb to tell her. Which I find incredibly cute.

He said we knew each other years ago, lost touch, and now Foster has a leash on his dick. I have a feeling she watered it down —other than the last part. It would make sense that Chase told her I disappeared on Foster without a word, and as his best friend, I'm sure Chase held opinions.

Foster assured me he wouldn't mention the real reason, but letting him is on the list for maybe one day.

A guitar twang surrounds us once we walk inside. The space opens into a large room with the axe throwing at the back, a small arcade on one side, and a full bar on the other. Wooden stairs right in the middle lead up to another floor. A sign posted beside them has RAGE AND SHINE burned into it along with an arrow pointing up.

Valeria leads the way to the throwing lanes. Wooden planks and metal lattice separate them, each with two bullseyes at the ends.

"Double or nothin' you can't hit that close a third time," Colton says as we approach.

He grabs a hatchet off an overturned barrel and passes it off to Chase. His brother grabs the handle with a cocky smirk and adjusts his chair to line up before flinging the axe down the lane one-handed. It buries in the wooden target, not far from the center.

As Colton curses, Chase swings around, ready to gloat when he spots us and smiles, first at me, and then he stays on Val.

"Now you're really fucked, little bro. My good luck charm just walked in." He pulls her into his lap and kisses her, mumbling something about being "Lumber-jacked."

Colton greets me with an eye roll once I reach him.

"What was the bet?" I ask.

"Everything."

My forehead scrunches, and I look up at him. "Everything?"

"Yep." He scratches his jaw, pursing his lips.

"How do you bet double or nothing on everything?"

He throws me a sideways glance, shrugging. "Fuck if I know. I wasn't supposed to lose again."

I laugh as he goes after the hatchet.

Felix and Christian are throwing in the next two lanes, so I watch them. They throw, retrieve, swap to larger axes, but the appeal is lost on me.

"It's an art form," Foster says from behind me.

Before I can look, his arm snakes around my waist, tugging me back against his chest. He moves my hair so he can nuzzle against my neck.

"Oh, is it?"

He hums an affirmative. "Watch Christian."

I do.

The manager sorts through his options until he picks one up.

"See how he tests the weight, judges the movement?" When I nod, Foster sweeps his thumb over my rib cage and continues, "His face tells you he doesn't like it." Christian sets it down and grabs another with a longer handle and larger head. "Now with this one, you see his lips purse? The tiny nod of his head? You know he's going to choose it."

Christian turns around with the axe and saunters to the top of the lane.

Foster's words caress my ear. "He's all confidence," he commentates, sending a shiver rolling down my spine from his low, raspy voice. "His hold on the throat, where the handle curves, stays loose. Now, when he throws, stay with him and not the axe."

Christian's arm lifts, the axe head drawing back until he brings it forward and releases. My gaze sticks on him through the *thwack* of the blade hitting the wooden target. His expression remains cool, and he turns, giving a smug nod to Felix.

"I still don't get it," I tell Foster, tilting my head to see him. It brings our lips inches apart, very distracting. "How is any of that art?"

He smirks down at me. "Because Christian has no fucking clue what he's doing. It's all a performative piece, convincing you and everyone else he was completely knowledgeable and in control the entire time."

I look as Christian slowly strides to the target and jerks the axe out from where it landed, several inches from the inner circle. And sure enough, when he comes up the lane, he notices us watching and winks at me.

Foster kisses my temple and then leaves my backside cold to grab the necks of two beers off a table where he must have set them. He tucks a bottle of water under his arm and swipes one more beer. "Last one's for you."

Following him with mine, I pluck the water from him too. His mouth lifts on one side.

"What?" I ask as we walk over to the brothers and Val.

He shakes his head. "I just still can't believe you're here sometimes."

But I am. And I can't imagine being anywhere else.

When we reach them, Colton takes two of the beers, passing one to Val, and Foster directs me to Chase.

"The water's for him."

Chase flashes me a smile as I hand it off. "Thanks. Drinking screws with my meds."

I nod, and Foster tucks me against his side. Since he left right after Colton and I arrived the other day, I haven't seen how the three of them interact together. But the dynamic I've witnessed between Foster and Colton for months seamlessly adjusts to fit Chase until I forget he hasn't been part of it all along.

Their competitive natures quickly kick in, and soon everything becomes a chance to show each other up. And not just with axe throwing. Who finishes more of their beverage in a single gulp, and which of them checks their phone first. Then out of nowhere, they're trying to throw *worse* than each other.

Half the time I don't even realize they're competing until one claims victory.

But no one cares in the end. No one keeps score—except maybe when they all text Colton and Chase's mom at the same time and Mrs. Wilde replies to Foster first.

Val's perched on one of the overturned barrels, cackling at them when I unpack my camera.

Foster and Felix notice and prove themselves well-trained, moving to side-by-side lanes without me asking. They bicker and laugh with each other, and it's exactly what I need.

With so little downtime for the guys outside of the break, we have limited B-roll of them like this. Dev has a handheld with him in Arizona, so I might have something to use from his trip. Otherwise, I'm starting to think I'll have to fly to LA after the tour for footage of the three together in a relaxed environment.

I need Colton to command chill time for them.

Once I finish, I drop down by my camera bag off to the side of the group where they've all congregated.

"Bad news, baby." Foster's walking over as I pull the zipper closed. "Colton bet my everything and lost." He stops beside me. "Chase gets everything that's mine, so…"

I shrug, pushing to my feet. "I guess that means I live in Austin now."

"Nah, I'll smuggle you out of here."

Val laughs from farther down. She's beside Chase, his hand on the outside of her thigh while they talk to the others. His thumb skims over her jeans, and she lights up every time she looks at him.

"How long have they been together?"

Foster glances over at them. "About three years." He grasps my sides, hands wrapping around my ribs.

"Were they together before his accident?"

Outside of what Foster said and Val saying he had a spinal injury, no one's told me anything more. I haven't asked either, not wanting to pry or open wounds. Chase is Chase with or without me knowing the details, and Foster will talk to me about what happened when he's ready.

"No, they met after."

His palm starts inching downward on one side.

"They were both at a tech conference," he says. "She'd been hired for a demonstration, wearing sensors while she danced that provided instant feedback on muscle engagement and form tracking. He was checking out the technology for the company where he works but spent more time checking her out instead."

Foster runs his fingers along the bottom of my shirt before trailing to my hip. "Chase claims he took her home, but Val says it was the other way around. Either way, Colt and I were in tuxes six months later."

I smile. "I like the idea of you in a tux."

"Yeah, well, you couldn't handle it." His palm reaches the outside of my thigh and slips just under the fabric of my skirt.

"Let me guess, I'd be throwing my panties at you?"

"You'll be doing that regardless."

When he steps closer, he cups my ass with his other hand. Then I see his eyes dart to the side. To Chase.

I look and see his friend's hand tucked between Val's thighs, barely moving higher before he glances at us.

"Are you two competing right now?" I land a glare on Foster.

He fights a smile. "That depends." Dropping the subtlety, he pulls me flush to his chest. "If I admit we are, will you help me win?"

His head hangs lower, so his nose almost touches mine.

"No." But I stay. I leave his hands on me. I help him win anyway.

"ARE we shitty people for still not telling Colton we already knew each other?"

We only have two days left of the tour break, and the

thought's creeping in more often. Along with others—whether I want them to or not.

But this one remains insistent.

Foster snorts. "No."

He's on his side next to me in his bed. His fingers link with mine, and he drags my hand up to press a soft kiss to my wrist. "Do you want people to know?"

I hesitate to answer him. None of it has to do with us or how I feel about him, but rather everything to do with all the heaviness attached to when we first met.

Telling Foster about my mom and what happened to Roman is too fresh. I'm nowhere near ready to share with everyone else, and the thought of talking around it to others sounds miserable right now.

The pause makes his eyes flick to mine. He studies me before kissing my wrist again.

"I honestly couldn't give a fuck when anyone thinks we met. The only thing I care about is you're mine. So long as you know that, we won't have a problem." Then he abandons my hand and moves to cup my cheek, his bottomless blue gaze penetrating, a question in them. "Now tell me, are we going to have a problem, Remi?"

I shake my head. "Not a one."

He releases a relieved breath, like the answer could be anything else, and then pulls me to him. My cheek rests on his shoulder, and I tilt my face up to see his, tracing the contours of his chest. "How mad will Colt be whenever we do tell him?"

"Oh, he'll lose his shit and unleash a level of petty you've never seen." Foster smirks at the thought. "Petty Colt's pretty damn entertaining, though. Almost more so when it's aimed at you."

"And you wonder why he's so quick to kick you from being his best friend."

Unbothered by the threat as always, he purses his lips. "Even if he did, I keep a spare."

I smile when he looks down at me with one of his own. He captures my chin, raising it more, and his eyes bounce between mine.

"I mean it, Rem. We're doing us on our terms," he tells me. "As long as I get to be with you, my terms are met. The rest is all up to you."

Him and his perfect words, never fighting fair.

He's always found a way through my defenses, disarming me even when I would fight against it. And that was when he was in parts and an ocean away. Foster as a whole carves his way into the places I hide from and makes me think I might not need to anymore.

While he showers, I throw on one of his shirts and crawl back into bed with my phone. Because I'm determined to make today a maybe one day, and this call requires some semblance of clothing.

Stretched out, I prop up on my elbows, waiting for my favorite smile in the world to appear on my screen. Then it does, and something instantly eases inside me.

"Remington Sinner." Roman's sitting in his car, his beanie pushed high on his forehead and jacket unzipped. "The hottest up-and-coming director of her time."

I snort and remind him, "You said the same thing after watching the video I shot on my phone of you blowing out birthday candles."

He considers it and nods. "You're right. The real reason that video was such a masterpiece was the subject."

I shake my head, my own smile spreading, and he chuckles.

"All right, catch me up, pretty girl," he says. "What's big enough to earn a call?"

My fingers twist in the bedsheet, lips tilting up even more. "I can't check in just because I miss you?"

His face speaks for him, clearly stating, *You can, but you ain't.*

And he's right. About the *just* part, anyway.

Roman and I have talked a handful of times since I left New York, but we've mostly kept up in texts. Texts with words.

The emojis stopped after everything happened. We didn't need them anymore, and they would have only served as a reminder of why we ever needed them in the first place.

Up until now, all of my updates have stayed documentary-related, or about Of Men and Wolves, or the tour itself. No mention of Foster—no mention of Adams in place of Foster.

Nothing between us fell into a category of things I would ever share with the man I consider a second father.

Until now.

"Do you remember…" I trail off and bite my lips together.

Very rarely am I the one to bring up anything related to my mom or our time at the lake house. Even the months after Roman was attacked, I avoid. He tests the waters now and then but never pushes too hard.

But right now, the safety in his dark eyes is enough I can push myself.

"One of the guys on tour with me is Foster."

A crease forms in his forehead. "Foster…"

"He was the guy I cried over after Daniel killed my mom."

The last part's hushed and feels brutal, but I breathe through it. I've practiced. Out loud and alone.

Roman's blink lasts too long when I say it, calmly and without tears. It's his only tell other than a puff of air that leaves him before he looks at me again. "I remember who he is, Remi. I need you to let me know, am I happy or on a plane?"

I sigh, my cheek landing on my arm. "So fucking happy."

The man slumps in his seat, head falling onto the headrest, and then he grins. "Damn. You look it too. He's been there the entire time?"

As I straighten back up, I nod, focusing on him while I push out more. "We weren't on the best of terms because I couldn't tell him what happened. It took until recently, but now he knows where I went and why. I told him everything—even about the lake house." Tears build fast at the memories, and I swallow roughly. Inhale and exhale. "Saying it to him really fucking hurt, Roman. I've hidden from it for so long."

"But you did it anyway. You're on the other side and still standing."

His head tilts, concern marring his face, so I force a small smile. His expression softens in response, and he manages to fill the silence with everything I need. Such a simple thing he wields like the world's most powerful weapon. At least in my world.

Roman glances to the side, and the dome light pops on a second later, accompanied by a ding as a door opens. He angles the camera to show Bea crawling into the back passenger seat with a shopping bag. "Say hi to Remi."

She glances up with a smile while shutting the door. "How's my girl?" Unbuttoning her coat, she reaches for the phone with her other hand. "We miss you."

Things changed between Roman and Bea after his attack while we were staying at her lake house. She said it took almost losing him to realize how deep that loss would have gone.

Having recently been gutted and the wound being a through-and-through, I understood.

I leaned on her a lot while he recovered. She was my first call when I finally got to him, barely conscious and broken. Then she was there for both of us every step of the way. In truth, she kept us afloat until we could swim again.

They became a *we* after Roman and I moved so I could start school. She would visit back and forth until she eventually stayed with him in New York. But neither of them loved the city. He denied it for a long time—and I know it was because of me. After I started working with Heath, Bea and I ganged up on him, and they moved to Philadelphia just over two years ago.

It was after the weekend I spent at Sound Clash that I helped them unpack at their new place. While I was there, I also helped them celebrate something else. Or someone.

"I miss you guys too," I tell her, only a high-pitched squeal overpowers my *too* and has Bea dramatically widening her eyes.

Roman chuckles. "I told you she'd wake up the second you got back."

Bea waves him off and rotates the phone screen so I can see Imane in her car seat and she can see me. She's beaming, black curls peeking from under an orange fuzzy hat. Her big brown eyes match her dad's, but the rest shines through all Bea.

"There's my baby," I coo.

Through the random word sounds, I catch a "Remi here," and my heart squeezes. She changes so much between updates, and I seek out every one.

"Say Thanksgiving wasn't the same without you, sissy." Bea coaches her while handing her a plastic key ring of shapes.

Foster and I spent it with Chase and Colt's family.

Imane answers in baby, ignoring the toy entirely and desperately reaching for the phone instead. And then the world ends when her mom won't give it up.

I wince at the cry and screech, but she's too fucking adorable to really care about eardrums.

Bea flashes me an apologetic face that she backs up with a, "Sorry. Love you."

She passes me back to Roman in the driver's seat, and he's wincing along with me.

"I'm so sad I missed this part with you." He smothers it in sarcasm, causing me to laugh.

"Yeah, I can sense the unshed tears. Get your girls home."

"Two of my girls," he corrects. He smiles but with a seriousness beneath the surface. "We're not done here. When you have time and are ready, I want to finish our conversation. Then you can tell me more about this Foster guy who's responsible for you being so fucking happy." Imane starts to calm behind him, so he lowers his voice. "I'm proud of you, Remington. Stay standing, and remember I'm here for it all. I've got you through the good, bad, great, and ugly."

The words act like his hugs, warm and grounding. What Roman's always been for me. Despite the cost to him.

"Same. Good, bad, great, and ugly," I repeat.

"We love you," he says, and I tell him I love them too. Then he adds, "Warn Foster I'm holding him responsible if anything happens to you. But I won't lie, I haven't even met the man and already prefer him watching over you to Xander."

His nose wrinkles in mock disgust, the call ending before I can even respond. Not that anything I say would matter.

Despite his best efforts, Xander still hasn't fully reversed Roman's first impression of him.

To be fair, when my roommate answered our apartment door last Christmas in only low-slung sweatpants—and I mean *low*—he didn't expect Roman to be on the other side. Neither did I.

It was Imane's first Christmas, and Bea's family was there visiting.

I hadn't wanted to impose; plus, I had a shoot the next day. So, Xander skipped his family's plans to keep me company, and we stayed in the city. We bought the saddest plastic tree, which leaned in a corner, and *The Year Without a Santa Claus* played on repeat.

Then late in the afternoon, he and Roman were face-to-face. Roman gruffly introduced himself as my dad and demanded Xander, *"put on a fucking shirt,"* before shouldering his way inside. He wrapped me in a hug and told me a video chat didn't cut it.

By the time he left, he'd relaxed toward Xander but still made him swear to never touch me and promise to keep me safe. I think most of his disdain he feigns at this point, but I kinda love it.

I'm writing the scene list for our first week back on the road when Foster comes out of the bathroom. Steam billows out from behind him, and I flash back to the band's dressing room in Prague. His dark hair's wet and messy, hands pushing through it.

My attention quickly diverts to his painfully gorgeous face before sinking to the dips and rises of his abs, then I drift lower to his tattoo, the trail of hair disappearing under the top of his boxer briefs.

"I have a sparkling personality, too."

I look up to him smirking at me. "It's not that great."

"Liar."

On his way over, he runs his hand over his taut stomach. He grabs a pillow and stretches out on his front beside me, tucking it under one arm. The other hand immediately creeps up the back of my thigh, dragging the bottom of his shirt higher.

"I talked to Roman," I tell him, lowering my phone.

His blue gaze settles on my face as he reaches the curve of my ass with his palm and stops.

"About you."

After a second, he cocks a brow. "How much about me? Enough I need to warn Colt to keep an eye out?"

I shake my head. "I skimped on the details, so I think you're safe for now. He remembered you, though. I told him you know everything, and you make me happy."

"Fuck," he rasps. "And I used to shoot for not as sad. Now I need to make you feel consumed by me like I am by you."

"We're there, I just skimped on the details."

I smile when he does, and then he studies me while I study him.

Today was definitely a maybe one day. Maybe tomorrow will be as well. And the way Foster's looking at me right now makes me believe maybe tomorrow's tomorrow could become one too.

The sliver of him inside my soul doesn't feel foreign anymore. Now that he's here, that part of me healed.

"Foster," I say.

He hums, running his fingers up my back. "Yeah, Remi?"

"Thank you for being real."

When he brings his hand up, he pushes it into my hair and pulls me down to kiss him. "Anytime, baby."

35

FOSTER

I HAVEN'T BEEN virginal the past five years. I wouldn't dare insult someone by trying to claim otherwise. Until my sexy witch and her dick spell returned, I fully lived up to the cliché, just far more discreetly than Felix and Dev.

With that in mind, I would never hold Remi's sex life against her. But I'd be lying if I said it didn't grind at me to have a guy on my tour who's fucked her.

The woman has me in a chokehold, and I'm becoming a possessive bastard.

Nah, fuck it. I am one.

And since Xander's part of her crew—she claims he'll be invaluable—and he is clearly not going anywhere, I cut calling him Wannabe once we're back on the road and start pretending he's a puppy capable of wielding a camera.

By the second show, it takes less energy not to glare at him. They swapped out a couch for one that folds out on the other bus for him, and Christian left Remi on ours for the remainder of the tour.

Otherwise everyone falls back into the groove quickly. The only real change is between me and Remi. We're not dancing around each other anymore. We feel right. No longer misaligned.

Of course it also means she's openly calling me on my shit.

After I drop my bag in our dressing room at tonight's venue, another hits the floor not far away. With attitude.

My lips twitch before I rake my gaze up Remi's tight jeans and top to the set jaw and eyes narrowed at me.

I lift a brow. "You have words to go with the ice?"

"Oh, I have plenty," she says, each one edged in brat. "It's you who seems to be lacking them. Specifically recorded ones."

I lick my lips to hide a smile and avert my gaze, bringing it back with a sigh. "I relent. Let's do my solo interview after a show this week."

She blinks like she expected more of a fight, but I have no reason to resist anymore. It wasn't the questions I've been avoiding but sharing the answers with the person asking them. I couldn't open up to her while simultaneously locking her out.

I want to share it all with her—I always have, if I'm being completely honest, but I can kick off the self-preservation mode. She can have the Adams North origin story.

"What's the catch?" she asks, still squinting at me.

"No catch. I'll answer every single question you ask." I crowd her against the wall and bring my mouth to her ear. "You just have to buy each one with a piece of clothing."

Her mouth pops open, and I smirk, walking away.

"What if I have more questions than clothes?" she asks my back.

"Guess you'll need to find a way to negotiate for them."

A quick glance over my shoulder verifies she's blushing, but she also holds a challenge in her eye. I wink before heading back to the bus.

Colton's stepping out of the bathroom when I push through the curtain to the bunks. He's fresh from a shower, and he tracks me while I grab my acoustic case. With a sigh, I roll my head toward him and flip him off for whatever he's thinking.

But I know what he's thinking. Then he voices it.

"How long are you going to do this to yourself?"

My face tips up as I consider his question, but I wind up answering with a shrug. "I wish I could tell you, brother."

He runs a hand through his wet hair and nods. "You mind if I hang out while you torture yourself?"

"It wouldn't be proper torture without your presence," I tell him.

When we go inside, I set up in another dressing room. It has a similar layout to ours, only with extra mirror stations. Colton flops onto his back on the floor. The exasperated sigh that follows doesn't go unnoticed.

I haven't recorded anything to send my mom for a while, but the asshole on the floor reads me better than I like most of the time. He knows the drill. He knows the mood. He knows me. Better than Chase, if I'm completely honest.

It's also because of Chase. Colton had always been my brother but as an extension of Chase. Then his accident broke both of us, changed us, bonded us how only he and I understand and in ways that can't be undone.

I'd make a lot of what happened different in a heartbeat, but not me and Colt. As much as I hate the reason we fused, I can't imagine a life where he isn't right fucking here every step of the journey with me.

And he has been. Even if it's simply existing in the same room when I need to not feel alone.

I start the voice note on my phone, setting it on the side table by the sofa. Nothing happens. My mind blanks, a heaviness washing over my limbs. Tired. But not in the final stretch of a world tour, seven songs deep in a new album way. I'm exhausted by the simple act of sitting here. By knowing any pride or joy my mom might experience won't reach the surface. By having to admit I dread every interaction at this point because none of it matters.

You can't save someone who doesn't believe they need saving.

It seems my mind and body have surrendered to reality. Just my fucking heart still holding out.

"What were you playing the other day?" Colt drawls. He has an arm draped over his eyes, the other tucked under his head. "You've been humming it whenever you think, and now it's stuck in my head."

I half-smile. "It's good, isn't it?"

His eyes might be closed and covered, but I'll bet my career they rolled anyway. "Just fucking play it."

Reaching over, I cancel the voice note of silence and restart. I restart the rest of me along with it. Because nothing about this song feels heavy. Not a damn bit of it scrapes.

Not anymore.

I shut off the recording after playing through once, press send, then settle in, working it for another hour. By the time we resurface, Colt's the one humming the song while I organize lyrics in my head.

COMING off the stage a few days later, I snag Remi and kiss her. Right there at the bottom of the stairs, my blood pumping and the crowd still screaming.

Fuck, it seems too perfect. Being where I belong, onstage, and then feeling settled by being with her the second I walk off. I need it to last—need her to stay.

"Hi," I say, and she grins.

"Hey."

"You need to go be a sexy director with your crew before I get you?"

She typically meets with them for a breakdown of what they filmed, anything they missed she needs to account for at the next concert. I have to share her until she boards the bus. And I suck at sharing.

But tonight she shakes her head. "I passed it off to Xander for the rest of the tour."

"Puppy?" I ask. "I didn't know he could do that trick."

A nod. "Told you he'd be useful."

I smile and press my lips to hers. "I'll be sure to tell him he's a good boy. Maybe I'll even throw a Frisbee for him."

As Remi laughs, a member of the tour's crew snags her attention. Audio, I think. She goes to talk to the woman before I reclaim her and head to the dressing room.

Dev and Felix have enough time on us that I pull her to me outside the door, leaning back against the wall. She sinks into my chest, face tilted up as she gives me a look.

"What?" I ask, sliding my hands to her ass.

"You could get your own dressing room."

My lips twitch at her suggestion. "Why would I do that?"

"So you wouldn't feel a need to avoid it after a show when Felix or Dev or both are either snorting coke or fucking women. Or both."

"Oh, it's both." I shrug at the rest and tell her, "The label and our agent already view the band as two parts—Christian acts like it too sometimes when he's following the money. A separate dressing room only feeds into it. If it backs up we're a single unit, I'll feel you up in hallways."

She nods while messing with my shirt. "Mac pushed for the focus of the doc to be on you. I told Heath I wouldn't do it, and if they press again in post-production, he said he'll back me up. I refuse to make a cut downplaying Dev and Felix into supporting roles."

I groan and kiss her. "Could you stop being so fucking perfect? It's pretty disgusting."

When she smiles, I kiss it too. "Okay, so I get the one dressing room, and I know why *I* avoid it after a concert."

"But…" I tuck my fingers under the top of her tight, ripped jeans.

"You used to go in," she says, squinting at me. "You never even hesitated until these concerts after the break."

I scrunch my face and turn my head away from her.

"You don't have to now, either."

With a sigh, I look back at her. "The second I walk in there, I'll have tits rubbing on me and need to guard my dick while dodging chicks on their knees."

A slight pink stains her cheeks, a jealous glint in her emerald eyes. "Is that any different than the rest of the tour?"

"Remi," I say, but she hits me with a, "Foster."

I smirk as she blinks, like she's forcing the next words out.

"Do I love the idea of you being in a room with gorgeous naked women getting railed? No. But it's part of the gig. Plus, I've watched women throwing themselves at you this whole time, and I have yet to snap." Her smile's fake as hell. "So, we should be good."

A loud as fuck moan comes through the wall behind me as she finishes. Remi glances down, lips pursed, and I shake my head. My fingers hook under her chin and lift to bring her face up again.

"Are you done?" Once she nods, I hang my head closer to her. "I haven't touched anyone since you've been on tour, Remi. I haven't even looked since I heard your name again. The reason it's different going in there now is I won't risk you thinking otherwise for a second. I don't want anything to do with what's on the other side of the door, and I won't even let the possibility worry you. A little change in my post-show ritual is nothing."

"I wouldn't care if you went in, though," she almost whispers. Her eyes bounce between mine until I press our foreheads together.

"Of course you wouldn't, my beautiful little liar."

She shoves at my chest with little behind it. But she doesn't deny the lie either.

I spot Colt sauntering toward us from down the hall. "You mind if we bail and go back to the bus?"

He nods, not even thinking about it. "I'll grab your shit." Then he throws a glance at Remi, reaching for the door. "Close your eyes and ears, lioness."

She rolls her eyes instead, but they drop at the sounds released when he walks inside. I'm smiling down at her as the door shuts again, her cheeks fully red.

"Tell me again how you want me in there," I tease, hauling her even closer.

Colton's in and out in under a minute, and we head for the exit. He lets security outside know the plan but then stops at the door. "They need a second," he says, listening in his earpiece. "The fans are being too fucking much tonight, apparently."

I shrug Remi's camera bag onto my shoulder, waiting for the go-ahead. And when Colton hooks his head for us to follow and opens the door, he wasn't exaggerating.

We're met with an onslaught of screams and flashes, but something else hangs in the air. A recklessness to the crowd.

Remi and I haven't discussed an *us* outside of there being one, but knowing she shies away from attention because of what happened to her and Roman, I doubt she'd love how much she gets with me in public. So I give her a quick smile and slip out first after Colton. Another member of security falls in behind me, and I glance over my shoulder, checking one follows with her.

I stop for normal autographs and pictures, but it all feels off. The walkway's narrower than usual—the barricades closer together. Claustrophobic as fuck. Especially with people grabbing and able to reach from both sides.

It all turns to a buzz at some point. Flash, *Adams*, scream, hands grazing me. One latches onto my shirt and jerks hard enough I have to step while signing a shirt. Colt knocks them off and then shakes his head, nixing the autographs.

"Let's just get to the bus," he shouts, guiding me forward with a hand on my shoulder.

I check back on Remi again. She usually walks out separate from us, ignored by everyone. Right now, though, she has her head down while the flashes go off. One look tells me she's fighting her anxiety with all the cameras, and it fucking kills me. I shouldn't have brought her with me at all.

Colton follows my line of sight, and I practically hear his eye roll over everything else. He tows Remi ahead, so he's covering both of us. The guy who was with her moves behind us.

Then a chant starts.

No, two chants.

One's for me, but the other…

"Shit," Colton shouts, and I realize it about the same time.

The second is a countdown from three already to one. Our heads whip around as a group of fans surges forward into the barricade. The metal scrapes over concrete, moving inward with the force and nearly tipping.

Fuck.

I pull Remi to me, tucking her against my side to save Colt from splitting his attention. A breath later, she's yanked away by someone catching her arm over the fence. Colt's right there to body block as I haul her back and tighten my hold, not chancing anyone fucking touching her again.

The countdown restarts, but I'm pushing Remi in front of me and up the stairs onto the bus. I'm right behind her, and Colt's right behind me, quickly closing the doors.

"Jesus, fuck." He swings his head toward us. "Everyone good?"

I'm already cupping Remi's face in my hands and scanning her over. Panicked green eyes jump between mine, her arms wrapped around herself.

"Are you okay?" I ask, needing her to say it.

"Yeah…" She glances out the tinted windows. "It's never been like that." She looks back at me. "Right?"

It hasn't. The other two shows back since the break were more intense when we walked out. But not this level.

I shake my head. "I don't want you walking out with me again."

A sad smile appears, but relief sneaks in there too.

Colton's barking orders through his radio, coordinating to get things locked down before they bring Felix and Dev out. He finishes and audibly sighs on his way over. "Fuck, I'm sorry, brother. My gut told me we needed more crowd control tonight. And those barriers were too close together."

I shrug it off, not blaming him in the least. "No apologies," I tell him. "But we can't deal with that every time."

He nods. "Yeah, it's time to restrict access to the backstage exit. I'll have it set up for the other venues. That shit's not happening again." Then he scans Remi and pats her on the head. "I'll put security outside the bus, but I should probably make sure everything runs smoother for Dev and Felix. You two can…" He waves us off, not finishing as he walks away.

I shut the doors behind him and turn around. "Come here."

Remi drops her arms, and once she's close enough, I pull her the last few steps. She appears less shook up, but I want to hide her away. And hide with her.

My gaze trails up the footholds in the wall.

"You mind if a sweaty dude takes over your refuge up there for a bit?"

"Hmm." She pretends to consider her options, so I remind her she has none, picking her up. "Foster," she squeaks and throws her arms around my neck as I climb to the loft.

I drop onto my back on her bed, dragging her down on top of me. She laughs but cuts off when I grab the back of her neck and bring her mouth to mine.

Fuck, I could do this for the rest of my life with her—having her melt into me and how she fills my chest. But there's still the ache behind my ribs, the guilt I keep avoiding. Just until after the tour and the doc wraps.

I bite her lower lip and tuck an arm behind my head. She folds hers over my chest, setting her chin on them while my eyes search hers.

"You swear you're okay?" I ask.

"Are you?" she counters. "I wasn't the one those people nearly stampeded trying to get to."

I lower my brows. "There were people out there? I never even noticed them."

She fights the smile, poorly. "Right. Now who's the liar?"

"Nah, baby, I only saw you." I brush my thumb over her cheek. "Awake, asleep, eyes open, closed—all I ever see is you, Remi."

When she fully smiles, I kiss her, then I really kiss her, knowing it's only partially a lie.

If I let myself, I could forget anything else exists outside of her. Outside of us.

I did forget before—about the world. Except, forgetting about the world doesn't mean it stops moving. It just leaves you completely oblivious to what's going on right in front of you. Until all those things you were missing blindside you. Like they did me.

36

REMI

I'm getting the shot tonight.

Of Men and Wolves will walk to the stage and cross in front of my projector. The venue's light gray curtains will work perfectly as a backdrop to cast a video of them performing. I have a lens to soften the edges, and I'll use a lower frame rate so the shot looks more vintage, and I can add grain in post-production.

I've told myself all along this is a self-indulgent shot, one for me. But deep down, I've always imagined it as the opening of the documentary. Audio of the crowd chanting layered over top, then a soundbite from one of the band members. A line or two to set the tone straight out of the gate.

By the time I set up the projector, I feel a charge running under my skin. I adjust the angle and then go to arrange the curtain, wanting the backdrop smooth except for one fold near the stage. The heavy fabric takes both hands to slide, requiring me to tug it into place while backing up.

I stop before running into the stage and am still staring up when I'm caught by the waist. A combination of a squeak and a gasp rushes out of me as I'm pulled behind the curtain. Then someone's kissing me. Someone so incredibly familiar, the lips and tongue and palm wrapping the front of my neck.

When my eyes flutter open, they meet Foster's. But with the audio techs just above us in the wing and his name echoing through the arena, he's Adams North right now too.

"What are you doing back here?" I drape my arms around his neck, fingers twisting in his hair.

"What I do before every show."

The last time I found myself in the dark with him by the stage pops into my mind. And I finally unlock his pre-show ritual. "You're listening to the crowd."

"They ground me. Hearing them reminds me they want me out there as much as I fucking want to be." His hold sinks lower. "What are *you* doing, director?"

"Setting up for a shot that haunts my dreams."

Foster cocks a brow. "If it's me bending you over and fucking you against the stage, then our dreams align."

"Tempting." I back away, which breaks his hold. "But staying a dream."

"For now," he says.

Following me out, he roughs up the back of his hair and then tracks the light beam to the curtain. "What's the vision?"

"An old video of the band will be playing when you guys pass in front. Your shadows will cut through, light highlighting your profiles." I admire the perfect fold on one side of the blank projection.

"You should stay recording after we take the stage and grab the audio of me greeting the crowd."

My eyes bounce to him, surprised I hadn't thought of that.

He smirks. "I'm kinda brilliant." Then he nods to the projector. "You need me to pass a couple times so you can check the angles?"

"Isn't this disrupting your ritual?" I ask.

His shoulder lifts and falls. "Worst that can happen is I ruin the entire show. And in that case, I'll just blame you for depriving me of your delectable cunt."

After dropping a kiss on top of my head, he walks away.

I only need him to cross in front of the beam half a dozen times before I figure out the best place to set the tripod. With the cart holding the projector angled, it should cast their silhouette and catch the video on their faces. If I film with the old video of them playing at 2x, I can slow the entire shot down in post-production, then the band will appear moody, slowly crossing.

"Here." Foster hands me his phone with a video pulled up. "I don't know what you planned on using, but this probably beats it."

I watch him, Felix, and Dev play together, an ugly orange shag carpet in a nook behind Felix and his drum set. I look at Foster, recognizing the background. "The music store in Houston where you had your meet and greet?"

"Finding a cheap lefty bass is a pain in the ass, so we drove from Austin after Dev tracked one down. Back then the place was owned by a Deadhead and named Grateful Fret. The guy let us jam while Dev got a feel for the bass."

When the band stops playing, the person filming lets out a *"haaaaah"* to emulate a roaring crowd. "Thank you, Houston," Colton shouts. "We're Nameless Because Our Guitarist Is A Broody Fuck. Good night!"

In the video, Foster glares at the camera. Beside me, he shakes his head before he taps the screen to pause it.

"The bickering is endless after that, but…" He steadies the phone with his hand behind mine so the other can zoom in on the wall over Video Foster's shoulder. The blurry image in the frame is barely distinguishable as a wolf. "I stopped being broody, and we left as Of Men and Wolves."

My smile is so big my cheeks ache when he steps behind me and takes his phone.

"This is vital lore, Foster West. Why am I only hearing about it now?"

"You hadn't earned it yet." His lips are at my ear. "This is the only freebie you get from me. Anything else you pay for by stripping out of one of these slutty little outfits you wear."

Then he's gone, striding across backstage. I'm still smiling when he texts me the video. I watch it again, my sole focus on the guitarist. Tortured eyes and hard-set jaw. A hint of a melody emerges while he plays, barely there but enough I recognize what it will evolve into eventually. The song that put them on the map.

"Echo."

AFTER BOTH OF the next two shows, I become prey as soon as the final song ends.

Like tonight. Adams North closes out the show with his guitar hanging. He has a hand on the microphone stand. His voice is worn and oh-so sexy.

And his heated gaze is locked on me offstage through it all.

People scream while he, Felix, and Dev walk off, and Foster hands off his guitar to one of the roadies before descending the stairs. Same as last time, he stalks toward me, grabs me by the nape, and then his lips crush to mine. His kiss is hot and claiming and everything.

I gasp when his hands drop to the backs of my thighs and he hikes me up. My legs wrap around his waist, my arms around his neck.

Once he has me breathless, he tugs at my lower lip. "Are you mine?"

I'm so his it hurts. But he means for the night, to which I slowly nod, and then he nods with me and carries me to the dressing room.

The door's open, no Felix or Dev. Foster takes my bag, tossing it on the floor, and lowers me onto the couch. He comes down on top of me, his mouth back on mine, my hands in his hair.

"Sinner, I need him," Christian says.

I turn my head, and he winks at me from inside the doorway.

Foster groans and drops his forehead onto my shoulder. "Fuck off."

The band's manager tugs down his sleeves, switching back to business mode. "Would if I could. You know how much I hate to be a cockblock, but I need all of you *and* your attention. So, be a good boy and heel."

He walks out.

Foster's lips find my neck before he climbs off me with a sigh. "You good to hang out for a bit? I don't want you leaving without Colt, and I have no clue where he is right now."

I nod, sitting up as he fishes his phone out of his pocket and checks the screen.

"Shit." He seems to mull something over and then glances up. A little smirk forms as he tosses his phone at me. "I'm expecting a call from a guy about a thing. I don't know how long this will take, so if he calls, let him know I'll call him back as soon as I'm done."

"A guy about a thing?"

"Yep," he says, leaning down to kiss my cheek. He pulls back enough to see me. "The passcode's how many times I think about you a day—184369."

"Uhhu, sure," I say as he heads for the door. The battery's nearly dead when I glance down. "On top of being your secretary, I'll charge it for you too."

He spins to walk backward and clutches his chest over his heart. "The sweetest thing anyone's ever done for me."

I laugh as he pulls the door shut. Once he's gone, I sink into the couch, fucking dizzy from him.

Felix left the charger he used earlier, so I plug in Foster's phone before moving my bag to the wall beside it. After I review the list of shots I wanted for tonight, I start to text Xander to see if they're still meeting. They might as well swing by here so he doesn't need to relay everything.

Despite the rough start, having him around has taken some pressure off. We have an extra set of eyes for potential shots and hands for the planned ones. Not to mention he knows how I work and easily slips into the assistant role or a leader one when I need it. He's also been respectful of me and Foster, back to being my friend—where he started, and I need him to end.

Before I hit send, Foster's phone lights up. I stretch for it, realizing I have no idea if the guy about a thing is saved in his contacts. If he is, I doubt it's as *A Guy About a Thing*.

Sitting back, my brow dips at the name. It takes me a second to realize the numbers separated by a dash is yesterday's date. Apparently vagueness is Foster's favorite language.

Not sure what else to do, I swipe to answer.

I haven't even brought the phone to my ear when I hear a shocked, "Holy shit."

Then, "You never answer. I mean, I knew you were still part of the club since you've texted me anytime you get a new number, which is a lot, by the way, but seriously?"

The voice and cadence and rambling rips through me until a shocked numbness takes over. Or maybe a disbelieving one. Either way, I can't move. Can't speak.

But she barely takes a breath. She never did. "I call you *every year* on Remi Day, and the one time I worked a double and call a day late, you pick up?"

I swallow, my heart thrashing in my chest at my name even through the numbness. When it becomes undeniable who called Foster's phone. Who knows Foster to even call him.

"Hellooo?" Sage says. "You—"

The door swings open, and I end the call. I look up as Colton slows down, scanning me over. I'm breathing hard even though it feels like I'm not at all. Dizzy for a completely different reason than when Foster left.

"You good, lioness?" Colton asks, two lines between his brows.

After a few blinks, my eyes fall to the phone screen again. I try to swallow, but my mouth and throat are too dry.

"Remi."

My attention jerks up, his expression even more concerned.

Then the sensations flood back in. The reality of what just

happened crystallizes in my head. Whether it was shock or disbelief freezing me before, it morphs into something else now. Anger. Or maybe hurt? No, this time it's very much both.

I grab my bag, pushing to my feet, and rush by Colton, not sure I could answer him if I tried.

"Hey," he calls after me, but I'm already charging down the hall. "Hold the fuck on, Remi." He catches my arm, but I wrench away.

"Let me go, Colt."

He darts in front of me, blocking my path. "Not until you explain what the fuck is wrong."

I look up at him, searching for words, for an explanation without exposing every bloody wound. "The world is full of liars and the oblivious," I tell him.

"Okay, cool." Then he shrugs and asks, "What the hell does that have to do with why you're upset?"

One side of my mouth lifts, the smile broken. "I always thought I was a liar." I force a breath through the threat of tears—I don't even know the reason behind them. But that's the problem.

I hand over Foster's phone. "Tell Foster we're doing his solo interview. Tonight. Center stage."

37

FOSTER

W<small>HILE</small> C<small>HRISTIAN</small> <small>DOES</small> his manager thing, pacing and talking about merch sales, Dev has his tongue shoved in his cheek, twisting the ring on his finger.

"What's wrong?" I ask, keeping my voice between us.

His eyes dart to me, an exhaustion in them that wasn't there earlier. "He's stalling. We aren't going to be happy when he finally gets to the point."

From his other side, Felix hangs his head back to see me, joining the conversation. "Our guy was lurking around on his phone earlier. Anytime either of us came close, he'd do a floor routine to avoid us being in earshot."

"Goddamn it," I say at full volume, causing Christian to stop and look at us. "What the fuck did the label want?"

Christian sucks at his teeth, taking a power pose with his hands on his hips. He sighs. "They want you in the studio a week earlier."

Felix's head drops back again, only this time he stares at the ceiling, his jaw working overtime. Dev swings his gaze to me again. We soul-read with the music, but in moments like this, it pops through too.

A week earlier. We only had nine days between our last show

and our first session. Originally, we were supposed to have a month. Mac pushed for sooner before we left on tour. They wanted it bad enough to kick in perks, but fuck.

I shake my head, and Dev backs it up.

"No." He steals a glance at Felix, and I do too.

Our drummer's not the only one wearing thin at the seams. Dev's showing signs, but Felix's crash-outs stand to cause more damage.

He brings his head up and throws a grateful look our way, but we've got him. We watch out for each other. Because at the end of all this—the fame and money—we'll still be family.

My Cali-boy roommate included.

Christian scans us, his arms drop, and he nods. "Then it's a no. All of you on board or none."

Then, not wanting to call attention to the fact he's more chill vibes than dollar signs at the moment, he checks his unnecessarily expensive watch. "Buses leave in two hours." He zeros in on Dev. "And they're leaving without extra passengers."

Dev blinks at him, feigning innocence, but it doesn't quite land after the other night. To be fair, the woman had no qualms with climbing into an Uber for a four-hour trip back home.

With Christian already on his phone, I throw a smile at my bandmates on my way out.

I plan on heading back to the dressing room, but Colton's there to snag me right outside the door.

"Hold up."

"Can it wait?" I ask, strolling past him. "I have somewhere to be."

"Yeah, you need to be center stage. Remi's setting up for your interview."

I pause and spin to him, confused given the requirements I laid out for her. "She said center stage? Now?"

He nods. "And I wouldn't fuck with her either. You didn't see the daggers she threw at me, demanding I tell you when and where."

My eyebrows draw in as Colt glares knives of his own. Aimed at me.

"I don't know what the fuck you did," he says, voice pitched low to stay between us, "but I've never seen her look so hurt. Even when we iced her out."

I shake my head, trying to figure out if Smith would have said something to tip her off when he called. But even if he spilled every detail, her being hurt doesn't make any sense. "Help me out here, man. She didn't say anything else?"

Colton hands me my phone. "Apparently she's not a liar?"

Even more unsure what the fuck is going on, I pocket it and run back to the dressing room to rinse off the concert. After the quick shower and a change of clothes, I return to the stage. The wet hair look is going to have to be part of the aesthetic.

I spot her on my way up the stairs, bent over her open duffel bag, grabbing her tripod. When she sees me, she abandons it and straightens. She waits by the single stool she set up for me, all business with a hard set to her jaw.

"What happened?" I ignore the mic pack she shoves at me, reaching up to cup her cheek instead.

She knocks my hand away. "Put on the mic so we can do the interview."

"No," I say, confused as fuck. "I don't know what's going on, but I need you to—"

"What's Remi Day?" she asks.

My chest constricts. "What?"

The words are wrong out of her mouth. It sounds even worse the second time.

"Remi Day," she repeats. The mic pack lands in her bag, and she folds her arms over her chest. "Apparently it was yesterday."

"*Fuck.*" It was. It was yesterday. I never even thought about the date. About the phone call I never received—or the follow-up text when I don't answer. The one I don't reply to either.

"I was going to tell you after the tour—when the stress of all this was off you. But I swear, Remi, I can explain."

"Great," she snaps. "Go right ahead and tell me why Sage calls you every year." All the hurt Colton mentioned surfaces as Remi shakes her head, eyes pleading for a safe answer. "How *could* she call you, Foster?"

I look up at the rafters high above us. The moment I've been fearing bears down. The moment I stand to lose her.

After a drawn-out breath, I force myself to meet her gaze. "Because I called her after I talked to your stepdad."

"I don't understand…" Her eyes dart between mine, trying to complete a puzzle without the final broken pieces. Sharp and ready to slice. "How did you get her number? What haven't you told me?"

I have to swallow, my throat tight and trying to keep the confession sealed away.

But she deserves better—she deserved better then, too, but I didn't know.

This time she lets me step closer, and I thread my fingers through her hair while I stare down at her.

"I told you I was coming for you, Remi. And I did. Then I really fucked up."

38

FOSTER

Before...

"Let me get you my card, son," Daniel says. "In case you hear from her." His gaze falls to the hardwood between us. "I don't think any of us will, but my wife loved her. If I can ever get a part of Rebecca back in my life, I'll find a way to forgive."

I nod, still not paying much attention. The razor edge between heartache and doubt I'm teetering on requires a hell of a lot of resources.

Daniel reaches into the pocket of a black police jacket hung on a hook by the door. "Damn." His hand returns empty. "I have some stashed in my office. I'll be right back."

He disappears through the arch, and I run a hand through my hair again. I'm still holding the funeral program in the other, and when I set it down, my gaze lands on what was beneath it. The corner of a blue sparkly phone case sticks out with half of a camera lens exposed.

I lift the program and uncover exactly what I expect.

Remi's phone.

My heart shutters to a stop for a beat, but in the next one, I swipe it, letting the rest fall back into place. I check for Daniel as I pass the archway, and then I'm out the door. Fuck his card. King of Deceit, after all.

Given I took it from the police chief's house, sticking around sounds like the worst idea. I drive a couple blocks before I park. The phone's dead, so I plug it into my charger, a spiderweb of cracks on the screen.

As the longest wait of my life commences, mine goes off again. As unhelpful as Chase's thoughts proved earlier, I pull it from my pocket. I need to do something.

"Hey," I answer, eyes on Remi's screen, waiting for it to come to life.

"Fuck, you make me feel like an ex with the way you ignore me," he gripes. Then, without a chance for me to respond, "Where are you, brother? You ducked out last night and have been MIA since. We're going to fucking climb."

"No, we're not." I say, earning a groan.

"Come. On. I want to scale a wall, see the world from above. Or at least the rest of the rock climbing gym," he says fast. "We need to get you out of this funk, so get your ass downtown. We'll drink away your sorrows after—find a roof, cry it out, rise from the ashes."

"Dude, I'm in Ohio."

He's silent for several seconds. "I thought you were kidding. You actually went after this chick?"

"She wouldn't just—"

"She fucking did, Foster. Jesus, what is it going to take for you to realize you got played? You need to watch her fuck another guy? Or will you still claim some bullshit excuse?"

"Could you not be a dick for once?" I bite back.

"Right. I'm the problem." A car door slams. "I'm not the one constantly choosing some imaginary relationship over his family. And before you defend her yet again, it was imaginary. Whatever you have in your head is wrong, and it's time you finally admit it. This bored cocktease used you for entertainment purposes and fucked off before your clingy ass found her."

My jaw clenches. The urge to lose it on him is as real as the last time he pulled this shit. But the words stay locked behind my teeth.

"What, can't argue because you know it's true?" he says after a beat. "Maybe you deserve this."

"Maybe I deserve a best friend who isn't so goddamn jealous anytime I want to have a life outside of him." I grip the steering wheel hard enough my knuckles turn white. "I get it, Chase. You don't have shit going for you, and you want me at the bottom with you. So, yeah, you are the fucking problem."

He's taking the brunt of the mess of thoughts and emotions inside me right now, but I'm so fucking tired of him deciding when he's going to support me and when he wants to turn on me. The last few months, it feels like I breathe wrong, and he's pissed.

Chase's laugh sounds cruel. "Yeah, brother. I'm jealous and want you at the bottom with me. So much for us being in it together—all sides, right? Guess that only applies until something better comes along." His car starts, music blaring through the speakers. He shouts over it. "Hell, Foster, your old man is peeking through. He chose his other kid over you. Now you're choosing the cu—"

I end the call. Close my eyes and breathe before I lose it.

Second time. The second fucking time he's used the truth to damage. Every word slashes at what's already been raw and throbbing.

My eyes land on Remi's phone in the cupholder when the screen lights up, charged enough to turn on. Swapping out mine for hers, I hit the power button. And then after a couple excruciating seconds, I'm staring at a passcode screen and a keyboard full of letters.

I run through conversations in my head I'm not even sure matter anymore before I start trying. And on the fourth attempt, when her phone unlocks, I can't tell if it hurts or soothes that it worked.

D-A-R-L-I-N.

Then I sit there. I stare at the plain black background, the apps for recording and editing, the text messages and photos icons.

What the fuck am I doing? Why am I here?

Now that it's all at my fingertips, it feels wrong to go through her phone, an invasion of her privacy. Although, if she left it behind, does it even matter? Fuck. It matters to me. I can't stop feeling like one more missing detail and everything will make sense, and at the end is Remi.

The doubt continues chipping away at me, and not only about going through her shit. I'm stuck in a loop of trying to decide my next step when a text comes through on my phone.

Chase.

Even though I still haven't read most of the others he's sent, with a swipe, I read this one.

> I am so fucking sorry, brother. Please answer so I can apologize.

But I don't. I hit ignore when his stupid picture pops up. Let him wade through the guilt. If I have to hurt because of what he said, he deserves some of the pain too.

Instead I decide to open Remi's messages. I'm in the running for the most recent unread messages, and I copy the number for my competition into my own phone, then I call.

WALKING into the coffee shop for the second time today, I scan the tables. I stall on the only familiar face—and the face itself is only newly familiar thanks to her contact photo.

I drag out the chair across from Sage and drop into it.

Her eyes flit up to me, a flash of disbelief in her stare as she looks me over. "Well … at least she had good taste."

"Has," I reply. "Here. It was on the table at her stepdad's house."

I set Remi's phone on the table between us, and she snatches it before I even retract my hand.

"The passcode's…" I trail off since she already has it unlocked.

She raises her brows but keeps her attention on the screen. "My best friend might not be a sharer, but you won't find anyone who knows Remi Sinner better."

The name's still odd, and I avert my gaze. My phone goes off, and I fish it out long enough to see Chase's picture before hitting ignore. Again.

"Damn, bitch," Sage whispers, bringing my attention back. She has the phone flat on the table. "What were you doing?"

I glance down at the text thread she's scrolling through—with R. All emojis. Single ones and combinations. Sage pauses every now and then, deciphering them maybe. That's what I'm doing upside down. A plane and pleading face a few weeks ago. Folded hands, a heart, the world from last month. A calendar and a shrug. Car, arrow, house.

But not a single one since the day before she disappeared on me.

The gut-wrenching one is what she sent him on Halloween. A heart and a fairy.

I swallow, regretting not going through the phone before coming here. Such a great fucking guy—upholding her privacy so I could be flayed open in public.

"You really think they were together?"

"I mean…" Sage's eyes rise to mine, and she half-shrugs. "I thought they might have been before she left with him. And seeing these messages…"

I watch the phone, my leg bouncing under the table. "But does it feel right? She just vanishes without saying anything to you? I can't believe she'd screw me over like that either. Planning shit with me and then running off with some guy—"

"He's not just some guy, Foster." An apology floods her eyes, and I hate it. "Roman's always been there. They've been close for a long time, even closer the last two years. Feelings evolve. I'm sorry you got caught up in it." She huffs, folding her arms on the table in front of her. "As for her ditching me? I was never part of Remi's escape plan. She just executed it sooner than I expected. I thought she'd at least tell me and give us a chance to stay friends, but I guess not."

I shake my head, teeth grinding, and then I scrub a hand over my face before dragging it through my hair. "She wouldn't do that to me," I finally get out.

The teary look I'm met with hits so deep in my chest I sit back. It isn't apologetic anymore but filled with pity, like I'm so wrong it should pain me.

I'm not, though. Despite what Daniel said, what Sage confirmed, Remi Saint would never hurt me this way.

But Remi Sinner…

A tightness creeps into my throat, and I tongue at my cheek, swiping Remi's phone as I stand. "Thanks for meeting me."

I swerve around people on my way out, needing air. Needing answers. Or maybe I'm just desperate for better ones. Ones which don't scrape. She's not supposed to scrape.

Pushing out the door, I head across the street toward the square. Going where, I don't even know, but I want distance from everything right now. I want to go lie on a park bench and call the only person in this world who feels like they were made for me. Who the universe lined up with my broken pieces. Unless it never did, and she used them to cut me instead.

My phone starts up again, and I ignore Chase without looking. As I step onto the curb, I hear my name.

I glance over my shoulder, and Sage has her arms crossed over her chest, her long sweater pulled tight around her as she rushes after me in the cold breeze.

"Wait," she says.

I turn the rest of the way around, and she sighs and comes to a stop in front of me, chewing on her lower lip. Her long ebony hair blows over her face, and she brushes it away.

"She talked about you."

My gaze falls to the sidewalk. I'm not sure if that makes it better or worse.

"She never gave me the juicy shit, but she admitted to having a Foster. Foster the wandering boy."

I shake my head. "Why are you telling me this?"

She shrugs with one shoulder. "Because I want to be wrong, and maybe you want to wander a little more." She pulls out her phone, thumbs moving. "Roman mentioned a lake house up north a couple times—he'd go there some weekends. I don't know the exact address, but I remember a few things."

A text comes through, and I check what she sent. The lake's name and details to help find the house. A huge tree in the side yard and a porch swing.

"It might be a long shot. I planned on checking once the idea of her abandoning me doesn't hurt as much." She blinks away tears and tips her chin a little higher to deny them.

"I'm sorry she left you," I tell her.

Sage nods and forces a sad smile. "I'm sorry she left you, too. Let me know if you find her? We can start a support group or something."

She has a begging in her eyes that I feel in my bones as I back away from her. I spin, heading to my car while another round of messages I won't read floods my phone.

I PULL up shortly after dark. A few cars were parked in driveways as I drove in, but otherwise the street's abandoned where it circles the lake. It looks like a majority of the community has been for the winter.

Except, on this stretch, lights come from inside one house. I stop across the street, a tree-lined divider separating me. A big oak towers in the side yard, and on the porch, there's a vague shadow in the corner, hinting at a swing.

I stay in the rental a little longer. I want a sign that what I'm doing is the right thing or if I should leave. Let Remi Sinner live the life she's chosen instead of the one I desperately wanted to start with Remi Saint.

A sinner disguised as a saint.

When I climb out of my car, the only sound is the leaves scraping over the concrete in the icy breeze. There's a picture window in front of the little house. It's cute, picturesque. The kind of place I imagine Remi would love, where she would chase shots.

I'd smile if I weren't feeling less and less like I belong here. I haven't brought myself to move yet when I see movement inside. And there she is. She walks into the room and then to the open kitchen, leaning over the back of a chair and looking at the laptop on the kitchen table. She moves the hair from in front of her face, and my chest constricts. It's her. She's fucking gorgeous. She's real. She's here.

I'm about to cross the street when headlights flash from a car rounding the corner. I stop, watching it slow and pull into the house's driveway and then wait for the door on the detached garage. Remi glances over her shoulder as the hum from the motor reaches me, and I'm frozen in place.

Someone just came home.

Came home to her.

As a guy climbs out of the car, Remi abandons her laptop. She rushes through the kitchen in that direction, disappearing while he grabs a grocery bag from the back seat. It allows me a direct, unmistakable view of him.

Roman. Her friend.

Within seconds she reappears through a side door. She runs across the wooden deck and down the steps toward him. He's barely turned around as she reaches him, but he manages to catch her, dropping the bag. Her arms go around his neck, his lock around her. She buries her nose in his coat.

And every millisecond is soul-crushing.

My nostrils flare as I watch them, reality unavoidable. The lies swimming in my mind.

She backs away, and he dips down for the bag before pulling her to his side and under his arm. Then they walk inside together. I nod to myself, forcing it all down.

Remi said she didn't want it to be real, and I'm the clueless fuck who decided it was.

The shock and disbelief of having everything I ever wanted within reach and then watching it be ripped away has already turned. She knew. She *knew* what happened with my dad, and she still led me on like that?

Even though my phone vibrates in my pocket, I dig out the other one. The sparkles on the cover glint in the moonlight. *You can always run to me, darlin'* repeats in my head. And I hate every memory cycling in there too.

"Goodbye, Remi."

I draw my arm back and launch the phone toward the house, bouncing it off the porch railing into a bush.

Climbing back in the car, I text Sage.

> You were right. About it all.

I crank the engine and tear down the street, needing to get the fuck away from here. To leave her with him at Echo Lake. The illusion of us over.

When I reach the main road, Chase has singed my last damn nerve with the incessant calling and texting. Sometimes it's not fucking about him, and he needs to back the hell off.

I dig out my phone at the stop sign, over it all.

"What, Chase?" I snap, not even checking the stupid picture on the screen. "It better be fucking life or death because I'm not—"

"Foster." The panicked voice that's not quite Chase's has never sounded so fucking serious in our entire lives. I glance at the screen, see Colton snarling in the contact picture, and he croaks it again, "Foster."

Even more broken.

"What happened?" I ask.

As Colt fights to talk through tears, existence altering the more he says, I stare into the rearview mirror at a sliver of the light across the lake. Light from the window of the house of the girl who I would have given up everything for.

The girl who was supposed to *be* my everything.

Only she wound up destroying part of me instead. And I might have just lost the rest because of her too.

39

FOSTER

Now…

SHE BLINKS AT ME, like her mind wants to reject what I'm saying.

"You…" Remi takes a shaky inhale, stepping back, so my hands fall away from her face. I want to move with her, touch her. But even though it kills me, I don't move, needing to serve my penance.

"I've spent all this time thinking it was my fault. I led Daniel to us. Now you're telling me you left my phone so he could track it when he noticed it missing?"

"I had no idea there would be a tracking app on it, Remi."

Her head quickly shakes, her fists clenching at her sides. "Roman almost died, Foster. He suffered for weeks—no pain meds because he refused to compromise his sobriety. I'd have panic attacks when someone knocked on the door or I received mail."

"I'm so fucking sorry. God, I would have done so much differently that night if I'd known."

That's the second time I've said it to her. If I'd known. But I didn't.

Doesn't mean I'm not to blame.

Remi licks her lips like she's about to say something, but then her eyebrows slant in. "Chase … his accident was the night you came to the lake house?"

I force a hard swallow. "Yes."

She tightens the space between us, not entirely, but she's close enough to feel. "What happened?"

My gaze averts to our feet, jaw locking. The need to avoid pounds through me, but I can't anymore. I can't stop.

"After our fight," I tell her, "Colt met up with him to go climbing, but Chase was upset and just wanted to drink. I guess Chase was pissed I abandoned him one second and calling to beg for forgiveness the next, and Colt began picking up on what I'd been missing for months."

I shake my head at myself before looking up. Sad green eyes stare up at me, so tragically beautiful, and I reach out enough to brush my fingers over hers.

She lets me. Fuck, I'm glad she lets me.

"I was too wrapped up in us at the time to notice what was going on with him. Looking back, it started before Prague, but especially while we were there. Chase would mope around for days and then suddenly drag me out all night. Minor things I said or did set him off. He'd take them as a betrayal, only to suddenly act like nothing happened. Like when he refused to talk to me for almost a week, avoiding me and staying in his room."

She nods a little, the movement slight. "I remember you'd said Chase was acting like you weren't there, but when he answered your phone a few days later, he denied ever being mad at you."

And I dismissed it as pettiness, even though he never held a grudge against me in our lives.

"He was mostly back to being Chase after that, but once we were back in Austin, he wanted to go out constantly and pushed to do risky shit. It was almost overwhelming. Then he lashed out at me again when I went after you. The patterns were obvious if

I'd have paid attention. Chase wasn't being reckless and moody. He was struggling with undiagnosed bipolar disorder."

"And this led to his accident?"

"When Colt decided something was off, he tried to take Chase home, but Chase was trashed and still upset." I blow out a breath, my heart cracking all over, fracturing down the same line as then. "We have a thing with roofs. Since we were teens, we find one to sit on and vent about shit. He said he was going on one that night, so he could call me again. We'd snuck onto the one of a little café a year earlier, and they were near it. It had a ladder on the side of the building. Colt tried to stop him, but Chase climbed it anyway. Halfway up, he yelled at Colt to follow him while trying to get his phone out."

"Oh my God," she breathes.

The sound of Colton's wrecked voice hammers through my mind. How alone he must have felt, watching him fall. Alone because of me. Then come the memories of the hospital, walking in for the first time, Chase's body fighting while he was in a medically induced coma. Not knowing with each surgery if he would make it out. The pain in his eyes when he found out he wouldn't regain full use of his legs.

I sniff back the assault and admit the harshest truth I've ever had to live with out loud. "If I would have answered or been there, it wouldn't have happened. Chase wouldn't have climbed up there, feeling like I hated him and like he needed to fix it. But I was chasing you. Chase was broken and bleeding on a gurney— Colton was destroyed in ways I can't even understand, blaming himself. And I was at a fucking lake."

Her lashes flutter over building tears. "And you thought I was there because I abandoned you and wanted someone else."

"It crushed me. Even if it wasn't real, I'd lost you, then I almost lost him. I was hurt and angry, and I stupidly blamed you for all of it."

Tears roll down her cheeks, and I swipe them away with my thumbs, cupping her face. As hard as it is to tell her, the worst part is recognizing all the damage I caused. To her. To him. To Colt. Myself.

"You did hate me," she rasps, voice weak.

"No. I couldn't deal with reality, so I put it on you because it was easier. But even then, Remi, I loved you. I'd never fucking met you, but I knew I loved you. And realizing how much of your life you lost on top of everything else because I threw your phone…"

She takes a shuddering inhale, shaking her head against my palms. "You've spent this entire time blaming me for Chase while I've been blaming myself for Roman."

"Both were wrong," I tell her. "None of this is on you."

"Isn't it?" She fully backs away and places the mic pack in her bag.

"Remi."

The bag zips, then goes over her shoulder. Then she flashes me the most heart-breaking look she's ever given me before walking past me. In a split second, I sense my world crumbling and spin, darting in front of her, bringing her to a stop. I don't leave space this time, my hand pushing into her hair.

"Tell me what you need." I tip her chin up, bringing her eyes to me. "So long as it doesn't involve losing you again, I'll give it to you."

She relaxes into my touch enough I can breathe. "I need time to process, Foster. Right now, I can't handle much more than that."

My brows dip as I fight the instinct to hold on tighter. After a second, I nod.

"I'm letting you walk away now, but I'm going to follow. I won't be right behind you, but I'm going to be there." I press my forehead to hers. "Because last time, when you had to walk away, I went in the opposite direction, and it took way too fucking long to find us again."

I kiss her, and her fingers wrap around my wrist as she kisses me back.

Thank fuck she's kissing me back.

"I'm yours, Remi Sinner. Always. And there's no ending where you aren't mine."

My hand falls away, and I step back. This time when she walks away, I hang my head back between my shoulders and look up at the rafters, fighting like hell to stay where I am.

40

REMI

FOOTSTEPS FAST APPROACH from behind as I rush down the hall toward the venue's exit. I glance over my shoulder but keep walking, despite my shadow's long strides after me.

"I can't right now, Colt." My voice shakes. My chest hurts. I feel seconds away from collapsing.

So many thoughts swim and swirl, mixing with the old ones. Anytime I try to latch onto an emotion, another sweeps me away. Foster was there at the lake. He came for me. Then he didn't tell me. And made me easy to find by ditching my phone. He knew Sage. He blamed me for Chase's accident.

Colton falls into step beside me. "We don't have to talk, Remi. I'll just feel better if I know you're safe on the bus."

A tear slips before I wipe it away. "Thank you."

Fans are unable to access the back lot with the adjusted security measures, deeming the escort unnecessary, but I appreciate it all the same. Especially since he doesn't say a word.

The night air chills my skin once we step outside, and I slow partway to the bus. I close my eyes, breathe deep. A warm presence lingers. I wouldn't be surprised if Colton eases closer specifically so I don't get cold. I shiver anyway. More from a decrease of adrenaline and emotion.

"Here."

When I look over, he's yanking off his sweatshirt. I glance at the bus, then back to him, and he tilts his head.

"You look like you need a second." He shoves the sweatshirt at me. "Take it. None of the band will come out without me knowing."

With a halfhearted smile, I push my hands through the sleeves. I only wear half of it, warming my front.

He strolls over to lean against the side of the bus. His expression stays harsh, body language rigid.

"You heard us," I say.

He nods, pursing his lips. "I heard enough."

"I'm sorry we didn't tell you. Are you mad at me?"

"Not really. I'm fucking livid at Foster, though."

I'm about to tell him it was me who didn't want to tell him, but he sighs and tips his head back.

"No one ever told me your name after they got back from Europe. Just that some chick broke Foster's heart, and he went after *her*. And then everything went to shit. Months went by with Chase in his recovery. There never felt like a good time to bring up the ghost girl. The one time I did, Foster asked if I'd do him a solid and forget about it entirely."

I nod, crossing my covered arms as I go to lean beside him. He angles his face to see me, solemn and with a haunting devastation to his eyes. Suddenly I wonder if it's always existed, and I haven't noticed until now.

"I'm sorry for what happened to Chase, too." I pick at a loose thread on the sweatshirt's hem. "I can't imagine what you went through."

His gaze lowers. "Yeah."

We fall silent, and I stare up at the sky even if the city lights block the stars. The pang in my chest grows as I think about the extent of the damage caused—one moment catalyzing so many others. It all comes back to me.

When I ran from Daniel, I set so much suffering in motion.

After a few minutes, Colton straightens, listening to someone through his earpiece.

"Be there in a few," he tells them. He tips his head toward the bus's door. "We can come back out after everyone else is on the bus if you want."

I shake my head. "I'll be okay."

And I am. Until I climb the ladder and crawl under the blankets. Then I'm not okay for a while.

WHEN I WAKE UP—THOUGH I barely sleep—the erratic emotions from last night have dulled to a soft blur.

The last couple weeks of challenging myself to not hide from the past so much, I imagine, make a difference in how I'm coping with the new information. The reawakened anxiety that accompanies it.

No panic attacks though.

It's early, so I expect everyone to still be asleep. But when I descend, all the emotions surge again. Foster's on the couch in sweatpants and no shirt. He's facing me, his back against the arm, both knees bent to prop up his notebook as he writes.

He flicks his eyes up to me and slides out an earbud. The apprehension's evident in his face while he waits for me to decide how the scene unfolds. I feel the new tear, which first developed last night. Hearing the strain in his voice when talking about Chase had part of me wanting to run into his arms. But the other part can't reconcile how he played a role in what nearly cost Roman his life—and broke me in ways I never thought possible.

Suffice to say, I hate this tear as much as the old.

Especially since Foster's no more at fault now than five years ago—I'm still the root.

"I don't know how I feel," I admit.

He nods. "You don't have to know. You just need to feel it."

What I feel is the tug. To him.

So I follow it.

Foster moves the notebook aside when I come to crawl between his knees to lie on his chest. He adjusts to accommodate. Once we've settled, he kisses the top of my head. My cheek presses against his heated skin, and he sets his music to play through the speakers. His fingers run up and down my back as I absorb everything him and fall asleep.

If dreams were premonitions, mine would be something about lights and tunnels and annihilating trains.

BY THE END of the night, my picture's plastered online.

Nothing concrete, but half a dozen shots of Adams North and *the girl* on tour with him. No mention of the documentary or my name, but fuzzy images of me with my legs wrapped around him, his hands on my ass. His mouth shamelessly devouring mine. Those are amplified by one of me tucked under his arm when the fans were rough.

It's the most visible I've been. Not only in the last several years but in my life.

"Baby, I'm so fucking sorry." Foster takes his phone from my hand, pocketing it.

We're tucked away backstage in a dark hallway, my back pressed to the wall. Christian gave him a heads-up right after the encore and sent him screenshots.

He braces his arm on the wall above me and tips my chin up with his fingers. His pale eyes shift between mine, analyzing what I imagine is a blank look. The rest of me blanks too. My reaction's not as bad as I expected. Blank beats unable to breathe.

"This is my fault. No one would care if I didn't maul you when I came off stage the last two shows."

I swallow, blinking out of the initial shock. "It was bound to happen."

"No. I promised we'd do this on your terms, Remi. Then I put a spotlight right on us." He shakes his head, and his nostrils flare. "How can I make this right?"

The answer isn't one I want to give, but I'm so overwhelmed and exhausted. "I think I should go back to New York."

His eyes crush closed when he winces. "*Fuck.*"

"The key scenes are done," I tell him. "Xander's more than capable of finishing up with the other two. He can use my questions for your interviews, and I'll be back for the last one when the tour wraps."

"Sounds miserable." Foster's lashes flutter open, and he adds, "For me."

I reach up and drag my fingers over his jaw. Stubble scrapes the tips. "It's just too much at once for me right now. My feet aren't even back under me after what you told me yesterday. About you, Sage, the lake, and now I realize why you resented me so much. Because of me, you weren't there for Chase—"

"That's not yours to claim, Remi," he says, cutting me off. "That regret is all mine."

I disagree but let him have it.

"Still, I haven't finished processing what all of it means. Then add the stress of filming and being on the road. And now my picture's going to be everywhere."

"You're safe." He clutches the side of my face. "If that's what you're worried about…"

I flash a small smile. "I know."

And I mean it. The panic over my photo being public is fading. I just needed the parts of me that believe no one will hunt me down because of them to catch up.

After living in fear, some preservation tendencies never fully vanish. The gut reactions remain, the instinct to run or hide threatens to take hold before all else. Fear is meant to protect us, and sometimes you need to talk it down. I might not have the healthiest dialogue with mine, but it's at least taking my calls.

I touch the side of his neck. "But if I stay, there will be more pictures. People will be trying to figure out who I am. It'll probably get more intense since, as far as I know, you haven't been seriously linked to anyone."

"No one," he confirms. "You're right, though. They won't stop anytime soon."

"I'm not ready for that added battle yet. Colton said Felix is having trouble because he's needing to fight his demons while under a spotlight now. I've witnessed him struggling more the longer the tour goes on."

His head bobs. "I'm watching him. We all are."

"Good." I knew he would be, but it feels better hearing him verify. "And like you said, we'll be under one now too. I can't do what I need to right now. You've already helped me heal more than I ever thought I would. I'm not all the way there yet, but I want to be—I think I *can* be whole again one day. So much of that has to do with you. I just need to give myself a better chance to get there before taking on the world too."

The muscles of his jaw tighten, gaze studying me for reassurance or an alternative, I'm unsure, but he must find whatever he needed.

"Shit." He gently brushes his lips over mine, a resigned sigh following as his thumb sweeps across my cheek. "I meant what I said last night. I'll let you leave, but I won't let you go. I'll find a way to be there, even if it's in pieces for a while. You know my conditions, Remi—anything you need as long as I keep you."

41

FOSTER

Remi's on a flight the next morning.

Deep down I knew she would be the second Christian showed me the two of us splashed over gossip sites and celebrity rumor accounts.

The pictures couldn't have popped up at a worse time, given what I hit her with the other night. I wouldn't want her dealing with the hounding she'd have been in for regardless, but the blow was more brutal.

Despite what she said, the sinking feeling I've lost her skirts around my edges. Ready to trickle in and threaten my sanity.

I swore to show up some way in her life while she's not here. Now I need to figure out how the fuck I'm pulling that off so it doesn't just feel like a cheap Band-Aid slapped over a four-inch cut.

Tension radiates through the bus once she leaves and tags along to the dressing room before our concert. Shockingly, I'm not the source, but it certainly involves me.

Petty Colt has been engaged after he overheard us from the wing. It's not as entertaining as usual. Mostly because he's hurt I didn't tell him who Remi was the second she showed up in Prague. I hate him resenting me for it, but I wouldn't change it.

He would have backed me up on not wanting her on tour and likely told Christian the reasons.

And I wanted her on tour. Even amid actively refusing to sign off on her directing, I wanted her there. Call it a self-torture kink, but once she'd dropped directly in my path, I opted for punishing myself over losing the chance of seeing her.

As we walk off after the encore, Christian's on a call with someone, telling him a flash flood damaged the venue in Atlanta. The canceled show creates an unexpected two-day gap in our schedule.

The extra downtime couldn't have come at a better time, and within a few hours, I've hauled Colton and his cranky ass with me on a flight of our own.

I'm in need of a hard reset, and only one rooftop will do.

THE PATIO on top of Chase and Val's house is better than anything Chase and I found on our own. The stairs come out next to the elevator, and one entire side is open for the view. Smooth flagstone underfoot, a fireplace, a dining table for entertaining, and a lounge area that makes you feel lazy just by looking at it.

Perfect for relaxation, philosophical moments, and a place to gain a little bro-spective.

Weed helps with the last one as much as the bro who guides me through it.

We haven't needed a four a.m. roof session in a long time, but he was waiting up here with beer and a joint even though he doesn't drink or smoke. Now I'm halfway through both, and Chase is staring at me while I watch the night skyline.

"You never told me you found her back then," he says. "We need another math lesson on what you tell your best friend?"

My mouth quirks up at the thought, but I grow somber again. "I didn't see a point. She was gone, and you were dying."

I didn't give details on the reason Remi disappeared on me, only that she had a good one, and he isn't pushing for more.

When he doesn't say anything, I glance over, and he's nodding. "Only for like a week. You've had five years since then to fill me in."

Tightness creeps into my throat, all the regrets splashing at the surface. "I didn't tell you because it was the reason I wasn't there for you that night." My voice is gravelly, and I have to swallow to clear it. "If I hadn't gone after her, we would have gone rock climbing with Colt."

His eyes dart to our sullen brother in a wicker chair who refuses to sit near me, but he's most definitely been listening to every word.

"Everything would be different," I continue. "You were on that ladder because of me. Because I went after her instead of being where I needed to be. I'd already missed so much in Europe…" I blow out a breath and drop my head onto the chair back. "At the time I thought she betrayed me and kept me from helping you. You lost so fucking much because I was chasing her. You were right. I fucking acted like my dad, and you almost died because of it."

A beat passes before wicker drags over brick. The scraping ends, and Colt drops into the chair he moved to be beside mine. He won't look at me, but he's here. Like he always is when I need him to be.

I take a hit and roll my head to see Chase on my other side. His jaw muscles are rippling beneath the skin, and he leaves me with his profile.

"First of all, you're nothing like that man. Next up, almost." Then he looks at me. "I *almost* died. I didn't. I'm here." He huffs a laugh, not amused but more matter-of-fact. "Nothing that happened was your fault, Foster. I told you that. *This* was the problem." He taps his fingers against his temple. "My brain was the enemy. The call was coming from inside the house."

Shaking my head, I lower my gaze. "And I should have—"

"What?" he says, cutting me off. "Stayed at my side twenty-four-seven? Diagnosed me? Fuck, brother. *I* didn't know what was going on, why the fuck would you?" He swipes my bottle cap off the table between us and tosses it over my head, so it lands on Colton. "You listening, fuckface? Because it's been a minute since you heard this shit too."

Colton's stoic and locked down, but his eyes flick to mine for a second. He blames himself for letting Chase climb the ladder, and I always counter I'm the reason he wanted to. We both missed the signs Chase was battling with something. Colt realized it that night before they left the bar, but he has his own hindsight to deal with—calls and texts with Chase while we were in Europe.

Chase sighs. "I have bipolar disorder. Chances are I wouldn't have gotten treated until something happened. So, if it wasn't that ladder that night, it could have been a million other things during an episode. I won't blow rainbows up your dick and claim I wouldn't change anything. What happened fucking sucks, and most of the world is *not* built for a paraplegic. But I survived. I adjust. I'm living. I went back to school and landed an easy-as-fuck job that pays more than rock star bodyguard."

Colt snorts and mumbles an, "Asshole," which could apply to me or Chase at the moment.

"I have both of you, and believe me, I do not envy the lives you live." He licks his lips, smiles. "And I have a hot-as-fuck wife who's smart, talented, so fucking bratty, and has an ultrasound appointment in about seven hours."

"The fuck?" Colton's out of his chair, hands on his hips in my peripheral, but I'm entirely focused on Chase.

He shrugs. "Val told me I had to wait until after her appointment, so if you want me to live to see my fucking kid, act surprised."

I'm grinning as I remember she pawned off her beer on Colt when we were axe throwing. "Congrats. It's cute you think it's yours, brother."

Chase pulls a face and flips me off. "Fucking bet it is. Don't make me detail it for you."

"We already know enough," Colton says, cringing. "I know more about the interworking of your dick and little dudes than I ever wanted to."

"Preach." I raise my beer bottle to that one. "No more demonstrations either."

Colt nods, eyes wide in his agreement on that one. "But ... I am going to wake up Val and tell her you spilled." He dashes for the stairs the second the last word's out of his mouth.

"*Shit.*" Chase grabs a votive candle off the table, intending to launch it at him, but he rethinks and sets it down.

I smile at him when his head swivels around. "I'm fucking happy for you and Val."

"I'm happy for us too." He tips his head back and forth, weighing it. "I am until Val comes for me. Which means, we better solve your shit while I'm still with you."

"Right." I pull smoke into my lungs, using it as an excuse not to say more.

As if Chase would allow it. He's still waiting when I blow it out, his brows raised.

"Someone close to her got hurt because of me. When I found her at the lake, I did something that caused her a lot of pain. All this time, she thought it was her fault, but I was the reason it all played out like it did." I groan and take a swig of my beer, shaking my head as I rest the bottle on my leg. "She said she just needs to process, and I'll see her when the tour ends, but ... I need more. I need to know she can forgive me, and we'll get what we lost out on before."

"So get started." When I look over, Chase nods like he's onto something. "You need more, do more. You need to know she can forgive you, start your groveling tour. If you want to make sure you have a chance at the life you lost with her, build it so when you have her back, it's already there."

I let out a puff of air and half-smile. "I have a head start on one of those at least."

My call with Smith finally happened, and what he said was so much better than I ever hoped for.

"Make a plan, Foster. Be the charming motherfucker I know you can be and then kick on the broody looks to guarantee results. She'll be there when the tour ends, and you'll realize she missed you as much as you're missing her." Then he shrugs. "They always say distance makes the dick grow harder and shit."

There it is. The bro-spiration.

I snort, shaking my head. "You are the worst."

"Yeah," he sighs out as I kill the joint. "And you're in love, brother. Again."

Exhaling, I correct him, "Still."

When I glance over, he claps me on the shoulder and grins. "Another thing that never ends, huh?"

Colton waltzes back over, looking put out. "She said she'd punish you in the morning. Ruined my night if I'm being honest." He pulls the wicker chair so he's facing me and Chase when he sits.

"You need to be done being petty, my brother," I tell him.

He wrinkles his nose. "Give me a good reason, and I'll consider it."

I slump back in my chair, looking at the horizon beyond him. "We have stops to add on the tour for groveling."

He sighs. "Fine. And we're renegotiating my contract for more pay."

Of course we are.

42

REMI

I AM ENAMORED with Adams North.

He's perfected being a dick. He's demanding. He's rough around the edges, soft, compassionate, stubborn, sweet, and each one of those bits of him shows in the footage Xander has sent through in the last couple days.

And it's not just him. Felix and Dev open up more, and the band's cohesiveness and dynamic take center stage.

The band members are interviewing each other randomly. They pop on the glasses for candid moments between themselves, whether it's in their pre-show huddle, showing their circled shoes, or sneaks behind the bunk curtain when one's asleep.

All of the new stuff is amazing, raw, real.

Of course I know exactly who is responsible. The man behind it all.

Because Foster's sending pictures and videos straight to me. Like he used to.

Between concerts and writing, which he also shares, he shows me forgotten places and accidental finds in different cities up the Eastern Coast.

And fountains. He seeks out a fountain in every city for me.

An annoyed Colt is a frequent flyer, accompanying Foster from place to place. But he looks annoyed at the activity, not the man, so at least he seems to have forgiven his best friend.

Then the video chats start—the neck of his acoustic while he works on a song, an argument between the band and Colton when Felix locks the door on him during a writing session. The bodyguard threatens to kick the shit out of the guy he's guarding if they don't take a break.

Foster even calls from center stage in the middle of their set. *"Just wanted to say hey."*

But one afternoon, he goes back to sending me a pre-recorded video.

"I fucking miss you," he says, camera on him.

He's walking outside in a black hoodie, no sunglasses or hat. Not much more than some bare tree branches appear behind him with the gray winter sky. When he stops, he softly groans.

"I've spent too much time fucking missing you, Remi. I'll warn you now, I'm going to be clingy as fuck for years."

He said he's going to be.

"Be ready when I come for you. But before any of that happens, there's something I need to do." He smirks, an eyebrow rising. "I'm going to knock on a door, and I need you to answer one."

When he flips the camera, my breath catches. For a second, I thought it would be mine, but it's not. Foster shows me a white front door with a winter wreath of reds and golds. Without anything more, I know it belongs to a quaint little house in the suburbs of Philly.

Then he knocks. "Open the door, Remi."

The video cuts right as the door starts to open. I look to the one in my apartment, a smile spreading. I'm already rushing toward it when the knocking starts. I jerk it open, and my favorite smile in the world waits for me—well, one of my favorites. Roman's shares its spot now.

"How was my timing?" Roman asks.

I laugh and throw my arms around his neck. "It was perfect."

His hug lasts longer than usual, and then he aims a narrowed look at me while pulling back. "No warning Adams North was going to show up at my door?"

My squint meets his as I move aside for him. "Did you even know what Adams North looked like before he showed up?"

"I am *not* that old," he says over his shoulder. He tosses his winter jacket and plops on the couch, and I'm right behind him.

"I can't believe you met Foster."

He nods. "Sure did. And I was right, I like him better than Xander."

"Not surprising," I deadpan. "But why was he there?"

One side of Roman's mouth turns up. "Foster thought he needed to apologize to me for what happened when we were staying at the lake."

My muscles stiffen as understanding dawns. "Oh."

He watches me for a second, like he can see the internal reactions I'm trying to tamp down.

"I always believed it was my fault they found us," I admit. "The timing lined up with when I took your car and went to Ashfield for my dad's SD card, and I thought someone followed me." I lower my gaze and breathe for a second while willing the edge off the memories and guilt they bring along for the ride. "But Foster told me he was there a day earlier. About taking my phone and throwing it, and I'm guessing he told you about the tracker on it—I'm so sorry, Roman."

"Yeah, yeah," he drawls.

His unbothered response makes me look up, and I repeat, "Yeah, yeah?" but with far more confusion.

"I get it, Remington. You're sorry. Foster's sorry." He ducks in closer, gaze locked on mine. "And now I'll tell you the same thing I told him. There's no need for an apology because there's not a damn thing to forgive."

"But—"

He holds up his palm, indicating he hasn't finished. "Even if the phone was the how and why, it's not yours or his to carry the guilt over. The evil of others isn't our responsibility. All we can do is try and cancel it out in whatever ways we find."

Biting back tears, I force a smile and nod an okay. But it's not. His kindness is a given. I wouldn't expect anything else. But it's not the *how* and *why* that matters here. It's the *what*—Roman dehumanized and beaten.

He sighs at me, shaking his head. "Foster gave me the same fake-ass smile." Roman pulls a knee up on the couch between us, twisting to face me with his arm stretched along the back of the couch toward me. "Here's the truth I need you to understand. It could have been the phone. It also could have been the guidance counselor at the high school."

I draw back a little at his statement.

With a week remaining in the semester, I had to contact the counselor to verify what I needed for graduation and confirm my transcripts would be sent to NYU. I'd already taken most finals and only needed to submit a paper. By then, everyone knew about my mom's death, so they didn't expect me in classes. She just needed an address to mail my diploma and documents for a scholarship.

"You said she had to keep any information confidential since I was eighteen."

"And Daniel should have been arrested for Rebecca's murder, pretty girl." He exhales slowly, looking down between us at the tan cushion. "I never told you this, but three days before they broke in, I filed a report with state authorities."

"What?" I ask.

He shrugs. "I wanted to believe in justice. It was supposed to be anonymous, but … it could have found its way into the wrong hands. *I* could have been followed. The corrupt pieces of shit might have tracked down people I knew and searched properties, finding Bea's. Rebecca could have mentioned the lake house to Daniel at some point. Or maybe it was none of those things," he says. "If that man was planning to look until he found us, he was going to find us, Remington. I'm just fucking glad it was me in the living room when they broke the glass with guns."

I tip my head to the side, resting my cheek on his hand. "I've always felt like such a terrible human for hiding. For just listening while they said such horrible things and hurt you so badly. Maybe if I would have offered to—"

Roman cuts me off. "Fuck off with whatever you're about to say. I never would have forgiven myself if they touched you. Hell, I probably would have died trying to end them all."

I blink away tears, and he brushes his thumb over my temple.

"You've suffered enough over other people's bullshit. We both have. And I'm so fucking proud of you for living your life again." His lips lift at the corners. "I can't kill the monster in your closet. But you can stop believing in him—"

"And it's damn near the same thing," I finish with him.

He nods and smiles my tied-for-favorite smile. "Even strung out, I was fucking parenting. Not only that, but my shit holds up whether you're eight or twenty-three."

I laugh and wryly remind him, "You also told me if I ever stole you anything worth pawning, you'd give me a cut in gummy bears."

Roman winces. "Let's not relive my greatest hits."

"Or the time you explained the importance of always knowing my dealer?"

He scrubs his hand over his face. "I had to open my goddamn mouth." But then he settles his gaze on me again, all warm and kind and safe. "I know you won't entirely believe that none of the blame lies with you or him right away, but swear you will piece by piece. Whittle away at it for me, yeah?"

I nod, listening and committing to it. "Yeah."

"Great. I can't ask for more. It can count as my Father's Day gift." Not giving me time to respond to that one, he adds, "And so you're up to speed on the rest of his visit, Imane cuddled on, cried on, and then threw up on Adams North."

My eyes close for a long moment, lips pressed together. "Please tell me you got pictures of at least one?"

"The first," he confirms, shifting to show me.

The idea of Foster snuggling an almost-two-year-old should not be so sexy to me or my ovaries. But it very much is. Then I see Imane on his lap, and I am unrecoverable. Her face is smooshed into the front of his hoodie while her little hands hold the strings, and he's looking down at her with a bewildered smile.

"Where are we at with Foster now?" Roman asks as he tucks the phone away.

"I love him." I sigh. "I have loved him, probably all along. But I think I'm finally ready to admit it. At least to you."

Roman gives a long nod. "I'm glad you said that."

My glare narrows, my curiosity piqued by his response. "Why does it feel like there should be more to that sentence?"

"Because there is." He roughs up my hair before standing. "Let's grab dinner."

"You're not going to tell me?"

"Nope." On his way to the door, he glances over his shoulder and cracks a grin. "You'll find out soon on your own."

IN THE FOUR days after Roman appeared at my door, I've received something from Foster every day. Flowers, a hoodie that smells like him, and a mug with a camera on it that says, *Keep It Reel*.

Then on Christmas Eve he sends an empty film canister which holds a key. No explanation, no indications of its purpose. I message him a picture of it with question marks, but he only sends more back.

Always cryptic and vague.

Roman convinces me to spend the holiday at his and Bea's house. And of course, Foster shows up in parts.

His gifts are already under the tree when I arrive. He sent a toy guitar for Imane—red and black like his—to go with the drums he sent her after his visit. So I guess a bass is next on his list.

Bea and Roman receive tickets to a theater in the city for next month, along with Foster offering up my services to babysit when they go.

I want to have an opinion about it, but honestly, I'm already looking forward to it.

After I return to my apartment, my Christmas gift shows up. A delivery guy hauls in three vintage cases that scream movie set. Once he vacates with his cart, I flip the latches on the first and turn all giddy, seeing the packed-away mount. I scramble for the next and actually squeal at the studio camera from the 1930s. The third is accessories, lenses, and the original manual.

Foster's present sits wrapped in the corner where our tree leaned last year, and I lug the cases over beside it.

The mysterious *soon* reveals itself the following day. Or what I'm guessing is the *soon*.

I'm reviewing the latest footage from the crew when there's a pounding at my door. But when I check the peephole, rather than a delivery, I see the back of a chick's head. A long black ponytail over the hood of her winter coat, and her arms crossed.

Figuring she's here for Xander—not the first time someone's shown up when he doesn't respond—I smother a groan and open the door to tell her he's not here. And not interested since he clearly hasn't talked to her recently.

"Can I help you?" I ask, already knowing the answer.

Except then she turns around, and the entire world folds in on itself.

"Oh my God, it's really you."

Sage rushes me, locking her arms around me. It would knock the air out of me if I had any, but it vanished the second I saw her face. I slip back into my body after a second, a quiet sob escaping as I embrace her back.

"How…?"

"Foster," she chokes out, pulling back and grasping my face, tears falling. "Or Adams? That's a mind-fuck on its own."

I scan her over like I do Imane, seeking out every change. She's the exact same yet wildly different, and I drag her back for another hug. We stand just inside the door for a long time, not talking while we cry.

When I finally pull away, I step around her to shut the door. "I can't believe you're here."

She spins, her eyes shiny. "I'm here, and I'm so sorry, Remi. I was a selfish teen and incredibly naive, and I let you down. I've wished so many times I could go back and help you the way I should have."

I shake my head, confused by her apology. "Did Foster tell you—"

"Nothing," she says. "He only told me you'd been on tour with him, and if you didn't want to see me, I had to leave."

"Don't leave." I tug open one of the buttons on her coat to emphasize, and one side of her mouth tips up.

She shucks off her coat, following me into the living room. I sit, she sits, and then she scoots closer.

"You weren't okay back then," she says. "Miles tried to tell me shit wasn't okay for you so many times, but I couldn't see it. I was oblivious to so much, and after you left, I still twisted it to be about me. I'd decided you two were together, so when Daniel told me you and Roman ran off together, I believed him. I said you guys were hanging out, feeling sorry for myself because I was the one left behind."

Fresh tears fall down her cheeks, and I tame my own, her words striking so many tender spots inside me while simultaneously warming them. The pain easy to absorb and breathe through.

"It's okay—"

"It's not, Remi." She grabs my hand on my leg, squeezing and reminding me she's with me. "It was never acceptable. Miles was so angry with me. After I met up with Foster and still thought nothing was wrong, he broke up with me. He said I needed to grow the fuck up and realize how the world really works."

That explains why when I searched social media for Sage Ricci last year, I didn't find her. I post videos and documentary clips on my account RSFrames, and someone in a shot reminded me of her. She always said she would lock Miles down ASAP, so it felt like a safe bet. The thought was fleeting, though, and I never looked up Sage Teller.

"I'm sorry," I say, but she shakes her head at me.

"He was right. My second year of nursing school, I took a class where we learned how to interact with patients who suffered domestic abuse. So much made me think of you. Things you'd say and do. The pillows—fuck, Remi, and the trellis." She presses her lips together for a second and exhales. "Your mom never stopped using, did she?"

"No," I whisper.

Sage nods. "In high school, I knew she took pills, but I thought it wasn't a big deal, or else Chief Kane would do something about it." Her gaze lowers. "And Roman taking you to your dad's funeral because she was sick?"

"She was high."

When she looks up, her face crumples. "Goddamn it. No wonder you skipped town."

Anxiety lodges in my throat as I consider telling her the truth, but then there's another knock.

"Hold on." I leave her on the couch and check the peephole, then I whip around to her. "Did you skip over a rather important detail?"

She shrugs, lips curving up. "I was getting there."

This time I'm at least prepared when I open the door—tears burn my eyes anyway.

"Hey, Rem," Miles says. He charges in and flings his arms around me. "Your parking situation sucks."

I laugh, but it's half sob, and then I shove him away. "You fucking broke up with her? You unworthy asshole."

He smiles and jerks me back into the hug. Tighter. Longer.

Once I pry him off of me, he takes off his coat and settles in next to Sage. Seeing them together in my tiny Tribeca apartment feels like a fever dream. In some ways it is, given the source of my everlasting fever sent them to me.

I've been thinking about Sage a lot since I heard her voice, adding her to my list of one days. I mentioned it to Foster, and I'll never be able to thank him enough for bypassing me to make it happen so soon. Am I in emotional overload? Absolutely. Would I want anything different? Absolutely not.

They ask me about the documentary, the tour, and Foster. I tell them about it all—especially him.

Then I learn everything I missed with them for the past five years. Sage finished school and works as a labor and delivery nurse, taking extra classes for another certification. Miles has remained with the company that created *Wanderer* as a developer, but he's remote now, and they live outside of Hunts in an adorable house on a hill.

By the end of the night, I've told them the practiced words: *Daniel killed my mom*. It's a lot of crying, but so fucking cathartic. Even though I'm perfectly fine not talking about it again for a long time. They know about Roman too. The favorites and the threats.

I think what hurts my heart the most is when I open the door and Sage stops before walking out of it. "I wanted to find you when I finally opened my eyes, but I thought you probably hated me for not seeing it in the first place. But I need you to know I've missed you every day. You never said goodbye, and a piece of me has always held out hope that meant it wasn't one. It's why I called Foster every year in case he felt the same way."

"Fuck," I say. "You are terrible for mascara."

"That's why we're not married, you know?" Miles steps between Sage and the open door, his head cocked at me. "You weren't here, and we both wanted you to be a part of it." He tosses me his phone, camera already recording, and he winks. "And now you are."

I smile, aiming it at them before Sage catches up. Then her eyes bulge when Miles drops to a knee, right there on the threshold. I ease the shot out, sure to have the right angle as he reveals a box from his coat's inside pocket.

That's all the farther he gets before she tackles him. He looks prepared, though, keeping his balance, and she ends up sitting on his bent leg, opening the box herself and squealing at me like I'm the one proposing.

But he swipes the ring. "At least let me do some of it."

I text myself the video, and after they leave, I curl up on the couch. Relieved. Drained. Happy. Although, I could be happier. I message Foster a picture of the three of us together.

And then he calls. The lighting is abysmal, his face only lit by the screen. "Damn, sending them there could have backfired on me so fucking hard. But you're smiling. I love your smile."

I am smiling. He's backstage, listening to the crowd.

"Thank you," I tell him, "for the best gift you could ever give me."

He scrunches his face. "I really wish you wouldn't have said that."

"Why?"

"Because now I need to figure out what's better than best so I can give that to you too."

43

FOSTER

I FEEL like she's mine again after Roman and Sage visit her. I won't stop reminding Remi or myself of it, but the dread nudging at my consciousness has lost the war.

Now I need to surrender to something of my own.

Despite the impromptu interviews between Dev, Felix, and me, I finally cave to the softball interview I've avoided since the start of the doc. Unfortunately, that means one-on-one time with the puppy Remi abandoned for me to take care of.

I agree to record after the concert, so Xander has time to set up while we're onstage. Our vibes might never be fantastic, but I'm tolerating him better as the days go on. He watches us like Remi would as if he were channeling her. No skirts and Remi legs I imagine locked around my head, so not as fun to look at.

When I dip into a shadow by the stage tonight, I stare at my screen for a solid minute, mental gymnastics engaged. It's my mom's birthday. She hasn't responded to the voice note I sent her weeks ago, but I force myself to call her anyway. Her voicemail picks up, so I resort to another text.

Happy birthday, Mama.

I relax with my duty done and close my eyes, absorbing the sound of the crowd, but a message breaks my calm.

Do not try contacting us again.

For a number of heartbeats, I just stare at the message from my mom, but by the time I scoff and shake my head, something has twisted inside me in a way it hasn't until now.

This time when I call, it goes straight to voicemail. I know. I know right then she—or *he*—blocked me.

And that twisting escalates until it snaps.

I pocket my phone and track down Christian outside the dressing room. "The label wants to schedule the documentary to release with our album?"

"Around then. Why?"

With a shrug, I snag the door handle. "I can't be curious?"

Curious about how long I'll have between what I'm about to do and the results.

"Adams…" he warns, but I'm already in the room.

Felix sets down a bottle of bourbon and nods. "You lost? Shouldn't you be lurking in the shadows right now?"

"Nah. I think it might be time to dispel some, tease a little light into my life."

I pluck the spy glasses out of Dev's hair from where he's lounged out on the floor. He opens his eyes, long enough to acknowledge me and goes back to visualizing.

When I find where Remi's guy Nate has set up for the night, I also find Xander. Exactly the two I needed.

Nate trails off when I reach them. "Hey … uh, Adams."

I flash him a closed-lip smile and slap him on the shoulder, swiping a mic pack. "He's going to need you." I dart my eyes to Xander.

"For what?" asks the puppy.

"My solo interview. I changed my mind. I wanna do it now."

He shakes his head. "I haven't set up the backdrop yet. We won't have time before you play."

"We have a backdrop ready to go. Now grab your camera and meet me center stage. Nate, you're with me. I need you to catch audio for me."

They exchange unnerved glances before I walk away, but I almost forget a key element and spin, still going. "And get Remi on a call. I want her asking the questions."

Nate's grabbing at equipment when I flip around, sliding the spy glasses on. Turning them on, I glance to check he follows so they can pair the audio with the video later. Once we reach the stage, I wait for him.

"Set up wherever, so long as I'm in range out there."

"Yeah!" His voice cracks. "You got it." He lowers to the floor with the receiver and recorder, and then he's slinging his headphones into place. "We're recording."

I nod, throat drying. I gauge whether the tightening in my chest is a sailor's knot or noose. The question is whether I'm about to stabilize after all this time or destroy something I can't get back.

A sense of serenity joins the fray when I realize they've become the same thing. Two ends to the same rope.

The stage lights are off when I walk on, but no one needs them. And they fucking lose it. I stop center stage and wave before doing a 180. When I drop onto my ass, I lean back and brace on my palm, then slip off the glasses, turn them, and angle so the camera captures me along with the crowd behind me.

The *Adams* becomes clearer and louder, my name pulsing. The mic won't pick it up, so if Remi decides to use this, she'll need to overlay another recording, but I hear it. I always hear it.

"I'll never get used to this," I tell the camera.

I talk about our first performance as a group—before I started using a stage name, but I leave that specific part out—and compare it to the arena I'm sitting in now. During story time, I play with the crowd. I raise my right arm to see what they'll do. After that side roars, I swap to the other.

Xander looks slightly bewildered as he crosses to me. Without prompting, he sits three feet in front of me and crosses his legs like he knows what I expect of him. It almost has me impressed until I notice the position of his phone.

Sure enough, he nods. "Yeah, no problem." He hands it to me, and the fucking match to my soul is right there on the screen.

"Hey," I say to Remi.

"Hi. I have a feeling this interview won't be what I had in mind." She has her knees pulled up to her chest, head tipped to the side to rest on a couch cushion. When I smile, she sighs. "I hate when you go rogue."

"Liar."

"Any specific instructions from either of you?" Xander's unfolded a tripod, and he switches on a light attached to his camera.

"Hold her for me." I hand him his phone, and he keeps Remi facing me. "You ready to show me what a skilled interviewer you are, Rem?"

She blinks at me. "You haven't told me anything, Adams."

"Feel your way through it, baby. We're giving the world a breadcrumb to run with. Think of it like a tease—you're good at that."

While she nails me with a glare, I nod at Xander, but I trust she'll catch on quick.

Once Puppy starts rolling, he nods back.

I steady myself, banish the cutting sense of betrayal I've endured for far too long. My heart's fallen in line with my head and body, and I say a silent, *"Bye, Mama."*

This time, all I need to blow up Andrew West's life is to provide the fuse.

44

REMI

JUST LIKE FOSTER SAID, he only offers a pile of breadcrumbs to indicate a trail.

The key is his wording. Hints he decided to separate himself from the toxicity of his family. Specific regions of the places he grew up. What his dad does for a living.

Once the documentary airs, whoever wants it will know there's something to find. Enough to unbury the line between Adams North, the man the world has fallen in love with, and the abusive asshole who managed to make him feel like he wasn't worthy of love.

Later, he calls from the bus to assure me I can use the footage in the doc. He tells me why he decided to set it in motion now, and for the first time I truly wish I'd stayed on tour. Simply for tonight.

But I know leaving was the right thing. I even pushed myself to start therapy. Holy hell, was that a first session.

In three days, I review his interview twice, playing with how to incorporate clips or soundbites. The candid asks and answers between the band members has shifted my vision slightly, and this alters it more. Not enough Foster will get out of the original solo interview questions, though.

"Sinner."

I rip my headphones off as I jump. "*Jesus.*"

Heath scowls in concern for nearly giving me a heart attack on his way into his office above their garage. He ran into the house for—"*None of your business.*" Which means he went to check on Jasmine and his newborn son. Who already glares like him at seven days old, might I add.

"Have you thoroughly threatened the nanny?" I ask.

Heath ignores me, so I return to my laptop and the new files from Xander.

Despite being back for nearly two weeks, I hadn't seen my mentor until yesterday. Between Baby Erickson's arrival and the holidays, Jasmine barred him from work until the New Year.

He called me on New Year's Day, and I'm pretending it's because he missed me.

My screen lights up with a text from Xander, and I cock my head at the audio file.

> For the shot we both know will be the prelude and likely THE fucking teaser.

My mind immediately jumps to the band and projector. I won't admit it yet, but he's right. We both know. But then I reread the file name. *INTV_ADAMS_S1_RAW001.wav*

ME

> Adams did his solo interview with you?

I'm even more confused he voluntarily sat down for it. I honestly thought I was going to have to video chat tonight or tomorrow with him and strip while asking the questions myself.

XANDER

> He asked me. And I swear his first answer is specifically for your shot.

After switching my headphones over, I put them on and play

the audio. It starts with Xander introducing the interview with date, location, and subject. Then he says, "Rolling," and asks the first question. The one I've wanted since before I flew to Prague. Before the dressing room and museum, when it was specifically for Adams North, guitarist and lead singer.

"*Tell me, Adams, why Of Men and Wolves?*"

"*Because we're of the same cloth.*"

There's a pause that sounds deliberate, and I hit stop, my gut screaming for me to pull up the video file of the band and their past selves. Then I play them together with the video at half speed like I imagined.

Foster's voice returns, low and gritty, the cadence hypnotizing. "*Man sees their counterpart in the wolf. In the wild, a wolf moves to remain alive, chasing prey, fighting for their place in the pack. For us, the movement comes from fear of being left behind. Our chase is for purpose. Our fight to find somewhere we belong. Like the wolf, we stay restless to survive, knowing nothing is ever promised. We stay hungry, which is how we're most alike. And it's that endless hunger that shapes the lives both of men and wolves.*"

The audio ends after the band has taken the stage, so only the projection of Foster, Dev, and Felix in the music store remains. I take off my headphones to listen to the audio already overlayed with the clip. The roar of the crowd, and then Adams North says, "*Tell me how y'all are doin' tonight.*" More screams. "*No better place to be, right?*"

After three beats from Felix on the drum and Foster's first note, I pause the clip, leaving it zoomed in on Projector Foster and his guitar.

I audibly sigh and crash back into my chair, a squeeze in my chest. He's so ideal I ache.

"For fuck's sake. Wipe the drool, Sinner." Heath's behind my chair, hovering above me, and I tip my face up to see him. "He's at least subtle with his obsessing."

As he walks away, I swivel in my chair. "What does that even mean?"

He grunts and wiggles his fingers at me to follow him to his setup of monitors. I roll my chair over and plop beside him in his, and he immediately grabs my armrest to push me farther away.

"You're too sweet to me," I say dryly.

"I'll correct that starting now." He opens a folder of video files and selects the one of the writing session in Seattle when Foster wore the glasses. "I was bored out of my mind last week, so I started reviewing older footage to see if anything has a new look. Jasmine pointed this out, and unfortunately for me, I couldn't unsee it."

After Heath skips about five minutes in, Foster's view shifts as he grabs the neck of his acoustic. Once he settles back, his head turns so we can see into the viewing area through the glass. Colton's slumped in a chair, talking to Christian in another, and I'm in a third, scrolling on my phone.

My questioning eyes shift to the director, and before I say anything, he makes an irritated sound and switches to a different video. Another of Foster from late October when Christian demanded he wear the glasses on stage in Wyoming. Heath speeds through it until the shot moves from the crowd to the side.

To me and my camera.

The dressing room. He looks up when I walk in and follows me through the room as I set down my bag. The shot settles on Felix and his sticks, but the angle keeps me and my skirt in frame the entire time.

Heath opens a fourth file.

"How are you remembering all of these? Did you make a list of file names?"

He huffs. "Like I care that much." His eyes dart to me like I'm not getting it. "It's a safe bet if he's wearing the glasses or using a cam, you make an appearance. I've also caught him watching you from the other two's perspectives. All angsty and pining."

My smile slowly grows, but with Foster it feels like it could stay forever. Always.

"And now you're doing the dopey thing too." Heath leans

back in his chair, finger pressed to his temple. "It makes sense he'd go after you. When we met last year, one of the first things he did was praise your work."

The comment takes a second to register, and then it lands *hard*. "Last year?"

He glances over. "He was at the party you skipped in LA last spring."

I immediately know the one he means because it's the *only* one I missed. "I didn't skip it. I was sick."

"Whatever," he says dismissively. "He mentioned the scene in the Scars&Stars music video where the camera circled the drummer with the rain falling, and the water bounced with every hit of the sticks—"

"My scene?"

"Everything that happens on my set is mine, Sinner." He hesitates and forces out, "But I was drunk and might have accidentally given you credit." An annoyed grunt. "And maybe said Remi Sinner is the only name to watch." Pause. "And you'd take my spot one day."

"You…" I shake my head a little to clear it and try again. "You told Adams about me nearly ten months ago?"

He nods, reaching for his phone, likely to avoid the other stuff he told me. And we are *definitely* circling back to it once I get past this part. Foster knew I worked with Heath before the documentary—then I remember the label told Heath when they first floated the idea to the band, they pushed his name as someone they'd want. For his style.

"Can you do whatever you're doing anywhere other than my desk, Sinner?" He nudges my chair with his foot and sits forward, grabbing his mouse. "I'm not drunk right now, so I don't particularly like you."

I stand to roll my chair away. "Careful, or I'll stop holding back and overtake you tomorrow. What was it you said? I'm the *only* name to watch?"

His lips perk. "Ha. Fuck off."

Concerned end-times are upon us, I abruptly stop. "Did you just … chuckle?"

The look he lands could devour a lesser prepared person's soul. "Never. Go order coffee or something useful."

WHEN FOSTER CALLS AHEAD of the concert that night, he's backstage with people milling around him.

I haven't talked to him since the Heath revelation because they had a meet and greet earlier. "I thought you were calling me when you were back on the bus."

"I'll call then, too," he says. "But I have a couple people who want to say hi before they play."

And then neon colors, feathers, and squeals fill the screen. The Forest Nymphs take over his phone.

"Oh my God," I say as he steps back out of the chaos that is the band I worked with at Sound Clash.

Bianca screeches a, "*Remiiiiii,*" then the phone jerks from the bassist to Jaelyn. They both have blunt bangs to their bobs now, Jae's hair's purple and Bianca's teal.

"Where the hell are you, woman?" Jaelyn throws a look over her shoulder to Foster and drops her voice quiet and unnaturally deep for her. "We're opening for Of Men and Wolves. Can you believe it?"

I can because they're amazing, but I'm handed off again before I respond.

Cys appears, not nearly as enthusiastic but a needed balance to her sisters. The drummer has buzzed off her long hair, and damn, she pulls it off. "Adams told us you're directing a documentary about them." She smiles. "Baby director all grown up, huh?"

"Baby band seems to be doing rather well themselves," I tell her.

Her sisters barge their way in for a flurry of goodbyes and

blown kisses. Once they vacate, she smiles. "We're up. Keep killin' it, film nerd."

I laugh as she's dragged backward by Bianca, the video tilting sideways to a random speaker until Foster rights it.

Just as fast as they arrived, they're gone.

"They are an experience," he says, slipping in his earbuds as he goes to a quieter space.

I'm shaking my head at him. "How is the band from my doc opening for you?"

He spins and leans on a wall. "I saw them play at Sound Clash two years ago."

"You were there?" I ask, my heart falling out of my chest.

"All three of us went. 'Echo' started charting number one a couple months prior, so we had to lay low all weekend to avoid attention."

"We were in the same place." I smile as he nods.

"I had no idea until I saw your video." His head tilts then, his look the reverent one. "Even then I would have torn that place apart to find you."

After I got back from Heath's, I reviewed Felix and Dev's perspectives from earlier in the tour.

Heath was right about the glimpses of Foster watching me.

Regardless of how invisible the crew and I tried to be, we showed up in frame from time to time when the band wore the glasses. Several times when it was me popping up, Foster looked like he might be spacing out, but his body was angled toward me, his gaze in my direction.

Heath missed something, though.

I watched Foster too.

While in the background, with or without a camera in my hands, my eyes would flit to Foster.

Then there are moments the lens captured us looking at each other. One of us first, and then the other. Our gazes often held, and the tension is palpable between us every single time. Whether harsh, hot, or longing, it threads us together, pulling and pulling.

"You said you haven't looked at anyone else since you heard my name again." It comes out softer than I intend, and I look down. "That wasn't in Prague."

His lips have turned up when my gaze returns. "I never said it was. I just couldn't let myself believe it was really you until I looked offstage that night. Even then, I couldn't."

I hate the screen between us. Between me and his cutting blue stare. His touch. His everything.

"Foster?"

The words crawl from my soul, where they've lived, to my heart, where they started. But before they finally reach the place they were always destined to be, his gaze flicks up. He groans a second later and gives a sharp nod.

"Sorry. Christian thinks he needs me for something. Tell me what you were going to say first."

I flash a smile. "Just that I miss you."

"You have no fucking clue, my beautiful thing. I'll talk to you after we pack up for the night." His eyebrow lifts, his smirk devastating. "You can reward me for being a good boy and completing my interview."

Then he's gone, and I'm on the floor in my tiny apartment.

Every part of me desperately aching for the wandering boy I've always loved.

45

FOSTER

WE'VE BEEN WRITING ALMOST nonstop for the last week.

Even our day off, we spent it with our heads buried in the music. We're in a groove, and the end is in sight. And not only for the album, but for the tour.

More than ever, I want to finish, so everything can be Remi the second we walk offstage. She'll have it rough convincing me to sit for our last interviews unless a lot of seducing is involved. So, not all that different than the other ones.

We're on the bus outside tonight's venue when I check my phone and see the text I've been waiting for the last several days. A smile tugs at my lips, and once I watch it through, I nod at Dev and Felix on the couch across the aisle.

"Colt break."

Felix rolls his eyes. "Fuck that. I can take him if he comes for you again."

Dev snorts. "I would fucking love to see a rematch, but without a solid door between us and him this time. Maybe we should skip it again."

I would. Honestly, at this point, I'm more concerned with completing this than the very real threat Colt holds to my ribs.

But I have something better than the best, and I'm not fucking waiting to give it to Remi.

Moving my acoustic to the cushions, I step behind the curtain to snag a hoodie and grab Colton's tablet from his bunk. He's been inside, checking everything over for later, but he's on his way back when I step off the bus.

"You going inside?" he asks.

"Nope. I have a woman to surprise." I clap him on the shoulder. "I'll stay in yelling distance."

He waits until I drop to the concrete by the back of the bus before disappearing into it.

After sending the video, I use my bent knees to hold the tablet while I video chat Remi.

She answers and shows me a white ceiling before she picks up the phone. Her hair's in a messy bun, wisps framing her face, and her pouty lips kick up at the corners. "Hey," she rasps in the voice that melts my heart and wakes up my dick. Fuck, I'm so gone for her. Gone, gone, gone.

"God, I want to see your tits right now."

She laughs. "One of those calls, I see?"

"Nah, but we can revisit later. Do you have your laptop with you?"

On a sigh, she shifts and holds it up. "It's like you don't know me."

Colton steps off the bus and props next to the door, just watching from a distance. Because for as much shit as he gives Remi, neither of them ever stops.

"I'm sending you a video, but watch it on your computer. I get that sexy face."

As I text it to her, she goes all skeptical on me. "Are you going to tell me what the video is? Because I don't find a cryptic Foster nearly as cute as you do."

"Fucking liar." I chuckle when she glares. "Fine. The video's from the guy about the thing."

She bites down on her lower lip to suppress a smile.

"Tell me when you hit play."

In the thirty seconds she takes to adjust and pull up the video, my pulse starts racing. Sending her Sage and Miles was risky, but this one has me nervous for an entirely different reason. This is what was already in the works when Chase said to do more, grovel, and build the life I've wanted with her.

Depending on her reaction, it could add a tick to all three.

"Am I actually allowed to watch it when I hit play?" she asks, brat fully engaged. "Or would you prefer I maintain the mystery and only listen?"

"You're going to watch it, and I'm going to watch you. Hit play."

I start it on the tablet, and then my eyes return to her. Her brow lowers as the camera pans the street, not showing much other than a few townhomes and parked cars. Without referencing the screen, I know the moment it comes into view. Remi's lips part. Her eyes dart to me and then back to her computer screen.

"Foster…"

Only then do I verify the front of the three-story Victorian is fully in frame.

"What is this?" she asks. "I thought they were starting demo right away."

"Which is why I bought it the next day," I admit.

I planned on paying for it to be renovated and sold, simply to keep the beautiful thing intact. But as my trajectory tends to do with this woman, it changed direction to aim at her.

The paint on the house is still peeling, but the porch steps have been repaired, a few boards replaced.

"They've already fixed the foundation," I tell her.

Her lips turn up, eyes fucking glowing.

"They stabilized the porch for now, but it wasn't in too bad of shape. They'll finish before they repaint the exterior."

The contractor walks inside with the camera, and Remi gasps. Why, I have no idea, this isn't the impressive part.

"It's a work-in-progress." I state the obvious with the ladders, drop cloths, and plastic sheeting. "Most of the crown molding has remained intact, so there's not much to do there other than paint. They're going to open up the floor plan throughout to make it flow or some shit."

She's beaming now as the video gives a wide sweep, pausing at the base of the stairs. "And the banisters—"

"—are going to be a fucking pain, apparently. The guy has to bring in a specialist to restore them so they don't lose the carvings."

"I love the carvings," she whispers.

And I love her. Deep love, scary love, addictive love, love I haven't even figured out yet.

"They fixed the wall to the parlor." She looks at me. "They didn't want to open it up, too?"

I slowly shake my head. "They expanded it by knocking out the wall to the next room."

She nods, and as she refocuses on the video, all my nerves and doubts vanish. I once told Remi she deserved the world. I plan on giving it to her. Because she's mine. It'll take a while, but giving her back a little bit of what she's lost sounds like a damn good place to start.

"But the room isn't a parlor anymore, Remi."

"What is it?" she asks, watching as the video approaches the door.

I wait until right before the contractor opens it. "It's a gallery."

She has a tiny dip in her brow. "A ga—"

The words stop, the rest of her stilling.

I don't need to look to know what she sees. All I need is to stare at her while she experiences what I'm confident checks the box for better than best.

Remi swallows, her head slightly shaking as she blinks away tears. "This is ... Foster?"

"I used the investigator who helped me with my parents. The private commissions were harder to track down, but most ran in the same circles. A lot commissioned more than once." I glance long enough to see the close-up of a snow leopard, but then I'm right back to her. "Not many stopped at a single one-of-a-kind from Dimitri Sinner."

I have the ultimate one.

She smiles and wipes her tears. "You bought all of these?"

"Every single one I could find. A few more are on their way—"

"Foster." She looks at me, and I look at the screen. The mantel. Stone with wrought-iron details. "Tell me those aren't…"

"They are," I say.

She inhales shakily, seeing the half dozen cameras the investigator recovered. "I don't understand. Everything he owned passed to my mom because I was a minor, and she got rid of it all."

"The investigator found records of a storage locker in your dad's name. Your mom must not have claimed it, and they auctioned it off. I expected it to lead nowhere, but a lot of the equipment in there ended up with a collector. And it wasn't just the cameras, baby."

She stares at the screen, and I can barely make out the reflection in her gorgeous eyes when the video pans to the easel beside the fireplace. Her entire face crumples when she sees the photo of the little auburn-haired girl. What I know to be gorgeous green eyes are closed, her face tilted up while butterflies flutter around her. In the picture, Remi has her hands out where a butterfly landed in her open palm.

"The butterfly garden." She swipes over her cheeks, only for a new set of tears to trail down them, but she doesn't care. "But this was just us. He'd taken me along once for a commission, but that picture's from when he took me back."

I smile at her. "You have another SD card to not look at. Only this one's personal pictures. I scanned through some Smith sent but stopped when I found that one. If you decide to look, I'll see the others then."

She is doing her little head shake, neither of us watching the video anymore. "I … you…"

"Tell me words, baby."

"I don't think I have enough," she says. Disbelief and something else duel in her eyes until the something else wins out. "I love you." She smiles, ending me—I said my ending was her. "I love you, Foster."

Better the second time, and I have no doubt it will hit even harder the next.

"I love you too. Fuck, I've *loved* you, Remi." I swallow and lick my lips before deciding fuck it. "Come to the last show. I told you I'd play your song for you at MSG, and I want you there when I do."

She smiles even more. "You wrote me a song, Foster West?"

"I wrote you all of them," I tell her.

She huffs a laugh and nods, and I nod along with her.

"Meet us before the show. Be with me after. I know that key has been driving you mad. It's to my place in LA because the house in Utah currently has a fucking padlock. But I'll be anywhere as long as you're there with me."

"Yes," she says. "I'll be there before and after."

I smile, the rest of my life smiling back at me. "I'll see you in two days then."

"I'll be seeing you in two."

The call ends. I close my eyes.

Remi doesn't come to the show.

46

REMI

I STILL CAN'T BELIEVE I'm here.

The last place I ever wanted to be again.

The last place I ever thought I *would* be again.

Other than the nurse at my side, the hospital hallway remains quiet. Blue carpet underfoot, wooden rails running along the two-tone walls, a random visitor or staff member we meet.

"It's such a tragedy." Her shoes squeak with every step, keys jingling too. "Some people will try to tell you he owed money, but no one believes it. Small-town gossip, you know? So, don't let the rumors get to you, sweetie. He's one of the good ones, but you know that as much as anyone. It's so lovely the way you and Chief Kane were able to reconcile after everything."

"So lovely," I repeat dryly.

The sarcasm earns me a curious side-eye as we turn a corner, but she won't say anything.

She won't for the same reason no one questioned the hospital's contact information being wrong. Why the department's HR couldn't provide the right phone number either, even though I was listed on their forms as well. Not a damn soul wondered why a labor and delivery nurse overheard the issue and easily tracked me down.

Because the misdirection's still in place, and it turns out I've been part of it all along.

This illusion shows the power of love and forgiveness. Where an upstanding community leader never stopped loving his late wife's troubled daughter, even after the pain I caused. So much so, he found me, and after all my regret and apologies, he forgave me for running off with Roman. We reconnected, bonded, grew close enough he entrusted me with his life.

He upheld the deceit in every aspect, never breaking character, it seems. Even when he filed required updates to paperwork at the department.

Such a fucking pity a compulsive lie finally outperformed him.

I was supposed to be in NYC tonight for Of Men and Wolves' final concert on their tour. I was going to watch Adams North take the stage, be there when Foster plays Madison Square Garden.

Instead, here I am, walking through Ashfield's hospital halls. Ready to fulfill the role Daniel cast me in.

"Remi."

When I glance over my shoulder, Sage is speeding down the hallway. She's in scrubs, hair gathered on top of her head, and has a hand latched onto the stethoscope around her neck to keep it from swinging as she rushes after us.

"Just a second," I tell the nurse, going to meet her.

She knocks me back a step as she throws her arms around my neck. It reminds me of when she'd be the only one who ever hugged me, and I close my eyes, embracing her back.

"I'm so sorry you're having to deal with this. They said your name, and when I asked why, one of the other nurses shared the gross story that bastard's been telling. I thought you at least deserved to know."

"Thank you. Even if it's the worst reason to call, I'm glad you did." I pull away, and she studies me.

"You want me to go in with you?"

Despite the knots in my belly, chest, and throat, I shake my head. "I need to do this on my own."

I've told myself the first part over and over since she called me twelve hours ago. While I booked my flight to Ohio. In the back of the Uber headed to JFK instead of to see Foster. When the plane landed, and as I rented a car, and at least every ten miles of the drive to Ashfield.

Even after saying it aloud just now, I repeat it in my head.

I need to be here. I need to walk into that room. I need to deal with the monster in my closet.

So I can fully live the life Foster's shown me glimpses of, and I know waits for me with him.

He bought me a house. He found more of my dad for me to hold onto without fear of losing it. He reminds me I'm safe, and his promises are secure.

Foster's given me back so much by simply being him and loving me. Now I need to take the last of it back myself and then run to him. Where I've always belonged.

"I'll be okay," I tell her. "I swear."

"Miles is on his way." Sage squeezes me again. "We'll be in the lobby if you need anything."

As she walks away, she checks on me twice over her shoulder before I return to the waiting nurse.

And I change my mind another half dozen times on the way.

Ultimately, I steel myself and walk with her into the ICU. The door latches behind me, and I can't even try to regulate my pounding heart.

We pass a few rooms, walking along the line of glass walls with their blinds closed. Until we stop at one, and she slides the door open.

"I let the doctor know you're here, and she's on her way."

The look she gives me then acts as a prompt for me to go inside. I mumble a, "Thank you," before she walks away.

Once alone, I cast my eyes to the pink curtain, partly drawn for privacy. It takes a second for me to settle into my body enough to step over the threshold. My fingers flex, tightening into fists at my sides as I cross the room. Every breath comes shorter, but then I round the curtain and see the bed.

My hands unclench.

Daniel lies lifeless, the ventilator causing an unnatural rise and fall of his chest. His heart monitor beeps, and tape secures the tube down his throat. Another hangs from under the blankets, draining blood into a container below. Bruises, swelling, bandages —he's unrecognizable.

It's no question someone really wanted him dead. Then again, they gave that away when they hit him with a car and then took a baseball bat to him. Just in case, I suppose.

I'm guessing money was involved. Any rumor no one wants to believe is most likely what they should when it comes to Daniel. Personally, I can come up with a plethora of reasons someone might attack him outside a sleazy bar.

I watch him for a long minute. So weak, even though he upended my life. But the man underneath always has been— spineless, desperate, and cruel. All the power comes from the illusions and the false crown bestowed upon him because of them.

"Who holds the power now?" I ask from the end of the bed.

My head turns when someone walks into the room. The doctor offers a small smile on her way toward me, ID badges clipped to one of the pockets on her white coat.

"You must be Remington," she says. "I'm Dr. Sullivan. We spoke on the phone earlier."

"Remi." I shake her outstretched hand. "Has anything changed?"

Her features soften even more, reassuring me nothing has since our conversation before I boarded my plane.

She told me then they kept him here rather than transferring him to a larger hospital due to unstable vitals. They consulted with a neurologist, and after reviewing Daniel's scans, he agreed moving him posed a greater risk. He recommended they monitor him for any increase in the swelling in his brain and reevaluate once his medical power of attorney arrives.

"I wish I had better news for you, but Chief Kane's condition hasn't changed much since the last update."

"Much?" I ask, bracing for bad news.

Half of her mouth lifts, only to instantly drop. "At all, I'm sorry to say. The most recent scans show the swelling hasn't increased, but he's shown no signs of improvement either. We've been in a wait-and-see position long enough that, now that you're here, it might be time to discuss next steps."

"Next steps," I repeat slowly.

"As I mentioned on the phone, the police department requires regular updates to a medical power of attorney form both there and with the hospital. Since Daniel named you but left no further directives, decisions on how we proceed will go through you."

She glances between me and the bed. "Would you like to talk somewhere more comfortable?"

"No. Here is perfect."

I can tell she wants to disagree but nods.

"We have three options moving forward. It's still risky, but we could attempt the transport to Johnson Mercy so Dr. Mueller can perform a procedure to relieve pressure on Daniel's brain. He can walk you through the operation before you decide, but I want to be upfront. The chance of Daniel surviving the surgery is around twenty-five percent. If he does, there's only a ten percent chance of him fully regaining brain function."

"And if I say no to the surgery?" I sound cold, but I don't care.

"We can continue monitoring to see if the swelling reduces on its own. He'd still need to be on the machines, and the chance of recovery is incredibly low." She pauses, and I look up, my gaze having lowered. "Or you can decide to discontinue life-sustaining measures, and we'll keep him comfortable."

My heart knocks into my rib cage. "You mean turn off the machines?"

I need her to clarify, to say it outright, even though she nods with regret.

"Right now, they're keeping him alive," she says. "Once we

439

C.G. BLAINE

remove them, he'd most likely pass away quickly, but we'll be able to prevent any pain."

I swallow to keep the answer from tearing out of my throat. It would be poor form after all.

I force a slow count to five, and then I slip into my role, offering a performance worthy of Daniel Kane when I play off a sad smile.

"I think that's what my stepdad would have wanted." I gesture toward the machines, not bothering to look. "He wouldn't consider this living. It wouldn't be fair to prolong his suffering."

Dr. Sullivan grasps my other arm with a sympathetic squeeze. "I know this is a hard decision, so don't feel rushed. If you need some time, we understand."

"No," I say, resolute. "It's okay. I'm ready to tell him goodbye."

The last part isn't an act. The decision is anything but hard. I think the possibility of this exact moment was the real reason I felt a need to come here.

I needed to stand over his bed so if any part of him can, he'll hear me say, "I'd like to withdraw all life-sustaining care."

Her expression is comforting. "Of course, Remi. You'll need to fill out some paperwork, and then we'll give you some time with him."

As I walk out behind her, the nurse gently places her hand on my back, guiding me down the hall.

"My heart breaks for you, sweetie." True sorrow hangs in her tone, even though the man she thinks the world is losing never existed.

"Thank you," I tell her, but I mean *I'm sorry*.

Loss is loss.

But unlike her, I feel like I'm gaining something.

The room she takes me to sits off to the side of the nurses' station, quiet and only large enough for a round table and four chairs.

"It won't be long."

440

I sigh as she walks away, and I perch on the edge of the table. A tick-tick-tick fills the space from the wooden wall clock, but after a while, a voice drifts in.

A voice I'll never not recognize.

My muscles freeze over, and a breath shudders out of me. My lungs resist drawing another because the atmosphere's changed.

The air toxic.

I expect the wave of panic that hits me, for the onslaught of memories following right behind.

But neither level me like they once would. Instead of drowning in fear and retreating, I emerge on the other side to something else. A familiar fury builds in my bloodstream, and a cool calm wraps it. The combination is potent, the same one that drove me to return to Ashfield all those years ago.

Now it drives me into the hall.

The nurse is standing in the doorway to the room beside Daniel's and glances over her shoulder.

"The Chief has some visitors, hoping for an update..." She trails off, reading me as I stalk toward her and quickly moving aside.

I charge into the small waiting room, and five police officers all snap their attention to me. I lock onto two, shoulder to shoulder. The favorites.

For a second, I'm terrified I might crumble being face-to-face with them after all this time. After their threats and warnings. Only Elvin's face pales at the sight of me. Marlo swallows before clearing his throat and looking anywhere else.

The panic radiating from them eases my own, and I can see all the way through them.

Weak but without the power or protection.

I glare a second longer, then my eyes shift to the others in the room, all in their black uniforms. I don't recognize the two guys by the couch, but the blonde woman by the wall I recall. She has a familiar apology in her eyes, but I refocus on the favorites near the window.

Elvin continues avoiding, but the trained attack dog takes a step forward. Only one.

Marlo stops, his voice tight. "Remi—"

"Get out." I deliver the command evenly, determined to hide the tremble beneath the surface, the seething. "All of you. No one is approved to visit."

Elvin casts a nervous glance at Marlo while the others shift awkwardly. I wait for an argument. A challenge.

No one says a damn word.

Even as my pulse races, I cross my arms and turn to the side, reinforcing their need to leave.

The woman relents first with a crease in her forehead, and the two guys trail behind her. She hovers outside in the hallway after they file out, but I'm watching Elvin and Marlo as they cautiously approach me.

I follow with my gaze, neither chancing eye contact. Then I remember they wanted an update, so I give one.

"You were right about what would happen if you ever saw me again, officers," I say as they pass.

It causes a misstep from Elvin, the meaning no doubt crystal clear to him. Unsurprising since it's his words I'm referencing. The last thing he shouted through the lake house, in case I could hear, was a reminder that someone will die if they ever see me again.

And here we are.

Their king is dead. Or at least he will be.

A layer of submission graces Marlo's final look at me before they disappear around the corner. I want to collapse or cry or break the second they're out of sight, emotional overload hitting hard. But the woman switches from scrutinizing them to analyzing me like she's trying to piece together the interaction.

Then she comes toward me, reaching into her jacket.

My gaze lowers to the card she holds out. I blink at it and glance up.

"Roman Moore was a good man," she says. "He was honest

and genuine in everything he did. What everyone said happened felt so out of character for him, and … well, none of it lined up with the Roman I knew, but people relapse all the time."

I stare at her, my heartbeat more frantic now than when confronting the favorites. For the first time, it feels like someone might acknowledge the castle in the sky is just a cloud.

"I wasn't wrong about him, was I," she says, not phrasing it as a question, regret weighing heavy in her tone.

It spreads to her face and stance when I shake my head.

"Roman's still all of those things," I finally manage. "He celebrated fourteen years of sobriety last summer."

She urges me to take the card, so I reluctantly accept. I read the name and see the phone number.

"I ignored my instincts when it came to you, and I refuse to do it again." She checks over her shoulder and then returns to me, talking lower to keep it between us. "Something clearly happened between you and them. My gut's telling me it was bad, and I'm so sorry for anything I did and didn't do that led to it. I doubt they'll try anything now. Not without…" Her eyes dart to the wall separating us from Daniel's room to fill in the *who*. "Just know I'll be watching anyway. I'll be watching everything from here on, Remi."

I believe her. I believe she'll truly see it too.

My lashes stave off a sting of tears. "Thank you, Julie."

"Will you also tell Roman I'm sorry?" she asks.

"I'll tell him, but he'll say you have nothing to apologize for. He's still a stubborn ass, too."

Her lips tip up the tiniest bit at the corner before she nods. She points at the card with her eyes as a reminder, then she retreats through the doorway.

After taking the deepest breath of my life, I slowly exhale. Shaky as shit, but I'm in control again, and I follow her out.

On my return to the private room, Julie's opening one of the ICU doors. I catch a glimpse of Elvin and Marlo through it, and whatever threat they posed seems far away. I'll never forget it, probably always sense it to some degree. But the air tastes clean instead of caustic, the mouth of teeth muzzled.

I banished the closet's shadows. Now for its monster.

EVERYTHING MOVES QUICKLY once I sign the papers, authorizing the doctor to remove the machines. In under fifteen minutes, the doctor's standing bedside, a different nurse across from her.

"Are you sure you wouldn't like a little more time?" she asks.

"No."

I don't hesitate with the answer this time. I don't need to.

All the pretending is over. I'm calling wrap and burning the set to ash. Daniel can burn with it, and he can do it alone.

When I move toward the door, Dr. Sullivan says, "You don't want to stay?"

I shake my head at her. "I've done what I came here to do."

Without another word, I walk out. I don't even waste a glance on what's about to become a body.

A lightness unfurls in my chest, a sense of completion accompanying it. No one ever said beautiful things needed to be tangible. And the sensation of finally leaving all this behind is absolutely a beautiful thing.

There's no question about who I want to share it with.

Foster won't be on stage for a while, so I pull out my phone to text him, opening one of the ICU doors. Once through, I look up, and it *whooshes* shut behind me as I come to a hard stop. My brow lowers at the sight farther down near the elevator bank.

Colton's leaning back against a wall, scrolling on his own phone.

"Hi."

Every part of me free falls at Foster's voice. My head jerks to the side, and he's there. Against his own wall, his head tipped back.

"You—uh, what?" It makes as much sense as him being here, honestly.

He cocks a brow, bringing his head up, and I try again.

"Why are you here? What about your concert?"

"Rescheduled it." He straightens, the bomber jacket he wore in Prague open with a dark tee underneath.

"Can you do that?"

Closing the space between us, he shrugs. "Probably."

His fingers skim my cheek on their way to push my hair back. They linger, and mine immediately grip the front of his shirt. Leather and cedar envelop me. I stare up at him as his other hand settles against the side of my neck.

"You're really here," I whisper.

"Mhmm," he replies.

I smile, and he kisses me, softly, gently, then he kisses me like the first time wasn't enough.

It wasn't. It can't be with him.

"I can't believe you're here," I say while he drags the tip of his nose along mine. "You shouldn't be. I want you here, but why are you here, Foster?"

He sweeps his thumb over my skin. "I have always come for you, Remi. I always will."

Tears fill my eyes, and I finally let them fall. Warm lips chase them before pressing to mine. Not caring where we are, I push onto my toes for more. I missed his lips and tongue and touch—him.

Even when I tried to forget, part of me always missed him. Part of me always belonged to him.

He said if I let him inside me, he might never leave. But the truth is, Foster West has been there all along. The wandering boy embedded in my soul and stayed there through it all.

Now all of him is mine. Really, truly mine.

47

FOSTER

WE PLAY MSG five nights later. Remi's in the VIP tent, watching every second.

And when I play her song, she's the only person in the world.

It's the song that started as whispers in Paris, then built more as my muse began to reveal herself in pieces. I wrote the lyrics while we found each other again, not even realizing what they were until they were complete. Spread across different pages in my notebook and in different places on my phone.

The guys and I finished the details in the final week of the tour.

I go rogue, performing it to a sold-out crowd.

But I made a promise.

We fly to Utah the next day so Remi can touch every picture and camera in the gallery.

"I think I like this place," she says, dropping onto the chaise in the center of the room.

"I know I like it with you in it. Maybe we should stay."

Hammers bang on the other side of the wall, saws buzzing, music blaring from the construction workers, and her lips twitch. "Home sweet home."

We don't stay—yet.

Nine weeks after Daniel dies, Remi receives a call neither of us expects. After we walked out of the hospital, she washed her hands of it all, ready for a life beyond the muted one she endured for so long.

But sometimes an opportunity is too delicious to pass up.

"I thought I'd get you to a chapel before a funeral parlor." I meet her at the front of the car, running a hand through my hair, and she tosses me a sassy look.

Colt's already reclined in the driver's seat, arm over his face. My brother's been dealing with shit the last two months— avoiding working through it might be more accurate. The need to feel in control and to protect everyone was always a trait in him, but it amplified after Chase's fall.

Since everything went down with Felix after the tour, his struggle has intensified again.

And my drummer is our next destination as soon as we finish here.

I sling my arm around Remi and pull her to my side as we cross the parking lot.

"I haven't been here since my dad's funeral," she says, leaning into me. "Sage said this is where they held my mom's too."

At the solid white double doors, I release her, but my hand settles on her nape once we're through. Soft piano music plays in the entry, a musty smell hitting us from the get-go.

"Hello," a man calls through an open door off to the side. He appears a second later, in a dark sweater and slacks, wearing a comforting smile. Well-practiced and intentional. "Oh, Remington." Closing the distance, he takes her hand from her side. "It's been a long time. Not quite the little girl I remember."

She tries to return his expression. "It's nice to see you, Mr. Stenon. We're here for Daniel's ashes."

"Yes, yes." He nods, releasing her hand and threading his fingers together in front of him as he walks, expecting us to follow down a side hall. "The kinship laws become so murky in situations like this, but you're his last connection through the hospital paperwork."

Remi glances at me out of the corner of her eye, and I squeeze the back of her neck. She didn't have to accept the piece of shit's remains, but if she refused, the funeral director said they'd go to the police department.

But my woman isn't letting Daniel Kane rest in peace.

I fucking love it.

We reach a staircase, and down he goes, but as we reach the bottom, he stops and turns by a closed door. His face dips closer to us, voice lower even though it appears no one else is here. "The entire affair has been odd between you and me. First the estate not having money for a funeral and burial, and then the department held a service, even though I couldn't release the remains. Then," he almost whispers, the gossip heating up, "he'd defaulted on the payments to the cemetery, and they reclaimed his plot."

As he rotates, Remi presses her lips together. The man twists the knob and steps into the room, and her lips turn up as she drags me along by the front of my coat.

At the next door, he indicates for us to wait. He's only gone for a second before reappearing with a gray plastic box, a sticker on top identifying the contents.

Mr. Stenon hands Remi the box, but I intercept it. She gives me an appreciative look.

"I'm sorry for the box," the man says with an expression to match the apology. "We don't have unclaimed remains often, but when we do, I like to provide an urn for dignity's sake. With you coming, I didn't order one for the chief."

"Not at all a problem." Remi tacks on a smile. "I'm glad you didn't spend the money."

Mr. Stenon nods, but when we turn to leave, he stops us. "Uh-uh." The quirky man holds up a finger before stepping back into the room. "I didn't think of it until after we spoke," he calls out, voice a little muffled. "But I meant to find you after you graduated. I wasn't sure when you'd be of age, so I was playing it safe. Then you were gone before I got a chance to…"

Remi's brows slant in as he trails off, and then he steps out with a white urn. The design is kintsugi-inspired, lines of gold meant to resemble filled cracks. I know right then, setting my hand on her shoulder, and she reaches up to grasp it, squeezes.

"Your dad's been with me a long time," he says, gently lifting it toward her.

Her head jerks to me, eyes shiny as I smile at her, then she looks to him. "This is…"

"Dimitri Sinner was such a pleasure to know. I knew I'd get him back to you one day. It just took a while," he says, emphasizing.

I stroke the back of her hair. "Time to bring him home, darlin'."

She breathes deep, taking the urn, and then exhales, "Yeah. Home."

COLTON WAITS in the car again as we make our last stop before leaving Ohio. We stayed in Hunts last night after seeing Sage and Miles—and he and I and Colt endured wedding planning that none of us wanted to be a part of—and we fly to Utah this afternoon.

Remi and I have been out here ten minutes, our asses on the cold ground. I'll sit here forever if she needs me to, though.

"Sometimes I realize I haven't thought about her in a long time, and I feel guilty." Remi crashes her head into my arm, eyes trained on her mom's headstone. "I just can't remember enough good to outweigh the bad, you know?"

I rest my cheek on her head, entwining my fingers with hers. "I do know. My relationship with my mom was very different than the one you had with yours. Mine showed love and affection but never once when I needed it. Crying and having my mom walk by, pretending I wasn't there so she didn't upset her husband, kind of beat the clapping when I learned to ride a bike into submission."

"We deserved better," she says.

"We get the better now." My gaze falls to our fingers as I link and unlink them. "It doesn't take away the before, but we get to live knowing we won't be treated like that again."

I move when she tilts her face up, showing me those mesmerizing orbs. "I'm still so mad at her for not being my mom."

I lick my lips before nodding. "I know, baby."

The sadness in her exhale mirrors the one I feel when the thought of my mom pops in. I haven't heard from her. I won't.

"What if now she can be?" When Remi looks over, I push her hair back, hand lingering. "She wasn't your mom because of her addiction. But you once told me you tried so hard to love her for the woman you thought she might be underneath. The addiction isn't in play anymore. Maybe she can be your mom now that her demons aren't weighing her down."

"I think I like that," she says after a second of consideration. "It means yours will be able to be your mom one day too."

She's right. Mine couldn't be my mom because she needed to be his wife. Even when she wasn't anymore. She can't be there for me now either, and I resent her for it. But when she doesn't need to be connected to him, pleasing him, glorifying him, I can try to see her for who she could have been without the mental blocks. Talk to her like I did, but hear what I needed in response.

Morbid to think about, sure. But I'm not rooting for the day to come soon. It might help me hurt a little less when I feel the sad, though.

"I'm cold." Remi wraps her arms around mine. "Let's go home and stay there."

"No better place to be," I tell her.

I kiss her forehead and then stand, dragging her up with me.

She cautiously approaches the headstone and touches the top.

On her way to me, she smiles, and I slide my hand into hers. We walk toward the car, and her eyes focus beyond the iron fence surrounding the county cemetery.

Remi slows, and I let her go.

Colton's leaning against the driver's door, arms crossed, when I open the passenger side.

"This one won't take long."

He nods. "No rush at all. Piss on the fucker."

I snort, snagging the box from the footwell.

Remi wraps her arms around herself as gravel crunches under our feet. Once we pass through the gate, she stops and holds out her palm.

"Your therapist check the legality of this, baby? I'm down either way, just need to give the guys a heads-up if a camera catches us."

Her mouth turns up, and she flutters her fingers to prompt me. It's legal. Colt checked. But I'd be right here with her regardless.

I'm so fucking proud of the progress Remi's made the last two months. She still has her moments of panic—such as when her name was first officially linked to me—but she breathes through them quicker each time. Not even the incident with Felix dragged her backward beyond the effect it had on all of us. Now she's here, more determined than ever to close the chapter.

After she scatters Daniel's remains in the ditch, I toss the box and bag in the trash can on our return trip to the car.

Colton insists on driving, so Remi climbs in the back seat with her dad's urn. He's going on the mantel in the gallery. She hasn't said it, but I know. He'll be nestled between the picture of us and the one of him and her—because we looked at the SD cards. Right there in that room.

Colt's eyes flash to her in the rearview. She told him everything after we flew back to New York, and I think he'd save her over me now. I wouldn't want it any other way.

"Everyone cool?" he asks.

"Yeah, brother." I glance over my shoulder, and she smiles at me. "Get us the hell out of here, and we'll be perfect."

And when we arrive at the house late that night, Dimitri Sinner goes right where I expected. She smiles as I wrap my arms around her from behind and press my lips to her neck, brushing over the curves of the urn. "I can't believe this room exists."

"It's real."

She rotates in my arms, and I kiss her. Her fingers twist in my hair when my tongue strokes hers, and a soft moan from her wakes up my dick.

"Now I want you real wet in our bed." I slide my hand up to her throat, palming her ass while she drags my mouth back to hers. I groan and back up, bringing her with me. "Or shower. Fuck, I'll bend you over the banister, so long as I'm inside you."

I make it to the door and decide fuck it, picking her up. Remi throws her limbs around me and laughs until I crash her lips into mine, then she's rocking against me as I walk through the house we decided to call home.

We only have two days before I need to be in the studio to pick back up on the album. Ideally I'd spend as much of it as possible buried in Remi. Literally, figuratively, or both simultaneously.

But Dev and Felix get in tomorrow, and we want to see them. Felix especially. I've only seen him once since he got out of rehab earlier this week, and then we left for Ohio. Remi hasn't seen him since before he went in two months ago.

Since then we've bounced between here and the coasts, refusing to lose time together. The last of her stuff is being shipped to my apartment, but we'll live here while we record.

A clause in our label contract requires all three of us for performances and in the studio unless agreed otherwise. It saved our asses from having to use a session drummer and finish the album without Felix. The guy would have flat-out refused the program otherwise.

Logistics turn messy for a while once we finish. We'll stay in LA most of the time. She'll work with Heath when he's there and complete anything outstanding with the documentary, and the band will have music videos to shoot and appearances. The documentary coincides with the album release, so we'll have crossover there. Of Men and Wolves also has to decide if we re-sign with Mac Records once our contract ends.

And if I know Christian, my Cali-boy roommate is already playing with scheduling another tour.

Then we'll have different reasons we want to visit Philly and Austin. Remi says Roman has a soft spot for me that he hopes I don't notice. I have one for Imane that I openly admit. That little girl is cute as shit.

Watching Remi with her gives me a lot of fucking ideas, and soon enough, a mini-Chase will be unleashed upon the world. And my best friend and I have a dangerous habit of one-upping each other.

But despite all of those things, I still plan to steal Remi away every chance. Probably even when there isn't one. My beautiful thing has a lot of beautiful things to see. I want to show her all the places I have before—only I want her to really see them this time. I want to wander with her, not know where we're going, but always be where we were meant to be.

I'm there by simply being with Remi.

I don't set her down until I toss her on the bed. She bounces as I strip off my shirt, and then her eyes are crawling down my chest and abs.

"My eyes are up here, baby."

Somehow, after all the ways she's taken my cock, that turns her cheeks pink. She kneels at the end of the bed, and I push her skirt higher up her thighs.

"When did you get this?" she asks, trailing her hand across the *restless* tattoo above my jeans. "I've never asked, but I've wondered a thousand times."

Her gaze rises to mine, searching for the answer, but I'll willingly give it. I'll give her everything.

"After Chase started to recover." I press her flattened palm over the ink, my hand over hers.

She stares up at me confused. "But you thought I—"

"I was going to stay restless because I'd never have you," I admit, stroking my thumb down her cheek.

"But now I'm yours." She turns her hand over underneath mine, links our fingers, and lies back. She pulls me with her, and I willingly follow, coming down between her thighs and bracing my other arm by her head.

"You are."

"So you're not restless anymore?" she says, her touch dancing along my jawline.

"Nah, I'm settled." I drop my lips to hers, feel her, taste her, love her like she's always deserved. "But now I'll never forget what led me to you every time."

EPILOGUE
FOSTER

Later...

"SHE'S GONNA FIGURE IT OUT."

I flip off Colton, leaving him to trail behind me. "Just stay out of my shot. You'll ruin the romance."

He snorts behind me, and I catch his eye roll on my screen as I slip in an earbud. By the time I video chat Remi, he's moved to the side, so when she answers, she only sees me and random people in the background.

"Why aren't you here?" she whines.

She's on the bed in her hotel room in Prague, pouty lips extra pouty.

"I'm a busy man, baby." I turn the corner and adjust the camera to center more on me. Once I'm inside, I can lose the hat and glasses, but Colt drew the line on wearing them in public.

"You swear you'll be here by tomorrow?"

I smile and nod. "No other place I want to be."

And she has no idea how much I mean it. It feels as if we haven't stopped moving the past year. Of Men and Wolves had our album release, which means we both had the documentary. Goddamn, her work is a masterpiece. I'm biased as hell, but I've experienced a lot of art in my life. The way she conveys the world through her lens and how her message is clear yet holds such nuance beneath the surface for those looking has always left me in awe.

She brought the same touch to the music video she directed for us a couple months ago. I love watching her in her element, and Heath Erickson was right about Remi Sinner being the only name to watch.

Although, the director would likely off his protégé before he'll admit he wasn't drunk when he said it.

"Tell me everywhere you've been since yesterday," I say.

She beams. "Not enough places. I have a list I'm saving for us —Piss Sculpture included. I still don't know what message you sent for them to write last time."

"Hmm." I tip my head, considering if I want her to know. "You'll have to seduce that one out of me."

I'm falling in love with this girl. That's what the men whipped their dicks around to spell out.

The sky is starting to turn pink as the sun lowers, but she doesn't seem to notice. The cobblestone beneath my feet and Remi on my screen could fool me into thinking I'm walking back to a flat I'm sharing with Chase years ago. I bought one, but I want to surprise her with it in person. I'm obsessed with the way her mouth pops open and her eyes widen before shooting to me.

It makes me feel like I'm center stage when the crowd starts singing our lyrics.

"I miss you," I tell her as I veer toward the cement steps ahead. "I always miss you, Remi."

I walk through the sliding doors and tuck my hat in my back pocket, then hook my sunglasses on my shirt.

"Well," she says, with all the attitude that gets my dick hard, "if you'd sign autographs faster, you could already be here with me. So, your fault, clearly."

Of Men and Wolves had a signing yesterday scheduled after Remi and I planned our trip. Then we met up to agree on tour dates so Christian could manager-away. We're starting in Europe this time. And we won't be sleeping on buses at any point.

That decision was unanimous—even with our manager and the security guard following me to the elevator.

There are too many of us for that now anyway. I'm not leaving Remi behind, and Felix and Dev felt the same.

"Careful, Rem. When your mouth goes bratty, I want to fuck it."

As the elevator doors close, I catch a head shake from Colt and a hushed chuckle.

She narrows her cute glare at me. "Kind of hard to do when you're not here."

I lick my lips to hide a smile before returning to the task at hand. "I want to be there," I tell her.

My pulse kicks up, a hell of a lot of fluttery shit going on inside me when the doors open again.

I flip the camera, step off, and take out my earbud. Colton taps me on the shoulder before he peels off, disappearing around the corner down the hallway.

"I want to experience beauty in the mundane with you," I say, stepping out of the elevator nook and into the hallway—going the opposite way from Colt. "I want to wake up to your gorgeous face every day." White rose petals decorate the floor as I walk, votive candles lining each side and most definitely a fire hazard. "I want to be the man you deserve because you deserve fucking everything."

"Where are you?" she asks as she studies the screen. I don't answer.

"You slowly became my world, Remi Sinner. Twice. You were in my head, taking over piece by piece until I couldn't fight it and fully surrendered." Red petals join the white ones at my feet. "Twice."

Remi's mouth turns up as my girl works out the scene I've set up for her.

"I wandered because nothing fit quite right. For a long time, the only place I felt like I belonged was on a stage. Then I looked off it and saw you. Those pieces clicked back into place, and I was fighting like hell again."

"You were such a dick," she whispers.

I smile, approaching where the votive path curves to end at a door.

"Because I was scared of being consumed by you again. Because you were always the only thing that made sense through it all, Rem." Slowing to a stop, I say, "We both survived the pain, and at the end of it, all those worst ideas culminated in the best mistake of my life." I pan the camera until it faces the door. "Us."

She lets out a soft sound I feel in my chest, already moving.

"Open the door, Remi."

She tosses her phone. I pocket mine, and a second later the door rips open.

"Hi," I say.

Her gaze falls to the ring I'm holding, and her raspy voice replies, "Hey."

She looks up at me, lashes fluttering and chest rising faster. I'm so fucking in love with this woman I drown in her and greedily breathe in more.

"I lost you. I found you. I fell even deeper." I lift her hand and line up the ring. "Now there's no way out for me. Tell me you'll marry me."

"Yes," she says, nodding as I'm already pushing her finger through the ring.

I catch the side of her neck with my other hand and kiss her as I press her farther into the room.

"Yes to everything," I remind her, the door shutting behind us.

She grabs me and pulls my mouth back to hers and mumbles, "Yes, yes, yes."

I warned her it was a dangerous game, but she keeps agreeing to play.

I break away, fingers in her hair, when I tilt her face up to mine. "Let's get married right now."

"Foster…" she warns, but I counter, "Remi."

"It'll be symbolic. We'll do the Roman-walk-you-down-the-aisle thing later, but I first loved you here." My forehead touches hers, then my lips. "I want to keep you forever here."

"You already have me forever. Heart, body, soul. Always."

God, I love hearing that promise from her. "I can't wait to call you my wife. I want to put babies in you…"

"Foster."

"Help me win, baby. Chase is taunting me like an asshole with Luka—"

"*Foster*," she says on a laugh.

Her head tips to the side, telling me to look, and I glance at the bed. At the open pregnancy test box.

"Fuck, Remi. Tell me it's positive." All she needs to do is smile, and I smirk. "We're back in the game."

Then I'm kissing her. Kissing her, keeping her, settled by her, and obsessed with her.

I'm devoutly hers, always.

A wanderer no more.

Unless she's at my side.

ACKNOWLEDGMENTS

This book almost didn't exist, and in all honesty, there's a version of me that didn't make it to the end with the rest of me. It was the part of me who forgot what my voice sounded like. The one that couldn't cut through the noise to find myself.

But I came out the other side, and *Before Now* was the first thing that made me feel again.

J: You always stay. You always support. You always have my love. Thank you for tackling me back from the edge as often as you do.

To Lauren, who constantly nudged about the book she started reading and never got to finish. *We* made it to another The End. Magic.

As for Brit, you've loved Fuzzball and Raccoon from the beginning, and I love you for holding onto them when I couldn't. Thank you for letting me borrow Sav and The Hometown Heartless.

To Jayla and Whitney, my sensitivity readers, thank you so much for reading my words and helping me shape my characters authentically.

My editors: Thank you Becky with Fairest Reviews Editing and Ellie with My Brother's Editor. You make me look like I know what I'm doing, and that's an art in itself.

To Kate with Kate Decided to Design, the tattoo goddess, thank you for an incredible cover. Your talent amazes me.

Emmily and Haley, take my imaginary hugs for the extra pairs of eyes you loaned me.

So much love for every reader and my ARC team. I will

always be grateful you let my words be a part of your world. And for the ones who stayed when I went quiet—thank you.

A special note to those still crawling their way back: You're still here and never too far gone. It's never too late. Scars are hot. Whether physical or on your soul.

And finally, to Remi and Foster. For dragging me, kicking and screaming until I remembered what it's like to bleed onto the page. Because of them, I did.

I plan on doing it some more—be ready.

xx

CG

ABOUT THE AUTHOR

CG Blaine writes unapologetically messy and emotional romance novels. She loves her characters complicated, the connections intense, and rip-your-heart-out feels.

She is obsessed with her vicious cat and aggressively cute bunny. Her favorite stories hit with the hurt and then apologize oh-so well.

Never miss a thing!
Be sure to stay in the loop and sign up for CG's newsletter.
You'll also snag a FREE short story.
Sign up at https://www.cgblaine.com

facebook.com/cgblaineauthor
instagram.com/cgblaine

ALSO BY C.G. BLAINE

www.ingramcontent.com/pod-product-compliance
Lightning Source LLC
Chambersburg PA
CBHW061538190726
48289CB00004B/1088